When exiled royalty and espionage combine, expect a romance as bold as the 1920s . . .

Olga Novikov is a princess without a throne. Her fiancé and her family slain in the revolution, she flees Russia and finds herself working as the head of housekeeping at London's luxurious Grand Russe Hotel. It's a far cry from the glamour of her former life, but she's grateful for the job—until a guest forces her to question where her loyalty lies. The charming nobleman challenges her at every turn—and arouses dreams of romance she thought she'd abandoned forever . . .

Douglas "Glass" Childers is living a double life. On the surface, he's the indolent Viscount Walling, but in truth he's an intelligence agent searching for a Bolshevik weapons master. The coolly beautiful and headstrong housekeeper is a distraction he doesn't need—unless she's the key piece in the puzzle he must solve. Trusting her could be dangerous—but loving her is an undeniable temptation . . .

Visit us at www.kensingtonbooks.com

Books by Heather Hiestand

The Redcakes
The Marquess of Cake
One Taste of Scandal
His Wicked Smile
The Kidnapped Bride
(novella)
Christmas Delights
Wedding Matilda
Trifling Favors

The Grand Russe Hotel
If I Had You
I Wanna Be Loved by You
Lady Be Good

Published by Kensington Publishing Corporation

Lady Be Good

The Grand Russe Hotel

Heather Hiestand

LYRICAL PRESS
Kensington Publishing Corp.
www.kensingtonbooks.com

For my friends and readers who have had the tough experience of starting over in a new country

Acknowledgments

Thank you to Judy Di Canio, Eilis Flynn, Mary Jo Hiestand, David Hiestand, Delle Jacobs, Melissa McClone, Peggy Bird, Marilyn Hull, Madeline Pruett, and my family for your assistance and support. Also, I'd like to thank my editors Liz May and Peter Senftleben, and the rest of the Kensington team; and my agent Laurie McLean and the Fuse Literary team for their support of the Grand Russe series.

Chapter 1

London, February 23, 1925

Though Lord Walling was his true title, some days it served as an alias. Douglas "Glass" Childers, Viscount Walling, reflected on the irony of his new posting as he surveyed the Artists Suite on the seventh floor of the glorious Grand Russe Hotel on Park Lane. His Hermès steamer trunk, shoe case, and vanity case were piled against the wall between the entryway and the sitting room, along with his Louis Vuitton hat box and a couple of *porte-documents voyage*—all the accoutrements of the modern traveling nobleman, whether he was a spy or not. He had only needed to transport his luggage a short distance, from Knightsbridge, in fact, where he lived just below Hyde Park.

Not that he liked people to know that. As far as his network of agents was concerned, he worked and possibly even lived out of a one-bedroom flat in Cosway Street, Marylebone.

"Nice digs, eh?" Bill Vall-Grandly, one of his operatives, said. He'd been posted here for a few days, and his less-impressive luggage waited just inside the suite door.

For now, Glass's usual activities were curtailed because of the threat to national security presented by certain hotel guests. Higher priorities prevailed, and he had to take his place as a spy instead of as a spymaster. Surveillance came first. "Indeed. Show me the operation."

Vall-Grandly, a rotund man with a kindly air who nonetheless possessed the steely nerves and stamina required of intelligence work, went into the sitting room and found the clasp holding a painting against the wall. As he opened it, he said, "Behind this is a shelf created by Secret Service technicians. It holds our listening equipment." He pulled on the headset for a moment to ensure that the recording device trained on the Russian trade delegation next door was working properly and pointed out the features to Glass.

Normally Glass supervised secret agents rather than acting as one himself. But staff had been thinned to unacceptable levels since the war ended. The present government didn't want to believe there were any current threats to Great Britain worthy of the expense of spycraft. Glass knew better. The service monitored German intriguers, Irish anarchists, and, worst of all, Russian bomb makers, among others.

For now, he'd had to pass management of his section to his chief and dig into the daily work of a spy himself. He'd lost his last operative installed here full-time in the suite to matrimony and an assignment in the north, monitoring the infiltration of trade unions by the Bolsheviks.

"Thank you. Have you heard anything new regarding this so-called trade delegation's dabbling in human smuggling?"

"No, but they've only been here a month. Plenty more time for mischief before their official meetings commence." Vall-Grandly pressed the painting back against the wall.

At least staying at the listening post should be uncomplicated work. Only last month this hotel had nearly been damaged by Bolsheviks, but they'd caught wind of the plot in time. The Metropolitan Police's Special Branch had sealed off the tunnels beneath the hotel proper, which had once harbored the tools of the bomb maker's trade, including a nice little nest where at least one Russian had been hiding. The hidey-hole in the basement had been dank and dark, as unpleasant as any Great War trench. Nothing like the rest of the hotel.

"I'll be going now, Glass. I have a dead drop that I have to monitor rather closely to pickup time, or the messages tend to be destroyed. Waste bin near a nursery playground. You need a break, just let me know. I'll be happy to give up a few hours of sleep to keep the operation going."

"Thanks, Bill. It is men like you who are going to keep these bloody Russians from wreaking any more havoc on London."

Lines creased diagonally under Vall-Grandly's eyes as he smiled. "Thank you, sir." They shook hands before the operative picked up his modest bag and glanced over the sitting room one last time.

Glass took in the luxury of the Artists Suite as he stepped away from the Russian-style painting of a dancer dressed as the Firebird. The furniture glowed starkly, all white to highlight the richly decorative Russian artwork on the walls. He had no knowledge of the artists' names or styles, but he could appreciate the sheer exuberance of the jewel tones. Reds, purples, blues, and greens all blazed as brightly as any stained-glass window letting in the sun. The stenciling high on the walls of the hotel's public spaces was absent here, so the eye could feast strictly on what was inside the frames.

"Be a pity if this place was destroyed," Vall-Grandly ruminated. "I've been told that ballet is the primary theme of the hotel, but art in general is a strong second."

"I recognize the Firebird as being a character in a ballet, but I have no idea who the sleeping lovely in the next painting is meant to be," Glass said. In a blue-and-white ball gown, the sleeper rested on a dainty pillow, her blond curls done up in a sapphire ribbon. The settee holding her petite body was upholstered in blue, pink, and cream stripes. It would never work at the Grand Russe Hotel, which had been decorated in reds and greens. He took in the rest of the painting at a glance, having trained his eye to detail: olive walls, floral screen, gold occasional table, a window, the bottom half of a painting, a bookcase.

A knock at the door made him turn away from his fledgling art appreciation. The floor butler, he expected, or the hotel's head of security, ready to verify his communication needs. He opened the door ready for one of these men.

Instead, he found a tall, ash-blond beauty in a severe black dress—a serviceable dress. Despite the bearing of an empress, she must have been an employee.

"Yes?" he asked.

"My lord," the woman said in an imperious Russian accent as she stepped in. "My apologies. I have come to collect a painting from the suite."

Vall-Grandly smiled broadly at the woman and laid a finger next to his nose before sliding out of the door and shutting it behind him.

The Russian accent lifted the tiny hairs on the back of Glass's neck. Yes, some of the hotel employees were Russian, but their employment didn't mean they were above suspicion. "Who are you?"

"I am Olga Novikov, the head of housekeeping."

"Novikov," he said slowly. "Shouldn't it be Novikova?"

"The English do not feminize their surnames, so I do not either."

She was trying to prove a point, but he wasn't sure what the point was. Unfortunately for her, Novikov was also the surname of the bomber his section was searching for. This woman could be a connection to the man he sought, but the cool beauty did not appear to be a woman who would give up her secrets easily.

He remembered a time when it was suggested that she be developed as a source for the Secret Intelligence Service. Now, her surname made her more of a point of suspicion rather than someone they'd pay money to for information. Besides, he had no one to run her as a source. He'd have to take her on himself.

"I've heard of you. Serene Highness, correct?"

"I am a great-great-great-granddaughter of Nicholas the First," she said, tilting her head.

"A distinguished lineage," he murmured, noting the perfection of her nose and her slim neck. He suspected a chain of ancestors who only married the most beautiful women in Russia. "I have just moved in, Your Serene Highness. The suite is satisfactory to me as it is."

She frowned. "I am merely Olga here. Titles are for guests, not staff."

He let his eyebrows settle over his eye sockets, knowing that when his eyes narrowed it gave him a most forbidding look. "If you say so. Are you the only Novikov on staff here, or is it a common name?"

"I have no relatives at the Grand Russe."

"Did many of your family escape the revolution?" he inquired.

"My family can be of no interest to you, Lord Walling." She took a step closer to him, enough that he could smell bleach and orange oil. "If I could collect what I need I shall leave you to settle in."

"A distinguished name doesn't mean I can allow you to take a painting from the suite."

She placed one hand over another, on top of the keys that she wore at her waist. "Not only am I head of housekeeping; I am also a personal friend of the hotel owner."

"And your point?"

"I am curating a Russian art exhibit for the hotel. I require the *Firebird*."

Glass might have let her take a painting but not that one. He was glad to know the woman, with her suspicious surname, had no idea that the *Firebird* had been permanently installed over the surveillance equipment. "I am convinced that the hotel manager did not give you permission to take that particular piece. It is the centerpiece of the room."

The princess drew herself up. "I'm well aware of the importance of Mr. Bakst's work," the princess said. "But it is not the room's centerpiece. That is the Konstantin Somov watercolor over the fireplace."

Glass stiffened at the name "Konstantin." Konstantin Novikov was the name of the bomber. He could not bring himself to merely send away the self-assured princess. "Let us take a look and see if I agree with you."

He stepped back so that she could enter the foyer and went into the sitting room. Above the fireplace was the work she had mentioned.

"It is a study for Somov's masterwork *Echo of Bygone Days*," she said, gesturing. "You can see the bodice is unfinished, as is the garden off to the right, yet the pale dress, and the dark walls to her right, makes this the perfect painting for this room."

Glass said nothing and merely stepped toward the *Firebird*, grateful his equipment didn't make any noise, at least until the recording device came to the end of the disk and turned itself off. "How can you say such a thing? This Echo girl is nothing but a bland apparition next to the doll face of the *Firebird*. Look at the dark eyes. And her dress! All those vibrant oranges and reds."

"You are teasing me, my lord," she said. "While I am a mere servant now, I assure you that I know art. Removing the *Firebird* will harmonize this room."

"I don't want it harmonized." He forced the corners of his lips up and turned them down again, knowing she was intelligent enough to pick up the falseness of his expression.

"My lord." She attempted to stare him down.

"Don't be headstrong," he chided. "I am a guest in one of the most expensive suites in this hotel. I expect my wishes to be respected."

Very deliberately, she bobbed into a curtsy.

"I must say you are far more beautiful than any of the women depicted in these paintings, though I can see the resemblance between you and this painting next to the *Firebird*. A relative of yours?"

The princess went to the sleeping beauty painting. "It is another Somov," she said. "But I do not know its history. Somov was a part of the Miriskusstva group, and I didn't know any of those artists."

"Why not?" he asked. He observed that the fiery light behind her eyes had softened. She'd gone deep, into the past.

"The artists I knew were Symbolists, friends of my late fiancé, not the homosexual crowd Somov ran in. They are mostly in Paris now, the survivors."

"Why aren't you there?"

"I—" She swallowed hard. "It is a long story, my lord. And I am taking too much of your time."

The smile he flashed was genuine this time. "I assumed you would refuse to leave until you had what you wanted."

"No, I need to return to work. I had a break, but that is long past now."

"Then you will have to leave empty-handed."

Her gaze sharpened again; the melancholy faded. "I insist we discuss the matter of the painting with Peter Eyre," she said, all show of obsequiousness departing the lines of her Athena-like body.

"I am sure the hotel manager will side with me," Glass said, "but I will not object to the conversation. Do you want to take the time now?"

She hesitated. "I should have someone come and unpack for you."

"That is the floor butler's duty, surely."

Her head swiveled toward the door just as he heard a click behind the *Firebird*. The disk was full. But she didn't seem to notice the out-of-place sound. "I can't imagine why he hasn't stopped by."

"Busy with other guests. All those Russians next door must keep his schedule full."

She shook her head. "I do not understand why that party has not been removed. Boorish, my lord. They are not our kind."

He inclined his head. "Thank you for the advice, Olga. I shall endeavor to steer clear of them."

"Let us go downstairs, if it pleases you, and see if Mr. Eyre is available."

"Excellent. I am very curious to know exactly how close your friendship is."

Her gaze darted frantically to his face, a quick movement of her eyes like a trapped bird trying to escape the otherwise serene expression. What was she afraid of?

All of a sudden, his curiosity was thoroughly piqued. The princess had secrets.

* * * *

Olga rarely felt petite. At twenty-five, she was a statuesque lady hovering on the edge of youth. Her nightclub days were about over, not that she'd ever been to one, not even Maystone's, the venue that was part of the Grand Russe Hotel, despite the separate entrance.

Viscount Walling, though, was a giant of a man. Not just his height gave that impression but also his bearing. She guessed he was over thirty and had been an officer in the war. He still carried himself like a soldier, with that upheld chest and shoulders that made a man seem massive.

He had thick, springy black hair, creating a further impression of height, and hadn't put a hat on when he'd left the suite to follow her along to the lift. His black brows matched the hair on his head in thickness and intensity, though the right one had a visible scar running through it, creating a space in the center that made the perfect symmetry of his features even more obvious.

Why was he staying at the hotel? Normally incurious about the guests, she was dying to know. With a title herself, and hoping to find some version of her old Russian life here in England, she'd studied *Debrett's Peerage & Baronetage* when she arrived. She knew Walling was the heir to the earl of St. Martin's. The earldom had plenty of money and surely still owned St. Martin's House on Hanover Square.

Maybe he had argued with his father. While she hadn't had brothers, she'd had cousins and could remember the fights the boys had had when first in the age of young manhood. They'd all died one way or another, in the war or the revolution. So many ghosts.

Lord Walling smiled at her as the lift operator held open the door for them. They exited onto the ground floor of the hotel. Her senses came to life as they turned the corner and arrived in the Grand Hall. The marble checkerboard floor and vaulted ceilings exaggerated every noise, from tapping ladies' shoes to men's canes to bellboys shouting guests' names. Words seemed to echo in the space, meaning secrets were never meant to be shared here. Everyone was bundled in thick coats, hats, and furs, trying to stay warm and dry in the incessant rain London had experienced recently. It seemed that spring would never come.

She slipped in a puddle someone's umbrella had left on the floor. Lord Walling captured her elbow to keep her upright. She felt more ungainly than ever as she struggled to stay on her feet. It served her right for the vanity of wearing inappropriate shoes. When Peter had promoted her officially to head of housekeeping, she'd stopped wearing her lace-up shoes and replaced them with black leather pumps. While she grimaced less when she caught her image in the wall mirrors on every floor of the hotel, she did present a hazard for herself on the marble floors.

"You can let go of me now," she said once she felt secure.

"Maybe I don't want to," he said.

She saw the twinkle in his eyes. It was far from the first time a guest had been fresh with her. Usually her manner and less-than-youthful age put them off, but not the bolder souls. "I want you to," she said with a direct stare.

He nodded and let her arm drop. "I apologize if I offended you."

"It is not my place to be offended. We'll have to pass behind the reception desk to reach Peter's office." They arrived at the desk. Hugh Moth, the front desk clerk, stood over his guest ledger. He was a nice boy, but next to him was Frank Russell, the concierge, who was a rougher character. She couldn't figure out how to stop him from asking her to attend the pictures with him. He'd been asking her for weeks on an annoyingly regular basis.

"Let us through, please," she said to Hugh. "Lord Walling has business with Mr. Eyre."

Hugh sneezed. He pulled a large white handkerchief from inside his coat pocket and wiped his nose. "Sorry, Olga."

She noticed his pale blue eyes were glassy. "You should be home in bed."

"I'd rather be here," he said and sneezed again. He lifted the folding part of the desk, gestured them through, and wiped his nose again.

She passed by, making sure no part of her touched the desk. The concierge smirked at her and winked.

"Friend of yours?" Lord Walling asked as they ventured past the rows of cubbyholes for guest mail and the key wall.

"Absolutely not. He's terribly impertinent."

"That way with all the female staff?"

"Not that I've noticed." In the back the switchboard operators were busy on their headsets, moving cables around as they connected guests to the outside world. Focused on the people speaking into their ears, none of them turned in their seats as she and Lord Walling walked past.

"Lots of girls to choose from," Lord Walling commented, swiveling his head as he took in the secretarial group in the middle of the business office. One of them, a pretty brunette who couldn't have been more than nineteen, simpered and blushed in his direction and stuck her pencil behind her ear. "Why is that man focused on you?"

"He is the concierge," she said. "It's a rather important position, and I'm the only woman in authority here at the hotel. I expect I would increase his prestige."

"So you are the bachelor girl in demand here?" he said, that twinkle returning to his eye.

"Rubbish," she said and knocked on Peter's door. When she heard the manager's voice, muffled behind the wood, she pushed open the door a few inches.

Peter Eyre stood behind his desk, gesturing toward John Neville, the new day manager. At twenty-seven, he was a year older than Peter, but the hotel manager's assured manner and aristocratic background made him seem much more mature.

At this time of morning, he wore a dark bespoke suit, cut tightly against his lean body. A gold chain created a half-moon across his waistcoat, and his coat was unbuttoned. Although Peter never seemed to take exercise, a steady diet of little more than cigarettes and champagne kept him trim. A slight air of exoticism had been inherited from his half-Indian mother, though few knew the truth of his family background. Sandalwood underlay the smoke from freshly smoked cigarettes, an American brand. The butt of one still smoldered in the battered ashtray engraved with the previous name of the hotel, now gone down in infamy as the Sodom and Gomorrah of its day.

He and Lord Walling knew how to look like gentlemen. While Lord Walling's suit was cut for more movement, his imposing height gave him just as much presence as Peter's more careful appearance. John Neville, on the other hand, was not quite up to snuff for his new role. She wondered when Peter would force him to reorder his wardrobe to better represent the Grand Russe.

Peter glanced at her. "Ah, Olga, what have you brought me today?"

"Lord Walling, sir."

The aristocrat in question smiled with closed lips, the skin around his eyes crinkling. Peter came around the desk and clasped hands with Lord Walling. The two men were an interesting contrast, the bon vivant versus the sportsman. She had felt the strength of Lord Walling's hand when he took her arm at the puddle and suspected he had limbs of steel.

"Just moved in, Walling?" Peter's sandy-brown eyebrows lifted.

Olga had the sense the men had met before. Had they gone to school together? No, Lord Walling was definitely in the middle age between Peter and his older brother, Noel, too old to be the contemporary of one yet too young to be the contemporary of the other. But they might belong to the same clubs, though Peter rarely left the hotel, preferring to hold court here.

"Indeed, Eyre." The way he said Peter's last name held a hint of amusement. Lord Walling obviously knew Eyre was not Peter's true surname.

While the men spoke, she recalled everything she knew about their seventh-floor guest. Lord Walling was the youngest of four brothers. All the elders had died in the war, of which he was also a veteran. She'd read the dates in *Debrett's*. Ypres for the second eldest, the Marne for the eldest, and Cambrai at the end of the war for the third. What a shock it must have been for a fourth son to find himself the heir, yet it was not so uncommon in the previous decade. Maybe it had been one of his brothers who knew Peter's elder brother, now a long-term resident of a hospital in Suffolk.

"Did we have luncheon plans?" Peter glanced at the clock on top of a file cabinet.

"No, your head of housekeeping wants to remove the *Firebird* from the Artists Suite."

Lord Walling said the words calmly enough, but Peter's reaction confused her. He stiffened, his shoulders going back.

"You said I could have whatever I need, and that suite has the best art in the hotel. I want the *Firebird* to be the centerpiece of my Russian art exhibit." She spoke in her most persuasive tone.

"If Lord Walling wants the art for his own private use, so be it," Peter said. "He has hired the room; therefore, the decision is his."

Olga felt her lips part. Normally she was better at hiding her reactions. But she didn't understand the strange behavior of either man. Peter seemed to be deferring to Lord Walling.

She forced her voice to remain calm. "I admit the situation is inexcusable. We should have removed the painting before he arrived, but you've changed the locks on that suite so that the master key doesn't open it."

Peter glanced at Lord Walling again. What was going on? Was he a secret investor in the hotel or something? She knew Peter's family had silent partners in ownership. They had needed them because the hotel had received a massive facelift after having been closed for a couple of years as a result of the infamous Starlet Murders.

"I'm sorry, Olga, but the painting will need to remain where it is. We don't need to disturb Lord Walling any further." Peter pulled his cigarette case out of his coat. "A butt, Walling?"

"Cigars only," the other man replied.

"We'll have to try the cigars my uncle brought back from a recent voyage. Maystone's, tonight?" Peter pulled a cigarette from the fine gold case and removed his Dunhill lighter.

"I might be able to stop by late," Lord Walling said.

"Come to the Coffee Room," Peter urged. "I'll be there until ten."

"Good morning." Their guest walked out of the office without glancing at her.

Once again, Olga had the distinct impression that Lord Walling was in charge, not Peter. How abrupt he had been. "I am sorry, Peter. I let my desires get the best of me. It won't happen again." She hurried after their guest.

* * * *

Glass expected that to be the end of the *Firebird* controversy. He assumed Eyre remembered that the painting was attached the wall now. If he had control over his staff, the princess would let it go.

But she was still a princess, and however life had humbled her, her spirit remained intact. He couldn't help but like her for it. She said good-bye to Eyre, who shut the door behind her, and stepped right to him, a picture of regal grace despite her sensible work attire.

"Have you been in the Grand Russe before?" Olga asked over the scratching of pencils in ledgers and the clacking of typewriter keys in the business room.

He regarded her. Because of what he did for work, he preferred to say as little about his private life as possible. Anonymity was the key to the game.

She shook her head. "No, I suppose not. I wonder why you are staying here, my lord?"

He narrowed his eyes and walked past the row of desks. They passed the switchboard. When he moved to the door where they'd come in, she took his arm.

"There is another way out." She took him toward a door on the left. It led onto a featureless corridor. "We aren't meant to come in this way because we need to have approval to see Peter."

"Why do you call him by his first name?" he asked. "It's very informal."

"We are old friends. I spent time in London as a girl. We played in Kensington Gardens together."

"Very old friends," he said.

"May I show you around the hotel?" she asked. "Since you are new here."

He needed to be at his listening post, but Princess Olga Novikova was a cipher that needed solving. Was she related to the bomber? Would she be a good source of information about the dealings around this hotel, a hotbed of Russian activity? For now, the woman was a higher priority than his post. If only he had more men to spare. "The penny tour, please."

She smiled, exposing good teeth and dimples on either side of her mouth. They transformed her face, giving her an impish quality completely lacking when in repose. "Penny it is, Lord Walling."

They went out of a door at the south end of the corridor and were back in the Grand Hall. Olga stood, head cocked, and began to gesture in a counterclockwise pattern. "The reception desk, of course. Past that are the stairs leading to the basement and the public bathrooms are at the base of the stairs. The Reading Room is on the other side of the staircase, then the dress shop."

"Very good."

"There is a tailoring service if you need repairs," she said. "Then on the other side of the front doors is the Restaurant. Next to that is the Salon."

"No ballroom on this floor?"

"No, that is one level up, along with meeting rooms, including a suite of rooms that can be used as a theater."

"That is where the bomb was laid, correct?"

She nodded. "Explosives, but without the fuses attached. But I wouldn't worry, my lord. Security is very good here."

He wondered if she believed that. For himself, he considered the Grand Russe Hotel one of the most dangerous locations in London.

Chapter 2

"The centerpiece of the hotel, in my opinion, is the Coffee Room." Olga tugged gently on Glass's arm, pulling him to the left as they traversed the Grand Hall. "When I was a young girl, it was a tearoom, and we came here for tea with our nanny."

"Who is we?" Glass asked as they approached the four-panel door.

"My sister, Fyodora, and me. She is a year older than me."

"Does she live in London too?" As they entered the room, the first thing he noticed was the smell of coffee and toast. Tall beverage urns, along with toast racks and a selection of jams and butter, stood on a table alongside the wall.

Obviously, he was hungry because the room itself should have been noticed first. The walls were covered in silver-and-blue geometric wallpaper, a sight that dazzled the eyes. While tables were spread across the floor, he could see a square of raised dance floor covering the parquet of the main floor, plus a small raised dais for a band. Right now, the room appeared unfinished because there were at least twenty thin rectangular wrapped shapes leaning against the rear wall.

"Is that your art exhibit?" he asked.

"Yes, the start of it. We are going to cover the wall in white silk, then put up the paintings. It's a magnificent space, don't you think? The *Firebird* will make the exhibit." She smiled at him.

For himself, he thought anything would be dwarfed in the magnificence of the room. The wallpaper was so showy, the flooring so ornate, that it could be likened to a royal palace. "I think the oranges and reds in the painting will clash with the wallpaper in here," he said.

"Oh, no," she assured him. "We're going to set up screens, you see, pairs of them, running down the center of the room. Paintings there, too. It will lead the viewers straight to the wall. They won't notice the wallpaper at all."

Despite himself, he asked, "Why this room? Why not the ballroom?"

"Peter feels that the evening scene is out of control," Olga said. "He wants to kill the champagne and dancing hours for a week or two. The faithful will return, but hopefully the others will find some new pattern to their evenings while the room is off the circuit."

"You've been reopened less than four months," Glass observed.

"Yes. The hotel has done marvelously well, despite the controversies."

"That's what you call a bomb attempt?"

She shrugged. "Nothing happened."

"As a senior member of staff, surely you are aware that more than one attempt to bomb the place has occurred. Men have been discovered living in your basement. A cache of weapons and explosives was found down there."

She pursed her lips into a pretty bow and clasped her hands behind her back in a military pose. His stomach growled. He had revealed too much. What was he trying to prove to this focused, arrogant young woman? Or was he merely trying to frighten her?

He needed a plan. He needed to strategize, to develop her properly. She was a target, at least until her connection to the bomber was uncovered. He needed to think like an operative.

"How did you come by that information?" she asked after glancing around to make sure no one else was in the room.

He noticed his hands were shaking as he moved toward one of the coffee urns. He took a cup, held it under the spigot, and let the coffee flow. Then he added sugar for good measure. He preferred tea, a good malty Assam, but this would have to do.

"I'd have preferred this remain a tearoom," he said. "This hotel used to be known for its tea service."

"We still have afternoon tea in the Restaurant. On the seventh floor you can order in a full tea from the butler. It's just as good as ever. Our kitchens are marvelous."

As he drank his coffee, standing, he hoped he had successfully deflected her from his remarks about the basement, but she was not the woman to let anything go.

"Lord Walling? Who told you about the basement? It's very private information, but I can assure you the situation was dealt with."

"Rumors," he said, deciding to go vague for want of a better idea. She had him in knots. This afternoon he would decide on a plan to manage her. He'd get to the bottom of her name and her loyalties. While he'd been repeatedly assured that Peter Eyre trusted her, and he even understood why, now that he knew they were childhood friends, he could not trust her.

The British government, of which he was an important cog, could not afford to trust her.

"I have a table at the Criterion tonight," he said. "Eight o'clock. Will you dine with me?"

"I merely want the painting, my lord," she said. "Don't think my interest in spending time with you results from some other motive."

"Dine with me," he repeated. "Where do you live?"

"Montagu Square," she said. "In a boardinghouse."

Obviously her family money was long gone. She must have been one of those unfortunates who escaped Russia by the skin of their teeth. He admired her for wanting to work instead of living off the charity of friends, but what a comedown. She fascinated him.

"Very good. I'll call for you at seven thirty." He set down his empty coffee cup on a silver-plated tray.

"I didn't agree to dinner."

"You can't possibly say no to dinner at the Criterion."

She hesitated. "I'm not sure I have the right clothing for such an exclusive spot."

He took a step closer, using his superior height to add weight to his words. She stared up at him, her eyes seeming larger than they had before. "You'll make do. I have faith."

Before she could respond, he strode out of the room, not trusting himself to speak with her any longer. She had him at sixes and sevens, not a good feeling for a master spy.

* * * *

Olga waited in the parlor of her boardinghouse that evening. She'd come downstairs to find Bert Dadey fiddling with his gramophone and sat next to the pleasant old man on his faded velvet sofa while he changed records. Her landlord was a music aficionado. Despite his advanced age, he loved jazz. She considered music more background noise than anything important and never knew the names of the songs he played. Art was her world, not music.

"You'll like this one, Miss Novikov," Mr. Dadey said. "'Revival Day' by Al Jolson. Nice to hear a religious tune when you've had a death in the house."

She listened quietly as he snapped his fingers and sang the hallelujahs, but it didn't sound very religious to her. Having seen all of his records, though, she knew he didn't have hymns or anything like that.

Above her, she could hear the movement of the women in the bed and sitting rooms upstairs creaking the floorboards. Alecia Loudon was to be married tomorrow, and Emmeline Plash was helping her with the final arrangements for her wedding suit. When Olga had gone downstairs, Alecia had been trying on shoes. Emmeline was trying to talk her out of wearing her favorite pink leather shoes in favor of something more restrained.

Emmeline had rallied after the death of her mother. It had to be said that they were all sleeping better, as the old lady had wandered in the wee hours. Whatever demons had been chasing her in her old age, they came out to torture her about two in the morning, disrupting the floor. Alecia had tended her in those last weeks of life, doing what she could to keep Mrs. Plash quiet, but only death could cure the old lady's nightmares.

Now, Alecia would marry the Grand Russe's head of security, Ivan Salter, born Ivan Saltykov, another Russian Peter had taken under his wing. Unlike Olga, though, he was not an old family friend. He was from a distinguished family, but nothing like hers. It had taken him three years to travel from Finland to England, working his way through Europe with his sister.

That was very different from Olga, who'd been packed out of Russia just after her fiancé's murder in 1918. She'd had luggage and a little money. Fyodora, just under a year older than her, had left too, a few months later, headed toward the east instead of the west. What had happened to her after that? Fyodora's fate was a mystery, but that was better than knowing she was dead. Everyone else was, those faces of her childhood, her fiancé's family, her own. The people she knew had fared no better than the French aristocrats of 130 or so years ago, though death had come by illness, firing squad, or murder, not the guillotine.

Something clattered to the floor above their heads. Mr. Dadey shook his head, the loose skin under his chin wobbling. "Sorry to see Miss Loudon go. Now there's a pretty girl. Not regal like you, but a nice English lass."

Olga couldn't take his words as an insult. She'd been a known beauty in Russia with at least five proposals of marriage by the time she was seventeen. Maybe it was her position, rather than her face or her form, that had given her beauty, though, because she hadn't received any marriage proposals since. If only Emmeline hadn't been forever underfoot. Maybe Peter would have offered for her, but the pair of them had some kind of sick relationship she didn't understand.

So she had stayed with Grand Duchess Xenia, her benefactress, and aged. As the Russian imperial's household continued to be reduced because of lack of funds, and no one proposed marriage, she realized she would need to make her own way. Peter's family were good employers, and they had always stayed in touch, so she'd asked his sister Eloise to give her work. This had come as a desperate move after a failed attempt to be a companion to a nearly deaf countess who mostly stayed at her family estate in Southwold. London had seemed a faraway dream in those months before she'd gone to Leeds and been trained as a chambermaid.

Mr. Dadey changed the record. She recognized Al Jolson's voice again.

"He's Russian," Mr. Dadey said.

"How interesting," Olga responded. She jumped up when she heard the sound of the front-door knocker. "Oh, Mr. Dadey, can you get the door, please?"

The old man chuckled. "Hooked a good one?"

"I never thought an earl's heir would be taking me to dinner at this point in my life," she said. It didn't matter what she said to Mr. Dadey. He was a dear and never gossiped.

"When you have bait like that face of yours, you ought to be able to land a duke." He sucked on his fake upper teeth, making them click, and lumbered out of the room.

Olga took her old House of Worth silk-and-fur cape from where it had been waiting on the arm of the sofa and moved into the front hall. A narrow space, only about four steps across, it was overshadowed by the staircase heading up to the first floor, where her room was, next to the more expansive private space of the Plashes.

Lord Walling dwarfed the tiny hallway. Mr. Dadey shut the door behind him, shaking his head about the rain. She saw droplets on her guest's hat and shoulders.

"That's a very nice cape, Your Serene Highness," her date said. "Are you sure you want to risk damaging the silk in this beastly weather?"

A touch of pride straightened her shoulders when he called her by her title. They were out of the hotel, and she could be a princess again, instead of a servant. That he remembered made her think the world of him. "I will only have to walk a few steps between the taxicab and the buildings." She didn't want her cape damaged, but she had no other evening garment to wear. Also, she wanted the warmth.

"It's a lovely piece."

"Thank you." Her old black Vionnet had too much class to ever go out of style. However, nothing but strings of beads held up the bodice, leaving very little fabric to keep her upper half warm. She waited to hear him make some comment about her work versus her stylish clothing, but he said nothing.

"A beauty, ain't she?" her landlord said proudly to Lord Walling.

Olga took care to introduce the men, pleased to see the respect Lord Walling gave the old dear, and then took his arm. He escorted her to the door; then they went down the steps to his taxicab. She shivered a bit as they drove to Piccadilly, despite the fur that composed the rest of her cape. March could not come more swiftly. She'd never had trouble with cold, but the London damp was difficult to tolerate. Lord Walling made small talk about the guests on the seventh floor, and she told him more about the paintings in his suite.

They pulled up in front of the rain-soaked pavement outside of the restaurant and passed between streetlights and under a fringed canopy into the restaurant. Only a few droplets caught her around the shoulders and were absorbed by the fur. She hated worrying about her clothes like she did, but she couldn't afford to replace them.

Inside, the restaurant radiated warmth and discreet wealth. Diners spoke in lowered voices, waiters hovering attentively nearby. After Lord Walling spoke to the maître d' they were seated at a table in a long, rectangular space framed by arches and thick columns.

"Have you been here before?" he asked.

"No." She straightened her shoulders and smiled at him.

He lifted his chin. "It might not be too exciting to someone of your background, but look up."

She glanced up and exhaled in wonder as she took in the gold mosaic ceiling. "How lovely. Thank you for pointing that out to me. It really is a beautiful space."

"I think you will enjoy the food as well."

"I cannot think it better than the Grand Russe's restaurant." She bit her lip after she said it. It wasn't as if she could dine there. Peter wouldn't mind, not really, but she would. She didn't want to spend any more time than she did in the place where she was a servant.

"It wouldn't be seemly to take you there," he said in a calm tone as he placed his palms on the table. "Besides, I cannot spend all my time at the hotel."

"How long do you think you'll be residing there?" she asked, careful not to say "with us" like she would if she were at work.

"I'm not really sure." His lips curved boyishly, like he was thinking of a joke he wasn't sharing.

"Are you doing renovations at your London home?"

He lifted his index fingers from the table. "A spot of painting. You know the sort of thing. Maintenance."

"So a short stay then."

"Not necessarily." He smiled at her, giving the distinct idea that he was offering up the notion that she might have something to do with how long he stayed.

What was it? A foxlike gleam in his eye? Had she become a viscount's prey? She stiffened. While she might be poor, she was far from desperate. Olga Novikova was still a respectable woman, despite everything.

"It's a very nice suite. I can understand why you would never want to leave once having settled in."

"Indeed." He left it at that.

The waiter arrived with the bill of fare. Lord Walling ordered wine and a roast beef dinner for them. She found nothing to object to in any of his selections, much finer than her usual cheese-and-toast dinner.

She decided to bring up her most pressing concern before their food arrived. "Have you had any further thoughts about releasing the painting to my exhibit?"

He smiled but didn't answer. The waiter conveniently came up to them just then, displayed the wine selection, and went through the ostentatious process of offering it to her date for tasting. Olga glanced around, not recognizing any of her relatives, though she did see three men with English titles, one dining with a lady who wasn't his wife. Most Russians lived in very reduced circumstances these days. Many of those who had escaped with wealth, or had bank accounts or property in Europe, had been fleeced because of their lack of knowledge about handling money.

Wine splashed into her glass. The waiter faded into the background, quickly followed by another with their first course.

"Were you very sheltered when you were in Russia, or were you out in society?" he asked.

"My childhood was delightful, but, of course, the war came. I would say I was sheltered; my sister and I both were. When my sister was seventeen, we were introduced to prospective suitors, men we'd known all our lives." She took a sip of wine. It tasted rather banal. "We both became engaged. Her fiancé died in the war. Mine was murdered in the revolution."

"Then you fled?"

"Yes. I went to Crimea first, helped by my fiancé's family who knew the grand duchess Xenia, sister of the tsar. I'd seen his murder, you see; I was there. They thought it best I go where I could receive protection for fear something would happen to me."

"Who was he?"

"A prince, an artist. Really, it was the artists who moved me to Ai-

Todor. Maxim's family supplied the money and his friends had the network that helped me escape Petrograd. Compared to some others, such as Ivan Salter, who also works at the Grand Russe, I had it easy. The dowager empress included me in her entourage when she was rescued by a British warship in 1919."

"Do you have many relatives in London?"

"Distant ones. I lived in the household of the grand duchess Xenia for a time, but, charitable as she is, she couldn't afford to keep everyone. Her jewelry was stolen, and she didn't have much else. She's moving into grace-and-favor housing now, courtesy of the king. I'm lucky I had Peter's friendship. He has given me a fresh start here in London after his sister Eloise trained me at her hotel in Leeds. The hotel has only been open about three months, and he promoted me last month."

"You must be very proud."

"Oh, yes. I am very grateful. I may not have to do chambermaid duties at all by spring. The hotel is doing so well that we're slowly bringing on more staff and I can focus on management."

"What about Novikovs? Do you have relatives here who aren't members of the imperial family?"

She took a delicate bite of her shrimp cocktail. The cocktail sauce was divine. "We aren't so numerous. Why? Do you know people with my surname?"

"No. But I've heard the name somewhere."

Her fork hovered over the cocktail sauce. She did have a second cousin here in England. His family had been forced into exile from Russia after a sex scandal involving his father, so her cousin had been here for a decade, though his parents were deceased now. He was trouble, though. "There was a branch of Novikovs who came here just before the war, my uncle's family, but most are deceased now."

"Did they help you?"

She shook her head and quickly changed the subject. "How do you occupy your time? I know you were a soldier, and of course, you will inherit a great deal of responsibility someday."

"The estate is still intact," he said, "even if our family is not. But my father and I are not close. I have a government job."

Grateful that he'd let her move on, she enthused. "Oh, how industrious of you. Anything interesting?"

He smiled as he took a shrimp. "A paper pusher I'm afraid. It helps the years to pass."

He was an odd bird. At thirty-one, according to *Debrett's*, going on seven years since the war ended, she'd expect him to be married, a father, especially with his families' crippling generational loss. As best she could tell, the title would go to a third cousin if it passed out of the direct line. Could he be considering her a candidate for his wife, or did he have some darker motive for asking her to dinner?

It was hard to be considered respectable when you had been a chambermaid. If only someone had been willing to marry her years ago when she'd first come to England, but she hadn't been a catch. All she had to offer was herself and a useless title that was more an impairment than an aid.

She took a deep breath and began to share stories about her extended family, leaving out the malcontents and difficult personalities and speaking of the great names. She left out the affairs, her grandmother's illegitimate child with her personal secretary, the midlife madness that had afflicted some of the men.

"And your fiancé?"

"Yes, my dear Maxim. He was an artist, as I said. I hope his work survives in Russia. I have very little of it myself, only a book of sketches he did for me."

"What kind of art did he produce?"

"He was a religious man and a Symbolist. He did a beautiful series based on the Ten Commandments."

"Did you love him?"

Red splashed across her vision. Her hands went to her lap as her heart fluttered. She tapped her fingertips unknowingly. When she felt the telltale pressure on her leg, she forced her hands to still. "I could not control the nightmares after he was killed. His death was such an abomination I could scarcely remember him alive." Her voice had sunk into a whisper.

"I have those kinds of nightmares," Lord Walling admitted. "I am sorry a gently reared lady has suffered in the same manner."

"It is the affliction of our times. I am grateful we have peace now."

"For now," he echoed.

Their main courses came. They spoke little during the rest of the meal. Tension made her shoulders and temples hurt, not because of Lord Walling's behavior exactly but because speaking of Maxim still upset her, even after all these years. She had no head for violence; that was the truth.

When he suggested they dance at Maystone's for a little while, she agreed. She knew she would not sleep well, so there was no point in retiring at a sensible hour, despite a full day of work ahead of her.

As he helped her from her seat, he asked, "You look bemused. Not your usual Monday night?"

"No. I am a reader of novels," she admitted. "We are also quite social in the boardinghouse. Mr. Dadey is a great music lover. We play bridge a couple of nights a week." Of course, that would all change now with Alecia marrying.

As he helped her into a taxicab, he asked, "Are you too tired to dance? You've had a long day."

"I've never been to Maystone's." She pulled her cape more tightly around her as the taxicab pulled away from the curb. He kept a polite distance from her, denying her the warmth of his body. "It will be fun."

When they arrived in the alley where Maystone's front door was located, just around the corner from the Grand Russe, Olga could hear music despite the closed doors. Maystone's had a wonderful house band, with a cornet-playing bandleader and a piano player who was considered so talented that even she had heard his name—Judd Anderson.

Lord Walling escorted her to a small table at the far edge of the dance floor after they entered. He ordered a bottle of champagne. Their table was against a mirrored wall and had a long white tablecloth to hide what was going on at waist level and a vase with a rose in it. Where the mirrors ended, a raised area where the band was tucked away began, alongside the polished wooden dance floor.

She spotted Peter dancing. His mistress's mother had passed away the week before, so she wasn't evident, but Peter never had a problem finding temporary female company. The woman foxtrotting with him wore white and still had the round face of youth, though the amount of paint decorating it made it likely she was an actress.

The crowd here was younger than at the Restaurant, the Bright Young Things set. Peter had been delighted to see the nightclub's name popping up in the gossip columns recently.

She leaned toward her date and spoke into his ear. "I just realized I've never seen your name in the gossip pages."

"You read them?"

"For mentions of the hotel," she admitted.

His lips quirked. "Of course. I'm a quiet man. I don't go in for the high jinks. I'm too old for that crowd anyway."

She thought she'd like to be in a column herself, with her title prominent as well as his: Princess Novikova and Lord Walling dancing the night away at Maystone's. In frustration, she huffed out a breath. If only she'd had jewels to pack on her way out of Petrograd instead of just clothing and books. But she hadn't been a very worldly girl, and her mother hadn't been one to share her jewelry with her daughters. "I'd never fit in either. Too sensible."

"Sensible and single-minded," he said. He lifted the champagne flute that a waiter had just filled and held it up to her. "To a life of hard work and good sense."

She lifted her own glass and made a face. "Must we toast to that?"

He set his glass down. "Very well, we won't. Shall we dance?"

She nodded, despite her work-sore feet, and took his hand. The band started a new tune, the band leader dancing in his tuxedo as he lifted his cornet. They stayed on the floor for two dances; then a couple was pushed onto the floor to do an exhibition of a new dance from Broadway. Their high kicks and gymnastics were exhilarating even if Olga couldn't imagine doing the routine herself.

At the end of the couple's performance, she couldn't hold back a yawn. Lord Walling noticed and brought them back to their table. "Is it time to escort you home?"

"I'm good for another hour, if I stop drinking champagne. I already had two glasses of wine with dinner."

"I have commitments early tomorrow myself," he said.

She realized he was trying to end the evening, not the best sign for a future relationship. "I'm happy to go then. You don't want to yawn through your meeting."

The doorman whistled for a taxi when they walked outside. Wind rustled through the alley, kicking up old newspaper pages as they went to the cab. Olga's cape blew up as she bent over to climb in, and goose bumps covered her arms. She was glad for Lord Walling's warmth beside her as the driver pulled away, going much too fast on the wet roads.

Lord Walling didn't seem to mind the speed, but when her hand accidentally brushed his coat-covered thigh, he captured her fingers in his and put her knuckles to his lips, surprising her with the gesture. Perhaps all was not lost.

When they arrived at her boardinghouse, he opened the door and stepped out first before escorting her up the steps of the old Regency-era mansion.

"I hope you had a nice time," he said before she could speak.

Instinctively, she leaned toward him, half closing her eyes. She had the wine to excuse her impulsiveness with this handsome man. He took the hint and touched his lips to hers. Before she could do more than feel the glide of his smooth lips against hers, she slid her hands up his arms and wrapped them around his neck.

He tilted his head and intensified their kiss. Her body tingled as she pressed against him. She felt alive for the first time that day. When his tongue brushed her lower lip, she parted her lips, allowing him to taste her.

She felt something on her foot, and alarmed, she jumped away, letting her arms fall from his shoulders.

A cat brushed against her, its tail knocking against her leg. It jumped off the step into bush below.

"My stars," she said with a laugh. "That startled me."

"And disrupted a very nice kiss," he said.

"It was wonderful." She smiled at him. "I hope you don't think your kissing skills will improve your service at the Grand Russe."

He let out a short bark of laughter. "Of course not. Merely the end of a pleasant night."

"Yes, well, I'm sorry I ended it so abruptly," she said.

He nodded at her and turned to the taxicab waiting below. "Must go. Busy morning."

"Of course, my lord. Best of luck with your meeting."

"Hmmm." He forced a smile and went back down the stairs.

She stared at his back until he entered the cab. She fumbled for her keys as it drove away. The evening would have ended better with a kiss alone and not their awkward exchange. "Blasted cat," she muttered, shoving her key into the door.

Chapter 3

Glass had his shoes kicked off, and his coat lay over the umbrella stand by the suite door. The sofa was too white, and the table, where his feet were propped, was too ornate to risk scuffs. Peter Eyre, or whoever had designed the hotel, must spend a fortune renewing upholstery and finishings. It made no sense to him how the hotel could make money.

He rubbed his fingers against his temples and finished the last half inch of whiskey in his glass. The peaty taste of the stuff had helped clear the impression of Princess Olga Novikova from his senses.

For all her regal manners, he sensed a little girl lost behind the glossy surface, the professional mien. Their erotic moment had ended in complete awkwardness. He had not thought of her as a chambermaid currying his favor with a kiss. If she'd been that kind of girl, Peter Eyre never would have promoted her into management. No, she'd created discomfort out of her own confusion. She'd had no idea why he'd invited her out, and therefore, it had ended badly.

He needed to work on his spycraft. The girl should have been dazzled by his savoir faire, but he must have let a little of the spy out of hiding. He hadn't questioned her smoothly enough about her family in his quest to discover if she had any relationship to Konstantin Novikov. That had caused her to be less than wrapped into a cotton cloud of kisses, and the cat had exposed her nerves.

He pressed his hands against his thighs and rose. Time to check on the Russians and change the recording disk before retiring for a few hours. His subjects tended to carouse until the wee hours, and it was just past midnight. He couldn't risk going to bed until they were within an hour of retiring because of the limited amount of time he could record on a single disk.

"Hello, Firebird," he whispered as he unhooked the painting. She looked sad to him, with her dark eyes and strangely shaped mouth. Now she was hiding deception behind her angular, heavily bosomed body. He couldn't help but compare the painted female form to that of the princess in her slinky black gown. It had been the wrong choice for February. Her nipples had pebbled from the fabric the entire time they were at dinner. He hoped she hadn't noticed him staring, but they had looked like ripe fruit, ready for the plucking, and he'd been thinking of them when he took her mouth.

Had he been too rough, too eager? He'd thought he had more restraint, but the thought of those straining cherries under her silk-and-fur cape had sent the blood rushing south.

He stared at the recording equipment. As he watched, the arm swung back over the disk. The recording was full. Forcing his mind to the task at hand, he put the headphones over his ears and blanked his mind. A native Russian would be better at this, but he had a good ear for languages, so he caught most of the conversations.

A party had begun in the hour he'd been skulking on the sofa. He heard female, as well as male, voices. Music played, but the people were closer to the microphone hidden in the wall than the gramophone was. Feet drummed against the carpet as people danced. There must be a drinks table just below the microphone. He could hear glasses and bottles clinking, and the partygoers had had an hour to fill up with vodka.

Setting the headphones down, he slid the used disk into a paper sleeve and set a fresh disk on the device but didn't start the recording. Then, he fetched a chair and placed it in front of the wall so he could listen for a while. Unlikely anything useful would come of a party, but he wanted to know where the girls had come from.

They knew this group of "trade delegates" had dealt in white slavery. Were the girls local prostitutes, or had they somehow come in from Russia?

For twenty minutes, he enjoyed the music, all Russian and Polish. By then, voices had become shriller, slurred. He heard someone fall, the loud guffaws of the witnesses. Just as he was thinking he'd turn on the recording and take a bath, he heard a man speak in a guttural bark.

"*Hvatit*," the Russian commanded. Stop.

Glass heard a woman giggle nervously, then the sound of something ripping—a slap, probably on a cheek.

"*Bop*," the Russian man growled. Thief.

The woman protested in English, hardly making sense due to her acutely drunken state. Another woman spoke, defending her. The man insisted on searching her. People moved away from the wall. Glass imagined them surrounding the woman.

She shrieked; then her voice was strangled. Had she been grabbed? Another woman protested, and he heard the sound of another slap.

"Hell," Glass mouthed. He turned the recording on. His gentlemanly code of honor warred against his need to stay above the fray as a spy. But the prostitutes probably had nothing to do with the case. After all, he now knew they were East Enders from their accents, not Eastern Europeans.

He swore again. The so-called trade delegation had no idea who he was.

Before he could second-guess himself, he went into the hallway and shrugged back into his coat, shoved his feet into his shoes. After he tucked everything back against the wall, he shut the *Firebird* against the wall, grabbed an unopened bottle of whiskey, and went to join the party.

* * * *

Olga had been up at 4 a.m. because she had to leave work early that day so she could be at Alecia's wedding to Ivan Salter, the head of security at the Grand Russe. Peter had allowed her to leave a change of clothes in his hidden private rooms, and they would arrive together.

At 10 a.m. she went to do a room check on the seventh floor. Because this was where the Grand Russe housed the aristocrats, the movie stars, the notables, she still took it upon herself to at least check the rooms once a day. Even with a new title, she did not put herself above cleaning if necessary. Not yet. She'd even take their pets downstairs for a bellboy to walk if necessary.

Unlike the floors with salesmen, the denizens upstairs tended to rise rather late. Ten was the absolute earliest she thought she might be able to check rooms. She started at the northeast corner, having seen the maids' carts at the southwest and southeast corners, respectively. By ten forty-five, she had worked herself around to the Artists Suite.

She gave a brisk knock since the Do Not Disturb sign was not placed on the doorknob. Impatiently, she pushed images of those kisses, the ones that had kept her up for half of her already shortened night, to the back of her mind. At work, Lord Walling was a customer, not a date. Besides, she'd ended their evening so awkwardly that he probably wouldn't ask her to dinner again.

As she waited for him to open the door, she wondered if there was a way to resurrect the situation. He had kissed her after all. There was an attraction there. What if she invited him to Alecia's wedding? There was no better way to see what a man's intentions were. A man who shied away from weddings wasn't ready to contemplate such a thing. A man who agreed to go to one was curious.

She knocked again after a minute and was about to turn away when she heard the lock slowly being disengaged. A moment later, the door opened.

Lord Walling stood in the doorway, barefooted with his hair in wild disarray, standing up in tufts. Bloodshot eyes peered at her as he attempted to smooth back his hair with both hands.

"What happened?" she gasped. "Are you unwell?"

One side of his mouth curled up. "I was drinking with the Russians next door most of the night."

"Why?" she asked. She shook her head. At work, she must be incurious about the goings-on of guests. "Would you like your room cleaned?" She didn't have a cart, but she had a bucket with supplies for fine-tuning the cleaning efforts if needed.

He chuckled. "They were having a party, loud enough that I couldn't have slept, so I joined in."

She hadn't thought him the type, but it wasn't her place, here at work, to have an opinion. She filed all these facts about Lord Walling away to consider them later. "Would you like your room cleaned?" she repeated.

"There isn't much to do. Not even the towels."

"Ashtrays? The bins? Glasses?"

"Oh, yes, all of that."

She inclined her head. "One of the maids is just down the corridor. I'll have her bring the cart."

"Can't you come in? I'd rather have you."

Last night she dined with him at the Criterion, and today he wanted her to empty his ashtrays? She abandoned all hope of a second date right then and there.

He stepped back but still blocked the door, putting his hand to his head. "Could you ask the floor butler to bring me a tea service? I need something to clear my head. The Assam I prefer?"

"Of course, sir." She set her bucket against the wall and went to fetch Thatcher, the butler on duty.

"Come right back," he called out.

She gritted her teeth and went to the den where Thatcher and the valets spent their time. Thatcher, a very thin South African who'd been a Londoner for some fifteen years now, was setting out trays.

"The aristos are waking up," he said in a cheerful lilt when he saw her.

"Precisely. Lord Walling has asked me for a tea tray. His Assam."

"He's the new one in the Artists Suite, yes? I must say I enjoyed having Sadie Loudon in there before, but I suppose she had to go north when her husband was transferred."

Sadie had briefly been a chambermaid at the Grand Russe but had decidedly married up and found herself a resident while still cleaning the floors below. Now, her sister, Alecia, was marrying the head of security and had taken a position as a switchboard operator at the hotel, to start after a couple days' honeymoon at a borrowed flat.

Olga enjoyed both of the Loudon sisters and was glad at least one of them would be around the hotel. Better educated than the average employee, they were pleasant conversationalists of genteel backgrounds. "I'm sure she'll visit. I plan to correspond with her, and I will tell her that you asked after her."

"Very good," Thatcher said. He placed a vase with a rose in it on the top center of a teak tray. "Don't touch the teapot. The metal will burn you."

"Understood."

"Would you like me to carry it for you?" Teddy Fortress's valet walked into the room. She couldn't remember his name but appreciated the quality of his care for the famed movie comedian's expensive clothing.

"I'm used to hauling buckets. I'll be fine," she said with a smile. After hefting the tray, laden with the pot and a cup, the vase, and a rack of toast with all the accoutrements, she slowly walked down one corridor and up the south-most side, where the Artists Suite was located.

She knocked on the door with her elbow, and Lord Walling opened it quickly. His hair had been smoothed down, and he wore leather slippers. She missed the sight of his bare feet. They had made him seem rather vulnerable.

His mantle of authority had not departed him, however. He sat with his coffee tray at a small table under the stained-glass windows. Glancing up at her, he asked, "Just one cup?"

"Of course, sir. I'll tidy up while you have your tea." Irritated, she turned away and went into his bedroom.

Lord Walling's scent, rich with exquisite cologne and clean linen, hit her at a visceral level. Last night she'd been pressed up against him, all his attention on her as he stole her breath away with his expert kisses. She'd lost all regard for place and time and had thrown herself into the experience.

Now she pulled up his sheets and tidied the blankets, wondering if she could have spent the night beneath them. Would she ever know the love of a man? Tonight these sheets wouldn't be quite fresh since he didn't want them changed. The pillows might smell faintly of his head as he lay down. She picked one up and plumped the feathers. A thought struck her. He'd been drinking with the Russians. What if they had supplied him with a companion for the night?

Breathe through your mouth. Quickly, she finished the bed, not wanting to know if more feminine scents were there, too. Nothing else was necessary. Even his clothing must be put away in the wardrobe as nothing lay out. No socks on the floors, no towels. She wondered who had trained him.

After that, she did a quick wipe-up in the bathroom, noting how tidy he was there as well. He'd be an easy man to work for, as a maid. She pulled back the curtains. Outside, rain clouds hovered over Hyde Park, making for yet another gloomy day. March was coming at the end of the week. While they wouldn't have much of a break in the rain yet, at least spring approached. She would never become used to this English damp. And she missed the White Nights, too, that time of year in St. Petersburg where the sun only set for two hours. She wanted to revel in the sun. Someday, when she was old, she hoped to see Italy. Russian aristocrats loved the country. The weather was so different from theirs. She could only imagine all that heat baking into her skin.

"Something happening in the street?" Lord Walling said from behind her.

Her heart leaped in her breast. She pressed her hand to it and turned around. "I apologize. Woolgathering. The sight of all those clouds."

He came up to the window. "An ordinary sight."

"That was the problem," she admitted. "I'm done with the bedroom and bath. I'll just take out your used glasses and return with clean ones."

Before she could turn away, he put his hand on her arm. "Can you tell me how many Russians are staying in the suite next door?"

"They have three bedrooms. I've heard a dozen of them came to the *Macbeth* performance, but I don't think all of them sleep there, at least, not at the same time."

"A dozen," he muttered. "Thank you."

He dropped his hand from her arm, and she left the bedroom. The exchange had been so brief that she hadn't even really realized they'd been alone in a room with a bed together. He had no real interest in her at all. Had last night merely been about loneliness or even simple impulse? All he wanted from her was good service and information.

She stiffened her back and gently placed a used glass into her bucket. Just one used glass. He might have been alone the night before, but it didn't matter. She doubted he'd be asking her to dinner again.

* * * *

Glass glanced over the sheath of papers his secretary, Lucy Drover, had brought him late Wednesday morning. All routine stuff that he would normally deal with in his office if he weren't stuck in the field. That was it had been routine until he reached the bottom of the file and found a report from Hull, a hotbed of Bolshevik activity.

The Secret Intelligence Service knew Irina Kozyrev lived up north and kept a close eye on her activities because she was the daughter of the "Hand of Death," the legendary Russian assassin Mikhail Lashevich.

He stacked his paperwork together and returned it all to the envelope. He went to the chair across from the suite's door, where Miss Drover waited for him. "I've signed everything that needed it. I need to obtain our best likeness of Mikhail Lashevich."

"Yes, sir."

"Bring it over to me as soon as possible."

The secretary added the envelope to her satchel, which also contained Glass's report and the disks that had been recorded. She'd brought a fresh stack of them.

"How are we doing with recruiting? I didn't see a report," he said as a final thought struck him.

"You would think, with unemployment as high as it is, that we'd find some good candidates."

"It's best to recruit young," Glass told her. "At the universities, or just out of the army. We need to have people in the right places, but we're stretched so thin that we aren't doing it properly."

"Do you have money to hire anyone?"

"One more operative," Glass said. "For the Big Smoke."

The secretary nodded. "I'll have that photograph or sketch or whatever we have to you this afternoon."

* * * *

At four, with the Russians absent from their suite, Glass went downstairs with his Lashevich sketch and asked to see Peter Eyre. Hugh Moth, the front desk clerk, led him behind Reception and through the business office to the hotel manager's private office.

Glass found Eyre alone, tapping the butt of a cigarette into a battered brass ashtray.

"What ho, Lord Walling?" he asked.

Glass sat in one of the visitor's chairs and picked up the small elephant on Eyre's desk. He let it slide through his fingers, enjoying the cool feel of the jade. "Have you ever been to India?" he asked, setting the elephant back in its place.

"No. I've been to the great European capitals and to New York, but nowhere very exotic," Eyre said, popping open the cigarette box on his desk. Glass waved his offer away.

"You're right." Eyre sighed, closing the box. "I mean to cut back myself. No more of this chain smoking. What can I do for you? I'm just back from a wedding, and I have no idea what's been transpiring in the hotel today."

"This isn't news about goings-on," Glass said. "We didn't have another party upstairs last night." He'd already made Eyre aware of the near-violent end of the party on Monday night. Eyre had wanted the Russians out of his hotel but had been overruled by the government because of the listening post that they'd set up.

"Glad to hear it. Prostitutes are a necessary evil in hospitality, but I don't want them being roughed up."

"Nor do I. This is about a Russian assassin."

"Surely we don't have any more Russians hiding in the basement," Eyre exclaimed. "Isn't everything sealed up now?"

"Mikhail Lashevich is probably in the north. His daughter lives in Hull. But he's an important player, and I expect he'll show his nose in London eventually. I wanted hotel staff to be alerted to his appearance in case he decides to meet with Ovolensky or his thugs."

"Understood." Eyre took the envelope Glass offered and opened it.

"That photograph is many years old, but hopefully he hasn't changed in appearance, much. The sketch is only about three years old from an operative inside Russia."

"He gained a scar on his cheek."

"Yes, but it could be covered by a beard," Glass said.

Eyre nodded. "I'll have one of the employees do a sketch of him with a beard and put all three images up in the Staff Lounge with one of my daily notes."

"Thank you. This man is a trained assassin. It would be best if he never came anywhere near London."

Eyre set the envelope aside. "Speaking of Russians, Olga finished the art exhibit yesterday."

"I'm surprised. She didn't take anything from my suite in the end."

"I think her artistic eye only wanted those oranges and reds in the *Firebird*. While your suite has some of the best art in the hotel, none of it had that color scheme."

"Fair enough."

"Want to take a look? I'll unlock the Coffee Room."

Oddly enough, Glass found that he was interested in what Olga had completed. He stood. "Very well."

Eyre stood as well and escorted him back to the Grand Hall and across it to the quadruple-paneled double-height doors. He unlocked them with an old-fashioned iron key and gestured Glass in before closing and relocking the doors behind him.

"This must be your favorite room in the hotel."

"Very much so. It is my throne room."

Glass heard the laughter in the man's voice as he turned on the lights. His vision was momentarily dazzled by the swirl of colors in the room.

"What an eye," he said.

"Olga is an artist," Eyre said simply. "She thinks of herself as the bereaved fiancée of one, but she has her own skill. In a way I am glad she didn't marry young. She might never have had the opportunity to develop her skills."

"What is her medium?" He slowly rotated to take in the full display.

"She paints. She has her own pieces in a gallery. Or at least she will. The gallery opens with its new installations tomorrow night."

"Good," he said, taking in the swirl of rich jewel tones on the walls of the screens that led toward a lighter-colored wall of art at the back of the room. "Her eye is very clever."

"I think her every waking thought was consumed with the layout recently."

Glass wondered if she'd been thinking about art when they'd kissed. No, he was reasonably sure she'd thought about a bit more than art in the past days regardless of her considerable talent. "As you say. She told me you are old friends. Did you know her sister and other family members growing up? She said she had cousins here as well."

Eyre shot him a sideways glance. "Suspicious of everyone, aren't you, Lord Walling?"

Once again, he'd used the wrong tone. If only there were a spy school where he could take a refresher course. "My interest might be romantic."

Eyre chuckled. "You and a chambermaid?"

"I thought she was management."

"I've promoted both her and Ivan Salter, but they are still doing their original jobs. Over time they will focus on management tasks. For now, Olga is more likely to be seen changing your bedsheets than sitting behind a desk working on charts."

"So you don't recommend I take her on a second date?"

Eyre's expression matched the confused look on the elongated, Cubist woman in the painting behind him. "You took her on a first?"

"Yes. I can't say it ended well." He pushed thoughts of that kiss to the back of his mind. "She seemed to think I was buttering her up to get better service."

"Hoping Pater will approve a Russian princess as your wife? I admit most of the Russians are penniless, but it's all relative. There are better-heeled princesses afoot in London."

"I take it you don't want to lose this one?"

"Her independence is dearly won." Eyre reached into his coat pocket for his cigarette case, glanced at the paintings around him, and seemed to think better of lighting up around them. "A No Smoking sign, I think."

"It seems wise," Glass said. "Back to my original question."

"Of course, my lord," Eyre said with a hint of a sneer in his voice. "Yes, I did know Princess Fyodora as a child, but I had no idea there were cousins."

"Odd. You'd think that England-based cousins would be exactly who the princess would have applied to for aid rather than her distant imperial relations."

"Obviously the families were not close. I would guess they aren't based in Surrey or London. I'd have found it hard to miss them if they had been."

Glass ran his tongue across his lower lip, catching a faint taste of marmalade from his breakfast toast. Dash it, he wanted the taste of Princess Olga Novikova on his lips again. As he stared at the dizzying array of Russian art around him, he began to formulate a plan.

Chapter 4

Her cousin Konstantin had shaved his beard for the occasion. Olga was happy to see that. He looked very different clean shaven. His face had seemed too narrow for his neck once he'd grown into adulthood. When he wore a beard his lower face and neck blended together, creating more harmony but making him look like someone who dwelled in a cave.

He lifted his hands when he saw her and came out of the shadows on the street corner. "You see, Cousin? I came," he said in Russian.

"That suit is older than my dress," Olga said, looking at him. How did he spend his money? He didn't wear a coat despite the chill air, but then he never seemed to feel temperature.

"We are Russians. We do not need anything new."

"Let us hope some Russians need new art. I could buy a new wardrobe if my work sells." Smiling at him, Olga straightened her glove, unable to hide her pleasure that her cousin had joined her. If he spent more time among regular people, maybe he would finally realize his illicit activities could hurt people. "Shall I take your arm?"

"No," Konstantin said quickly. "You know I don't like attention."

"I wonder why," she said, "with the terrible things you've done."

"It's all finished now," her cousin said, bumping her shoulder as they walked down the street toward the Imperial Art Gallery.

"No more bombs?" she said, careful to speak low and in Russian, not betraying her sense of relief.

"Not unless I need money," he said, looking at her sidelong as they walked under a street lamp. "Will you give me some?"

He blackmailed her, and when she didn't give him money, he did stupid things. She was reminded of poor, beleaguered Grand Duchess Xenia and her large family, forever asking for handouts, still attempting to live a royal life in reduced circumstances. In her case, she only had Konstantin, but he was a bottomless well of need, just as his parents had been to her father when she was a child.

"I'll give you everything I earn from my art." She stopped two doors down from the gallery and put her hand on his sleeve. He hated to be touched, and she usually respected that, so she hoped he understood the import of her statement. "But only if I have your promise that you will stop making bombs, for once and for all."

"I can't promise that."

"You have to promise. If that plot against the hotel had succeeded, I'd have lost my position. I might even have been killed. Where would your money come from then?"

He shrugged. "I'd make more bombs."

"Have you no family feeling? No conscience?" she demanded. As soon as she said it, she glanced away. He probably didn't. Ninety percent of the time he behaved more like an animal than a man. She'd learned long ago that she couldn't count on him. To think she'd reassured the dowager empress that she had family waiting in London to care for her back in 1919. What a lie that had been.

"I'm being chased by the police," Konstantin said, ignoring her questions. "I'm on the run. Always, I must pay rent, and then I cannot stay in the rooms because they are discovered."

"Yet people who want bombs can always find you." Her recrimination did not find a target. He didn't even glance at her.

Ahead of them, two cabs pulled up simultaneously on the street. Guests were arriving for the gallery show. Too many people would be around them, some of them Russian speakers.

"Never mind," she said. "Put on your glasses. They help hide those distinctive eyes of yours." The lightly amber-colored glass in his spectacles distorted the color of his eyes.

"Yes," he said, taking them out of his pocket and perching them on his nose.

No matter what, she kept trying to bring Konstantin out in the world. Maybe he'd notice that more people existed in the world than just him and stop doing such destructive things. One of these days he might hurt people and not just property before she could figure out how to make her only living relative stop.

* * * *

Glass had obtained the name of Olga's art gallery from Peter Eyre at the close of their rather unnerving conversation. Much more subtlety was required of him in the future, especially given that the princess still might be involved with the Bolsheviks somehow. At least being seen as a suitor was better than being recognized as a secret intelligence agent with the scent of prey in his nostrils.

He alighted from his taxicab in Grafton Street, happy to see the princess rated a gallery exhibit in Mayfair, despite what she did to earn a daily wage. Raindrops pelted his hat as he exited onto the pavement. He walked into the gallery behind a rotund couple, the woman dressed in a shapeless mink coat and the man in mothball-scented gray wool.

Inside, the Imperial proved to be a warren of small rooms. He wondered if it had once been a tavern. To his left, he saw one room filled with photographs of society beauties. Ahead of him appeared to be prints of the ragingly popular Scottish landscape variety. Not surprisingly, most of the gallery's patrons were clustered around the landscapes. He'd read about the American lust for limited edition prints and the enormous sums being exchanged for them. This gallery could well afford an exhibit of obscure Russian artists if they were also selling prints by Cameron and his ilk.

He took a right, following the general flow of traffic. A temporary coat check had been set up behind cloth-covered screens. He handed off his damp Callaghan of London coat and best Lock & Co. snap-brim fedora. The fur-lined wool coat would not only be warm enough to get him through a Russian winter but also worked perfectly for surveillance on London's damp streets. The fedora, on the other hand, only suited occasions like this one. He preferred a battered homburg for surveillance. Easier to hide under. Beneath his coat, his blue-and-gray-checked Savile Row suit had remained dry, despite the provocation of the late February weather.

"Douglas? Is that you?"

He tucked his coat check ticket into his coat as he turned around. A pretty woman in her mid-thirties had her head tilted so far sideways that she looked to be in danger of falling over. Faint lines creased in her forehead as she righted herself.

"I'm sorry. It's Walling now, isn't it? You ended up with the title."

"Margery Coulimore," he said slowly.

"Margery Davcheva now." Her lips curved up in a smile of embarrassment.

"That's right." He nodded. "I remember now. You married, what, about four years ago?"

"Five, yes." She touched his arm. "Danny had been gone more years than that by then."

He patted her hand, sorry that she felt any sadness upon seeing him. "I know. You mourned long enough. My brother would have wanted you to marry, have children. I didn't realize you'd married a Russian."

She waved at a young woman in a stunning embroidered dress and her elderly male companion. "Yes. We opened this gallery a couple of years ago."

"He is an artist?"

"No." She stared over his shoulder, nodding at someone else. "I used to dabble myself. It seemed like a good business to be in. I knew the right people, the right customers."

He vaguely remembered the smart set Margery and his second brother, Danny, had run in before the war. They'd had their wedding date set when war broke out, and Danny had enlisted with a group of friends, saying he'd be back before Christmas and they would reschedule the wedding. He'd never come home. "As I recall, that's perfectly correct. And it looks like what you are selling is all the rage."

"We do very well. I'm trying to recall exactly how old you are. You haven't married, am I correct?"

"No, I've stayed busy with work."

"I can introduce you around." She twisted the heirloom-quality triple rope of pearls draped around her neck. "I know positively oodles of people. I have at least two girl cousins in their twenties, lovely young women. I could invite you to a dinner party next week, pair you up with someone delicious."

A woman walked up to the coat check. He recognized the orange silk-and-fur cape. The princess. The man next to her wasn't familiar. Had Olga brought a date to her opening?

"Who are you staring at?" Margery asked. She did her head tilting thing again, bending sideways from the waist.

Olga pulled off her cape. Her companion didn't aid her. Underneath, she wore a dress that was much boxier than the slinky black number she'd worn to dinner. This dress was gray blue, probably silk, though he didn't really know fabric, with a lot of black embroidery on both the bodice and the skirt. It looked expensive but a bit dowdy on her long frame.

"Is she your type, Douglas?" Margery queried. "Blonde? Statuesque?"

"I know Her Serene Highness," he said.

"Do you? I wonder how." She broke off when Olga took her ticket and turned, glancing straight at them. Margery lifted her hand and wriggled her fingers in a wave. "I must go to her, darling. She's one of my artists, you know."

"She's why I came," Glass murmured.

"How lovely. You must buy something. She's desperately poor, you know, like so many of the Russians. My husband was so lucky to have a

father with a large deposit in the Bank of England before the revolution."
She brushed past him in a cloud of chiffon and went to Olga, taking both
of the princess's hands in hers.

Glass took the opportunity to stare hard at Olga's companion. He wore
strange spectacles, more like sunglasses than normal glasses. Some sort
of light sensitivity. Given that he had Konstantin Novikov on the brain,
he examined the man against what little description he had. This man had
no beard, but his basic body type matched. That could be true of so many
men. The glasses hid his eyes. And, according to Sadie Loudon Drake, the
bomber's eyes were supposed to be quite unusual, a cloud of amber around
the iris and that surrounded by blue. Glass knew he'd have to keep an eye
on the pair, but it wouldn't hurt anything if he looked at Olga's pieces.

He might even find a birthday gift for his father, if she had any talent.
Turning away from the coat check, where another half-dozen damp
Londoners were unbuttoning coats, he went into the Russian gallery. There,
he found quite a variety of offerings, from icons to paintings that seemed
to mirror Picasso's many changes of style to landscapes.

He found Olga's signature first on a nature scene. A picnic was set out
on the banks above a sluggish river. No figures were in the scene or in any
other of her paintings. Nonetheless, they each had a sentimental mood. He
didn't think his father would appreciate any of them since he wasn't an
emotional man. On the other hand, they did evoke emotion in him.

He was considering the starkest of the half-dozen paintings, depicting
a burned-out barn on the edge of a wood, when he heard high-heeled
shoes behind him.

"You've been staring at this painting for some time," Olga said. As he
turned toward the princess, a twig-thin woman in black took his place,
muttering to herself. "What is it that appeals to you?"

"It's terribly sad, Your Serene Highness." He smelled lemons, a scent
that seemed commonplace until it mixed with her skin and hair and became
something exotic. "I feel the sorrow coming off this in waves."

"A stable boy died in that barn. He became trapped when trying to free
the horses." She came alongside him, her profile regal and remote. "I can
still remember the screams."

"How old were you?"

"About nine. It is one of those images that lives on in nightmares. I
thought by painting it I might let the memory go."

"Did it work?" He watched her as she stared at her own work. She was
as still as a statue, but her head had jutted forward just a bit on her neck.
Her neckline was free of jewelry. She must have once had heirloom pieces

like Margery, but they probably hadn't made it out of Russia.

After a long moment she released a breath. Her shoulders relaxed. "I don't know. I have so many nightmares running through my brain."

So did he. Best just to push the tangle of them into the recesses of his mind and focus on the present. "Why no people?"

"I went with a theme. It's not that I never paint people." She gestured across the set of six small paintings. "I had a fantasy that someone might buy them as a set rather than having different types of work."

"You are very talented," Glass said. He considered telling her he would buy her work but thought it best to wait and see if anyone else did. He was no art connoisseur who would get her work seen and purchased by others. If someone like that wanted her paintings, she would be better off with them buying her work.

"Thank you," she said softly.

"What do you do now? Mingle, try to sell your work?"

"I couldn't be so forward, but I'm happy to answer questions if anyone asks them."

The room had started to fill. A dozen or so had entered, doubling the crowd.

"I've known Margery for years. She would have married my brother in 1914 if war hadn't broken out," he remarked.

Olga's eyes saddened. "She would have been the countess someday?"

"She was engaged to my second brother, not the eldest."

"I see. She doesn't seem ambitious that way."

"No, definitely more artistic."

"We were that way too, Maxim and I." She rubbed her lips together, darkening their rose tone. "At least, I think we would have been. I'm beginning to realize how young I was then."

"I saw you came in with a companion. Throwing me over for another man?" He meant it as a joke, but as he said the words, they came out more harshly than he'd intended.

The princess looked genuinely confused, but her expression turned to relief as the gallery owner came their way.

"There you are, my love," Margery said, bustling toward them. "Oh, don't spend all your time with Walling. There's a shy art critic over there in the corner whom you must impress." She took the princess's arm and steered her away.

Glass shoved his hands into his trouser pockets. Nothing he could do but chat with the mystery man himself. He glanced around the room but could see no sign of the fellow who had arrived with the princess.

Of all the bad luck. He did a circuit of the room for twenty minutes and saw no sign of his quarry. The man had left, and he still didn't know if he might be Konstantin Novikov. He didn't even know if the bomber was related to the princess.

What might it mean if she was? What did Princess Olga know about the man's activities? Was she a spy or Bolshie activist or completely ignorant of the man who shared her name?

He'd have to get close enough to find out—whether he liked it or not, whether she liked it or not. He'd have to court her more persistently. But for now, he decided to cede the floor to the real critics and art-world folk. He went for his coat. Time to return to his listening post and check in on the Russians.

* * * *

One of Olga's least favorite tasks was cleaning Peter Eyre's private quarters. She knew it was a trusted job because bits of hotel paperwork were scattered about. No one but her was allowed to have a key to Peter's private domain. But on a Friday morning, after a Thursday night much too late and full of champagne, she didn't want to be in a stuffy space full of the scent of old cigarette smoke.

The first thing she did in the sitting room was turn on the electric fan to circulate the stale air and prop open the door between the sitting room and Peter's official office, which at least had windows high in the walls. Because of Peter's location in the hotel, his personal space had no windows, no way to easily get fresh air in and out.

Once the air had started to move, she pulled her clean feather duster from her bucket and began to restack the magazines and newspapers on Peter's tables and dust around them. She picked up the overflowing ashtray on the main table between the sofas and chairs, carried it to a bin in the corner, and wiped it clean.

"What is that sick-making noise?" a woman with gravelly voice demanded behind her.

Olga's midsection caved in as she skipped a breath. *Emmeline Plash.* The woman who had managed to poison Peter's life to the extent that no other woman ever had a chance with him, for more than a night, at least.

"Just the fan, Emmeline," Olga said, half turning. "If your head is aching, moving the air will help."

Emmeline's parents had been friends with Peter's parents, and her little brother, dead in the war, had been Peter's best friend. Emmeline had been engaged to Peter's older brother at one time. Somehow, after the war, she'd become Peter's mistress, a financially motivated arrangement as he had paid some of her bills, and her mother's, for years. Mrs. Plash and Emmeline had lived at the Grand Russe for a few weeks when it opened, but Peter had moved them to Bert Dadey's boardinghouse when Mrs. Plash wandered one too many times and Emmeline lost her mind and attacked Peter physically.

"Turn it off," Emmeline snapped, flinging herself into a chair. "And bring the ashtray back to the table. I want it."

What was the witch doing here? Why hadn't Peter learned his lesson with this woman? Truly, she did have a sweet side, and definitely a glamorous one, but she also had violent tendencies, not to mention an unending need for money and attention.

Olga finished wiping out the ashtray and set it in front of Emmeline. The woman sniffed and opened Peter's cigarette box. "Raining, I suppose?"

"Yes," Olga said. If she had asked Peter's family for money instead of a job a couple of years ago, would she have a place in Peter's bed instead of on his payroll now? Olga wondered, but still a virgin, she couldn't imagine what that would be like. She'd been raised by a pious and conservative family. Becoming a mistress, even to survive in the style her position demanded, would have made her a sinner.

She'd never even considered it then. Lord Walling had been the first man to awaken her senses since Maxim died. He was the first man to appear in her dreams, to make her restless at night.

And yet, he hadn't even bought one of her paintings at the gallery show. Deciding to return later, she turned away from Emmeline. She didn't want to change out the towels and bedding when the mistress was in the suite.

She picked up her bucket. How far had she sunk in life to be offended by Lord Walling's disinterest in purchasing her paintings? Of course he didn't want to purchase art that made him sad.

But she had no one to rely on, so the blow was sharp, even if she didn't want it to be. Her closest relative just wanted her money. No one she knew could afford luxuries like paintings, especially those priced by a top gallery.

"Aren't you going to finish your work?" Emmeline called out behind her.

"I'll let you have your peace." Olga walked out of the sitting room, head held high, before Emmeline could ask her to do something demeaning.

She didn't even tidy the office; she just tucked her bucket inside the utility closet there and stepped out, closing the door behind her.

Instead of cleaning, she decided to do a hotel floor check. She had quite new chambermaids on the lower floors. By then, it would be time to busy herself on the late-rising seventh floor.

Frank Russell at the reception desk spoke to her as she went by. "Olga?"
"Yes?"

The concierge's farm-boy grin widened to alarming proportions as
he pointed to a crystal vase, filled with the most gorgeous red and white
hothouse roses. "These came for you."

"*Bushwa*," she said, shocked. "For me? Are you certain?"

"As certain as I am that I'd like to take you to the pictures tonight.
What do you say?"

Olga ignored his impertinent request as she lifted the vase and pulled
out the envelope underneath it. She slid her finger under the envelope flap,
noting the excellent quality of it, and removed the card. *"Congratulations on
a fine showing. I'm still thinking about that painting. You have tremendous
talent. Your servant, Lord Walling."*

All her bitter thoughts about the viscount vanished. Maybe he hadn't
bought her painting, but it had moved him. And he'd bought her a
Lalique mermaid vase. She hadn't had a vase of her own since she'd left
St. Petersburg.

Smiling, she tucked the card in her pinny and picked up the vase.
She'd put it in Peter's office for now. If she took the vase down to the
staff lounge, it might vanish before the end of her shift. Even if the vase
survived the day, the girls would probably pluck out the flowers, one by
one, and take them home.

* * * *

Glass opened his door and found Olga, an expectant look in her eyes
instead of the usual chambermaid indifference. "No bucket?" he asked.
"Decided to trust the chambermaid this time?"

"I haven't done my room checks yet. I came to thank you."

"Come in." He pulled the door the rest of the way open.

Olga stepped into the small foyer but stood in such a way that he
couldn't quite close the door. He suspected it to be a practiced move,
something to dissuade hotel guests from attempting to take advantage of
vulnerable female staff.

He wasn't an average guest, though, and she ought to know that. She'd
trusted him to take her to dinner, after all. "How about having a cup of tea
with me? It's just after eleven. I could use one."

She shook her head. "It's against hotel policy to fraternize with
guests like that."

"You went to dinner with me."

"Peter doesn't expect to control my activities outside of the hotel."

"I am to understand you would take tea with me outside of the hotel then?"

She nodded. "I'm curious to understand why you sent me those lovely flowers."

He heard a click emanating from the region of the *Firebird*. The recording disk was full. The Russians had been meeting, and he needed to keep recording. "Why don't you join me for a proper tea this afternoon? What time?"

"Just after three?" she suggested.

"Where shall we go?"

"The A.B.C. is the closest café."

"I can do better than that."

Her manner stiffened. "It is good enough."

He didn't want to insult her pride by pointing out that he would pay. Of course he would. He looked her over and realized that she must not want to go anywhere nicer because she was in uniform, not a smart dress of her choosing. "Excellent." He rubbed his hands together. "I'll meet you by Marble Arch just after three, next to the coffee wagon."

She inclined her head and stepped back into the corridor. Without further ceremony, he closed the door and bustled to the painting so he could change out the disk. His Russian wasn't good enough to understand Ovolensky's visitor, so he needed to record the meeting and have the conversation translated.

He spent hours standing with headphones on, attempting to untangle the Russian, so he was thrilled to leave the suite for a spell and ventured onto the chilly, damp streets. The sharp bite of raindrops felt good on his face, and he didn't mind the smell of exhaust hanging in the air after too many hours of the overheated air in the hotel. When a larger raindrop hit his chin and drizzled down his neck, he tied his muffler more securely and peered across the street, looking for Olga.

Someone tapped his shoulder. "Lord Walling?"

He turned around. Olga had come up behind him. "Where did you come from?"

"Staff entrance." She pointed to the stone steps the employees used, hidden from view by a half wall.

"Ah. Shall we?"

He held out his arm. Instead of taking it, she opened her umbrella and handed it to him to hold. He found himself walking back down the street past the hotel, the umbrella held over them both, carefully synchronizing his steps with her to keep them protected.

"I have to say I'm suspicious of shops like the Aerated Bread Company.

They have something like four hundred outlets in London alone, don't they? And then there's Lyon's. There is something to be said for the more bespoke tea experiences," he said.

"Like Redcake's, you mean?" Olga asked.

"Don't you think the quality is better?"

"Their prices are ruinous. They have been royal family favorites since Queen Victoria's day for good reason. I went to the Kensington Redcake's once with Grand Duchess Xenia." She pressed her lips together and pointed at the name of the Park Street tea shop, painted on the stone above the doorway.

"Are you and the grand duchess close?" He tilted the umbrella so she could push open the tea-shop door. When she was halfway through, he quickly closed the umbrella, shook it out, and entered the shop.

Olga stepped into line at the counter, behind two men. Glass listened to their conversation for a few seconds out of habit and dismissed them to focus on the princess.

"Not at all. We do maintain a correspondence, but she travels a fair amount and has a large family. I don't like to trouble her."

"A tsar's sister," Glass said. "Yes, I'd be intimidated by her."

"She's lovely," the princess assured him. "No airs, at least not around family. I owe her and the dowager empress my life."

He smiled gallantly. "Then I am a supporter of them both."

When they reached the counter she ordered an egg on toast. He asked for a ham sandwich and suggested cake for them both, along with their tea.

"You need more than just toast and an egg," he said. "You work hard."

"Very well." Her downcast eyes showed she was embarrassed.

He doubled their order of cream cakes to prove his point; then they walked into the crowded dining room, full of pairs of men having business meetings. A few women dotted the room as well, though mostly with male companions. The men in front of them at the counter had been discussing bank business, and most of the room looked to be patronized by a similar type of businessman.

"So much for the ladies' dining room," he said, finding them a small table against the wall. Women bustled around the room in black dresses with white aprons delivering orders.

"Not many women have money to spend like men do," the princess said. "It is hard to earn a living. Prices are reasonable here, but why expose yourself when you can eat at home?"

He held out a chair for her, and she sat gracefully. "Does Mr. Dadey allow you to use his parlor to entertain guests?"

"I spent time with Alecia Loudon and Emmeline Plash in the Plashes' parlor," Olga said. "I don't see many other people." Emmeline was a different person in her own space and when she wasn't over-imbibing.

"Miss Loudon is now Mrs. Saltykov, correct?"

She frowned. "Salter. How do you even know Ivan's original surname?"

"I must have heard it somewhere," he said, cursing her attentiveness. Why did he let his guard down around this woman? He couldn't trust her.

Chapter 5

"Ivan probably told you his original name." Princess Olga shifted on her hard tearoom chair. "He pays particular attention to the seventh floor. His cousin, Georgy Ovolensky, is staying next door to you."

Glass nodded. Of course she thought he needed all this explained to him. On Monday, as far as she knew, just five days before, he had been a newcomer to the hotel. Now he could blame any unusual knowledge he had on Ivan. They spoke every night about eight to keep each other appraised of security issues and the Russians' movements.

"I do see him daily," Glass said. "Do you work six days a week as he does?"

"Yes, Monday to Saturday. It will be simpler after tomorrow."

"Why is that?" He placed his napkin on his lap.

"I am moving into the hotel."

"You don't say."

"Renovations have been finished on the tenth floor. Peter is offering rooms to senior staff. He just told Ivan and me on Tuesday. We, and his new bride, of course, are all moving in on Sunday."

"Is it an improvement over Montagu Square?"

"I'll miss Mr. Dadey," Princess Olga said reflectively. "He is a very nice man. I'll be happy to see less of Emmeline Plash, though the only time I enjoy her is at the boardinghouse."

"What is her connection to the Grand Russe?"

"She is a lifelong, err, friend, of Peter's."

"But he doesn't employ her."

"She has an income. I don't know what she'll be inheriting from her mother. I would assume she'll have to share whatever is left with her older brother. He lives in eastern Canada somewhere."

"Her income might have been her mother's," Lord Walling said. "I hope she really does have something." He watched a light switch on behind Olga's eyes.

"I hadn't thought of that," she admitted. "Good heavens. I hadn't thought of that possibility at all."

"I hope for her sake that it ends well. I've seen some rather sad cases."

"There are too many women and not enough men in our generation," she agreed. "We women were allowed to come into England, but the government wouldn't allow any grand dukes to come, so Grand Duchess Xenia and her husband are forced to live in different countries."

"It must be a choice at some level."

"Perhaps," she said. "But not entirely. Don't you find that you never so much want what you cannot have?"

"I do not tend to think of myself very much." He smiled at the waitress who had arrived with their tray. She placed his sandwich in front of him, the princess's toast in front of her, and put the cream cakes in the center.

Princess Olga sighed happily. "Such decadence."

He wanted to ask her if Peter was reducing her pay, now that he'd asked her to live at the hotel, but knew he didn't have the right to learn if she was being exploited.

"It seems you are quite alone in London," he said. "If you could have anyone to tea in your new rooms, who would it be?"

"My sister, of course," she said, cutting a minute piece of her toast with the edge of her fork. "I would dearly love to know what became of her."

"What was her last known location?"

"She headed to China. I seemed to be in danger because of my fiancé's death, and she had no reason to go, at first."

"What of your parents?"

"My mother died of influenza. It was difficult to get nutritious food, medical care. My father was murdered. I'm sure you remember how bad it was after the war."

"Yes. It was terrible," he said.

They chewed in silence for a few minutes. When his mouth was clear of ham, he asked, "I know I am prying, but I admit to curiosity. Was that your cousin I saw you with at the Imperial Art Gallery last night?"

"Did we look related?" she asked and placed her last bite of toast in her mouth. She had eaten more quickly than he.

He'd like to encourage her to eat more. She was too thin. Her collarbone had jutted from her black gown when they'd gone to dinner. "Around the eyes, I suppose."

She leaned forward slightly. "In what way?"

"You both have eyes a little larger than is common. Thick eyelashes, as well. He has thick brows, unlike you, but I chalk that up to feminine magic."

She smiled. "Yes, we are related. I see him sometimes."

"What is his name?"

"Novikov," she said and picked up the plate in the center of the table. "Cream cake?"

"Yes, thank you." He took a cake and waited expectantly for her to continue. Instead of speaking, she seemed heavily distracted by the two young fools at the next table, who were babbling excitedly about a game of Ping-Pong.

He knew the subject matter could not be of any interest to her, and her body language told him that she didn't want to say more about her cousin. His internal antenna picked up static. Was this the elusive Konstantin, the Bolshevik bomber? How would a member of the Russian upper class wind up tied to the Bolshies?

"He must have the title of prince as well," Glass commented.

"Actually, no." She lifted her hands. "In my grandfather's day, there was a petition to transfer the title. My grandmother was the only heir, and being female she couldn't carry the title. The title was transferred to my grandfather, who was her third cousin, I believe, and the title carried on. And the names are confusing, too. Cousins marrying too many cousins."

"Until now."

"Until now," she said, "since my parents only had two daughters. There was a son, but he died when he was two weeks old."

"Did you see him?"

"No, it was before I was born. I think my family is not very healthy. Everyone married relatives in previous generations."

"I don't imagine you will do that unless you marry this cousin." He pulled his second cream cake from the plate. She hadn't yet touched either of hers.

"No, I would not do that. I don't believe in marrying without stability."

"He has no money either?"

She glanced down. "Whatever he has, it is not managed well."

"You could take the reins."

Her lips curled. "After what I've told you, about dead babies and family lines all but dying out, you think I should marry my second cousin?"

He smiled. "Ah, but you are probably related many more ways than that."

She put the outstretched fingers of one hand to the front of her forehead. "Keeping up is exhausting. I actually thought I was more closely related to the imperial family before I left Russia, but then the grand duchess showed me a genealogy chart. Somehow I had missed a generation."

"It happens. My title goes back more than three hundred years, but one has to wonder if the title really continued unbroken for all those generations."

"Unlikely. Three hundred years or more?"

"Right. One has to believe that the bloodline circles around again, in the end." Too many people lied. But he'd had a considerable amount of conversation with the princess since she'd changed the subject. He returned to his original question again. "What was his name, this second cousin?"

"Konstantin Novikov," she said. Their eyes met. She quickly glanced away and reached for her first cream cake.

Bingo. He had no idea how common her name was, or how common the combination of Konstantin Novikov was, but he needed to find this man. When he returned to the hotel, he'd make a telephone call to Detective Inspector Dent at Special Branch and put a tail on her. Since she'd probably only rarely leave the hotel once she moved in, she shouldn't be that hard to watch.

* * * *

Olga stood in an empty guest room on the second floor at nine on Saturday morning. "The first thing you want to do is clear the surfaces of trash and ash."

The new chambermaid, Florence, gaped at her. John Neville, Peter's new day manager, had taken over the hiring. Why had he taken on a girl as dull-witted as Florence?

She put her hand on her hip. "Are my instructions too much for you, Florence?"

"You have a funny accent," Florence said. "I can't understand you."

Unfortunately, Olga could understand the girl just fine. "You will have to learn. I do not have time to humor you."

The girl's expression didn't change. Olga walked around the room, pointing at wrappers, dirty cups, half-full ashtrays, and other debris. She waited for Florence to clear everything away, attempting to hold onto her seniority and her authority despite the complaint about her accent. As excited as she had been by her promotion, she'd have been far better off with a husband than a useless title. After all, she still cleaned rooms, even the room of the man she was seeing. She, who had been born in a palace, now pointed out bloodstains from a shaving accident in the sink to a girl who had insulted her.

She squared her shoulders and took a deep breath. Giving into self-pity bought her nothing. No, she simply had to get on with it and keep hope alive with Lord Walling. For whatever reason, he had some level of interest in her. Her life could still change.

She pulled out the small notebook from her apron pocket and turned around. A sharp pain exploded on the side of her knee. She yelped, instinctively raising her leg and hopped around. Florence stood, mouth open again, holding a broom. She said nothing.

"You hit me," Olga said through gritted teeth.

"Didn't see you there," the girl said, finding her voice.

No apology. Had she done it on purpose? Olga narrowed her eyes. "You do understand that I am your supervisor? I am in charge of you."

"Wot's that? I don't understand." The girl let her mouth hang open over rabbit-sized front teeth. Her eyes bulged.

Olga thought frantically. Did she have the authority to fire this ghastly creature? She was very afraid she didn't, since she hadn't been asked to do the hiring. Pulling the tattered remnants of her dignity around her, she limped through the room toward the door.

"What do I do next?" Florence called.

Olga stepped through the door and shut it. She pulled out her key and locked the door from the outside. Perhaps she was losing her mind, but she didn't want the girl loose in the hotel while she received permission to sack her.

Tears welled in her eyes as she went to the staff lift. Peter would tell her what to do.

* * * *

At one, Glass arrived at St. Martin's House, Hanover Square, for lunch with his father. His operative, Bill Vall-Grandly, was monitoring the Russians for the afternoon. He had plenty of other duties, but he'd worked in the suite before and was the only man in London at present fully apprised of the situation.

His father's butler, a half-decade older than Glass with a hitch in his step from injuries suffered during the war, escorted him into the small drawing room on the first floor used by the family. Glass took the opportunity to circle the room and visit with his lost brothers and mother, who stared down at him from the walls. How was it that he, the least of his family, was now the heir to all this wealth and position? He'd expected to make his way in the world. So intent had he been on that path that he'd kept working after the war and had changed his fortunes instead of learning the family business, all the estate and money management. He was a poor choice for earl, and his father grew older every day.

"Beautiful, wasn't she?" his father asked from behind him, entering the room. He stepped in front of the portrait of Lady St. Martin's.

Glass's mother had been what they called Black Irish in appearance. She was the daughter of an Irish Peer. Glass had never had contact with any of those relatives. Although wealthy and titled, they didn't come to London. Her mother, being English herself, had brought her for a season, though, and they had taken the fashionable world by storm. His parents were engaged three weeks after meeting and married two months after that. He rather suspected his oldest brother had been an eight-month miracle. She'd been a daredevil, his mother, unlike her more staid husband. Unfortunately, her death had reflected this, a fall from a horse while riding at their Derbyshire estate early one June when he was in mid-childhood. They had been picking wild strawberries, and she'd challenged her two eldest sons to a race. Glass had been left behind with the buckets to wait for the servants to pick him up in a gig. He hadn't seen her fall. He hadn't been able to eat strawberries since.

"You need to find yourself a beauty," his father said gruffly. "Makes it easier to fill your nursery when your woman is easy to look at."

"You liked Mother, though, didn't you?"

The earl lifted his pocket watch on its chain and peered at it. "Luncheon in ten minutes."

"St. Martin's House runs better than the trains," Glass said. "But what say you about my mother?"

"You must not remember her very well. You were, what, four when she died?"

"Eight," Glass corrected.

"Then you are older than I remember. Not good, Walling."

Glass curled his upper lip in response.

His father glanced at the portrait, clasping his hands behind his back. "I was obsessed with her. She had the tiniest waist, the fullest bosom, and the daintiest feet I'd ever seen. Her laugh made me feel like a king."

Glass nodded, waiting for him to go on.

"She gave me four sons. I wouldn't have minded a daughter, but we had none of those. You're from good stock. Find a girl—doesn't need to be wealthy; we have plenty of money—and get us an heir."

Glass considered before speaking. "I've met a Russian princess. Distantly descended from a tsar. Grand Duchess Xenia was her benefactor."

"Was? She's alive, isn't she?"

"Yes. But the princess had known the Redcake family as a child, and Eloise Redcake took her under her wing and taught her the hotel business.

She's working for Peter Eyre at the Grand Russe now."

"As what? A secretary?"

"She manages the chambermaids. Hard work for someone of her background, but she's a strong soul."

"Healthy?"

"I believe so."

"You should marry her. No money but a title, royal blood. Nothing to complain about there. You obviously respect her. Is she a looker?"

"Beautiful. Not like Mother at all. Fair."

"Change the look of the family." The earl moved a few steps to the right and stared at a portrait of his four black-haired sons painted in 1913. His own hair had been a dark brown, and Glass's hair didn't match either of his parents' precisely but was a mixture of both tones.

"She probably would."

His father chuckled suddenly. "Mixing Irish and Russian. That will be an interesting bloodline."

"I haven't seen any fire from her." He thought about that. "It might be there, however. I'm not sure whose side she's on politically."

"A Russian princess? Why, she's a White, of course, a royalist."

"I would believe that wholeheartedly if it weren't for the issue of the bomber wreaking havoc in London having the same last name as she does."

"You don't say."

"She's admitted a branch of her family, without a title, has lived in England for a time. I saw her cousin briefly, and he might be the man we know as Konstantin."

"Can you really trust any of these Oriental types?" his father said. "Oh, I know, many Russians lived more in Europe than Russia, even before the war, seem to be European, but then something like that revolution happens, shows what savages they are. Not like us at all. How long has she been in London?"

"She came in 1919 when we rescued the dowager empress."

"Who at least was European. A Danish princess," his father said and smacked his lips.

The butler appeared in the doorway to summon them to the table.

His father turned to him. "Bring her to dinner one night. Make the arrangement with my secretary. I'll sort her out for you."

As he strode to the door, Glass followed him. He never tried to put on airs with his father, too aware he'd been the youngest son, the least important, until well into his twenties. At work he was a competent leader, but here, he didn't try to expand on the role he'd been placed in at birth.

At the dining table, he took careful stock of his father, who was closing in on seventy years of age. He didn't look it, having the hard, hearty appearance of a country squire, but the years would catch up with him all too soon.

"We should spend more time together. I need to learn the family business," Glass said as a footman poured the wine. All around them were tapestries of hunting scenes, ordered by some eighteenth-century earl. They had scared him when he was a child, with all the gore of the kill so lavishly displayed, and he'd been happy to always eat in the nursery.

"You should move into this house," his father said. "I understand you are a busy and important man, but if you are on-site, it will be easier to work together with what little time you have."

Glass nodded. "I'll consider it. We are so short-staffed that I'm on a surveillance job myself at the moment."

The earl snorted. "Don't they know how important your work is? You're all that is standing between the people and madmen like this Konstantin."

"I know."

"What is it going to take to discover if your princess is part of his conspiracy?"

"I need her to trust me."

"How are you going to manage that?"

Glass picked up his spoon and scooped up a small amount of beef broth. "She's an artist. Just had paintings go on sale at the Imperial Art Gallery."

"Any good?"

"Yes, but not your sort of thing."

His father shrugged and picked up his wine glass. "Doesn't matter. Can hang the paintings out of the way somewhere. Don't need to look at them."

"It's Margery's gallery. She married a Russian."

"I remember her." The earl drank deeply and set his glass down with a clatter. He'd gained five years of pain in his eyes with the mention of Margery. "Why not give her the business? I'll contact our solicitor to buy the paintings."

"Olga Novikova. That's her name."

"How many works?"

"There were six. It's possible some were sold by now."

"I'll purchase what is left. You tell her about it, that you brought her business. That ought to soften her up."

"Yes, sir," Glass said, cheered by the thought. At least he wasn't buying them himself. They would hang in Hanover Square. He'd have to make sure they were placed somewhere his father's guests would see them.

* * * *

On Sunday afternoon, Olga stood on the bank of the Serpentine in Hyde Park, waiting for Konstantin. A peaceful atmosphere filled the park. On the grass, sheep grazed, natural lawnmowers. A couple shepherds chatted on a bench, but otherwise, the area remained empty on this rainy day. She stretched her shoulders back, pushing out her chest. Her arms and much of her upper body hurt after moving her property from Montagu Square to the Grand Russe's tenth floor.

She stared at the family of swans passing near to the bank, slightly jealous of their uncomplicated lives. Was moving into the hotel the right thing to do? Would she find herself a slave to her work, never leaving and developing that wan skin people who never went outside had?

At least she had the park nearby. With its delights so close, how could she find a reason not to venture out every day? She could buy a better coat too, with the money she saved on lodgings. Bert Dadey hadn't charged too much, but free was better.

All in all, Peter Eyre had treated her well. It wasn't his fault that this wasn't the life she'd been raised to expect. Maybe by the time she was thirty-six, half a lifetime past her engagement to Maxim, she'd have forgotten the privileges of her youth.

Instead, she should focus on her neat little room. No longer did she have to stare at that dark blotch on the ceiling in Bert Dadey's boardinghouse, evidence of water problems on the floor above. No more faint odor of mildew, either. She'd only had time to sit on her new mattress so far, but it had no lumps, and she had a double bed instead of a single. A proper closet, too, with a built-in set of drawers, and for now, she had her own bathroom until someone moved into the room next door. Heaven, really. So modern. The walls were a neat white, ready for art to be hung. The eighth through tenth floors of the Grand Russe were set in from the lower part of the building and were therefore smaller and cozier. The eighth and ninth were being renovated with an eye to becoming convenience apartments, long-term rentals that were able to take advantage of some of the hotel amenities. All the managers had been tasked with deciding how to fill the rest of the tenth. Chambermaid dormitories? Security guard dormitory? Or even space for the secretarial workers. So far, she shared the floor with the Salters, the night and the day managers, and the concierge. The Restaurant's chef had turned down a suite, as had the hall porter. Plenty of space remained.

Despite these engrossing thoughts, she saw her cousin before he saw her. Konstantin had a nondescript black bowler tilted over his eyes, though he didn't have his amber glasses on. Why couldn't he remember to wear them? He didn't appear to have shaved in the three days since she'd seen him, and red stubble flecked with gray showed on his jawline.

She saw the moment he caught sight of her, just a pause, a hitch in his walk; then he circled a pair of sheep and came down to the bank.

He reached into his pocket and handed her a heel of bread. His lips curved upward slightly, the closest to a smile he ever came. "Thought you'd like to feed the swans."

How sweet of him to remember. The bread felt stale and rough underneath her mittens. "Wonderful. I never think to bring any myself."

"I know. Strange, with all that free toast in the Coffee Room at the Grand Russe."

"How do you know about that?"

He shrugged.

"You really should avoid the place," she admonished.

"I don't go in there now, not since they made certain changes on the lower level. I could outsmart them, but I don't have a reason to as long as you help me."

She crumbled the bread between her fingers, ignoring his implied threat, and tossed a piece toward the swans. It bounced off the white-feathered back of one. She clapped her hand to her mouth. "Oh, dear."

Konstantin rolled his eyes as the second swan ducked his bill to pick up the piece. "You didn't hurt it."

"Where are you staying now?"

"Nowhere after tomorrow. Rent's due. Can you lend me some money?"

She sighed. At least she didn't have to pay her own rent on Monday. "What do you need?"

"Three bob should do me."

She frowned. "That's too much."

"I have to move around. Some weeks are more expensive than others. I'm in a good part of the city this week."

"If you would change your associations, you wouldn't need to run."

"Just give me the money, Cousin." His eyes had gone hard.

She wondered if this is why he'd left his glasses off, to intimidate her. Knowing as she did how his mood could switch from the sweet person who brought bread to swans to the man who built bombs, it was effective. She wondered, as she often had, what Konstantin's father had done to exile him to England. The tale varied, but a woman who'd been burned came into the telling every time. She suspected he had plunged an unfaithful mistress's hand into a samovar. It was the version told by an elderly aunt, and it made sense to her. It also made her afraid of what Konstantin might be capable of doing to her.

"I made very little more than that," she whispered. "I know rent can be half of salary in London, but three pounds is so much more than that. How am I supposed to live? To eat?"

"Toast." His eyes bored into hers. "You get all the free toast and tea and champagne you like. Deviled eggs, too. I've seen them out in the evenings."

"I'm the help. I can't eat in the Coffee Room. I'm not a guest."

"You can sneak in. You're a clever girl." He held out his hand. "The money."

She straightened her aching shoulders with effort. He'd never asked for so much. Had he calculated what she had and decided to go for every shilling, now that she'd moved into the hotel? A move only as old as an hour ago, and he demanded everything she possessed. She swallowed hard. He was her cousin. She could stand up to him. "No. I need a new coat. My clothes are still what I brought from Russia. Rags, some of them."

He put his hand on her shoulder and moved his face close to hers. He slowly tightened his hand as he spoke, digging into the already taut muscles along the back of her shoulder. "I need to stay moving. You don't want me to be arrested, to drag our illustrious name through the mud."

As she bit back a cry of pain, he tore off her coat. Two buttons fell into the dirt. He pawed through the coat until he found the hidden pocket within another pocket and pulled out her change purse. After he emptied the purse and tucked the contents into his pocket, he let the purse slide from his fingers. She grabbed for it.

Face still impassive, he threw the coat in the dirt at her feet and walked away. When he reached the grass, he started to whistle.

She shivered hard, a full-body rejection of what had just happened. Crouching, she picked up her coat. Her fingers shook too hard to close them around the buttons. She fumbled until her coat was back around her, cupping her shoulders with comforting warmth. Then she picked up the buttons. She tucked them inside her mitten and tightened her hand into a fist around them.

She didn't feel the peace of the place any longer. The clouds, gray and broad, had lowered in the sky, and the wind swept the trees. She could hear the branches, still bare, fluttering. Turning away, she walked up the low hill, her knee aching, ready to return to the hotel.

"Ya awright, miss?" one of the shepherds called as she walked by the bench where they sat. "Ya needs a hot drink o' tea."

"Yar pale, lovey," said the second man, holding up a sturdy, leather-covered vacuum flask.

She turned to them, her mouth working to say something in anger, and saw their sun-etched faces, their friendly smiles. The hand that wasn't clutching her precious buttons folded into a point toward the path where Konstantin had disappeared. "Didn't you see what he did?"

"What did ya do ter him?" the first man asked.

She gritted her teeth and squeezed her hands, feeling the button. The other hand went to pull her coat closed. "Nothing. He wanted my pay."

"Yer husband has a right to it."

"He's not my husband."

The second man's mouth worked. She could hear the click of his dentures. "Ya'd best break it off then, lovey. Man like that is as likely to beat ya as kiss ya."

"He's my cousin." Her voice broke on the last word. She put her hands to her face.

"Next time, don't bring the money," the first one advised. "Why, he'll hit ya for it, but if ya hide it good, put it in a bank or summat, he'll find a new victim. Listen to what Thomas Sykes say, lovey."

She clutched her coat more tightly, her heart pounding in her breast. If she didn't come when Konstantin made contact, he'd find her. He'd be in her room some night, a proper burglar. She'd never bothered with a bank account, but perhaps it was time. Or she could ask Peter to store her earnings in the safe. Maybe it was time she stopped treating him like family, but, oh, he was the only family she had. Her entire being rejected the loss of her one remaining cousin from her life.

The shepherd handed her the flask. She forced a smile, opened the stopper, wiped it with her coat, and took a trembling sip, despite her nausea. The tea was still hot, and sweet.

"It's perfect," she said, feeling the sugar coat her tongue. "I'm sorry I can't pay you." She closed the flask and handed it back.

"We're proper knights in armor," Thomas Sykes said with a chuckle. "Get ya home, girl. I'd be putting the lock on."

She nodded. What was the point of explaining it wouldn't stop her cousin?

Chapter 6

"I'll bring you more towels, my lord." The blond, buxom young chambermaid bobbed a curtsey and scrambled for the door.

Glass had never seen this chambermaid before. She had a country accent and a naive manner. She'd probably be eaten alive by some of the more autocratic guests on the floor, like the grand dame opera star Ethel Arrathorne, who had moved into the Opal Suite last night. His bedroom wall seemed to share with her bedroom, and he'd been subjected a series of vocal warm-ups that morning that made the hair on his arms lift.

He'd had a glimpse inside the suite that night as porters moved in her trunks. Absolutely stunning, a mix of white and variated blues, building on the opal theme until one might have thought they inhabited the inside of a mineral specimen. He hoped the delicate inlaid tables and mirrors could withstand the force of her singing.

Yawning, he went to the *Firebird* and made sure it was securely closed. He'd just changed the recording when the chambermaid had knocked. As he pushed the painting flush against the wall, he felt it vibrate as if someone had slammed a heavy trunk against the wall. He frowned. What were the Russians doing?

A knock at the door prevented him from putting on the headphones. He found Olga at the door, fluffy white towels covering her arms.

"Hello, strange princess," he said. "Haven't seen you for an age." He tried to sound flirtatious.

She walked in, and he shut the door behind her to prolong their chat. "You weren't here when I checked the room on Saturday, and I'm not on duty Sunday."

"Did you move in upstairs?"

"Yes." She nodded briskly and moved toward the bathroom.

He stared at her, narrowing his eyes when he saw her limping. What was wrong? He followed her into the bathroom.

She placed hand towels along the sink-side rack and set the rest of them on the rack above the bathtub. When she turned around, he pointed to her leg.

"What happened?"

"Florence happened." She scrunched up her nose in distaste.

"Is that the new girl?"

"Monica is your new chambermaid, but she's been with us for a bit, now. Florence had just started last week. Nasty piece, that girl. I had her sacked after she made fun of my accent, then hit me in the knee with a broom, accidentally on purpose."

"Bloody hell," he exclaimed.

Princess Olga flinched at his profanity.

"I'm sorry," he apologized. "The heat of the moment. Why ever did she do that?"

"She didn't like my accent." The princess rubbed her nose and then her eyes.

He could see her fingers came away wet. Concerned, he approached her, placing a gentle hand on her arm. "You're tougher than this, old girl. What's troubling you?"

She sniffed.

"Something wrong with your new digs?"

She shook her head. "No, my room is perfect." She sniffed again and then sobbed, a loud, abrupt barking noise. Her hands went over her face, fingers spread.

Good Lord. He threw caution to the wind and put his arms around her, cradling her head until she rested it against his shoulder. Openly sobbing, she wrapped her arms around his waist and held on.

He let her cry until the sobs settled into an occasional shudder. His shoulder was soaked with her tears. He pulled away just enough to pull his handkerchief from an inner pocket and hand it to her before gathering her back to him.

"I'm sorry Florence was beastly," he said. "Prejudice is an ugly thing. I'm sure she didn't know any better. Does your knee ache dreadfully, darling?"

"It's irritating," she said and sneezed. She used his handkerchief on her entire face, went to the sink, wrung out the cotton square, and wiped her entire face.

"Then what is so wrong?" he asked when she seemed restored.

Her lips quivered again. He winced, thinking he'd better let her cry on his other shoulder this time. But she took a deep, shuddery breath.

"Not a mind reader," he said in his gentlest tone.

She stared at him. Her sepia eyes had never seemed so full of secrets. He needed to know the truth, or they could never proceed, either as a courting couple or as friends. "Princess," he whispered, "let me help you."

The corners of her mouth jerked, as did her cheeks. She blinked hard. "I have no money."

"Why not? Did the boardinghouse take all your pay?"

"No, about half, what you'd expect, but my cousin always has a hand out. Yesterday, he tore off my coat when I told him he was asking for too much money and stole my coin purse. I had every shilling I own in my pocket because of my move. I hadn't decided where to hide my money yet. He took everything."

He went very still. He hated bullies. "How much?"

"Five pounds. Three months wages minus food, shelter, Christmas presents, and what my cousin has taken."

That was all? It should have been more like twenty pounds. "I'll replace the money for you. This is disgusting. Did it happen here at the hotel?"

She shook her head. "No, in the park. That's where I met him."

He leaned against the bathroom wall, trying to make himself look casual, like he had no hidden agenda. "This is your English cousin? The one who was raised here?"

"He was my age when he came to England." She pressed her lips into a thin white line before she spoke again. "Konstantin's father did something terrible to his mistress just before the war. Burned her or suchlike. He was exiled and came to England with his wife and son. He's my second cousin."

"Konstantin."

"Yes." Her voice lowered to a thread. "He's a bad man. I give him money, and he promises to be good, but then something happens. He has evil friends, and when I don't see him, that's when I worry most of all."

"Because he is earning money from evil?"

She nodded. "The shepherds in the park told me never to meet him with money. They said he'd hit me once but then leave me alone. I think he'll find me here in the hotel, though. He has always had a gift for locks, for secreting his way around. Strange, really. He's not a small or inconspicuous man."

"Some have that gift." He had operatives with astounding criminal talents.

"He's been here, in the hotel. Spent nights, eaten the food in the Coffee Room. He respects nothing." She pounded a fist into her palm.

"Please tell me the next time he contacts you. I'll meet him instead and fix this."

Her eyes went wide. "No, he's family. I couldn't betray him."

"Don't you know you mean something special to me?" he asked. "Please, let me take care of this for you." Little did she know what he had in mind or how much power he had.

"Maybe," she whispered. She took a step toward him.

Instead of wrapping her into the hug he wanted, he brought her into the sitting room and made her put her legs up on the white couch. He took a bar towel and opened the ice bucket. A little ice remained, swimming in a sea of cold water. He wrapped the ice in the towel and put it on her black-stocking-covered knee.

"Poor princess," he said. "You've had a dreadful few days. We'll make it all better now."

She sniffed. "How?"

"My father wants to meet you." He imagined how delighted she'd be to see her paintings installed at St. Martin's house. Would she come to his father's next dinner party? Normally he loathed the stuffy formal occasions, but she might adore it.

"Why?"

"I told him about you on Saturday. He was quite taken with the notion of you."

Her eyes seemed larger than ever as she stared up at him. He leaned forward on the back of the sofa to bring his face closer to hers.

"Really?" she asked.

"Yes. I think he's going to take a look at your paintings. We know Margery, you understand."

She nodded. "That's very nice." She tilted her face up to him.

He walked around the sofa and sat on the edge of the coffee table. She turned to him, and a long pause ensued while they stared at one another.

"You have beautiful eyes," he said. "Beautiful everything, really. Stunning." Without meaning to exactly, he leaned forward, ready to capture her mouth under his.

She arched back against the sofa cushion and sat up straight. "Lord Walling!"

Genuinely confused, he asked, "What? We've kissed before."

"On a date. Not here at the hotel. I'm at work." She stared down herself, as if suddenly realizing she was reclining with a damp ice pack on her knee. He could see her stockings were already soaked.

"I apologize. The moment, you understand." He cleared his throat, which had gone tight.

She sat up and spread her skirts back over her knees. "I must return to my duties."

Her brittleness was palpable. "Princess Olga," he said in a low voice,

"I meant you no disrespect."

"The rules are different here." She stood and took the dripping towel into the bathroom.

He didn't follow. She'd veered from one emotion to another over the past fifteen minutes. Besides, he had what he needed from her. Or at least, he had what he needed for His Majesty's government: *Konstantin Novikov.*

For himself, he wanted something rather different. An image of her smiling up from his pillow, the white sheets contrasting with her slightly darker skin, came to mind. He forced that away. *Not at the hotel.*

She walked back into the sitting room and moved past him rapidly, hardly limping at all. Her well-bred, haughty expression left no room for apologies or kisses. Even a few minutes of ice had helped her, though it had ruined their relationship. He sat, motionless, as the door closed. Alone again.

But he couldn't worry about the princess now. His Majesty's government needed him too much for that.

He rubbed his hands over his face and remembered that noise he'd heard along the wall just as she had knocked. He needed to get on the headphones and see what he could learn.

* * * *

Olga had not seen or thought of Emmeline Plash since she'd seen her on Friday. Now that they were no longer boardinghouse neighbors, she wouldn't see the nice side of her any longer, just the rude woman who surfaced under the roof of her lover's hotel.

When Hugh Moth at the reception desk asked her to unpack a new arrival on the fourth floor just after her luncheon break, she thought nothing of it. But there stood thirty-four-year-old Emmeline in the center of the small suite, one arm over her ribs and supporting her other arm, which held a long cigarette holder.

She gasped impatiently when she saw Olga. "I thought you'd never get here. Have you got a light?"

Two bellboys came out of the bedroom, followed by the bell captain. Olga surveyed the small space, not nearly as fancy as one of the five Duchess Suites on the fifth floor that Emmeline had inhabited before she physically attacked Peter. This suite did have a wireless installed, and the furnishings were well upholstered and of good wood, but the walls were bare of ballet-inspired artwork. The space was almost too small for pacing.

"What are you doing here?" Olga asked, attempting to gauge how long the woman might inhabit the space. How completely did she need to unpack?

To the level that her trunks needed to be installed in basement storage?

She turned to the bell captain, but Emmeline's hiss made her turn around.

"A light?" she demanded again.

"Allow me, miss," a bellboy said. He stepped forward, bony wrists emerging from the red uniform jacket that apparently he'd grown out of in the past three months, and pulled a hotel-insignia lighter from his pocket.

After he lit her cigarette, she tapped the lighter. "Leave it, boy." She turned her attention back to Olga. "I'll need you to unpack me, Olga."

The bell captain caught Olga's eye and, in a quick flash, turned his lips down in irritation before his face went impassive again. The three men left the room, knowing Emmeline would never bother to tip any of them.

"Have you left Bert Dadey entirely?" Olga asked, stalling. If she had to spend hours unpacking to the woman's specifications, she'd have to stay late tonight. Peter never allowed extra hours to be paid without his personally authorizing them. Not to mention her leg had begun to ache again. She should have put it up in the staff dining room, but the room had been full, and she didn't want to show weakness.

"Yes, of course. Peter didn't want my mother in the hotel hiding in the bathrooms and behind the ferns, stealing random objects, but now that she's gone..." Emmeline shrugged.

Olga couldn't deny that Mrs. Plash had been a point of pain, but Emmeline's actions had sent her away. How had she found her way back inside? The mysteries of human sexual activity never failed to fascinate her.

If only Peter had better taste. "You had better show me what you want done. I can give you an hour of my time; then the fourth-floor maid can finish up after the next shift change."

"Oh no, Olga. You must act as my personal maid." Emmeline gave her a snaky smile.

Had she offended the woman at some point recently? Olga couldn't remember a time, though she had heard a rumor that Emmeline had been furious to be living in a boardinghouse where chambermaids resided.

"No, I mustn't, Emmeline. I am sorry, but I have other duties. You'll need to hire a maid of your own."

Emmeline sneered. "We both know that you had best do what I say. If you want Peter to order you about instead of me one last time, I'll have him brought upstairs so he can tell you himself."

"You'll have him brought?" Olga echoed. "Last I heard, your family sold their stake in this hotel over twenty years ago. He is in charge, not you."

Emmeline looked down her cigarette holder as she took a long drag. "If you'd ever lose that holier-than-thou virgin-princess act, you'd discover men can be led along quite easily. I assure you that a smart woman is in charge of her man, no matter what title the man holds."

Olga shook her head. "Your appetite for self-delusion is vast, Emmeline. I happen to know your entire history at the Grand Russe, and I doubt you'll be here for long."

Emmeline pointed to the open bedroom door. Her voice lost the singsong air it had held, going flat and cold. "Unpack me."

"If you had Peter Eyre wrapped around your finger, you'd have a ring on yours," Olga said in a low voice. With every word, she knew she'd risk everything. "I'll give you one hour, and that will be an end to it."

"You'll finish the job," Emmeline said, crossing her arms back into their previous posture, apparently having decided she'd won.

"Not without overtime authorization," Olga said. "I'll let you work on that, shall I?" Calmly, slowly, she walked toward the bedroom to see what Emmeline had brought.

* * * *

During the Russians' habitual three-hour dinner out of their suite, Glass took a taxicab over to Cosway Street and the one-bedroom flat where he met with his agents. When he entered he found Bill Vall-Grandly and Tim Swankle waiting for him, perched on chairs around the small table. Tea had already been made by the section's secretary, Lucy Drover. Redvers Peel arrived just after him, completing the arrivals for his staff meeting. He'd heard stories of rooms full of special intelligence agents during the war, but he only had three people operating locally at this time.

He seated himself and poured a cup of Assam. "Lucy, go ahead and sit with us. I wouldn't be surprised if we don't have to activate you as a proper agent soon."

"I'd like that, my lord," Lucy said eagerly.

Glass nodded and rubbed one of his eyes. It had been an overlong day. Hours on the headset after that ghastly scene with Princess Olga. He had to force himself to the matter at hand.

"Swankle, it must be about time to sever your connection to the Grand Russe. Would you say the new head of security, Ivan Salter, is ready to be our source?"

"I've only been there two months, sir," Swankle said. Twenty-eight, he looked no more than twenty-four, and his snaggle-toothed grin and countryish manner fooled people into believing he had a far lesser mind than he did.

"We were concerned that the Grand Russe would be a hotbed of

Bolshevik activity."

"We weren't wrong," Swankle said, mirroring him with a tea mug. "Just not the way we expected, with this bombing."

"I know you were involved in clearing up all that, but there really are very few Russian employees, and with Salter in place, and me currently on-site, I think it is time to give notice and move on. I'm thinking of turning you into a journalist. You can volunteer at one of these Bolshie papers to try to discover which government secretaries are sharing their beds with the wrong people."

"Very good, sir," Swankle said. "Salter moved into the hotel on Sunday, and I think we can trust him to keep us informed. I'll tell him who I am and set up a dead-drop system with him before I go."

"Give a week's notice," Glass said. "That will give Lucy time to have your new papers organized."

Swankle nodded.

"Vall-Grandly? Peel? Anything of note to report?"

Vall-Grandly monitored several sources and mostly had a desk job. Peel had been undercover at the docks, watching cargo coming in from Russia. That was all his section did: Russia. Half of his operatives were outside the Home Counties area, with a few scattered inside the Home Counties but too far away to make a meeting like this.

Neither of them had much to report. Intelligence work was like that. Quick bursts of activity followed by weeks of monitoring and reviewing.

"Very good." He forced a smile. "Lucy, would you retrieve a family tree for Princess Olga Novikova? Go back to Nicholas the First, and I want to see every relative. For everyone still living, I want to know their present whereabouts."

Miss Drover opened her notebook. "Anyone in particular I should focus on?"

"Konstantin Novikov."

Vall-Grandly spoke up. "The bomber?"

"I think so. I've seen him now, and I could definitely identify him," Glass confirmed. "I believe the bomber and the princess's second cousin are the same person."

"Anyone else?" Miss Drover asked.

"Drill into the history of anyone who spent time in the United Kingdom," he instructed. "Also, why don't you find out where Princess Fyodora Novikova is, if she is still living? Last our local princess heard, her sister was headed toward China."

"I'll reach out to Shanghai," Miss Drover said. "Thank you, sir."

"Excellent. Drover and Swankle have their new orders. Vall-Grandly and Peel, stay the course. We'll meet again the same time next Monday evening, if nothing changes." He stood and thrust his hands into his pockets.

"Any word on the budgets, sir?" Vall-Grandly asked. He'd had to start wearing spectacles recently because of the rigors of so much desk work.

Glass forced a smile. "Nothing good."

* * * *

Peter Eyre nodded at Alecia Salter, who sat at the switchboard being trained for her new position. "All settled in upstairs?"

She nodded. "It's a lovely suite. Thank you so much, Mr. Eyre."

"We'll change your husband's hours as soon as we can so you don't have to work opposite shifts," he said.

"We still have midnight at the nightclub's back door." The new bride's gaze softened with romantic happiness. She fairly glowed with it.

Peter's brain hazed over for a moment. Men weren't meant to have jealous thoughts, but what little brother didn't wish he could have some of the accomplishments of his older brother? Jealousy was something he'd fought against since his childhood, forever overshadowed by Noel, eleven years older than he and good at everything.

Little did the bastard know how lucky he'd been to be jilted by Emmeline Plash. Peter had taken her on out of a sense of improving on his brother's rare failure, and look where it had landed him.

"I'm so glad it's worked out for you. Very touching ceremony," he said to Alecia and turned with a jerk, simultaneously pulling out his cigarette case.

Then he saw Olga, who'd asked to speak with him at the end of her shift. The blond beauty appeared a little worse for wear. She had dust stains along the hem of her black dress, and her white apron had colorful streaks across it.

He waved her over, and they went into his office.

"If I may." She put her hand on the edge of the door.

"Yes, you can close it," he said and put a cigarette to his mouth.

He realized she'd gone pale. Dropping the cigarette to his desk, he poured water from a carafe and handed her a glass.

She took it and drank it down. "That was entirely too much Emmeline," she said. "She stood over me while I unpacked. Unwashed clothes, heavy perfume, three years' worth of powders. A dreadful mess."

"Is that what is on your clothing?"

"Yes, makeup and dust from the bottoms of the trunks. I'm going to have to find the time to wash and iron my clothes tonight." She passed a hand over her forehead and set the glass on the edge of his desk.

He poured a glass of water for himself. An attempt to be healthier. Water or tea during the day; champagne only after seven. Also, he attempted to only have as many cigarettes as fit into his case once each day, though he hadn't had a perfect day yet.

"I can't do this, Peter," Olga said, lifting her eyes to his. "I can't be Emmeline's maid. I'll move back the boardinghouse before I allow myself to be on call to her all day and night."

"I didn't ask you to be," he said.

"Why did you allow that disturbed creature to return to the hotel? She's already tried to strangle you once."

"She wasn't sleeping before because of her mother's illness. Once Alecia went to care for Mrs. Plash, Emmeline slowly calmed down. She's been very sweet."

"She's manipulating you," Olga said. "I wouldn't call her a fool. She's keeping you from having a life. You don't find a nice woman to marry, to have a family with. One day, she'll be over forty, you'll be over thirty, and you'll both be alone."

"I don't know what the future holds."

"You know it doesn't hold her. You'd have married her by now if you were ever going to."

"Her mother—" Peter started.

"Is an excuse, one she'd never have allowed to get in the way of a marriage if you'd offered. But you won't. Deep down, you know she's a horror."

Peter leaned back in his chair and tipped his head toward the ceiling. The medallion surrounding the ceiling lamp still had the initials "GH" for Grand Haldene, the former name of the hotel.

"Peter," Olga said sharply. "Can't you admit she's bad for you? Send her away to a spa town, somewhere in France. You can afford it. Maybe if she's out of your hair for a couple of months you could move on."

"I know you resent her," he said. "But like you, I've known her since childhood. And I helped you, didn't I?"

"Your sister helped me. Once I was trained by her, I became an asset to you."

"I promoted you," he said. "I could have left you as a chambermaid."

"That would have been a waste," Olga insisted, "after your sister took all that time to work with me. Besides, I still do plenty of maid work right now. What does Emmeline do? Earn her suite on her back?"

Peter drank another glass of water. "Don't be coarse, Olga. It doesn't become you."

"Oh, don't think I consider you any better than she is," Olga snapped. "You are who you spend time with."

"You were such a quiet girl. What happened?" he mused.

"The revolution happened. Maxim's death. All of it. I cannot allow life to happen to me any longer." Olga leaned forward. "I'm telling you now I will not be your mistress's maid. Today was the end of it. She screamed at me when I left, demanding I continue to serve her, even though I had clearly stated how much time I had and that I couldn't work overtime without authorization."

"I'll authorize the overtime," Peter said quickly. *Is this about money?*

"I'll refuse," Olga said. She spoke each word with thorough emphasis. "I will not be that woman's maid."

"I need help with her. Her drinking is out of control." He pointed at the empty carafe. "I have the discipline to rein myself in when I'm going too far, but she doesn't."

"You only think you do." She stared hard at him. "I'll never believe you are a disciplined man until you rid yourself of that woman. She's a danger to both you and the hotel."

"Come now," he chided.

"Think about Richard Marvin? The actor? How he let the Bolsheviks set up a bomb at his performance of *Macbeth* in the hotel all because he'd become romantically entangled with a Bolshevik whore? You break with Emmeline while she's still allowed on the premises and who knows what damage she'll let inside your home."

"First, that Bolshevik whore is Ivan Salter's sister, so be careful what you say. Second—" He paused, uncharacteristically unsure of what to say next. Olga had a point.

"She's your weakness, Peter. I don't know what skills she has in the bedroom, but I know you don't actually like her. Pay her off. A trust would be best, something she can't waste."

"She already has a trust. But she spends more than she has."

"You aren't equipped to run this hotel and deal with a troubled woman who is out of control. Why on earth did you move her back in?"

"She promised it would be different this time."

Olga shook her head. "Her mother was never the problem, just an excuse. I don't want to talk in circles. Sack me if you like, but don't expect me to answer Emmeline's summons again. I don't work the fourth floor. I only supervise the chambermaids there."

"What should I do?" Even to him, his voice sounded

uncharacteristically hopeless.

"If you are going to keep her here, hire her a dresser. It won't fix anything, but it might keep disaster at bay long enough for you to put your head on straight."

"Olga." He trusted her to help him.

"I've known you for many years." She stood. "And I'm aware that your history with her has a great deal to do with Noel and what happened to him. I feel terrible for you both, but no one our age has escaped great suffering. Don't ruin the rest of your life, and please don't hurt the hotel. You owe your employees your best efforts." She turned, very straight-backed, and left the room, shutting the door behind him.

Peter pulled his cigarette case from his coat and opened it. *Empty.* "What is eating at me?" he muttered. "What isn't eating at me?"

He saw a lone cigarette on his desk and remembered he'd pulled it out earlier. He stuck it in the corner of his mouth but leaned back instead of lighting up, remembering the days where he never had a problem so big that his big brother Noel couldn't fix it. But he and Emmeline were long past anything Noel could make better. Unfortunately, it seemed he'd wrung the last drop of patience from Olga. He'd have to deal with Emmeline on his own.

Chapter 7

Olga limped into Glass's suite with her bucket at ten on Tuesday morning. She sketched a faint hello with her hand and upturned lips, but her smile didn't reach her eyes.

"You don't look much better than you did yesterday morning," Glass said, surveying her limping gait as she crossed the entryway into the sitting room. "Couldn't you stay off your leg at all yesterday?"

Her back turned to him, she said, "Long day. No ice on the tenth floor."

He frowned. Hadn't she thought to ask for help? "You could have brought some up. Ask Thatcher for a bucket and some ice. I'm sure he'd help you."

Her shoulders slumped. "He would, but then he'd probably tell someone. I wouldn't want Peter Eyre to think I'm putting on airs."

Glass blinked. More was wrong than her knee. "I've never heard you say his surname before. What is wrong?"

"His mistress has moved back into the hotel," she muttered, running her finger across the mantelpiece. She brought it to her eyes and moved on, apparently finding no dust to concern her.

"You were hoping their relationship was done?" Did the princess want Eyre for herself?

"I was hoping I was done with her," she snapped. She opened the first set of curtains and ran her finger across the lintel. "I don't like how it affects my relationship with Peter."

"Where is she staying? On the seventh?"

Her accent, never strong, thickened dramatically as she spoke. "No, the fourth. A downgrade from before. She and her mother were on the fifth in an enormous suite after the hotel reopened. We were very friendly when we lived at the boardinghouse this past month, but now she is here again and has returned to her old tricks."

"That shouldn't concern you. You have no pretense of cleaning on the fourth."

She returned to her bucket and picked it up. "She expects me to act as her maid. Now that I live here, it will be so easy to send for me whenever she wants."

He exhaled from his nostrils. "You think Eyre moved you in here to be available when this woman returned?"

She finally looked at him. "I hope not. After all, I'm not the only person who moved onto the tenth floor on Sunday. But I can't do it. I can't deal with her." Her lips slid back, exposing her clenched teeth.

He walked over to her and pulled the bucket from her unresisting hands. "You need an afternoon off."

"It's only Tuesday." Her shoulders trembled.

"And you need time for your art," he continued. He set the bucket down and put his hands on her upper arms. "I had a note from my father. He bought four of your paintings. The other two sold to clients of Margery's."

Her jaw relaxed immediately. "Are you certain?"

"Of course."

Her face lit with blinding happiness. She clasped her hands together in front of her. "I'm so appreciative that your father purchased my work, but that it sold to strangers as well warms me."

"And the money doesn't hurt."

"No. It goes quite a ways toward refilling my coffers," she said, "even after my expenses. And I will not feel like spending money on paints and canvas is a waste of money I could spend elsewhere." Her smile vanished.

"What?"

"If my cousin doesn't take it. I need to outsmart him."

"I am so glad to hear you thinking this way. You need more than the Grand Russe."

"Thank you for understanding my feelings," she whispered. "In art, my title is a good thing. Mrs. Davcheva can charge more for my work."

He wanted to do more than touch her arms, but he'd learned that kissing her in the hotel would be a mistake. Still, he wanted her close. "For now, let's pretend I have a dreadful mess here in the suite. Take an hour and relax."

"Applesauce" was her quick response. "I was not promoted because I am lazy."

"No one will know. I'll break a glass if you like."

"Don't you dare!" Lightly she moved away from him.

He let his arms drop to his sides. "You need to rest that knee before anything else happens. Why don't you take a bath? I'll bet the suite's tub is larger than what you have upstairs, and I have salts, perfect for aches and pains."

"You must be mad, Lord Walling."

"It's Douglas," he said. "Here in private, I'm Douglas." He wondered why he gave her that name. No one called him that. He'd been Glass to his family and colleagues for many years, never Douglas.

"Douglas," she said, trying out the name. "You must be mad."

He caught the hint of a smile. "I'll leave if you want me to. Really, the salts will do your knee a world of good."

Her teeth closed over the corner of her lower lip. "I can't."

"You need to be strong, Princess. If you are in pain, you will show weakness to this woman. It's just a bath, some ice."

Something in her changed as she spoke. That slumped air of defeat lessened. He could see her draw herself up.

"Very well, but I will not cheat my employer. May I return at the end of my shift?"

"You may."

"And you will leave?"

"The bathroom has a lock," he suggested.

"You will leave?" she repeated. "I don't want any nonsense."

He chuckled. "A bit of nonsense might make you feel better."

"I'm not that sort of woman, Douglas." Her tone had sorrow in it. "Since Maxim, there has been no one."

"No kisses in seven years?"

She shook her head. "Not until you. I was faithful to his memory."

"No one you could count on?"

"No, but you are proving yourself to be someone I can rely on." She clasped her hands to her chest, the perfect picture of a movie heroine. "Asking your father to purchase my paintings, it was most kind."

"I liked them for myself," he explained. "But people are more likely to see them at St. Martin's House. He has parties, you know. He invites collectors."

"Most kind," she repeated. "Now, I must take up my bucket again and finish checking your room. What will you do today?"

"Have some notes to write up from a meeting yesterday."

"What do you do, exactly?" she asked.

"I am the heir to an earldom," he temporized.

"Of course." She cleared her throat. "I'll be on my way then." She walked deeper into the suite, swinging her basket. Still limping, but at least she wasn't slumped over in despair.

Six hours later, Glass heard a knock at the door. He opened it and found Olga, breathless and nervous.

He gestured her in. "Ready?"

She nodded and slid into the entryway.

"I see you changed your clothing."

She clutched her pink cardigan over her loose gray dress. "I wanted something clean. I discovered the chambermaid on the sixth hasn't been dusting under the beds. I had to do it."

"Two bad days in a row," he commented. She had a difficult life for a princess. He wondered what kind of mental gymnastics it took to successfully transition from one kind of life to another.

"I look forward to hiring the staff myself," she said. "I'll make sure we don't hire lazy girls."

He led her to the bathroom. "I believe you. The girls you have on the seventh seem to be doing a good job."

"The best we have for the seventh, with a focus on the Russian employees because of the trade delegation." She paused at the doorway of the bathroom. Her mouth rounded, her eyes alight with pleasure.

He'd gone out and purchased candles. Long tapers lit the mirrors and reflected light back into the room. He'd found a sachet of dried rose petals in a store, and they scented the room. The tub sparkled, the glass jar of salts ready on the lip.

"Those are mint salts, so only add a little at a time," he warned. "The sensation of too much mint can be very shocking to the system."

"I'll be careful." She grinned at him, giving a glimpse of what the young princess must have looked like at eighteen. Her fingers drifted across his cheek, followed by her lips. While she only gave him a quick peck, he understood what even that intimacy cost her.

Gently, slowly, he angled toward her cheek and kissed hers in return. "Feel better, my dear. Stay as long as you like. I'll go down the Reading Room and catch up on the papers."

* * * *

More than an hour passed before Olga rose from the bathtub. Nothing had disturbed her as promised, although she'd heard an odd clicking in the sitting room. She hadn't bothered to investigate since it hadn't repeated itself.

Douglas hadn't been wrong. His tub easily held double the volume of the ones upstairs. Although her knee needed the heat the most, the rest of her body felt relaxed for the first time since Christmas. By the time the water cooled, she felt like an elderly stalk of celery, wrinkled and wobbly.

She stood, stretched, and unpinned her hair. The thick strands picked up water on her shoulders and drifted halfway down her back. Slowly, she dried off with one of the fluffy towels on the bathroom rack, enjoying the luxury as the towels upstairs were not nearly of the same quality. Then, she wiped away the condensation from the cheval mirror in the corner and took stock of her entire body, a rare opportunity. She still had a bruise on the side of her leg. It had gone yellow. The rest of her seemed a bit scrawny. Strain had whittled her down. Not so statuesque now. She hadn't realized.

Physical labor hadn't entered her life until this past year while she trained to be a chambermaid. Her thighs had once been round and dimpled. Now she saw firm muscle on them, and her calves were carved down to nothing. She put her hands on her hips, thinking she'd have fit into her corsets from a decade ago, if they were still in style.

Her body wasn't the kind to drive men wild. Maxim had been too respectful to attempt to ravish her and had held to sweet kisses. She sensed something darker in Douglas, something that spoke of moonlit rooms, crisp sheets, and heated flesh. Would he like her strong shoulders and muscled body? Or did he prefer a girl who could afford to put on flesh?

She didn't know. But she liked the look of him. The worst thing would be to fall, to give herself like one of these modern girls. It still made sense to behave like an aristocrat, a typical upper-class virgin worthy of any man. But for the first time in years, Douglas had brought different thoughts from places she'd long since forgotten.

Dreamily, she redressed. A few minutes later, she found herself hovering in front of his half-open bedroom door. She stared at the crisp white sheets and blankets, imagining them mussed and smelling of him. But she didn't go in. No, she forced herself into the sitting room. She walked briskly through, remembering she had no right to do anything but clean the magnificent space, complete with stained-glass windows just under the ceiling. All the love the architect and designers had lavished on the seventh floor was not evident on the smaller eighth through tenth floors.

With a sigh, she left the suite and turned down the corridor to the service lift. Five minutes later she had her door unlocked. Her bedsit had no kitchen facilities, but a curtain could be pulled between the sleeping and sitting area. She had two comfortable chairs with a large square table in between, plus a smaller table with two café-style chairs tucked in around it. The decorator Peter had hired had offered her a choice between a loveseat, one large chair, or two smaller ones. She'd thought the latter choice the most flexible.

The bedroom area held a double bed covered with a yellow-and-white patchwork quilt that Bert Dadey had given her, crafted by his sister's hands many years ago. A trunk rested at the base of the bed, which was hers. There was also a small dressing table and a closet. It wasn't bad, nicer than the maid and valet rooms in the main hotel.

Though her bed looked awfully inviting, it was too late for a nap and too early to go to sleep. Instead, she thought about her conversation with Douglas and pulled her sketchpad from her trunk. It hadn't left that spot since she'd begun work.

Why? So many scenes at the Grand Russe, not to mention Maystone's, ought to be recounted. The mad scene in the Grand Hall, with everyone scurrying around, the diners at the Restaurant, the dancers at Maystone's. Peter holding court in the Coffee Room. The musicians should be immortalized; all the bellboys managing the guests' dogs were adorable. So much she could sketch.

Inevitably, once she put charcoal to paper, though, what emerged wasn't a bustling hotel scene but an image of Douglas.

She had his eyes right away, his nose, his thick shock of nearly black hair, and his brows. His mouth challenged her with its mobility, the paired humor and strength. But she knew his body just well enough to get that right. In an hour she had quite a good likeness.

When she finished, she discovered her hands knew more about him than her eyes did. He had a trio of grooves carved across his forehead, and his long upper lip had a definite bow. Freckles dotted the skin below his right eye. His earlobes were rather puffy.

She stared at the sketch, wondering how those earlobes would taste, if they'd be soft and plump against her lips. A shiver passed through her at the delicious thought of nibbling him there.

She'd been the one to tell him not to kiss her at the hotel. At a moment like this she thought she'd been mad.

With a flourish, she signed the sketch. To do a full oil painting, she'd need him to pose. She regarded the sketch again. Maybe not. Maybe she already knew him well enough. Something about the nose seemed a little off. It wasn't hooked at the end but softer somehow than she'd drawn it.

She picked up her charcoal again, trying to perfect his face. Adding a body, more of a doodle really, she let her thoughts drift. When she glanced down at the page, she discovered she had done quite a good likeness of his face but had sketched him in armor atop a horse. Did his family have an ancestor portrait of such a man on horseback? Next, she drew him with an Elizabethan ruffle around his neck, imagining a sixteenth-century forebear.

But after that, she was done, her mind finally drained.

She yawned, tossed the sketchbook on the table, and curled up in her cozy chair. Sleep might have been possible in the larger chair she hadn't chosen, but not this one. No head support. She stood up, cooled from her bath now and pleasantly weary, and went to bed.

* * * *

Glass rolled over in bed, stirred to wakefulness by noise. He sat up, instantly alert. Life in the trenches had taken away his ability to relax, half asleep, like he had as a child. He clenched the knife he kept under his pillow. The noise came again: a knock on the suite's outer door.

He turned on the lamp and checked the clock. Three in the morning. After he shoved the knife back into its resting place, he grabbed his dressing gown and pulled it on as he went to the door.

When he opened it he found the Russian head of security, Ivan Salter.

"What?" he asked, his gaze instinctively sweeping the corridor. At times, the Russians kept a man posted across from their door but not tonight.

Salter handed him an envelope. "There are two men waiting for you downstairs, my lord."

"Do you know them?" Glass licked his lips, tasting sleep at the corners of his mouth.

"Detective Inspector Dent," Salter said, his mouth twisting. "I know him. Not the other."

He lowered his voice. "Special Branch?" He slid his finger under the sealed edge of the envelope.

"Probably. He's not one of the men I've seen in the suite."

Glass pulled out a note. "*Dress and come down. Bad news.*" It was signed by Dent.

He turned the note over so Salter could read it.

The Russian shook his head. "It's not the hotel."

"This time," Glass muttered. "You remember how to contact Bill Vall-Grandly? You'll need to get him in here as soon as you can."

"I will telephone him straight away, sir."

"Thank you."

Salter didn't leave. Glass lifted his eyebrows.

"May I ask a question?"

"I might not answer."

Salter nodded, and Glass backed into his suite so that the night watchman could come in. He shut the door behind him. "What is it?"

Salter straightened the lapels of his red watchman coat. "I wondered if you knew why Tim Swankle gave notice. I've always thought he was more than he seemed. Is he one of yours?"

"Does it matter?"

Salter cleared his throat. "Should I know him if I see him on the street, or would he be playing at someone else?"

"Ah, I see." Glass scratched his chin. Whiskery. These days he had a heavy beard, something that hadn't yet developed when he went off to war. "Follow his lead, Salter. If he acts as if he doesn't know you, then it is best to let him alone."

Salter's nostrils flared. "I thought as much. Thank you for your honesty. Shall I wait for you?"

"No, get Vall-Grandly."

Salter nodded and left the suite. Glass locked the door and went to the *Firebird* first. He opened up and put on the headphones, ensuring no one stirred in the Russian's suite. Just in case, he switched out the finished recording that he'd changed just before retiring and put on a new disk. Whatever had happened to bring Dent out in the wee hours, the Russians could be involved. They were his section's patch, after all.

He dressed quickly but did take the time to shave. A British gentleman looked his best. Even so, not twelve minutes had passed since Salter had come to his door by the time he locked the front door of his suite and headed to the lift.

At the reception desk, he found Dent, an experienced man about a decade older than he with Black Irish looks, leaning against the counter. Next to him was a man he didn't recognize, but Detective Robert McCall came toward him from the main hotel door.

Dent moved away from the desk and approached McCall, the triangle of men meeting at the banquette seating in the Grand Hall.

"Report?" Dent asked.

"About two hours ago," McCall said. "Explosion near the Edgware Road Underground Station."

"Heading toward Marylebone or Paddington?" Glass asked.

McCall tapped his temple, his disordered hair waving. "Marylebone. Mean anything to you?"

"We run operations from a flat near there," Glass said. "Where exactly did this happen?"

"Newsagent on Lisson Street."

"What is nearby?" Dent asked.

"Art gallery next door was damaged, too, but the dynamite was set in the newsagent's. Easy pickings, that shop. Not much in the way of a lock."

Arrows flashed in Glass's mind. Marylebone. Art gallery. Dynamite. Too many coincidences.

"What gallery?"

"The Pankin Gallery."

He hadn't heard of it. "You're thinking Konstantin?"

Dent raised his eyebrows, making the circles under his eyes widen. "Why?"

"I've learned something about him," Glass revealed. "His closest living relative in London is an artist. That's not the gallery she shows at, where he's been seen with her, but they might have ties to it. Is it Russian-owned?"

McCall pulled his notebook from his pocket and flipped through a few pages. "Viktor Pankin."

"Is that Russian?" the unidentified man asked.

"Yes," Glass and Dent said together.

Glass turned to Dent. "Haven't heard the name before, however."

Dent shrugged. "Nor me."

"I'm concerned by how close this was to my operation," Glass said, "but it's probably a coincidence given the art gallery."

"We need to get Konstantin off the streets," Dent said. "Are you ready to nab him?"

Glass put his hands on his hips. "I don't have a location yet. His cousin has been terrorized by him for years. I believe her, but I also know she's been shielding him, perhaps because of her fear or merely loyalty. He's got money. Took five quid off her recently."

"What is our first course of action?" asked Dent's man.

"Who are you?" Glass asked.

"Stone. Detective Allen Stone." Stone looked to be in his late twenties. Smaller than the others, though still at least average height, he had lean, foxlike features; dark brown hair; and suspicious gray-green eyes.

"Just transferred into my command," Dent explained.

"How do we know this is the work of your man Konstantin?" Stone asked.

"First, he's a bomb maker. We don't know that he ever sets a bomb," Glass explained. "He uses dynamite. I'll have to see the remains to know if it truly matches his modus operandi."

"They are combing through the site now," McCall said.

"I'm suspicious because of the Russian component."

"I have to say that the newsagent isn't Russian," McCall said.

"Fair enough," Glass admitted. "We need to build a dossier on both the newsagent and the art gallery owner, see what connections we can find."

"Who has hired Konstantin in the past? We broke up the cell that went after the Grand Russe," Dent said.

"That's the only case we know for absolute certain. But we've found the same signature triggers in three other places around the UK," Glass explained. "It's likely they are all him. All three of the other bombs were up north."

"Hull?" McCall said.

"That area," Glass said.

"I'm going to assign Stone to you," Dent said. "So you have someone to make arrests. What do you want to do now?"

"Sent McCall back to the bomb site to gather what we can. Let's verify the trigger signature," Glass said. "I think we should re-interrogate everyone in custody from the Grand Russe bomb attempt."

"I'll get on that," Dent said. "And you and Stone?"

"His cousin just moved in upstairs," Glass said grimly. "We have to find out if she's made contact with him since he stole her money."

Stone frowned. "She's a guest?"

"Employee," Glass said. "Tread carefully. She's also a Russian princess."

Stone cocked a hip. "You are telling me that the relative of a Russian imperial is a bomb maker?"

"Her family tree is a long ways away from the imperial family," Glass said. "Much closer to the bomb maker. From what the princess has said, he's just an evil sort of chap."

"Evil chap with a skill," McCall said. "More's the pity."

"With me," Glass said, nodding to the Special Branch detective. He sketched a wave at the other two men and went to the lifts.

The main guest lift did not go to the tenth floor, but he knew the hotel rather well and simply went to the service lift. Another bank of lifts was being taken out of mothballs, as it were, so that new residents of the higher floors could access them as they opened. For now, only staff had a reason to rise that high so the service lift had to do.

Stone nodded his approval as Glass took his place at the controls. "I never expect an aristocrat to know how to do anything."

"I am a fourth son. I knew I'd have to fend for myself. Learned a few things."

"Soldier, of course."

"That I was."

"I've some unlovely scars to show for my bit," Stone said. "Nothing to scare the ladies in public, at least."

"All I have visible is the one on my eyebrow," Glass said. "The worst is on my leg. Took shrapnel."

"I was out after Cambrai. Landed in the tank corps. I made it to the end of November twenty-first but then—"

"It ended?"

"Yes. There was so much mist and smoke and noise that we didn't even know we were on fire at first. Burned badly enough that it was my war's end."

"Plenty of battles still to fight, now that you've joined Special Branch."

"Yes. Bloody Bolshies," Stone replied. "Not a royalist, you understand, but those animals have destroyed an entire country. To think they were our allies not that long ago."

Chapter 8

Glass spread his stance to account for the lift's steady rise to the hotel's tenth floor. "Not the same place anymore, Russia."

"No." Detective Stone's gaze swung across Glass's face. "What am I to call you?"

The lift shuddered, and he shifted again. "Glass on duty. Lord Walling in social situations or when we are trying to do our work quietly."

"Very well." Stone cleared his throat. "Sorry none of your brothers made it home."

Glass focused on the lift controls. "Thank you, Detective."

When they exited the lift they found a silent floor. He knew more of the rooms were uninhabited than not and hoped they could speak to the princess without waking the rest of the floor and causing a scene.

Unlike his digs, he knew the princess had only one room, so a simple knock at the door would probably wake her. What he didn't want was any awkwardness with her thinking that he'd come to her door for a tryst. That would lead to making explanations to the detective that he didn't care to offer.

He nodded to the man. "You knock, Stone."

Stone nodded. He was the police officer, after all. First, he rapped smartly. After thirty seconds, no answer came from inside. His cheek twitched, and this time he banged on the door, rattling the frame. "No way out of there?"

"Not easily. The only exit that doesn't involve fire ladders would be to go through the bath into the unoccupied adjoining room and then out the door to our right."

"Keep an eye on it," Stone said, lifting his fist.

The door opened. Olga peered out, clutching a stained wrapper of indeterminate color around her neck. A thick braid lay across her shoulder and was tied with a faded pink ribbon that lay over one breast. She glanced at the detective, blinking hard, and wiped her eyes with her free hand, adjusting to the hallway light.

"What?" she asked. Her gaze traversed the corridor, lighting on Glass. "L-lord Walling?"

The detective pulled his badge from his coat and showed it to her. "We need to speak to you, ma'am."

"What is this about? I've been asleep." She blinked again.

"It's just before four in the morning, Your Serene Highness," Glass said. "May we come in?"

She pressed her lips together hard, and her cheeks trembled. "Yes." She turned, her shoulders going back.

They followed her into the small room. She went straight to the back middle of the room and began to pull a curtain across.

"I'd prefer you didn't do that, ma'am," the detective said. "Are you trying to hide something?"

She turned back, still holding the curtain. "My unmade bed. You woke me."

Stone stepped forward and walked around the curtain. Glass heard his footsteps as he checked the space. Glass closed his eyes for a moment and checked the front of the room. He opened the bathroom door and looked behind the tub curtain. When he exited, he could hear a closet door open and close.

"It's clear," Stone said. "Seen your cousin Konstantin lately, Princess?"

Olga glanced at Glass. "What is happening?"

"A bombing next door to the Pankin Gallery. Do you know it, or Viktor Pankin?"

"What was bombed?"

"A newsagent. The gallery took some damage, too."

"Why do you think Konstantin is involved?"

"Why do you think he wouldn't be?" Glass countered.

"He promised," Olga said and muttered something in Russian.

Glass wanted to suggest they all sit. He pulled one of the chairs away from the small table and nodded at the upholstered chairs. Stone and Olga both seated themselves. "Did you believe this promise?" he asked as he sat.

"He took enough money from me to lay low for a while."

"Maybe he'd already delivered this bomb to whoever laid it," Glass said.

"Does he set off his own work?" Stone asked.

"It's an art form for him, these bombs. I don't think he is quite right in the head. He sells them like I sell paintings."

"What is his ideology?" Stone asked, whipping out a notebook.

She shook her head, her expression mournful. "He has none. No allegiances. I am his prey, nothing more. So ashamed." Her head sank into her hands.

"Where is he?"

"I don't know."

Stone glanced at Glass. He spread his hands out and moved them up and down, indicating that Stone should keep the situation calm and respectful. "Can you give us the general overview of his movements?"

"He always comes to me." She lifted her head. Tears gleamed in her eyes. "I'm sure you know he was here at one time, holed up in the basement."

Glass nodded.

"He claims he spends a great deal of money on rent. He moves weekly, I think. I don't know how his clients find him. He knows I disapprove. I've tried to make him stop, but I have no power."

"You need to give us something," Stone said.

"Why is Lord Walling here?" Olga asked, her head trembling on her neck. "I don't understand."

Glass licked his lips, acutely uncomfortable. "I work for His Majesty's government, ma'am."

She took a sharp breath. "I don't understand why. You're a nobleman."

"I am a fourth son. I needed a profession," he said.

"Yes, but you must assist a government minister or such, correct?"

"Not exactly." He kept his eyes on hers and watched for the light to dawn. She was a woman of intelligence; it did soon enough.

"You're here to spy on the Russians?" she asked.

He saw her hands shake. "Yes. They've been involved in some unsavory activities. But your cousin has become a greater danger."

"I see." She swallowed hard and stared at her hands. "I'll tell you as soon as I see my cousin again. I'll tell you everything I can find out. But I don't know anything right now. The friendly part of my relationship with him is over now. The last time I saw him he became so cruel."

Stone rattled off several questions. He went back to her first days in England six years ago, spent an hour taking her through the development of her relationship with her cousin, trying to pinpoint acquaintances, favorite places, and habits.

Olga seemed to know nothing. Glass wasn't convinced she wasn't hiding a few things, though he had no idea why. She truly seemed to have given up on her cousin.

"Is there anyone else who might harbor him?"

"I'm the only member of my immediate family in England," she said. "I think my sister is in China, if she's still living, and I have no brothers, no parents." Her hands shook.

"It's very cold," Glass said. "Can I fetch you a blanket?"

Stone rose before she could speak. "I think we are done here for now. I have a few ideas."

Her gaze lifted to him. "I gave you something useful?" She seemed shocked.

"Places to begin," he said. "People to interview." He nodded at her.

Glass rose as well. His eyes met Olga's for a moment. Her face had no expression, but her skin was paler than he'd ever seen. She was a wounded bird, yet all the more magnificent for it.

"I am glad you want to lock him away," she said before they departed. "He needs to be kept from the world if he will risk people's lives. I have always feared he may have done worse than the bombs."

His hand on the doorknob, Stone turned back. "Why do you say that?"

"I've always thought he killed his mother. She died in a fire in a garden shed. It never made any sense to me."

"You have evidence?"

"Just the way he spoke about her when I came to England. Sneering, prideful. I always thought there was more to the story than I knew."

"Anything else?"

"He courted a girl, I don't know, ten years ago, no, a dozen. Her family, the entire family, was killed in an automotive crash a couple of weeks after she said yes to another man's marriage proposal."

"Lovely," Glass muttered. "So he's tried arson and maybe even sabotage before turning to bomb making."

"Maybe," she said in a dull tone. "But I think he has a strong bent for revenge. I try never to give him reason to hate me. Who else do I have?"

"Do you feel safe from him here?" Glass asked.

"Of course not. He's always come in before at will. Has the run of the place really."

"Do you think anyone on the staff helps him?"

"They wouldn't need to. He's clever."

"Thank you for your time," Stone said. He held his pencil over his notepad. "I'd like the name of that family who died."

She gave it to him and they left. Glass took a look back at her before closing the door. Often, witnesses seemed smaller after a conversation like this, diminished by a realization of the evil they'd encountered. But she appeared stronger, as if the discussion had given her power. He realized she'd needed to share these thoughts with someone, thoughts she had perhaps kept locked inside for years.

* * * *

Olga flinched when she heard the knock on her door on Thursday evening. She hadn't slept much after Douglas had arrived with that police officer on Wednesday morning, and she had spent the day moving like a turtle. Despite her concern over her cousin and his actions, she'd slept well on Wednesday night. Douglas hadn't come to her again, and he hadn't been in his suite either yesterday or today. She wasn't sure he'd even slept in the hotel the previous night.

As she went to the door, she worried. Was he resting anywhere? She hoped he'd gone to his home or to his father's house. The idea of him out chasing Konstantin without sleep or a change of clothing disturbed her.

The idea of her cousin in similar circumstances, however, did not trouble her at all. Had he spent her stolen five pounds on explosives, fuses? Who had hired him to make the bomb? How had Konstantin become this person? A decade older than she was, he'd been a full-formed adult by the time she'd come to England. When she'd visited England as a child, he'd had no interest in her. Indeed, her family's meetings with his family had been brief and perfunctory due to their disgrace.

Therefore, Konstantin had been nearly thirty before she'd known him. She understood now that he'd probably never seen her as anything but a mark.

Hoping for Douglas, she opened the door but found Peter, his hands free of cigarettes or champagne glasses for once. Freshly shaved and pomaded, he slouched elegantly, hands in his trouser pockets.

She peered at him. "Are you growing a mustache?"

"Never been able to," he admitted. "Thought I'd give it a go."

She perused his face. "I don't know that it is going to fill in right there, on the right." She traced across his upper lip with her finger. Then, when she noticed the red rip in her cuticle, she closed her hand into a fist. Cleaning destroyed the hands.

His gaze narrowed. "What is troubling you, Olga? You aren't speaking to anyone."

"The government is looking for my cousin. I assume you know the entire story now."

"Why don't we talk about it?" Peter asked, putting his hand on the doorframe.

Fear made her pulse race. Was Konstantin about to cost her this position? She didn't want to, but she invited Peter inside. What they had to say to each other might best be said in private. "Please come in."

He glanced around the small front area. "Chose the two-chair option I see."

"What of it?"

"I'd have thought you would choose the one reclining chair." He sat in one of the chairs, and she took the other on the opposite side of the square table.

"I didn't expect to have many visitors," she admitted, "though I seem to have miscalculated. I made the right choice, though I did it for looks rather than comfort."

"You could have both kinds if you like," he offered, "though it would make the space tight."

"I would like that," she said. "Thank you. I haven't money to spend on decorations or anything else, so there is room for the chair."

"Why not? I pay you fairly."

"My cousin has taken most everything I earned since I went to work for your family at the start of last year. Before that, I stayed with Grand Duchess Xenia, and she didn't pay me." She paused. "That is, I've managed to save a little for art supplies but not much else."

"Why did you never tell me about your cousin? I'd like to think of myself as your protector. I'm certainly your employer and your friend, too." He frowned at her.

"Konstantin was never your problem. You didn't know him. I thought I was paying to keep him from making bombs." She laced her fingers.

"He became my problem when he made the bomb that came into my hotel and was my unwelcome guest, besides."

"I am sorry about that. I had no idea at first. Then I thought, well, if he's living here he won't make any more bombs to attack the hotel. It became the safest place in London."

Peter pressed his lips together. They were colorless when he spoke again. "Do you understand what was found in his basement lair? Not just dynamite and blasting caps and fuses but weapons, too. A regular little arsenal next to his cot."

"I had no idea he would be capable of gathering all that." Her voice had gone to a whisper. "His father was a very paranoid person, a kind of mental disorder I think. He'd make wild accusations but take no responsibility for his own actions. Or so I heard."

"I think you have to be very disturbed to make bombs. You risk killing yourself as well as others."

"It is his art," she said.

"I'm sorry he is your closest family."

"In England, at least." She swiveled her head to glance at the small family portrait she'd managed to bring to England. Her parents, long gone. Her sister, missing.

"You'll tell me if you see him again?"

"I'll tell everyone, including Lord Walling. Did you know he was some sort of policeman? I was so shocked. He's the heir to an earldom. Doesn't his father exert any control over him?"

Peter's lips curved, taking a decade off his face. "He's not the type to be controlled by anyone. Besides, he is the fourth son, meant to have a career, and a grown man when his last brother died in '17. Why not have a career?"

"What about the family estates?"

"His father is firmly in charge still. I'm not sure there is a place for Lord Walling there."

"He's kissed me," Olga said, "taken me to dinner. I fancied I might be a match for him."

Peter shook his head. "This is what comes of living quietly for so long. You don't know how to tell who is on the up and up. He's over thirty, never been married. If he was going to fall in love or marry for duty easily, he'd have done it by now. No, he's married to his work. You know that, of course."

"I just didn't know what it was," she said.

Peter clapped his hands on his legs. "You need a night out, something to paint for your next series. Congratulations on selling out at the gallery, by the way."

"Lord St. Martin's bought most of them."

"Not all." He smiled at her. "I didn't even have an opportunity to get to the gallery, so you know I wasn't the one buying anything."

She knew he would have and was happy her sales had come so quickly. "I didn't expect it. You've hung my work in the hotel."

"I like what you do. Your river view done in soft Impressionist colors is my favorite."

"On the first floor?"

"Yes. I should probably be your patron instead of your employer, but my parents don't believe in that sort of thing. Too practical, both of them. I had to offer you work."

"And I had to take it. It was either that or grow old in grace-and-favor housing with the grand duchess."

He tapped the arm of her chair. "Why don't you come to Maystone's tonight?"

She started to say no, but he held up his hands. "I won't allow you to demur. Change into your best frock, and we'll meet you downstairs."

Her eyes narrowed. "We?"

"Emmeline," he said, "of course."

"Peter," she protested. Was there anyone she was less interested in spending the evening with?

"I'll be the one dancing with her," Peter said, reaching for his cigarette case and taking it out this time. "You focus on your sketchpad."

"I won't be called down to help her dress?"

"I had a talk with her. I was hoping you could help me keep an eye on her but not if it means you spend three hours a day being her lady's maid." He shook his head. "Not that, but I'd appreciate you being social with us."

She sighed. "You both need a keeper."

"You're my conscience, Olga." He lowered his voice and glanced at her through irritatingly thick sandy eyelashes. "At least, I had thought you were. But that's the issue with us both, isn't it? Propping up people we care about whose lives are falling apart?"

He stood abruptly and walked out. Olga stayed in her chair, knowing he was right. She couldn't judge him on the subject of Emmeline after the things Konstantin had done. They were both good people but too weak, she and Peter. How could either of them move on, stuck as they were?

* * * *

Just before midnight, she sat at a small table just off the dance floor at Maystone's in her old Vionnet. Peter and Emmeline had danced for an hour before he cried off to speak to some friends of his family. He and the two other men were huddled against the drapery on the wall. While they had danced, she had sketched, five pages of couples in movement. Two or three of them had real promise. She had the idea of breaking the couples down geometrically, playing them against the band and the dance floor. There must be a way to show both the static space and the movement.

Emmeline stood abruptly, clutching her handbag. The table rocked. "Going to powder my nose."

"You can do that at the table these days," Olga said, putting both hands on the table to steady it. Champagne had already sloshed down the side of Emmeline's glass. "Powder and lipstick for everyone to see."

Emmeline sneered. "It's a euphemism, darling. You're such a child." She vanished into the crowd behind them.

The band had been on break since Peter stepped away, but before Emmeline returned, they appeared on their small stage again and struck up a dance tune. Two men arrived at the table. Olga recognized Emmeline's twin cousins, Harold and Gerald. They were often at the Coffee Room in the evenings, but she didn't know they made it into Maystone's later on. Both had their cousin's heavy-lidded eyes and mousy brown hair, but they weren't bad-looking, had broad shoulders, and always dressed correctly. One of them held out his hand. "A dance, Your Serene Highness?"

She could almost wish they were just a few years older, if only they weren't tied to Emmeline. "My pleasure. Which one are you?"

"Harold." He inclined his head.

She stood up and went to the dance floor, happy to live a little, even if her feet did hurt. As she reached it, she saw Emmeline returning, a bounce to her step that hadn't been there before. Her eyes looked unfocused. She'd taken something; that was the reason for her euphemism comment. No wonder she never had any money, if she was spending her income on cocaine.

Harold danced well. Gerald had taken Emmeline onto the floor and attempted to trade partners with his brother when the dance was over, but Harold refused and spirited her away to the far end of the floor.

"I wanted to speak with you," he said in her ear as the band struck up a waltz.

"Oh?"

"Yes, I saw the show at the Imperial," he said. "Do you know I was trying to come up with the budget for one of your paintings, but when I returned to see it again, it had all sold?"

She blushed with pleasure. "You didn't. I had no idea you were an art lover." In fact, she didn't even know his surname. Was it Plash?

"Very much so. I took a first in art history at Oxford. Gerald studied geology. I know we look alike, but otherwise, we don't have much in common."

"Other than spending most evenings at the Grand Russe drinking Peter's champagne."

He grinned. "Well, there is that. Free to us, you know, because of Emmeline. Peter's a good chap."

"I know. He really is."

"In love with him?"

"Who? Peter? Oh, I knew him as a child, just like Emmeline. I didn't know her, though."

"Or us," Harold said. "Say, why don't you come out with me sometime? See a picture? Since you aren't in love with Peter."

"I'm too old for you," she said. "But I'd love to sell you a painting if you can afford one."

"Rather have me spend my money on art?"

"Yes." She squeezed his shoulder lightly. "Which painting did you want?"

"The still life with the array in front of the window and the river beyond?"

"Right. That was meant to intrigue the Russian clients because I had painted in a photograph of the tsar on the table."

"So it was sold to a Russian?"

"Yes, someone visiting from Paris. It was the first piece that went."

"You must be very happy."

"Oh very. What did you like best about it?"

"Everything—the color, the mood, the scenery." He waggled his eyebrows. "Could you do one for me with Grand Duchess Anastasia instead of the tsar?"

She laughed. "Of course. I'll happily take your commission."

"Then I'll save my pennies. Draw up a contract if you like."

The song changed again while they spoke. She saw Gerald leaving the floor and didn't think of it again until a dark-skinned female singer came on stage from a hidden corner to the far right and began to belt out an American Old South spiritual number. Harold pulled her to the far side of the dance floor, and they leaned against the drapery, catching their breath while the woman sang about cotton and working the fields.

Just as the singer reached the peak of a soaring crescendo, Olga blinking away tears at the deep emotion, she noticed someone sitting on the piano bench with Judd Anderson, the piano player.

She nudged Harold with her elbow. "What is your cousin doing?"

Harold reoriented his gaze from the singer to the piano. Emmeline leaned her head against Anderson's shoulder and put her arm around his back, forcing him to sway in time to the music. Olga heard her laugh under the singer's vocal.

"I'm sweating feathers," Harold exclaimed. "What is that minx doing? Peter will kill her."

"How can you get her off stage?" Olga asked.

Harold took her hand. "We'll have to dance up to the front, then drag her off. If I can get her into hold you can leave gracefully."

Olga nodded, sad to ruin her lovely interlude with Harold. She hoped he really wanted the painting he'd asked for. As the spiritual ended, the singer moved on to a sad show tune, and they danced toward the stage. The piano player had stopped playing, but the new song had a lot of horn.

When they reached the stage, Harold climbed up and went to his cousin, taking her arm. Emmeline tried to shake him off as Olga gracefully attempted to make herself as unobtrusive as possible. She felt a hand on her shoulder and turned to see Peter taking her into hold. They danced in front of the stage while Harold pried Emmeline's arm off Judd Anderson. He pulled her off the side of the stage. Tears had dripped black mascara down Emmeline's face.

"It was so sad," she heard Emmeline cry; then she buried her face in her cousin's shoulder.

When Olga glanced at Peter, she saw his lips in a thin line, the edges downturned. "I'm sorry," she whispered in his ear.

"What did she do?" he asked.

"She said she was going to powder her nose. Told me it was a euphemism."

He growled. "Who gave her the blow?"

"I think she already had it, Peter."

"I'm going to find out, and then I'm going to kill whoever gave it to her." Peter dropped her hand and strode away, leaving Olga in the middle of the dance floor partner-less.

When Olga reached the table after trying very hard not to let anyone catch her eye, she found her sketchpad and pencil had vanished. Leave it to Emmeline to create enough drama to ruin every last part of everyone's evening.

* * * *

On Friday morning, Glass bit back a yawn as he opened the front door of his suite to housekeeping's knock. He hadn't been here the past two mornings, and he hoped Princess Olga was at the door. Exhaustion kept him from more complex thoughts.

She stood at the edge of the carpet, mirage-like in her black dress, apron, and cap, that blond hair underneath two neat waves around her temples curving into a tight bun at the apex of her neck. He couldn't keep the smile off his face. "The sight of you is good for sore eyes!"

She stared at him, an incredulous look on her face. "How can you sound happy to see me after what has happened?"

He took her hand, the one not holding a bucket, and pulled her in. "How can I not be? You aren't at fault for your cousin's actions."

Before he shut the door, he saw the lift door open. Two Russians flanked three cheaply dressed young girls. The men wrapped beefy hands around the upper arms of two of the girls and pulled them off the elevator. The other, stumbling and probably drunk despite the midmorning hour, followed in their wake. One of the men knocked on their suite door, and it opened a crack. He shoved the girl he held through the crack and pushed the drunk girl in. The second man moved his charge through the door then followed, leaving the first one in the hallway.

Glass ducked past his doorway and shut his door. He didn't want them to think he paid attention but wondered if he would have to pull out his party-eager viscount act and join the group to protect the girls. The thought of a drunken rout at ten in the morning did not please him.

Chapter 9

Glass checked his watch. Twenty minutes until the floor butler was due to knock. He considered asking Princess Olga to get him but didn't want the Russian in the hall to notice her beauty and try to take her to the party next door.

"You stay out of Ovolensky's suite, don't you?" he asked the princess.

She turned from wiping a smudge on a window pane. "Only men serve that suite."

"Good. I was afraid you might ignore that edict because of your supervisory role."

"I'm still a woman, and being a Russian princess might cause additional problems."

"Best they don't know," he said.

She frowned at him. "Don't you want to talk about Konstantin?"

"Yes, but right now I'm more concerned about those three girls."

"They are being paid," she said in a monotone.

"For sex," Glass said bluntly. "Not to be beaten."

The princess set her bucket down and fisted her hands at her sides. "What?"

"It's happened before. We have a listening post in the wall. Do you remember that morning when you came in and I'd been up half the night?" *The night we kissed.* "I was over there trying to stop them from hurting the girls they'd brought in."

She blinked and shook her head as if her body rejected what he was telling her. "Why is an earl's heir running a listening post?"

He forced a smile. "Why not? I am a section head, but we are so ill staffed that I had to take my turn here. Ovolensky and his men are here until May."

She wiped under her eyes. "You have more to do than protect prostitutes. Let Peter handle that."

"His hands are tied because we have refused to allow him to kick the delegation out of the hotel."

"Because of the listening post?"

"Exactly. I'm glad you know the truth now. I didn't want to hide myself from you."

"It does make any kind of honest discourse difficult," she said.

"Now we don't have to hide: you and your cousin, me and my work. It is good."

Her lips trembled. "Where does it all leave our friendship?"

"I hope we are becoming good friends."

"Just friends? Only friends?"

"I dream about kissing you all the time," he admitted. "I don't know how to live this life I currently have and be a man who can kiss you."

He could hear her breath rushing through her nose as she sighed. "I understand completely. I don't know either. We are both trapped in our duty: me by the need to make a living and my family and you by duty to your post."

He took a step closer and stroked a finger down one shining wing of hair, following it behind her ear, to where it twisted around the back of her head. Then, he spread his fingers and massaged down her neck. She took a step closer to him, her head tilting. He felt her breath on his skin, smelled floor polish and ammonia and orange oil.

Her lips parted. He tucked his chin down, ready to kiss her. A loud thump jarred the wall between the suites. His arm jerked, and he let Princess Olga go so he could sprint to the listening post. He pulled at the painting, ignoring her soft exclamation of shock as the *Firebird* swung away from the wall, and put the headphones on.

He heard a shriek. One of the prostitutes. How long had they been inside? Ten minutes? And one of them was already being hurt? The activities on the other side were deteriorating.

"Has housekeeping finished next door?" he asked the princess after he'd pulled the headphones off.

She pulled a small clipboard from her bucket. "They haven't signed off."

"I wish there was a telephone in this suite," he muttered. "I don't want to go down the hall and let the Russian guarding the door see what I'm doing."

"You could go downstairs in the guest lift, then come up in the service lift," she suggested.

The wall thumped again.

"I doubt they'd let a cleaner in," he said. "I'm going to have to stop this myself."

"You won't get past the guard."

"Yes, I will." He narrowed his eyes. "Give me the skeleton key that opens their door."

She pulled a keyring from her apron pocket and unhooked a key. "What are you going to do?"

"Stay here. Lock the door. The floor butler is due to check on me in about ten minutes." He checked the recording. It didn't have much time left. He switched the disks quickly and closed the painting.

"Douglas," she protested.

He shook his head. "Don't open the door to anyone else."

Moving fast, he went out the door of his suite, shut it securely behind him, and was at the Piano Suite before the Russian, standing on the opposite side, realized what he was doing.

Glass had prepared. The key, correctly aligned, slid right into the keyhole. He kicked the door open with his foot. It slammed against the wall, the key still in it. The air moved as the Russian guard came at him from behind. He bent his knees and felt for the man's arm; then he used the man's forward motion to flip the Russian over his back. The man fell into the entryway of the suite, Glass somersaulting in behind him.

He ripped the key out of the lock, put it between his fingers to use as a weapon, and quickly took stock of the room. Ovolensky stood, rubbing his knuckles. One of the girls cowered on her knees, her hands in prayer position. Another wiped blood from her mouth. He didn't know where the third was, in one of the three bedrooms that opened off the sitting room probably, servicing a Russian.

"I'm tired of whores, Georgy," Glass growled at the so-called diplomat. "It's not yet eleven in the bloody morning, and you are interrupting my sleep with this banging and shrieking."

Ovolensky had recently shaved off his thick mustache, revealing an extremely thin upper lip that did not match the obscenely shaped lower lip. Beads of sweat dotted his forehead. He said nothing in response to Glass's outburst, merely pulled a handkerchief from his trouser pocket and wiped his forehead. He had no coat on, just a waistcoat and shirt. Glass thought he saw blood on the fine wool.

"I do apologize, Lord Walling," Ovolensky said smoothly. "This one had been paid to be faithful to me while she was here, but once a whore, always a whore."

"Or you aren't paying her enough," Glass growled, breathing harder than he'd like. "Rates are a bit higher here than in Petrograd."

"Don't take me for a country mouse, Lord Walling. I do not take insults lightly."

"I don't care," Glass responded. "Keep the noise down." He glared at the girls and pointed toward the door. The two in the room rose shakily to their feet and scampered to the door, still open, and raced to the left, toward the lift. He had no idea how to get the third girl out there.

The guard he had thrown lifted his head. He must have been knocked out.

"What martial art do you practice?" Ovolensky asked, looking Glass over.

"Judo," he said. "Where is the other girl? Don't want to hear her screaming next."

"She's busy," Ovolensky said, looking down his nose. "She belongs to my colleague and is presently entertaining him."

"You keep beating up girls, and the police will be called," Glass said. "Peter Eyre is a friend of mine, and I don't want to see his hotel's good name dragged through the mud."

The Russian chuckled. "We're men of the world, Peter and me. Girls are a way to pass the time."

"Then visit a brothel," Glass said. "Go down to Villiers Street off the Strand. Any perversion you Russians prefer can be found there."

"I have no trouble finding what I like," the Russian said.

"No more of it here," Glass said. "Or I'll have you thrown out of the hotel." He turned around to stomp out. The guard began to move, still on the floor. Glass kicked at the man's knee as he walked by. The man grabbed his leg and howled in pain. Glass hoped he'd incapacitated the man and wished he could do the same to every one of the Russians.

The adrenalin left him as soon as he closed the suite door behind him. He went down the hall to tell the floor butler to get the male cleaning team into the Piano Suite, hopefully dislodging the third prostitute, and went back to his own rooms to explain himself to the princess.

He let himself into his suite with her skeleton key and found her pacing through the sitting room.

"Are the girls safe?" she asked, coming toward him.

"Two of them. I'm hoping the floor butler can rescue the third. I didn't like my chances, fighting my way through all the Russians." He brushed at his sleeves.

"Where had the other gone?"

"Into one of the bedrooms." He saw how upset she was. "Listen, the girl who was being hurt got out of there. Maybe the other girl isn't being injured."

"Just used," the princess said bleakly. "I should stop feeling any sort of pity for myself. I have honest work. I'm being paid for my art."

"I have never seen you have a self-pitying moment," Glass declared.

Her smile was tentative. "Thank you. I need to get on with my work."

"Wait a few minutes until the situation next door is resolved." He coughed. The brief fight had winded him. Not as athletic as he once was.

She shook her head. "I'll go the opposite direction. The Russians won't even see me."

"If you must, I will be your bodyguard." He went to the window and picked up her bucket. "Shall we?"

"Oh, you couldn't, Douglas."

"Of course I can. I'm a man of leisure, right?" He winked at her.

"You don't want the Russians to get an idea about you and me," she said much more seriously. "They might do something to me to punish you for breaking up your fun."

"Are you incapable of worrying about yourself for your own sake?" he asked. "You want me to cower in here while you wander the corridors at will? I won't have it."

"You can't do my job with me all the time."

"I assure you, Princess, that this is your last day working on the seventh floor. I'm going to tell Peter he can't allow any more female staff here until the Russians have gone."

"You can't," she gasped. "I am management!"

"You are too precious, Princess Olga. I want you safe."

"I can." Her eyes bored into his, and her sweet, stubborn little chin had hardened.

"You can what? Do you know hand-to-hand combat techniques? When that Russian barbarian rushed me from behind, I knew how to flip him off me." He gestured with his hand.

Her hands went to her mouth. He saw her cheeks work as she bit her palm. "You didn't tell me that."

"These men are animals. I'm taking you on your rounds for today, and that is the end to them until the Russians are gone."

* * * *

Olga felt like she'd spent most of Friday pacing. She hadn't, of course, but those minutes in Douglas's hotel suite had felt endless. She couldn't monitor the action next door while he'd been gone.

Now, after a long day, and an evening of furious painting on the commission for Harold, her hands ached, and she knew she was done for the night. She glanced at her canvas. After roughing out her design with graphite, she'd opened the windows of her room and squished a few colors onto a clean palette. Tired, she'd focused on simple things: the table, the window panes. She'd save the fine details of the curtains, the portrait of the grand duchess, and the scenery, for Sunday, when she had an entire day free.

If Harold hadn't left an envelope for her at the front desk, she probably wouldn't have painted at all, but he'd already paid her ten pounds toward the commission. And she wouldn't have to give half to the gallery owner! For now, she'd hidden the money in the inner pocket of her dressing gown. She simply had to remember not to launder it.

Staring at her feet, she saw they were moving, pacing again. The wind blew into her room, and she felt a wet spray of droplets. She ran across her space, pushed behind her bed to pull down the windows, locked them closed, and brushed the rain from her smock. The paint smell had gone, and she didn't want her bed to be soaked.

Now, the room needed to warm up. She turned the radiator on. When she pivoted she caught sight of her sketchbook. Idly she flipped through the pages. The caricature of a man on horseback in armor capped by Douglas's head caught her eye. He had surely been a knight in shining armor to those prostitutes he had rescued. Her heart melted at the thought of his gallantry. He'd taken a risk with his safety for the right reason. Before she thought too deeply about it, she pocketed her keys and left her room. One staircase led down on the opposite end of the floor from the Russians' suite. She could reach Douglas's rooms from the other side. The only way she'd get into trouble was if they had a guard posted in the hallway again.

Without inquiring too deeply about why she needed to see him, she moved quickly down the three flights of stairs.

Not five minutes later she knocked on his door. It might have been wiser just to enter, but she didn't want him to attack her. Now that she knew he was skilled in combat she wouldn't risk it. Thankfully, the corridor was empty. The Russians must not be making trouble.

His door opened. Douglas peered at her and frowned. He reached for her arm to pull her in. "I thought I told you to stay off the floor."

She was so close to him she could smell the wine on his breath. He'd probably dined in his room, alone, monitoring his listening post. The aroma of meat in burgundy sauce hung in the air.

"I don't think I ate dinner," she said.

"I didn't eat all of mine. Do you want it?"

She shook her head. "I didn't realize until I'd smelled it. I was painting and thinking."

"About what?"

She stared at his face, the long, taut jaw and stubborn chin, that froth of black hair rising from a widow's peak at the center of his grooved forehead.

Her fingers went to his half-moon lower lip. "This."

His eyes narrowed in confusion. She stood on her tiptoes and set her lips against his. Desperate to explore, she touched the tip of her tongue to his lip and tasted salt. He parted for her, but she didn't know what to do. Maxim had kept her so innocent all those years ago.

Douglas muttered something and took control. He pushed her up against the wall and tortured her, gently, with his mouth and tongue, teaching her angles, tastes, sounds. She curved her fingers into his hair, learning the shape of his head, and surrendered to him completely.

The sounds she made shocked her back into consciousness some minutes later. She pulled her head back, bumping it against the edge of a painting, and saw how swollen and damp his mouth was. She'd done that. Her fingers went back to where they had started, feeling him. She leaned forward again, another kiss, but he pulled back.

"What are you doing?" he asked. "You're not the sort of woman who comes to a man's rooms late at night."

She stiffened as his words hit her. What *was* she doing? All she'd thought of was wanting to be with him, but she had no right to be here. He'd think her loose when all she'd wanted was to be around him.

She shook her head and wrapped her arms around herself. "I'm sorry. I don't know what I was thinking. It's been a most trying day."

She wrenched open his door and ran down the corridor back to the staircase. She went inside and climbed all the steps, panting by the end; unlocked the door to the tenth floor; and stepped into the corridor. When she'd closed and relocked the door, she leaned against it, bending at the waist trying to catch her breath.

Had she survived Maxim's death and the flight from Russia, fear and poverty only to lose her mind over a handsome viscount spy?

* * * *

Glass sat at his table in Cosway Street on Saturday afternoon. He finished his last gulp of malty Assam and set down his cup. His team members had just left with their new assignments. A telegram had come during the meeting. He'd been told more operatives would be assigned to him on Monday, a necessity for the Konstantin hunt.

He had a hard time focusing on the bomber when Olga Novikov was taking up so much brain power. What had the princess been thinking last night, to come to the seventh, expressly when he'd ordered her to stay away for her own safety, and enter a man's rooms, late at night, and offer him her sensual mouth?

He'd pegged her as a most aristocratic virgin. Yes, there had been moments when he'd wondered about her relationship with her late fiancé, Prince Maxim, wondered about the things that older man had taught her. But he'd been dead seven years, and his impression was that she'd been touched by no man since.

He'd thought her looking for marriage, not a lover. Never, ever would he have mentioned her to his father if he'd thought any different.

What was she trying to say about herself with that kiss? He let his head fall into his hands. If he assumed his impression of her was right, why would a princess, looking for marriage, brave the seventh floor to kiss him?

Tilting his head to the ceiling, he forced himself to consider. She'd hoped for a romantic proposal because she'd risked everything for love? That seemed more the act of a very young girl than someone who'd reached twenty-five. But she'd been engaged at seventeen and wrapped in imperial cotton wool since until she'd gone to work as a chambermaid. Maybe she was closer to that young girl than he thought.

Her manners seemed older, but she was a princess, schooled in proper behavior. Still, he really couldn't see the situation any other way. The kiss had been a major gesture. She would be hoping for one in return.

If he wanted to keep her under consideration as a possible bride, he needed to do something. If he wanted to keep in her good graces so that she told him about Konstantin's moves if she learned anything, he needed to do something.

"Blast it," he muttered. Tim Swankle had made the transition to journalist over the week and was no longer involved with the hotel, but he had Bill Vall-Grandly in his suite for the day, so he didn't have to return immediately.

He took his tea things to the sink, rinsed them out, set them on the sideboard, and set out for Grafton Street to take advice from Margery regarding possible gifts for an artist princess.

Margery wasn't in, but her sales manager suggested a set of horsehair brushes for his artist friend. After a quick look through the gallery to see what the princess's paintings had been replaced with, he went to the shop the sales manager had recommended and picked out a handsome wood case and filled it with the most expensive oil painting brushes in the shop.

He returned to the hotel in the early evening, after a soothing visit to his home. His man kept the place feeling lived in, with frequent airings and dustings. Quite relaxed after a couple of hours of going through his personal mail settled in his favorite armchair in front of the fire, and with a case full of unread magazines under his arm, he went to the Reception Desk.

"Do you ever have a day off?" he asked Hugh Moth, the ever-present desk clerk. Behind him, the business office waited silently for Monday, but the Grand Hall echoed with the water-spattered footsteps of Restaurant guests and those waiting for the opening of Maystone's in the Coffee Room.

"As little as possible," he said. "I have a widowed mother, a widowed sister, and her two little ones to support."

Glass stared at the young man, who couldn't be a day over twenty-one. "I'm glad you can work the hours then."

"It's an easy duty," Moth said. "I even have a stool I can sit on when no one is at the desk."

Behind Glass a man passed by with a hideously pungent cigar. The tobacco must have become wet and been dried again. "Tell me, can you have something sent up to the tenth floor, or would that service be just for guests?"

"To Ivan?"

"Olga."

"Oh, certainly, my lord." Moth banged on a bell, and a lad zipped from the bellboy waiting area in between a couple of large potted ferns. "Can you take my lord's package up to room 1004?"

"Yes, sir," the bellboy said smartly, pushing his slightly too large red cap off his forehead. Glass handed him the package and a coin and the lad ran off whistling.

"Cleaning supplies?" Moth asked.

"Excuse me?" Glass said.

"Some of the seventh floor guests have very particular tastes. Mrs. Arrathorne will not allow anything lavender-scented in her suite."

"I see." He didn't want to say anything one way or another. Who knew what crazy idea he might have to come up with to keep his intelligence operation going? He'd already had to make unusual requests like frequent security and floor butler demands. "Well, the princess is in charge of housekeeping."

"Yes, sir," Moth said.

Glass, remembering Moth's family, flipped the clerk a large coin and turned away before he could see how the young man reacted. He heard the coin hit the desk and Moth's exclamation as he fumbled to catch it before it hit the door. Obviously he hadn't been hired for dexterity, unlike the bellboys.

This morning, he'd seen one catch a guest's cat in midair when it squirmed out from under her arm. That had been a praiseworthy feat. He wondered if the bellboy had been a pickpocket in a previous career, or possibly a circus performer. It took a great deal of skill to catch an agitated cat and not get scratched.

"I say," he said, turning back to the reception desk, "do you know which bellboy caught the cat? Must have been about eleven this morning."

Moth quickly tucked his new guinea away and pulled off his glasses. "Jeremy, I believe. I was helping Teddy Fortress with correspondence and didn't see the entire adventure."

"Is he still on duty?"

"No, sir. The younger lads only work ten-hour shifts, and we have two shifts a day."

"Send him up to my room when he's on duty next," Glass said. "I might have an assignment for him."

"Yes, my lord." Moth looked over his shoulder, and Glass stepped aside for two men who held luggage in their gloved hands. New guests for the hotel on a rainy March night.

* * * *

The package had come quite late. Olga had set it aside, afraid it was something from Konstantin, some demand. Either that or canned jellies or some similar small token from the grand duchess. When she pulled away the paper and string, however, she found a flat rectangular box etched with the image of an artist at their easel.

She opened it and sighed with delight: a painting box, with compartments for all sorts of things, and brushes, of good horsehair, rested inside, too. What a lovely gift.

She paused, her hand over one of the brushes. Lifting the box away, she shook the paper, looking for a note. She found one; it must have been on top of the lid before sliding away.

In bold handwriting, the note said, "One gift deserves another." Her gift giver had signed it "Douglas."

She dropped into one of her chairs, clutching the note to her chest. One gift deserves another? What did he mean?

She remembered the shy touch of her lips against his. But the encounter had ended so awkwardly. He hadn't seemed pleased with her attempt to see him. She agreed she'd been scandalous. It was only that she...

"Couldn't stop thinking about him," she said aloud.

What a muddle. She slid the paper across her mouth, remembering. Had he been sorry he'd rejected her? Or sorry she had run instead of talking about it like a mature person? But who could talk about kisses late at night?

She closed her eyes and leaned her head back. Just a little too low, the chair hit the back of her skull uncomfortably, making it hard to think.

Peter's promise of a comfortable chair had not materialized yet. Instead, she paced the room, every few seconds brushing past the delicious box. It would be a pleasure to finish Harold's painting with those. Today was her day off from the Grand Russe. She could put on her smock, nibble on the rolls she'd taken from the kitchen basket at the end of her shift the night before, and stay in all day.

A few minutes later, she found herself in front of her easel, not inspired. She needed a cup of tea. Quickly, she washed in her for-now private bathroom, and dressed, then went to the den on her floor. The hotel's live-in staff weren't allowed to eat in the staff dining room or cadge anything from the Coffee Room when they weren't working, but they did have the den, which had a small kitchen.

When she entered, she found Alecia Salter kneeling in front of the stove, checking something inside.

"It smells delicious," Olga commented.

The new bride turned and grinned. Pink-cheeked and glowing with life, she looked nothing like the mousy secretary she'd been when Olga first saw her two and half months earlier.

"New apron?" Olga asked.

"Yes, I sewed it while I was living at the boardinghouse. Do you want one now that you have your own kitchen?"

Olga laughed at the absurdity of the idea. "I don't know how to cook. I'm happy to have the stove to make tea."

Chapter 10

Alecia shook her head in mock alarm. "Then what are you going to live on? Mr. Dadey's housekeeper isn't here to keep you fed any longer."

"I can make do for one day when the hotel isn't feeding me. My paintings are selling, finally, so I can afford to run over to the A.B.C. for some eggs."

"How exciting," Alecia exclaimed. "I heard you had done well at the gallery."

"And here as well," Olga said. "One of those Plash boys offered me a commission."

"Harold? Gerald?"

"Harold," Olga said. "He has hidden depths and a purse to match."

"How exciting. Is he sweet on you?"

"No, he's a child," Olga said. "I doubt he's a day over twenty-three. I don't even know if Plash is his last name."

"Oh, I think you're right. I believe they are related to the late Mrs. Plash's sister, not someone from her husband's side. But truly, now that I'm married I see all kinds of romantic possibilities for everyone," her friend said. "Love should be in the air. And my switchboard duties are four days a week, so I have a lot more free time than you or Ivan."

"I have cast my eyes over the seventh floor," Olga admitted.

"Who?" Alecia checked the oven again, then opened the door. A blast of warm, bread-scented air filled the room, and she pulled out a tray of cream scones studded with currants.

"Goodness. I'll just pay you to bake for me," Olga exclaimed.

"You needn't pay," Alecia said as she set her tray on the stove. "But if we make it a regular thing, you could help me with the grocery money, and then I'll deliver you food."

"That is very kind of you," Olga said. "But I hope you spend some time outside of these four walls. We both need fresh air and fresh things to look at."

"Even if they are opulent walls. I suppose it means nothing to you."

"It means a great deal, having my culture around me," Olga said. "I missed it terribly when I worked in Leeds last year. The Haldenes have a wonderful little hotel empire, but it's very British of course."

"Who are the Haldenes? I know this hotel was once the Grand Haldene."

"Peter's mother was married twice. Her first husband's name was Haldene, and they had an inn in Leeds before he was murdered. She and Peter's father went into business with her Haldene brother-in-law, and others, to open this hotel over thirty years ago. Ultimately they had four or five hotels, and Peter's sister, Eloise, runs the larger one in Leeds."

"Not her husband?"

"No, no husband. I didn't become close to her. She's more professional than anyone I've met. You know how remote Peter can be. She's even more that way."

"I see." Alecia poked at the top of one of her scones and scooped it up with the edge of her apron to check the bottom. Satisfied, she placed it on a plate and added the others. "Who is this gentleman on the seventh? One of the film stars?"

"No. Lord Walling."

"Ivan knows him. And Sadie's husband." Alecia raised her eyebrows suggestively.

"That should tell you something."

Alecia moved her tray to the sink and filled the kettle and set it on a burner to heat. "I try not to think too much about the fix my sister has landed herself in, marrying someone who is obviously not the salesman he claims to be."

"People like him are protecting England as much as any policeman or soldier."

"But they are deceivers," Alecia said. "I understand the need for double-dealing. We've made decisions in my family that I wish we hadn't been forced to make with regard to Ivan's sister, but I wish we didn't have to."

"Our world isn't black and white," Olga agreed. "I have my own secrets."

"Everybody does at the Grand Russe. Are you sure you want a man who spends time in the shadows? I can understand why you'd want a viscount. That's your world. But the rest is something else."

"You can't help but crave who you crave," Olga said. "He's the first man to intrigue me since my prince was murdered."

"Then you have to see where it takes you," Alecia said. "My husband took me from a mouse to an entirely new woman."

"And you're happy?"

"So happy," Alecia whispered and giggled. "And we have our own little suite! No more valet room, no more bed in a boardinghouse or cot in a friend's flat. Oh, it is such a relief to start our life. You will still be my friend when you are a viscount's wife, won't you?"

"Of course. We Russians have to stick together," Olga said automatically. "And us too, women without much family to rely on. We have to make our own circles."

"Exactly."

"But I don't know that I'll be able to marry Lord Walling. We seem to send mixed signals."

The kettle whistled. Alecia poured a stream of water into a waiting Brown Betty teapot. "You have to work at it. He's too big a catch to risk losing."

Olga bit her lip, considering Alecia's words. Her friend knew, as did she, how real the risk of becoming a surplus woman was for their generation, since so many men had died in the war. She had to keep trying, even if she made missteps. "He sent me a gift last night."

Alecia set the kettle back on the stove. "How exciting. Something good?"

"It was perfect," Olga admitted. She went to the icebox, found butter, and set it and a couple of plates on the table.

Ivan came in then, so she set another plate and some teacups and changed the subject. While she wanted to keep talking about Douglas, she'd be embarrassed to have the conversation in front of Alecia's husband.

After she finished eating, she returned to her room and applied a little lipstick, just enough to stain her mouth a cherry shade. She didn't like the heavy makeup some girls were wearing these days, but she wanted to look nice.

Hoping Douglas was downstairs, she took the lift to the Grand Hall so she could have a bellboy send a note to Douglas's room, mindful that he didn't want her on his floor due to the Russians. After the bellboy took her note, she went into the Coffee Room to enjoy her art exhibit. She'd checked it each day at the end of her shift but hadn't enjoyed the works for any length of time since choosing them for the show.

The exhibit would probably have to be taken down at the end of the week, and the Coffee Room restored to full size, but she thought it had served its purpose. Glancing around at the colorful works, she drew in inspiration. One beautiful work, depicting white horses coming onto a beach from frothy sea-blue waves, made her think she might add a horse to the landscape she'd painted in the picture window in her little commissioned painting.

Staring at the brushwork of the thirty-year-old work, she didn't hear

Douglas come in. "The horses of Neptune, right?" he asked.

She smiled at him. "Yes."

"The joys of a classical education." His mouth twisted wryly. "Thank you for not coming to my room. I want you to be safe, Princess."

"I know," she said, putting her hand on his arm. "But I missed you."

The corners of his eyes creased with pleasure. "You did? That's a lovely thing to hear on a rainy afternoon."

"I received that beautiful art box."

"Did you like it?"

"The box? Very much. The sentiment concerned me, though."

"What do you mean?"

"I don't want a gift for a kiss. Do you know what I mean?"

"You're afraid I sent you something because you kissed me, even offered yourself to me?"

Her heart skipped a beat. Was that what he thought? Was that what she had done? Of course, a different sort of men might think that way, but she didn't think it of Douglas. "I didn't mean to."

He pressed his lips together. "I know you are an innocent, but you took a risk. A different sort of man would have taken advantage."

"You're good, though, a good man." She hesitated.

"Thank you." His eyes were grave. "And the box wasn't a response to your kiss, wonderful though it was. It was in response to your bravery at trying to break through your shyness and reserve. I know you didn't want to kiss me in the hotel, but the reality is that we are forced to be here most of the time."

"Yes, but I don't have to be here today. Do you?"

He tilted his head. She liked the roguish effect.

"I could make arrangements."

"Please do."

"It's not a day for walking. Would you like to see a picture?"

She already had a plan. "Yes. I saw an advertisement in a paper. How about *A Romance of Mayfair*? It's about a duke who falls in love with an actress."

"Does it have a happy ending?"

"Of course."

He smiled at her. "Neither of us has our coat, but if we duck right into a taxicab and go to a theater, we should be fine."

"We can check the start time in the Reading Room." She gestured to the door, and he followed her out and across the Grand Hall to the center of the Reading Room, where all the London papers and others were laid over wooden dowels. They chose a couple and looked through them until they found where the movie was playing.

"We'd better leave five minutes ago," he announced.

"Oh, dear."

"I'll make a quick telephone call from the reception desk. You hold a taxicab for us and I'll be with you in a minute."

Olga nodded, and they left the room together. She went out, happy for the overhanging canopy over the main entrance of the hotel, and had the doorman whistle for a taxicab.

She and Douglas sat shoulder to shoulder in the taxicab. Olga felt naughty without a hat, coat, or gloves. When had impetuousness become part of her nature? She supposed Douglas was a different sort of creature altogether, forged by wartime and spycraft. Who knew what he might get up to?

"You have a very *Mona Lisa* smile on your face," Douglas observed. "What are you thinking of?"

"Adventure," she admitted. "I thought I'd spend the day with my paints, but here I am."

"This is what comes of late-night kisses," he said, as the taxicab pulled in front of a theater in Regent Street.

An usherette opened the door for them and they breezed in, chased by the wind. In the blink of an eye, they were seated in the back of the upper level with the aid of an usherette's torch, the movie screen below them. A thousand people or more were spread out on the main floor, and the screen already flickered with a Pathé newsreel.

They watched the reel about the removal of the Eros statue at Piccadilly and the flower seller who still sold her wares as scaffolding was erected around the statue.

"This city can't stand still," Douglas muttered in her ear.

"Not all of us are lucky to live where we work," she said back. "I'm sure we need the new Tube station."

"Not a fan of underground spaces, not after the trenches," Douglas said.

She jerked her head toward him at those words. She'd never thought about that, how many men in London must have flashbacks when they ventured into the underground stations. "I'm glad you can afford taxicabs."

His lips quirked, but his eyes were sad. Boldly, she found his hand on the armrest between them, squeezed his warm fingers with her chillier ones, and didn't let go until the film program had ended.

* * * *

Glass woke up the next morning with not the romantic film scrolling through his brain or even the feel of Princess Olga's chilly fingers warming under his on the plush theater armrest. No, what had stuck in his brain was that famous statue of Eros being covered.

All those men milling around, caps hiding much of their faces. Men in overalls were hovering about the scaffolding. The soot-streaked buildings and constant traffic, everything blending into the leaden sky. The noise and movement of cars, horse-led wagons, double-decker buses. All of London passed through Piccadilly. A place to blend in. A place for… Konstantin to hide?

He heard a knock on the door and went into his small entryway to speak to the floor butler. After he took his messages, he scribbled a note to Bill Vall-Grandly to ask him to come over, then ordered breakfast.

After he bathed and dressed, he ate his eggs and toast while reading his secretary's, Miss Drover's, summary of his section's activities over Saturday and Sunday. A possible sighting of Konstantin on the east side of the West End had him deciding to look for the bomber where instinct suggested. It wasn't confirmation by any means, but they knew the man loved concealed places, and with a Tube station being punched into the earth, new underground spaces were being created in Piccadilly.

He'd just changed the disk behind the *Firebird* when another knock came at the door. Bill Vall-Grandly, looking a bit more rotund than usual in an unflattering brown plaid suit, was accompanied unexpectedly by Miss Drover herself.

Glass let them into the suite. "I was going to have you run things here, Vall-Grandly, while I nip down to Piccadilly Circus."

"Checking out that report about Konstantin being seen near the Queen's Theatre?" Miss Drover asked, tightening the curl at the ends of her bob with her fingers.

"I saw a newsreel about the construction of the underground station at Piccadilly."

Vall-Grandly snapped his fingers. "He does love low places."

"Exactly."

"Busy place, Piccadilly," Miss Drover said.

"Quite. What brings you by, Miss Drover?"

She opened a leather case and pulled out a sheath of papers. "Requisitions for Les Drake's new operation up north. I need your signature to disburse funds."

"In return for that, why don't you stay at the listening post?" he suggested. "Generally, I don't like women about this floor because the Russians have beaten up some prostitutes, but if you stay inside the room you should be fine."

"Just show me what to do," Miss Drover said eagerly, unbuttoning her coat.

He showed her how to open the painting and quickly demonstrated the equipment. "They usually have a meeting about eleven, but since you don't speak Russian it will be gibberish to you."

Her smile was bright. "I have been taking lessons."

He'd known she was ambitious, but he hadn't expected this. "I wasn't aware of that. How?"

"My mother has a Russian cleaner, came from Petrograd just after the war. I'm paying her to teach me Russian. What am I listening for?"

Glass regarded his ambitious secretary with respect. A profoundly mousy woman in her late twenties, she must have thought she had lost her chance of finding a husband to work so hard in her career. Unfortunate, because she had a sharp mind and great energy. Any man would be lucky to have her. "Street names, ship names, anything that sounds like it is related to smuggling."

"Excellent," Miss Drover said with a brisk nod.

"The floor butler will be by in about twenty minutes on his next round. Order something, tea or whatever, and if you need to contact anyone, he'll take the note downstairs. We're a finely oiled machine."

"Very good," she said smartly, pulling the stool he used sometimes up to the wall. "How long will you be out?"

"One never knows," Glass said, slipping on his hat. "Hopefully we'll make progress on the Konstantin matter."

Vall-Grandly followed him out of the door. They crowded into the lift with his fellow guest on the seventh floor, the actress Mrs. Arrathorne, and her entourage, which included a maid, a small black yapping dog with very sharp teeth, and an extremely attractive young woman in a blue coat with a fur collar.

"My daughter, Lord Walling," the actress said. "May I present Miss Ruby Arrathorne?"

"Charmed," he said, inclining his head.

"A pleasure to meet you, my lord," she said. Her gray eyes were grave, her manner contained. While her mother might want her introduced to a lord, this young lady couldn't have cared less. A secret beau, perhaps, of whom her mother was unaware?

The lift jerked to a halt, and the door opened on the fourth floor. A salesman joined them, reeking of the cologne he sold into shops. Glass had been in the elevator with him before.

"Lord Walling," the man exclaimed. "A pleasure to see you again, sir!"

"Beecham," Glass responded. "Ready to make your sales quota?"

"Indeed I am, sir," Beecham said, squeezing the handles of his valise until the leather squeaked. "An exquisite new product just came in this morning. Top notes of rum and pineapple. Might I have the honor of sending a sample up to your suite?"

The look in the man's hangdog eyes was so hopeful that Glass couldn't resist. "Why not? We'll see what the ladies think of it."

Beecham's gums displayed themselves. "Very good, my lord. As soon as I return I'll have it sent upstairs."

Glass turned to the front of the lift as it stopped on the ground floor, happy to get away from whatever scent poor Beecham had poured over himself that morning. He didn't smell pineapple or rum, so he must not have sampled the new goods.

Vall-Grandly followed him out. "What a headache," he said, rubbing above his eyebrows. "That odor."

Glass ate up the marble floor with rapid steps and lifted a finger to Johnnie, the doorman.

Johnnie touched the bill of his cap. "Taxicab for you, sir?"

"Chucking it down out here," Vall-Grandly observed. "I know we'll get wet, but why not start out dry?"

"Get us a taxicab," Glass said. "Queen's Theatre, Johnnie?"

"Yessir," Johnnie said, in his strong American South accent. He put his fingers in his mouth and blew. A taxicab waiting down the block puttered up to them.

Glass flipped the doorman a coin and pointed Vall-Grandly toward the cab, close enough to the awning that they were only exposed to the wet for a couple of inches. Still, he felt the sharp stings of rain on his back as he bent over to enter.

After too much time in heavy traffic, they pulled onto Shaftesbury Avenue, in front of the rounded edge of the theater. Taller than the buildings around it, it hulked on the corner. They could have walked there as quickly.

"Why didn't we bring umbrellas?" Glass muttered as he paid the driver.

Vall-Grandly shrugged. "Good weapons in a pinch but unwieldy otherwise. We aren't going to see much in this muck."

"Let's scout around, see if there are any shafts opened up yet for the underground station construction."

"Right you are," Vall-Grandly said. "What did the report say?"

Glass began to sing "I'm Just Wild about Harry" inserting the name "Konstantin" for "Harry" at every repetition.

Vall-Grandly chuckled. "Not much, I take it."

"No, but we know Konstantin likes to harass his cousin, so he never travels far from the hotel."

"How many times have we almost caught him?"

"A few." Glass grimaced. "Come on, Konstantin, you rat. Where are you lurking?"

They wandered through the dark, rainy streets. Early March did not look different from February. Periodically, Glass stepped under an awning and tipped rain off his hat. When they reached the former home of the Eros statue, not to be replaced until 1931 when the construction would finally end, Glass looked around for the famous Mrs. Bonner of flower-selling fame but didn't see her.

"Let's go into the station, see if we can find any hidey-holes," Vall-Grandly suggested, "though we might need one of our pets from Special Branch to get us access."

"Very well." Glass led the way to Jermyn Street.

"A bun and a cuppa sound about right," Vall-Grandly said, seeing the little bakery on the right side of the entrance.

"I wouldn't mind," Glass agreed. Despite his coat and hat, rain had gone down the back of his collar, soaking him all the way to the skin. Most of his body was damp.

They walked past the Arabic arched awning on the side of the bakery and went indoors, shaking off droplets like wet dogs.

"Tea," Vall-Grandly groaned, beelining for the counter.

The clerk, a pretty brunette with a short, angular cut like a movie vamp, smiled at him. "Anything else, sir?"

"Two cups, please, and a couple of currant buns. Got to stoke the fires," he said, pulling coins from his pocket.

Glass stared into the station through the window at the back of the shop. He scanned the people inside, looking for a tall fellow with the triangular jaw and thick neck. When his gaze went back the other way, he thought he saw a similar form. He squinted, unbelieving, as Vall-Grandly came up behind him, holding a cup of tea.

"It's him," Glass said, grasping his agent's coat sleeve instead of the tea. "Konstantin."

Vall-Grandly said nothing, just tossed back the contents of his cup, heedless of the temperature. He set it on a table and tucked his bag of buns into his pocket. "Let's go get him then."

"You take the left and I'll go right; then we'll bear down on him from either side," Glass instructed. He took the other teacup, and Vall-Grandly went out the door. Sipping his tea, Glass watched him, marveling that his agent could swallow the steaming contents down. The man must have had a throat of iron. As soon as he'd warmed his throat, Glass set down his cup, went out the door, and moved to the right, setting a parallel track for the man he thought he recognized.

He kept his gaze moving, not wanting to tip him off, just taking quick mental snapshots: gray cap, loose blue scarf around the thick neck, long, baggy gray coat over dark trousers. When he was four feet away, he glanced toward his agent and saw him coming up, a couple of feet farther back. He paused in the middle of the old, high-ceilinged station, a fatal mistake, his wet shoes squelching on the damp concrete.

Konstantin's gaze, shadowed beneath the stained cap, stopped on Vall-Grandly, moved away, and moved back to him. Had he recognized the agent? Maybe they had overlapped in the common areas of the Grand Russe? They had both been there.

Glass darted forward, ready to tackle the man before he legged it. Instead of running, though, he stood his ground. That didn't seem like Konstantin. Glass stopped two feet away at a different angle, confused.

Vall-Grandly had his hands out, low, ready to tackle. But the other man shifted his stance, and his coat opened. Glass moved behind him, close enough to see the paralyzed expression in Vall-Grandly's eyes. He followed his agent's gaze down to the other man's waist level and saw what had petrified him. The narrow metal cylinder of a gun was pointing right at him.

Glass stopped moving and opened his coat. He reached for his Webley MK VI service revolver, tucked into a specially designed holster pocket. Not standard issue for Secret Intelligence, of course, or the police for that matter, but left from his army days.

Vall-Grandly's gaze shifted to Glass. Glass saw Konstantin rotate his weight onto his right side, clearly made nervous by the agent's change of focus.

"Put the gun down, Konstantin," Glass called, moving forward, his gun outstretched.

The man shouted something in Russian, gibberish to Glass's ears. Vall-Grandly, out of paralysis, stepped forward, and Konstantin's coat fell away from his arm.

What the hell was the Russian doing with a Thompson submachine gun? Did he have ties to the IRA, the Irish terrorists who were known to have purchased some of the American-made weapons? He jabbed his gun into the back of Konstantin's neck, feeling the flesh buckle, but instead of setting the submachine gun down, the Russian raised the barrel, one hand in front of the drum magazine on the fore grip and the other on the trigger.

The drum on the gun rattled, not a stealthy weapon. He tried to reach for the gun, but Konstantin raised the barrel, pointed at Vall-Grandly's face, and fired. *Rat-a-tat. Rat-a-tat. Rat-a-tat.* The brass went flying in all directions.

The agent's right cheek disappeared in a hail of bloody bits. He crumpled to the ground, blood, teeth, brains all scattered around him. *Dead.* Bill Vall-Grandly was dead. Glass discharged his weapon, thinking it pointed at Konstantin's neck, but his shot went wide. He must have jerked his arm away in the shock of the moment.

The world seemed to stop moving, and Glass could see the scene: his dead agent, Konstantin's wide back, the Thompson still firing, passersby ducking, screaming, running, clutching their companions. Then the universe began again, the horror all too real. A little trace of smoke drifting from the Thompson, but his gun was still cold in his hand with just one wrong shot fired.

He grabbed for the Russian as the wailing began from others in the station, but his target had already moved. A man had collapsed off to the left, his newspaper across his chest, his arms flung wide. He'd been standing just a few feet away. Another clutched a bloody leg as a woman knelt next to him, her hands hovering over the wound.

Hoping he hadn't been the one to shoot either man, he flew toward Konstantin, gun at the ready for a close-in shot that wouldn't hurt others, but the large man turned. Instead of firing again, he threw his weapon at Glass and ran.

Glass leaped over the gun and gave chase. He couldn't fire. People had crowded around the two bodies, the bloody living man too, instead of running away. Konstantin darted out the station door onto Jermyn Street, instantly anonymous in the rain except for his height.

Following, Glass dropped his gun into his pocket and reached for his whistle, hoping that blowing it would bring the police. Fumbling, he continued following his target, finding the whistle just as Konstantin ducked into the road in front of a fast-moving taxicab. Glass blew, waiting to cross the road until he had a moment when the road was clear. His feet slipped in muck, horse dung mixed with rain, and he slid onto the pavement and took a header into a lamppost. Dazed, he slid down with his back against the post, falling to his knees.

He struggled back up, ignoring the stares of passersby, and craned his neck at the corner of Duke of York Street, hoping to find his quarry again. Konstantin had vanished, helped by the rain and the general grayness of the day. A smart man, he'd left his gun behind. Otherwise, the screams of passersby would surely have alerted him to the Russian's progress.

He rubbed the front of his head, and his hand came away bloody. When he felt around, he found he'd cut above his right eye somehow. He wiped away blood, maybe tears, too, he didn't know.

Where were the police? How could Bill have died like this, bleeding out in the middle of Piccadilly Station? He could do nothing but head to Special Branch and explain what had happened to Detective Inspector Dent, get the police searching, and start filing reports of his own with his superiors.

Holding a handkerchief above his bleeding eye, he went toward a hotel so he could catch a taxicab to Dent's office.

As the taxicab sped him to his destination, he wondered if he had gone soft. Why hadn't he checked where he was firing? He'd seen people he cared about die before, and he'd needed to take Konstantin out. Had he made the mistake because he didn't want to kill the princess's cousin? That couldn't be it. The man needed to die.

What if Konstantin went to Olga for aid? Had he put his dear princess in danger?

Chapter 11

At the end of her shift, Olga went to the staff lounge to toss her apron into the laundry bin and retrieve a clean one from the rack so that she could go straight to work in the morning from her room. She hadn't glanced at the staff board yet today, so she took a moment to check it. The notice was almost a day old at that point as they were updated in the early evening.

Greetings from Peter Eyre. 9 March! The Grand Hall is meant for guests of the hotel and the businesses inside. If you see "ladies" loitering, who do not appear to be visiting the Salon, Restaurant, or Shop, please tell Mr. Dew or Mr. Neville so they can assess the situation and remove any professionals from the premises. Please offer any concerns regarding this order in full detail to your supervisor. Your servant, Peter Eyre

Nothing was said about "ladies" who were anywhere else. Peter didn't want transactions originating in the hotel, but there were plenty of ways to bring in the prols.

"Olga."

She glanced away from the board and saw John Neville entering the staff lounge, trailed by a number of chambermaids just coming off shift. She went forward to meet him as the girls made a beeline for their timecards. "Mr. Neville."

Neville wore his new Savile Row suit well, though she wondered if any muscle at all existed on his thin frame. He seemed only held up by his bones. This did no harm to his attractive face, just made his pale skin look delicate over the strong bones.

"Mr. Eyre would like to see you in his office."

She forced a smile past the exhaustion of a long day. Up and down too many stairs over the day had made her knee start aching again. "Should I be prepared?"

Neville shrugged. "Our guest Lord Walling is with him."

"Something about the seventh again," she said, her heart leaping at the sound of Douglas's title. "The Russians?"

"I really couldn't say," the day manager said. "Truly."

"Very well. Are you coming along?" She tucked her fresh apron under her arm.

"No, I wasn't requested. I thought I'd inspect the laundry." He nodded at her and went out the far door. A corridor, where the laundry bin was, led to the room where the hotel washing was done.

She went upstairs, holding onto the bannister as she climbed the steps, wondering what the denizens of the Piano Suite had done this time. Or maybe her cousin had done something. She closed her eyes for a moment when she reached the Grand Hall. Was he dead, this closest relative of hers in England?

She pressed her lips together. If so, good riddance. He had long since stopped deserving any pity from her. A liar, a bully, and surely a murderer, destroyer of property, ruiner of peace. That was her cousin.

She forced a smile as she went by the concierge and Hugh Moth, who looked weighted down by cares greater than his years. The secretarial staff started work an hour later than the chambermaids and they were still busy at their desks. She waved to Alecia Salter at the switchboard, then went through to Peter's office.

Peter and Douglas both stood when she entered. The room smelled like cold ashes, but Peter wasn't smoking. She saw a fresh cut above Douglas's eye. It created a T-shape when added to the old scar.

"What happened?" she asked, unable to read his face. "Did you fight with Georgy Ovolensky again? Or his men?"

"I had a report," Douglas said, his voice hollow, "of Konstantin hanging about the Queen's Theatre. You remember the newsreel about Piccadilly? When I realized construction on the new Underground station had begun, I knew the area suited your cousin perfectly."

"You found him?" she asked. Her knees wobbled.

Peter moved from behind his desk, showing the grace that normally only revealed itself when he danced, and pushed her into a chair.

Douglas turned the chair by him to face her and sat down, putting his hands over hers. "I'm sorry, Princess. We chased him into the station. He had a gun, a submachine gun, and when Bill Vall-Grandly approached him, well. You remember him?"

She shook her head.

"Spells me upstairs sometimes?"

"Shorter, a bit heavy?" she asked, digging through her brain. He didn't have too many visitors.

"Yes, that's him." His fingers went to the cut.

"You should bandage that," she said.

"Listen to me, Princess. Your cousin opened fire in Piccadilly Station. Killed two men, wounded a couple of others."

Black spots swung across her vision. The room grayed. She blinked hard and grabbed for the armrests of the hard wooden chair, trying to anchor herself. Behind her, Peter put his hands on her shoulders.

She touched Douglas's knee, her fingers light as a butterfly's wings. "Your agent is dead? This Bill?"

"Yes," Douglas said soberly. "I watched him die. And I didn't take my shot properly. I lost Konstantin on the street. He could be anywhere."

"You're in danger, Olga," Peter said.

"I'm sorry," Douglas said, his mouth creasing down.

She couldn't fit the words into anything coherent. "Sorry for what? Not killing my cousin?"

"He opened fire in a tube station," Peter said, squeezing her shoulders. "What do you expect? He's a rabid dog."

She cast her gaze down to her hands, realized they were trembling.

"She needs a cup of tea," Douglas said.

"She needs to stop caring about her cousin," Peter said more harshly. "If I had only known. I should have protected her better."

"You can't even protect a few prostitutes," Douglas pointed out. "How can you guard a headstrong princess?"

"I'm the closest thing she has to family." Peter's voice came out strangled.

"I didn't know you thought that way," Olga said. It explained a few things.

"Of course I do," he said. "I know my sister seems cold, but she feels the same way."

"She trained me," Olga said, "which earned me the money that Konstantin stole. What if he bought that gun with my five pounds?" Her eyes filled with tears.

"That isn't your fault," Douglas said. "The only thing you need to do is keep him away from your money now. I can't imagine you would escape unscathed if he finds you again."

"But you don't know where he is!"

"No, I don't." Douglas sounded calm, a leader in a crisis. "I should have taken more men into Piccadilly, but it was more a hunch than anything else. I made a mistake. Usually we get there after he's gone."

"What about Dent and his men?" Peter asked, speaking over her head.

"They are combing the streets now."

"Olga needs a bodyguard," Peter said.

"She needs a telephone installed in her suite." Douglas's voice harshened with irritation.

"You need one too," Peter said. "I'll put the order in. Who is going to keep an eye on Olga?"

"Someone from Special Branch," Douglas told them. "She needs an armed police guard. I'll have Dent send someone over."

Olga stared at her lap again. She understood the necessity of a guard. Konstantin would come for her money. He'd fired the gun of his own free will. It wasn't like a bomb, where he would have clients to hide him. He'd made the mistake, and he'd have to look to his personal contacts for aid.

Peter's hands left her shoulders. "What do we do for now?"

"I'll take her to my suite," Douglas said, "after I telephone Dent. We have the system set up where I'm being checked on at least once an hour."

"And we have a night watchman patrolling the seventh floor at least half the time," Peter said, coming out from behind her. "I'll have to hire more."

"Any thoughts?" Douglas asked.

"I'm not clean," she whispered. "I scrubbed stains out of rugs in this uniform today. I need a fresh dress."

"Why is she still cleaning?" Douglas demanded. "She is management."

"Short-staffed," Peter explained. "Sadie didn't last long. Then we had to sack her replacement."

"A new girl started again today. That's why I'm so dirty. I was training her," Olga explained.

"You've got to do better, Eyre," Douglas barked. "You seem to be chronically understaffed."

"We've only been open a few months. We had no idea how much traffic we would have, and we don't have a lot of job applications on file. These things take time. How could I have known we'd end up with a violent Russian trade delegation on our hands?" Peter reached for the elephant on his desk and closed his fingers over it.

Douglas stood and held out his hand to Olga. "You could have guessed, naming the hotel as you did." He pulled Olga from the chair and deposited her neatly at the door. "Go sit with Mrs. Salter while I make my call; then I'll take you to your room."

Olga walked out, head held high, but her heart pounded. Now Douglas would be her bodyguard, and she might have to share his suite tonight. What effect would that have on their relationship? At least her cousin wouldn't be able to find her.

* * * *

The hour had grown late. Olga had brought her materials down to his suite. It seemed appropriate for her to paint in the Artists Suite. Since Peter had suspended her from her duties for now, except that when she could have a watchman accompany her, she'd have more time to pursue her art.

Douglas had watched her paint for hours between checks on the Russians. Only a couple of them had been around, and they weren't speaking of anything but novels and films. It didn't seem to be code for anything nefarious.

At eleven, Olga placed her brushes in cleaning solution and removed her paint-stained smock. She stretched, lacing her fingers behind her back. He heard her let out a tiny gasp as her muscles relaxed. Pleasure, or pain. Her breasts pressed against the linen shirt she wore. It had a band around the hem and rested above her skirt, untucked.

The blouse looked so easy to remove. Idly, he wondered what she wore underneath. He thought he could see the faint shapes of her nipples under the fabric, though the light wasn't terribly good. The stirring below his waist warned him that this was a dangerous path to follow in his thoughts.

He forced his eyes from her breasts to her face. She was watching him.

He shook his head. "Sorry."

Her expression was solemn. "I find you attractive too, Douglas. I wonder if it's safe for me to be here."

"I promise I'll be a gentleman," he vowed. He was too heartsick to take action. Poor Bill would never see another pair of breasts.

She came toward him and sank onto the other sofa cushion. Her pale yellow clothing floated above the white upholstery like a yolk on a fried egg. He was getting silly, needed sleep.

"Why are you smiling?"

"My own humor," he said. "Don't mind me."

"The situation is absurd." She crossed one leg over the other, leaning toward him. "Family should protect me. A British spy shouldn't need to protect me from my own mad cousin."

"That's not what I was thinking. Nothing of the sort. I hope you would always come to me for help."

"I don't know if I would trust you," she admitted. "You do have a certain slyness about you, an unusual sort of grace. Not the regular sort of nobleman."

"And here I thought I was rather stolid."

"People who think that have never kissed you."

His gaze went to her mouth, as if summoned there. "Are my

kisses so unusual?"

"I've been kissed by four men," she said in quite an academic fashion. "Maxim, of course, and a couple of the Imperial relatives, bored boys."

"Did you like it?"

"Only Maxim." She paused. "And you."

He couldn't help himself. "Would you like more kisses from me?"

Her voice dropped to a whisper. A sexy little catch appeared. "You know I would, but it's dangerous. Where am I going to sleep tonight?"

"If you don't feel safe here, I'm sure you could stay with the Salters."

"I'm not going to interrupt the newlyweds. That's cruel."

"Safety first."

She leaned toward him and put her hand on the back of the sofa inches away from his neck. "Are you telling me I'm not safe with you, my gentlemanly friend?"

"Oh, Princess." He put his hand on hers and traced up the bare back of lower arm. The yellow fabric of her blouse ended at a band around her elbow, loose enough to push up all the way to her shoulder. He boldly stroked his fingers up her biceps, finding muscle that shouldn't be a surprise, considering the buckets she hauled all day.

"Yes?"

"I could show you such delicious things." He found the back of her arm and drifted his fingers across the taut skin.

"Have you a great deal of experience?"

He considered this. "More than you and I'll leave it at that."

"You were a soldier," she said.

"I've certainly never kissed a princess before you."

"I'm not a princess as the British think of them," she demurred. "I'm just an aristocrat like you."

He echoed her. "I'm not descended from a king, though, unlike you."

"No?" She put her hand over his before he moved his fingers any closer to the slope of her breast.

"No. Way, way back, we were merchants in the favor of James the First. He ennobled my ancestor."

Her breath touched his cheek. Had she moved closer, or had he? He doubted she realized her pleated skirt had hiked up over her knees. Inadvertently, she had exposed more than a foot of her thigh. He could see the woven edge of her stocking.

The sight was unutterably erotic. His hand left her shoulder of its own accord and settled on her leg, on the edge of the stocking.

"Delicious things," he said again, as if he were a record stuck on repeat.

Bill would never have a moment like this again, but life was for the living. He pushed his dead operative's memory into the recesses of his thoughts and locked it away.

She took a breath that pushed out her breasts and leaned her cheek against his left shoulder. He wrapped his left arm around her shoulders and moved his other hand higher up on her leg.

Her lips touched his first. She surrendered her body to his, flowing against him, opening her mouth and taking him in. He focused on the tastes of her mouth first, the potatoes they'd had in cream at dinner, the bottle of wine they had shared, perhaps unwisely. Her bun came undone when he pushed his fingers through her hair, dislodging pins and the scent of lemons.

But an earthier scent was in the air, too. Her arousal became more apparent as he inched up her skirt. His princess was ripe, ready for love. Her attraction to him was not just some pretty thing, a battle of words, a pursuit of his family money or position. No, her body wanted his, and this thought aroused him more than any half-imagined sight of her nipples.

Boldly, he slid a finger up the side of the lingerie cupping her sex and slid it along the warm, wet heat. He thrust his tongue into her mouth and caught her gasp on his breath. Learning her anatomy, he didn't go for the source of that sexy, damp passion but to the nub of her pleasure, a place a gently reared princess might not even know existed.

He rubbed along the soft hair of her mons, then down again, to the apex of her sex, and touched her there. She jerked against him but into him, her thighs slipping farther apart in encouragement.

He moved his mouth to her ear. "Move against me, sweet. Show me how it feels."

She didn't respond. Had he been too bold? But when he pressed her there again, her hips tilted, and he knew he had her. He rubbed her below and kissed her face, glorying in the sounds she made, a woman awakening to sensuality.

When she found completion, he had a sense of satisfaction that he desperately needed in some part of his life. Olga rested with her head pressed against his upper arm on the sofa back, her expression blissful and unfocused. Slowly, not wanting to disturb her, he pulled his hand away and smoothed down her skirt.

The scent of her hung heavily, erotically, in the air. His erection pressed against his clothing, but this moment had been about her. He couldn't ask for anything more. Every next step had to come from her.

Eventually, she licked her lips. He wanted to get her a glass of water but didn't dare move.

"One hears stories about this, but I've never experienced anything like it," she said, very low.

"You've been deprived." His voice was hushed too, suiting the intimacy of the moment. Just them, cocooned in luxury, on a late winter evening.

"You are going to teach me to want you, now that I am a woman of some experience."

"Someday you'll want to have a past," he suggested. "To remember in your old age."

"Maybe," she said. "But I can't fall, Douglas. I won't risk it."

"I want to please you, not hurt you."

She swallowed hard. "I've been very sad today since you told me what happened. I'm so sorry your operative died, and I'm sorry my only close relative in England is lost to me forever."

He didn't respond. "Do you feel any better now?"

"I would if you promise me Konstantin will be safe."

What nonsense was this? "He's a killer, Princess. I can't promise that."

"You can promise me that he'll be locked away, that he'll be cared for, given the opportunity to atone for his sins. I understand now that he can never live like an ordinary person, but he's sick, like his father was."

"Others are at risk because of him."

"He needs to be locked away," she repeated. "Promise me you'll try to capture him, not kill. He's my only relative, Douglas. He's all I have of my family." She squeezed her eyes shut, tears leaking from her closed lids.

He winced. "I hate to see you like this."

Her voice came out as a harsh whisper. "You lost your brothers. You understand, don't you? I can't lose anyone else."

He heard the old horror in her voice. "Yes, I understand. But I'm more concerned about you. Do you feel like you might be able to sleep?"

She nodded.

He slid his free arm under her knees, picked her up, and took her into the bedroom. When he reached the bed, he laid her down on top of the covers and folded the other side of the bedcovers over her. She was still dressed, but if she'd relaxed, it was better that she sleep now instead of changing and waking herself up.

He put his hands over her eyes and gently stroked down. "Sleep, now."

"What about you?"

"I'll be fine in the sitting room. Don't worry about me."

"You have to work?"

"Don't worry about me," he repeated and tread as lightly as possible as he left the room, his ghosts returning.

* * * *

On Tuesday afternoon, Glass had his tea in front of him at the flat in Cosway Street. A rare glimpse of sunlight came through the dormer windows, though it didn't bring warmth. He wrapped his fingers around his cup, breathing in the malty tea. A break was exactly what he needed after the morning he'd had, discussing Bill Vall-Grandly's death with his superiors.

Instead of quiet, though, his admittedly open hours at the flat were interrupted by their special knock at the door. Feeling like he'd gained ten years, he went to it.

His entire remaining London team stood there: Lucy Drover, Redvers Peel, and Tim Swankle, plus Les Drake.

"Down from the north?" he asked Les they took off their coats.

"Bill's sister called Lucy," Les said. "The funeral's already been planned."

"I haven't heard."

"It's tomorrow," his secretary said. "Late morning."

Glass glanced at his staff. "We can't go, you lot. You understand that, don't you?"

Les, an athletically lean man in his mid-twenties, who could go from almost royally distant to a man-of-the-world salesman in a heartbeat, lowered his eyebrows. "I can go. I'm working out of Hull. I'll take Sadie. Bill's cover was sales, just like mine. It makes sense that we'd have met on the road."

"I don't like it," Glass said.

"Bill deserves our respect." His secretary's voice was full of tears.

"That is not the point. Respecting one man can point fingers at the others. Don't forget that the way people like us are often found is to locate one of us and follow the trail back to the others."

"Just me and Sadie," Les repeated. "I won't lead anyone to the rest of you."

Glass drummed his fingers on the table next to the door. "Very well, but I'm going to let this flat go and find us a new meeting place. Time to start clean. I've had this one for long enough."

A knock came at the door again. Glass frowned.

"It's the new man," his secretary said.

"I've been assigned someone new? I wasn't told that this morning."

"I just received the forms," Miss Drover said. "They are in my handbag. But his name is Teddy Mount."

Glass pointed into the next room where the meeting table was and waited for his team to move in before he opened the door. He pulled his Webley from his holster and hid it in his left hand behind the door.

When he opened the door a crack, he found a man in his thirties, a slim, dark mustache decorating his upper lip. He wore a cap, and his suit was gray and baggy. Glass didn't recognize him. The man took off his cap, exposing wavy hair with a few hints of gray at the temples.

"I'm Mount, sir," he said.

Glass nodded and moved away from the door so that the new man could enter. He let the man see his gun as he holstered it, but he didn't flinch.

"Ex-soldier?" he asked.

"Survived the Western Front, yes, sir," Mount said.

"What have you been doing since?"

"The Germans," Mount said. "I'm good with languages. My Russian is good enough to be sent over to you, what with things heating up."

"You know we lost a man yesterday."

Mount nodded and set his cap on the table by the door. "Shot at Piccadilly Station. I'm very sorry to hear it."

"I didn't take out the perpetrator," Glass said. He pointed to his forehead. "Got this chasing him."

"You're a desk man," Mount observed. "I'm still in the thick of things. Been following a smuggling operation on the coast."

"You look fit enough," Glass said. "Come and meet the lads and our secretary."

Mount shook hands all around with the Russian section; then they settled into their meeting.

"I've one big piece of news," Peel announced.

"Tell me," Glass said.

"We've located Princess Fyodora Novikova in Shanghai," his man reported. "She's a taxi dancer at the Del Monte."

Glass frowned. "What's that?"

"A grand place. Only the best Russian hostesses work there. The youngest, most beautiful. It has a garden and a veranda. Unfortunately, rooms upstairs as well."

He had wanted to be happy for Olga, that her sister still lived, but she still might be lost. "So she's a prostitute?"

"I don't know about that, but whatever she is, she's the best at it."

"Let's get in touch with Secret Intelligence there," he said to Miss Drover. Surely he needed to do something for the poor, broken princess. "I'll release the funds for someone to offer her a ticket to London, even if I have to pay for it personally."

Miss Drover looked up from her notepad. "What do we do when she arrives?"

"Bring her here, or wherever our meeting place is by then. I'll debrief her and hopefully reunite her with her sister. I'll make sure Peter Eyre will allow her to share her sister's room at the Grand Russe."

"Are you going to make use of her?" Mount said curiously. "Is she really a princess?"

"Yes. A twenty-six-year-old taxi-dancing princess," Peel said. "She'll have lived a hard life since she was about twenty. I understand if a White Russian had money in foreign accounts they went to Europe. If they didn't, they ran for Vladivostok, and when the Bolshies took the town, they crossed into China or Manchuria."

"Her sister, Princess Olga, escaped earlier with some of the more European-focused imperial family members because her fiancé was murdered," Glass explained. "But her sister didn't leave then. Neither of them had money in foreign accounts, but because Olga was sent to the dowager empress, she was able to leave on a British battleship in '19 with trunks of possessions."

"The family should have sent them both," Miss Drover said.

"They may not have had that option. There was so much chaos, and when you consider how many members of the imperial family perished, it may not have seemed very safe to send anyone to them."

"I, for one, am very glad you are restoring this woman to her sister," Miss Drover said. "Bravo, sir."

Les nodded his approval. "Olga is a good girl. If her sister is anything like her, she'll be a survivor."

"She'd have to be. In Shanghai, Russians are the lowest of the low," Peel said. "To work at the Del Monte. She's at the top of pyramid of penniless Russian women. There is very little opportunity. They aren't offered jobs in shops, and even if they find husbands they usually have to work."

"We'll get her out," Glass said. No matter what shape she was in. "Let me know if you have any trouble, Miss Drover; otherwise, I expect her to be on the next ship out of Shanghai. In terms of assignments, Les, I assume you'll be on the first train north after the funeral."

"Yes, sir." Les nodded.

"Peel, I want you to liaise with Special Branch regarding the Konstantin search. This Shanghai princess is also Konstantin's cousin, and we might be able to use her to catch him."

"Especially if she appears seeming to have money," Peel said. "Konstantin will come out of his hidey-hole to gather more funds."

Chapter 12

"Exactly." Glass smiled at his operative. If only Princess Fyodora were already in London. "We need to keep her completely out of sight until we decide what use we can make of her. For the rest of you, Swankle, stay the course with your new journalistic career. As for you, Mount, Bill was embedded in the local activist activities. He took over where Les had begun. He had a sales cover. We'll have to put you in with another angle."

"I'm well used as a translator," Mount suggested. "Anything where being bilingual is of use."

"Let's work on your papers," Glass said. "Maybe we can get you into the so-called trade delegation next month. Don't go anywhere near the Grand Russe. We want to keep you clean."

"What should I do for now?"

"Work with Miss Drover to establish an identity. Then offer your services anywhere in the city that is servicing Russians. Charities, hospitals, schools. Start meeting people."

"Very good," Mount said, smoothing his mustache with two fingers.

Glass nodded and poured himself another cup of tea. The change of his roster, and the emergence of the new princess on the scene, might change the dynamic of his mission. Whatever happened, he hoped Konstantin would be brought in soon—or wiped off the face of the earth, like Bill Vall-Grandly.

* * * *

Douglas had left the hotel, muttering something about a meeting just after lunch. Olga stayed with her latest charge, the new chambermaid, until three; then John Neville took her on as he did inventory in the Restaurant with the chef. She'd managed to persuade him to escort her to her room so she could change out of her dress, and she picked up her sketchbook on the way out. Amusing herself with sketches of the kitchen and its busy workers passed a few hours easily enough, but then it was 7 p.m., and Mr. Neville needed to go home.

Lionel Dew, the night manager, brought her into the nightclub, which was opening earlier right now since the Coffee Room didn't have the usual champagne and appetizers in the early evening because of her art exhibit.

She sat at one of the small cocktail tables with her sketchpad while Mr. Dew and Mr. Friend, the nightclub manager, discussed stocking the bar. Eventually, the band came in and began to warm up. The only one she knew by name was Judd Anderson, the piano player with the golden hands. He had a good-humored face. Even his most vague expression held a hint of a smile. The rest of the band was good, but even the talented band leader/ cornet player didn't match his charisma.

The band settled into a rhythmic tune after they'd warmed up their instruments individually. So far, the singer hadn't appeared, and instead of listening to words, she could appreciate the syncopation. When they started into a tango, she dropped into a reverie. The pulsing song returned her to the previous night with Douglas, his fingers making her body writhe. He'd taken her to heaven, something Prince Maxim had told her about, had prepared her for mentally, but had never managed to make happen. She'd had *la petite mort* for the first time, and it had felt like a miracle. How could she deny herself that again? She needed to exercise caution though. Douglas was her cousin's enemy, and not exactly her friend. He was a spy, a deceiver.

But he was also someone who seemed to genuinely want to protect her.

She stared down at her sketchpad and drew Douglas with a gun in his hand. Could she trust him?

Emmeline sauntered into the nightclub. She stopped at the table.

"What are you doing?" Emmeline asked. She wore a loose sweater and skirt in pale pink wool, not yet dressed for the evening, though she had a full face of makeup.

Olga turned over her sketchpad. "Just gathering ideas."

"Is Peter opening his playground to staff now?" the other woman sneered.

"I've been here before," Olga said in her most neutral tone.

Emmeline snorted and stalked off, leaving a cloud of heavy perfume in her wake. She didn't normally douse herself with the stuff. Walking straight to the stage, she stepped up the pair of steps on the side and leaned against the piano, her back to the dance floor.

Mr. Anderson's affable face didn't betray anything, though she could see Emmeline chatting at him. Olga wondered if Peter knew about his mistress's latest hobby. Was Judd Anderson actually having relations with Emmeline, and when Peter found out, would he sack one of the main reasons people crowded Maystone's every night?

* * * *

Lionel Dew escorted Lord Walling into Peter's office that evening, having been under orders to bring the spymaster to him as soon as he arrived at the hotel. He'd finally rung through to Quex, chief of the Secret Intelligence Service. Peter wasn't exactly certain who Lord Walling reported to directly, but he'd used the contacts of his uncle, the Marquess of Hatbrook, to make his way to the former director of Naval Intelligence who had run SIS since soon after the end of the war.

They'd spoken for an hour, Peter impressing on him the idea that the so-called Russian trade delegation was damaging the reputation of his business with their antics, and surely surveillance could be better managed in a house, which they could set up with a full staff of informers and listening posts. They had also nearly led to the hotel being bombed, which could have killed hundreds of people, including British government ministers. Eventually, Quex had agreed and said he would assign someone to find a suitable location to house the Russians, possibly nearer to the site of the upcoming meetings.

Peter straightened his tie and used his handkerchief to gloss his desktop, which was unusually free of debris. He hadn't had a cigarette since just after tea, only three total that day. While he felt dizzy, a week from now he'd be grateful he'd cut back.

Dew, decidedly middle-aged and the oldest of his staff, walked in, followed by Lord Walling, fifteen years younger and a dark devil to Dew's angel.

"Thank you, Mr. Dew," Peter said, rising slightly. He gestured Lord Walling into a chair but stayed behind his desk.

His night manager closed the door on the way out.

"Where is the princess?" Lord Walling asked in a tone that showed whatever had happened during his day, he was entirely in business mode.

"At Maystone's under the eye of my manager there, Cuddy Friend."

"Anyone can get into a nightclub."

Peter picked up his elephant, letting the cool jade soothe his fingers. "We have men on the door."

"Konstantin is better than anyone you might be employing," the lord snarled. "She ought to be locked up in the hotel somewhere. Even your office would be a vast improvement."

"She's been at Maystone's less than an hour, after being passed around management for most of the day. She's never been alone, and no one has spotted Konstantin."

"This isn't good enough."

"Olga is an old, dear friend of mine. I wouldn't put her in danger." Peter folded his hands over his chest. "To that end I've taken measurements for both general and her specific safety."

"Oh?" Lord Walling's dark countenance went sardonic. "Doubled your night watchmen?"

"No, I've spoken to Quex."

Lord Walling's expression didn't change. "You don't say."

"Yes, we're removing the Russians by the end of the week. You've demanded that Olga not be allowed to work on the seventh due to their presence, which sorely affects her ability to perform her duties. As we all know, Konstantin was drawn to the hotel at least partially because of the delegation. We also will remove the problem of the prostitutes."

"You can never remove that difficulty," the lord said.

"I don't care if there is sex for hire under my nose," Peter said, squeezing his fingers until they burned, "but I'll be damned before I let any more girls be beaten here—or murdered."

Lord Walling stood slowly, making sure to let Peter see how tall he was, how physically imposing. Peter wasn't impressed. His father had been a soldier, and he was related to some of the most important people in England. He wouldn't be intimidated by a viscount. He stood, too, but instead of taking some menacing pose, he leaned his torso back, tucked his hands into his trousers, and put on his most insouciant expression.

"I respect your position here, Eyre," Lord Walling said. "But you won't win this battle. I will overrule you no matter how much pull your uncle has, or your mother, or anyone in your entire bloody family." He poked his index finger into Peter's desk, rattling his brass ashtray. "You will not dictate my operation to me or create problems. You and I are in business together until I say it is over."

"Quex is your superior."

"I'm certain that you told him your version of the facts, not mine."

Peter didn't shift. "But Olga."

"But nothing. She is my problem, not yours."

"She is both my friend and my employee."

Lord Walling's gaze hardened absolutely. "She is a pawn on my chessboard, Eyre, not yours. Stop trying to play my game."

Peter kept his gaze on Lord Walling's for a moment, matching wits, not giving an inch, his brain moving furiously. He'd have to send Olga back to his sister in Leeds. The situation was unsupportable. Olga wasn't a pawn but a young woman. His telephone rang, and his gaze instinctively moved to it, costing him his staring battle with Lord Walling. As he picked up the phone, the spymaster wrenched open the office door and was gone before Peter could even say his name into the speaker.

* * * *

"You seem irritated tonight," Olga said. Douglas had arrived after Emmeline had gone, brushed off by Judd Anderson, who obviously knew better than to mess with her.

Douglas had held out his hand to her, saying nothing. She'd closed her sketchbook and risen. He hadn't touched her when they departed and had taken her straight to the lift.

The floor butler had been walking down the corridor on the seventh floor. Douglas had ordered dinner for them both without asking what she wanted and had taken her into his suite, vanishing into the bedroom for a time.

He'd come out when dinner was announced, trading their cart of food for envelopes, letters he must have written in the interim.

Now, he read a book while she stared at the *Firebird*. It was nine, too early for even a chambermaid to go to bed.

A click came from behind the painting. "I think your recording just stopped."

He set his book down, a collection of Agatha Christie short stories. After he rose to go to the painting, she peered down at the cover of the book. She didn't like mysteries; her life had too many problems as it was.

Pulling the latest issue of *The Illustrated London News* from a pile of newspapers on the table in front of the sofa, she went to take a bath.

When she came out an hour later, he had disappeared. The previous night's sensual delights had been forgotten, she surmised. She decided to ready herself for bed, though it was still rather early. When she had her nightgown on, she went back into the sitting room to paw through the day's papers again. He had a decent selection of yellow press papers, and she could never resist a gossip column, even if she'd long since given up hope of socializing at the utterly exclusive Riviera Club overlooking the Thames, or dancing the night away with the Prince of Wales at the Embassy.

She was curled up on the sofa, reading an account of a fancy-dress party gone awry in the Daily Sketch, when she heard shouting in the corridor outside of the suite. She sat up, dropping the paper, but at just that moment, Douglas reappeared. "Problems?" she asked.

"A fight next door," he said. "I went to break it up. I'm sure you couldn't hear the thumping in the bath since it doesn't share a wall next door."

"Prostitutes again?"

"No, between two of the men this time. Ovolensky has taken off to who knows where."

"That's who was shouting at the hall?"

"Yes, he was threatening to change suites because I'm such an old woman." Douglas grinned roguishly.

"Isn't that a problem for you?"

He sat next to her as she picked up the newspaper and folded it. "There aren't so many suites that can be opened to three bedrooms like that one. The next step would be moving them up to the eighth floor, which is going to be outfitted as furnished apartments. Since none of them are ready, I'd have time to set up a listening post before they could move."

"But they'll go to another hotel."

"A few well-placed calls will keep other hotels from taking such a disagreeable bunch," he said.

"Understood."

"You are becoming braver," he observed.

"What do you mean?"

"Sitting out here in a nightdress and wrapper"—he surveyed her gown— "though I can't say you went for sex appeal."

She fingered the ruffled high neck collar of her cotton gown. "True. And you weren't here."

"Even so." He winked. "A princess in her night dress. My life is certainly looking up."

"Yours may be, but I don't know about mine." She stared at her fingers. One of them had an ink stain from the newspaper, and none were without nicks and calluses from her daily work regime.

"We'll catch Konstantin," he said with confidence. "He can't hide forever, and he's a murderer now, a fugitive. I wanted to ask if you'd do a sketch of him."

"He's a master of disguise. It's amazing how a beard transforms him, and he'll use hair dyes." She thought guiltily of the mangled sketch she'd produced before.

"He can't hide the way his head sits on that thick neck of his," Douglas told her.

"A muffler?" she suggested.

"Maybe," he said. "But not likely. Also, as spring comes on, no one will be wearing them."

"It doesn't feel very springlike now."

"No, but you have to stay positive. I know it's hard." He picked up her hand and rubbed away the ink stain with his handkerchief. "I am sure good things are coming."

She wished she had the same sense. "Would you like it if I wore sexier gowns?"

His gaze moved up and down her again. Instinctively, she pressed out her chest instead of attempting to hide it. "You're beautiful in anything." His voice had gone a little hoarse.

"You think I'm beautiful?"

"In this light, your skin has the quality of pearl."

"All of it?" Daringly, she unbuttoned the top of her collar, and when he sucked in a breath, she undid the next one. As he stared at her chest, she kept going until the slopes of her naked breasts had been revealed. Her body remembered the way he had touched her before, how she'd come apart in his arms, and yet, he hadn't taken advantage. All of a sudden she could think of nothing else, wanted nothing else.

He slowly lifted his hand, his gaze on her eyes. She said nothing, allowing him to slip his hand into her nightdress and cup her breast. When his palm brushed her nipple, she gasped.

"A good feeling?" he asked softly.

"The best," she said. How she wanted another little death.

His other hand went to her dressing gown and undid the tie. He helped her slip it off her shoulders, the thin wool pooling around her waist. Her nightdress gaped, but she still had a couple of buttons left. She undid them now. Nothing was revealed exactly, but he showed her what the placket was there for when he bent his head to her breast and kissed her, one hand on her left breast and his lips on her right. He learned the shape of her with his mouth and licked her nipple.

She gasped the second he made contact, her head going back against the sofa. By the time he went to his knees on the carpet and leaned between her legs, she was lost to the sensation of him plucking and stroking her nipples. She'd had no idea of their sensitivity. When his hand moved away, she cried out against the loss of it, but then she felt his fingers moving up her thigh, and she knew what he was going to do. She was too aroused to do anything but spread her legs apart, eager for his magic touch on that most private place on her body. His mouth roved her breasts, setting her on fire as his fingers played under her skirt. She pressed against him, rotating her hips, bolder than the last time, with no thought of anything but the moment's pleasure.

Spinning higher and higher, breathing hard, she came apart under his touch. Her eyes stayed closed as she panted.

"Look," he said softly.

She opened her eyes. Two of his fingers were glistening, and as she watched, he sucked them into his mouth, that same mouth that had done such wonderful things to her breasts.

"Delicious," he pronounced. "You are exquisite."

"I can't stay here, can I," she said, still panting. "I'm not safe with you. I'll want this again."

He ran his hands along her thighs, outside of her rucked-up nightdress. "You are safe, Olga. I'm only thinking of your pleasure."

"But you're a man. Don't you want more?"

He stood, and she could see the bulge even behind his generously cut trousers. "It wouldn't be right to ask for anything. Giving you pleasure is amusement enough." He smiled at her and walked away, his back to her.

Could she really continue to enjoy this without consequences? On one hand, Douglas did know how to keep a secret, but she didn't want to fall any farther and not have a place to land. How could this end in a positive way if he didn't offer marriage?

And would he? Offer marriage to a girl who so wantonly desired his touch on her body? He had already trained her so well. She shook her head. No, she couldn't stay here. Even if she had to live with Emmeline, she'd be safer. Even more importantly, she'd have more self-respect.

But oh, she would miss Douglas's caresses.

* * * *

Glass had, of course, not gone to Bill Vall-Grandly's funeral, but he and Quex stood in the trees as the coffin was lowered into the earth at the cemetery. It was a show of respect that perhaps only a spy could appreciate since they didn't make themselves known to the family or other mourners.

They walked out of the cemetery together after the first shovelful of dirt was thrown into the grave.

"Peter Eyre is awfully tired of those Russians," Quex said, tipping his fedora down. "Are we getting anything useful from all the time we've invested?"

"I don't see how we can walk away, as Englishmen and gentlemen," Douglas admitted. "They are beating women, fighting among themselves. I'm sure someone will be killed if we don't have someone there breaking up the situation."

"So we're there to protect prostitutes and Russian thugs?"

"They've already tried to bring in human cargo once. If we aren't at the listening post, we'll miss the next time they try."

Quex shook his head. "I don't think it's enough, Glass. I think you're missing the forest for the trees, which is unusual for you."

"There is also the matter of Princess Olga. Konstantin often targets her for cash, and she lives at the Grand Russe."

Quex's jowls drooped farther as he spoke. "That's a bit different."

"She's been sleeping in my suite since Konstantin shot Vall-Grandly."

"With you?"

"Yes, sir."

Quex shook his head. "This can't last like it is. I'll overrule the move to eject the Russians for now, but next week at this time, we'll be making plans if you haven't come up with significant intel about either the Russians or Konstantin. Understand?"

"Yes, sir."

"Let's face it, we have more trouble with the Bolshies than one rotten egg trade delegation. What's going on in the north?"

* * * *

That afternoon, Glass returned to the hotel, mindful of being there at the end of Olga's shift so that she didn't get passed around the hotel staff. Hugh Moth shook his head sadly as he handed Glass his key.

"What?"

"I heard Mr. Eyre grumbling about you at luncheon," he said. "I always bring him his tray. You've done something to make yourself unpopular."

"Maybe he doesn't like my friendship with Princess Olga," Glass said.

"Could be," the young man admitted. "It's obvious they have a special friendship."

"Anything else going on?"

"Another Russian arrived today. Oh, and I have a letter for you." He turned to the guest cubbyholes and pulled out a letter.

Douglas glanced at the letter and saw it was from his father. "What's his story?"

"I don't know. He had me send a bellboy up the Piano Suite with a note, and then Mr. Ovolensky came down personally to gather the chap."

"So he's staying there."

"Seems so. He had a case, but he didn't seem like he was new to England."

"Did he speak English?"

"Yes, but a very heavy accent."

"What does he look like?"

"Very cruel, dark eyes. Narrow-like. And a bayonet of a nose. Gray whiskers, like he had forgotten to shave today."

"Age?" Hugh Moth had a nice eye for detail.

"Mid-fifties?" Moth guessed. "Couldn't see his hair under his hat."

Glass sucked on his inner cheek as he considered the news. They didn't know much about Mikhail Lashevich, the famed assassin known as the "Hand of Death," but the general description matched. Was it coincidence or a terrible new problem?

Either way, he only had a week to sort things out here at the Grand Russe. Quex was losing patience with his operation. He'd already had to move Tim Swankle and now this. But his instincts told him to stay in the hotel. It felt like the kind of place where things happened, went wrong.

"Thanks, Mr. Moth." He tossed the desk clerk a coin and walked toward the basement staircase.

* * * *

Olga caught sight of Douglas as soon as he appeared in the staff lounge. She rose from the elderly upholstered chair where she'd been reviewing staff assignments. "What are you doing here?"

"Coming to collect you for the rest of the day," he said, pulling off his hat, shaking it off, and replacing it. He seemed tense, even more solemn than usual.

"What is going on?" she asked. "I can go to Maystone's or sit at one of the secretary's desks for as long as I need to."

He smiled, though it looked forced. "No need for that. I'm sorry. I attended Bill's burial today, and I'm low."

"Oh, I'm so sorry." A couple of chambermaids came in, chattering. Their appearance stopped her from patting his arm like she might have otherwise.

"Yes, well." He grimaced. "Can you gather your evening gown from your room? I'd like to take you to dinner at the Savoy Grill tonight."

"Why? Will it cheer you?"

He made a choking sound. "My father is available, and we'd discussed him meeting you."

Olga couldn't help the expression of pleasure that crossed her face. What a good sign. Her fears from the night before were assuaged completely. He wouldn't take a woman he was trying to turn into his mistress to dinner with the earl.

"My Vionnet is clean," she said. "I can be ready in half an hour."

"Let's go up and fetch it down to my suite. I need to put on evening dress myself."

She felt herself beaming the entire time they were gathering her clothes and taking them to the seventh floor. An evening out. They'd eat French food and drink wine. And all that after a long day training dizzy young chambermaids. Life was a strange journey.

* * * *

Lord St. Martin's was already seated at a central table at the Savoy Grill when they arrived. He rose and nodded at Olga as Douglas introduced them. While he had his son's height, she suspected his hair had never been as full or dark as his son's and had thinned to a sliver of gray brown around his ears and the back of his head. His eyes pierced her, though. She didn't feel disliked, but she sensed he knew exactly how old her clothing was.

"A very good evening to you, my lord," she said as a waiter seated her.

"I'm glad to meet the young lady who has so entranced my son, Your Serene Highness," he said, picking up his glass of red wine. "Not one for the ladies is Walling."

Olga had spent enough time in intimate clinches with him by this point that she knew very well that a total lack of interest was not Douglas's problem. "He is obsessed by his work, I think, my lord."

"Very true, very true. And not inappropriate in a young sprig of the aristocracy."

"Yes, but I suppose you'd like grandchildren," she said with an impish desire to shock the old man.

He chuckled loudly. "And what about you, Serene Highness? Want children of your own?"

"Yes, of course. I've lost my close family. My parents are gone; my sister vanished into China after the war."

"No brothers."

"I think there was a baby boy, but he died almost immediately." She shook her head. "I don't really remember."

"What took your parents?"

"The revolution," she said simply. She'd been in England by the time her father had been murdered. Her mother had died not long after, probably of complications of influenza brought on by deprivation.

"Bloody awful," the earl pronounced. "Do pardon my bluntness."

"Oh, I agree," she assured him as waiters set menus in front of them.

She was delighted by all the French dishes and knew she'd go to bed extremely content that night.

* * * *

"She's a happy girl," the earl said to Douglas an hour later, as the waiter cleared their table. "Good bloodlines, if you appreciate Russians. Going to marry her?"

Only centuries of aristocratic breeding prevented Olga's mouth from dropping open. The British didn't look down on White Russians as much as some societies did, like the Chinese, and her title being real helped matters, but still. The earl must have wanted Douglas to marry very soon to accept such a bad bargain as herself.

Douglas reacted by laughing. He shook his finger at his father. "You won't be happy until you're dandling a baby on your knee. Why don't you remarry, sir?"

"Oh, that is for the young," the earl said. "No, I insist. I'll go to the bank and pull out the Crewe diamonds for you. Must be something you can make into a modern ring fit for a princess."

Olga's gaze went to Douglas, then to his father, and back again as she tried not to laugh, or squeal.

Douglas cleared his throat. "I have a busy schedule, sir, but there is no harm in inventorying the diamonds. I know Mother didn't like them, so no one has probably worn them since your mother died in the 1870s."

"Yes, very out of date," the earl said, turning his head to Olga. "But good stones. Been in the family about one hundred fifty years before that. They probably need to be recut."

"I love old styles," Olga said. "Not that I expect any declarations from your son, of course. That is up to him."

"Do you love him?" the earl asked in the tones of a blunt sportsman.

Chapter 13

No one had ever asked Olga if she loved a man. Such a sharp and intimate question. Did she answer the earl with the truth? For a moment, she stared at the snowy white napkin on her lap as if the folds would give her the answer. "I could not regard any man I have known for just two and half weeks any more highly than I regard Lord Walling," she said solemnly, without exactly giving the earl what he wanted to hear.

"Well said," the earl declared, tapping his knife on his plate. "Keep an eye on him. If you don't make him take you out, have a bit of fun now, he'll stick to his ways, and you'll be a lonely wife indeed. Not how my wife and I were. She was a gay sort."

They sat for another hour, lingering over coffee and French tarts while the earl reminisced about his long-dead wife. When he reached stories about how much she loved the theater, he suggested they attend *No, No, Nanette* with him at the Palace Theatre the next night.

"I've heard of that show," Olga exclaimed. One of their former guests at the hotel had worked on the musical for a time.

"The premiere was tonight," the earl said. "But I never go to the theater on Wednesdays. What do you say, Walling? I have my usual box."

"Certainly, if I am free. The princess needs a treat."

"I can't take her alone," the earl warned. "Tongues will wag."

"If I am free," Douglas repeated.

For the first time, Olga saw lines of exhaustion in his face. His work might not tire him, but his father did. Interesting.

When they finally entered the taxicab to go home, Douglas let out a long sigh.

"Was it hard to hear so much about your family?" Olga asked.

Douglas patted her hand on the seat between them. "No, I was delighted to see my father in such an excellent mood. I'm afraid I cannot offer a large family circle to any woman. The war, you understand."

"How I know it," she said, enjoying the warmth of his glove over hers. She wondered if he had decided what, exactly, he was going to offer to her. "We all have had to start over, those of us who survived."

Butterflies moved the abundance of good food around in her stomach as the taxicab pulled up in front of the hotel. Johnnie Miles, who must be on a double shift, opened the cab door for them and nodded at her.

She felt like a proper guest as she and Douglas walked across the marble floor of the Grand Hall. With her in her fur-and-silk cape and the handsome man next to her in full evening kit, they fit into the jaunty crowd. As they waited for the lift, she heard two women in diamonds and silk enthusiastically discussing her Russian art exhibit in the Coffee Room, and her heart beat with fierce pride. But once she and Douglas were upstairs, the mood between them returned immediately to business.

He helped her remove her cape and draped it over his arm. "I have to tell you, Princess, that we've had a new arrival next door. Managed to get a sketch out of Hugh Moth downstairs. The lad can draw."

"Really? I had no idea." She looked at her cape. "I find it is best to store that as flat as possible. Is there room in a drawer or in the closet?"

"Yes, there is an unused shelf."

"Thank you. I'll place it there while you take off your coat, and then you can show me Hugh's artwork."

Thirty seconds later, he followed her into the bedroom. "It's less about his artistic ability and more about the man he drew."

"Of course. I misspoke."

When she came out of the closet, he went inside and came out with a sheet of white drawing paper. She took it from Douglas's hand and stared at it. The instant she recognized the face, she forgot any plan to take off her shoes, relax, or ready herself for sleep, much less think about a possible marriage proposal.

"Your hand is shaking," he exclaimed, pulling the paper away. "Who is it?"

Blood, across a snowy white shirt, dripping from his neck. His eyes gone glassy, then emptied forever. Those long, thin, talented fingers clutching, then slackening as he crumbled. The gun, moving toward her as she screamed. The man watching as she ran down the Nevsky Prospect, not killing her, no flash of heat and pain in her back, her breath catching in her throat as she pulled open the rear door of Maxim's automobile and begged the chauffeur to drive her home.

"He murdered my Maxim," she whispered. The tears came instantly, and her hands wouldn't stay still as she lifted them to her face.

Douglas dropped the paper and wrapped one hand around her head and the other around her waist. He pulled her down on the bed with her on his lap, in her much-too-chilly Vionnet.

"I bought this dress for him," she sobbed. "Maxim never saw it. It came all the way from Paris, and then it just went into a trunk when my parents sent me away. The first time I wore it was in England."

"I'm sure he'd have loved it," Douglas said soothingly, stroking her back.

"I'll never forget." She wiped her streaming eyes. "How can I? And now that man is next door. Why has he come?"

"Is he Mikhail Lashevich?" Douglas asked.

"He is the Hand of Death," Olga said. "That is all I know."

"One and the same," Douglas said. "Sodding hell."

"Is he here for me?" Her voice trembled, sounding weak. She forced herself to stiffen her spine, to stop crying. It didn't help Maxim then, and it wouldn't help her now. She thought the profanity Douglas had used, "sodding hell," and felt better.

"I don't know why he is here," Douglas said. "But his daughter lives in Hull with her husband, who is a trade activist. We've been monitoring him. I'm not surprised that Lashevich has made it into Great Britain, but I want to know why."

She pressed her fingers into her dress, careful not to use her nails and damage the silk. "I am not important."

"You saw his face," Douglas said. "I am so sorry, but that might be enough of a threat for him. All I knew before now is that the man matched Lashevich's general description."

Her legs felt cold under the silk. "I can never forget him. That will make me a threat to him as long as I live."

"I can never forget the face of the man who killed my brother Byron," Douglas said. "He was my second brother. He was running dispatches between commanders, and we ended up in the same trench during an attack. The Germans swarmed us, close-in fighting. Dreadful business."

"Did you see what happened to Byron's killer?" she asked.

"Found him in the mud a couple of hours later," he related, his voice expressionless. "Facedown. I kept his glasses for a time, stomped them to bits on November eleventh, when the war ended. I still thought I had one brother left, but he'd died in October. Buried in Masnières."

"Sodding hell," she whispered aloud. "Then it was just you and your father."

"War is cruel. I never thought I'd be the survivor, but I've never stopped fighting for my country."

"War is cruel, and revolution, and violence," she agreed. "Did it come back to you, those memories, when you watched your man die?"

"It made me want to see your cousin's mouth full of mud," Douglas said in that same eerie voice, "his eyelashes encrusted with dirt."

"If Konstantin is in business with my Maxim's killer, I will kill him myself. I know how to use a knife, and I will carry one with me from now on."

Douglas stood up, sliding her to the bed. He went to one of his drawers and pulled out a leather case. Turning, he opened it, displaying knives in smaller sheaths.

"Three-inch blade enough for you?" he asked.

She went to him and chose a sheath. She unsnapped it and pulled out the blade. It didn't need to be tested; she could see how sharp it was. "It will do."

In agreement, they nodded at each other. "Keep it with you at all times," he said.

She lifted her skirt just high enough to reach the top of her stocking, slid the sheath between the silk and the garter, and hooked it on. The leather felt dully cold, but it would warm slowly enough.

"You are a very sexy girl, Princess."

"We were both forged in war, Douglas. It is time I stopped being so soft."

He set the knife case on top of the dresser and came toward her. She stood her ground as he ran his fingers over her mouth.

"I don't want you to be hard, but I do want you to stay strong. I can't give you a quiet life, at least not if you want to be at my side."

"Do you want a wife who stays in the country, raises your children?"

"No, I want a woman to warm my bed," he said roughly.

His words licked heat down her chest, doing funny things with her nipples. She wrapped her arms around his waist and pressed her torso against his. Thinking he'd kiss her, she tilted up her head, but instead, he gently removed her arms and stepped away.

"It's more important than ever to monitor the Russians," he said. "Ivan should have changed the disk earlier, but I need to check on things. You rest, and we'll sort out where to stash you tomorrow."

Limply, she sat on the bed as he walked away. How quickly he dismissed her and returned to his work. But how completely he magnetized her. She couldn't keep her eyes off him.

How could a conversation about death have shown her for the first time that she was completely taken with her noble spymaster? She had promised to be strong, yet was more vulnerable than ever. *She loved Douglas.*

* * * *

He heard knocking through his dreams. Glass woke, sliding the newspaper off his chest. He'd slept on the sofa after monitoring a vodka drinking session between the old Russians and new for half the night. A glance at the clock over the fireplace as he walked by told him it was nine in the morning. The princess had managed to leave without waking him.

Lucy Drover stood at the door, a small crate in her arms. "Telephone for you, sir."

He stepped aside and let her in. "Telephone?"

"The wiring to this floor should be completed by Monday. Orders from above." She set the crate down along the wall.

"Why? What's happened?"

Lucy's thin upper lip slid over the lower, covering it. Was she about to cry, his doughty secretary? "My lord."

"What?"

"Another bombing, sir."

"Sodding hell." He went to the window, flung aside the curtain. The day had some clarity to it, despite clouds, and he could see across the park. No smoke in that direction out of the ordinary. "Where?"

"Piccadilly, sir. A theater there."

"The Queen's Theatre?"

She nodded.

"That bastard. Very well. Get word to DI Dent. Tell him to call all of Konstantin's known associates into Special Branch. Have everyone who works in the area around the theater interviewed since this is the third time we know he has been in the area."

"The princess?" Miss Drover asked.

"Not her." Glass swallowed and tasted the bitter mouth of a morning started unprepared. "She's been with me since three yesterday afternoon."

"That doesn't mean she doesn't know anything," Miss Drover said in the assertive tone characteristic of her.

"I'll question her myself. You may go." He stared out of the window as his secretary moved way. "Wait."

"Yes?"

"Send a note to my father with my regrets. We will be unable to attend the theater this evening."

"We?"

"Yes. Say we."

"Very good, sir."

He stood erect until Miss Drover had let herself out of the suite. Only then did he let his head drop against the glass.

Had he lost his edge where the princess was concerned? He should have her called in like everyone else. No favorites. Why was he trying to protect her?

He saw a woman on Park Lane below. For a moment, he thought he recognized his princess. When the woman turned her head, he saw it was just another tall blonde, not Olga at all. Was he seeing her in every woman now? Maybe he had actually fallen in love with the woman his father wanted him to marry.

* * * *

Just before luncheon in the staff dining hall, Olga went to see Peter. She'd been run off her feet all morning because there had been a party across three of the seller's suites on the fourth floor, and the mess had been more than the regularly assigned chambermaids could manage to clean by themselves.

Alecia Salter waved at her as she weaved between the switchboard station and the secretarial desks. Behind her friend, workmen were setting up another switchboard, either a replacement or most likely, an expansion. Some hotels did have telephones in certain rooms, and with the full-service flats being fitted upstairs, the Grand Russe needed the same technology. Douglas would appreciate a telephone. It would save so many disruptions.

"You don't look supervised," Peter said, glancing up from a tall pile of paperwork. "Who has been with you today?"

"Every chambermaid I could muster to work on the fourth. After a tidy like that, I can understand American Prohibition. The things those commercial travelers did to the rooms!"

"We'll charge them cleaning fees."

"One of the rooms needs a new carpet." She pulled her report out of her apron and handed it to him. "Do you want me to give it to John Neville?"

"I'll do it," Peter said. "Who is staying with you this afternoon? Walling around?"

"I don't know. But I can't stay on the seventh anymore."

"I didn't hear any more about Russian parties," he said. "Isn't Walling enough to protect you?"

"You must have heard about the new man with the Russians," she said, her voice starting to crack.

"Yesterday's arrival?"

She nodded.

Peter frowned and reached a hand across her desk. She took his fingers in her own and clutched them. "What is it?"

"He's the man who killed Maxim. Douglas says he is a famed assassin."

Peter's fine features went slack. "Bloody hell."

She willed the warmth of his fingers into her cold ones. "I can't go back upstairs. What if he sees me? Famous assassins are unlikely to ever forget a face, and I can identify him."

Peter pulled his hand away and stood. "You can't stay with me. It's not proper." He snapped his fingers. "We'll put you in with Emmeline. It's perfect. You can both do with a bit of company."

"You wouldn't, Peter." Her voice broke completely, and she let her head drop into her hands, shoulders shaking.

"No more work today," she heard him say through her tears.

The door behind her opened, and she heard Hugh Moth speak, something about a bombing. Peter swore again. "Have her things moved into Miss Plash's room, Hugh, would you?"

Then he was gone. They were both gone. She walked around Peter's desk and found a fresh handkerchief in his upper-right drawer. After blowing her nose, she saw his drinks tray and decided to indulge in an inch of something. Her nerves needed steadying if she was going to have to spend time with Emmeline.

Twenty minutes later, she'd had an additional finger of very smooth orange-flavored liquor, and no one had come to fetch her. She felt belligerent. If she had to stay with Emmeline, fine, but she wouldn't survive without her things. She had Harold's painting to finish, just the fine details, really, and didn't want it damaged. She'd carry the painting herself.

After she opened Peter's office door, she went to the left and out the door into the side corridor. She'd expected to find a bellboy to go upstairs with her, but no one was around. When she sidled into the service lift, she could see a fair amount of activity going on in the Grand Hall. She ought to find out what had been bombed, but first she wanted to secure her painting. It was worth a lot of money to her.

As she stepped onto the lift, she saw policemen walking by. Obviously, the Grand Russe was secure. She didn't need a bodyguard.

She operated the lift herself, ascending to the tenth with no trouble. It took more time than usual to unlock her door. She wondered if the liquor had hit her too hard. Hadn't she slept well? She remembered she hadn't eaten yet and had had a hard morning. Luckily she had a half-full shortbread tin under her bed, and that would sustain her since she'd missed luncheon by now. She weaved a little as she crossed the room and half sat, half fell on her bed. Had she really only drunk two inches' worth of Peter's orange whatever it was? She let her head drop to her pillow. What did it matter?

* * * *

When Olga checked her list at ten the next morning in the staff lounge she discovered that no one had brought Emmeline tea since the lead chambermaid on the fourth floor had not shown up for her shift that day.

Ivan Salter had checked on her at the start of his shift because Douglas had telephoned the hotel to make sure she was safe, though he would be out all evening. He hadn't spoken to her directly. She had agreed to sleep on the Salters' sofa since she refused to stay with Emmeline and had woken with a crick in her neck but had otherwise slept well enough.

A strange night, like so many others recently. Her dreams had been dreadful, angry, swirling colors, indistinct figures. She'd think she saw her sister, and when she reached out, Fyodora was miles away.

Olga put up her hands and pressed them away from her, trying to ban the spirits that had mocked her through the night. She muttered a Russian prayer.

"Have you turned witch on us?" someone with a friendly voice asked.

"I'm sorry, Mr. Neville," she told the day manager. "Do you ever have that feeling that your dreams are chasing you?"

"Bad night?"

She rubbed her neck. "I slept on a sofa. It didn't agree with me."

"I'm sorry to hear that, but I'm sorrier to see you alone. That isn't supposed to happen."

"I'm short-staffed today. I came down to check my list, and now I need to gather a tea service from the kitchen and take it to the fourth."

"That isn't your job."

She grimaced. "It is when it is Emmeline Plash."

"Ah, I see. Let's gather it up then."

Olga nodded and left the lounge, followed by Mr. Neville. The kitchen was busy with trays for the seventh and luncheon preparations for the Restaurant. She stopped at the order station and asked for Miss Plash's usual tray. A chef's assistant poured boiling water into a prepared teapot and placed a toast rack next to the butter and jams.

Mr. Neville shook his head as the man covered the tray with a cloche and placed it on a wheeled cart. "I could never manage my day with a breakfast like that. I need the full English."

"I'm partial to mushrooms and tomatoes myself, but I can do without the meat," Olga said, following the man pushing the cart.

He took it as far as the service lift. She opened the door at the gate and helped him lift the cart over the divide; then, Mr. Neville popped in beside her and operated the controls.

"Is she pleasant in the morning?" he asked, as they arrived on the fourth floor.

"I don't know. This isn't my usual duty," Olga said.

He wheeled Emmeline's cart to her door. When they arrived, she knocked briskly. When no answer came, she knocked again.

By then, they had waited at least two minutes. The tea would be brewed by now and needed to be served. Emmeline was a perfectionist about her tea. She put her ear to the door and hearing nothing, she frowned.

"I'm going to unlock it," she told Mr. Neville. "It's not like her to be up and out at this time of morning." She pulled out her master key and unlocked the door.

The sitting room was dark and smelled of cigars. She crossed to the window and opened the curtains. On the table, an open bottle of champagne rested in a silver bucket full of water. Two empty glasses huddled next to it. Emmeline's lipstick decorated the edge of one.

"I'll check her room." Olga found the door into the bedroom cracked open slightly. She pushed it aside and went immediately to the window to let in light. Then she turned to the bed.

And screamed.

Chapter 14

Following Olga's scream of horror, John Neville ran into the room. He stopped inside and swore when he saw Emmeline Plash. Olga had only just reached her side to assess the situation. Emmeline stirred weakly in bed, her eyes swollen and surrounded with bruises. Olga pulled back the blankets and found the sheet balled up next to her, dotted with dried bloodstains. Brown stains covered the pillowcase as well.

"I'll have the lift operator get help," Neville said, staring at a red-brown stain on the white carpet.

Olga picked up the other pillow, but the case had been smeared with some kind of hair oil and reeked of that and male sweat. The oil smelled vaguely familiar. "Go."

She went into the bathroom, filled a glass with water, and grabbed a clean towel. After she set them on Emmeline's table she went into the sitting room and was able to pull two round bolsters from the sofa. She used those to help Emmeline up.

"Who?" She dampened the towel and used it to wipe around Emmeline's eyes.

"Peter." The woman's cracked lips curved. One cut at the side of her dry mouth opened, and blood smeared.

"It wasn't him," Olga said, not a speck of doubt in her mind. "A Russian did this."

"How do you know?" Emmeline tried to smile. Blood zigzagged a thin trail to her chin.

"The pillow. How dare you try to blame Peter, who has taken more of your abuse than any man should?"

"The greater insult is his," Emmeline mumbled.

"Why?" she demanded.

"He didn't marry me." Emmeline moved her tongue around her mouth, wincing. She must have had loose teeth.

"You have more from him than you deserve. I will never understand why he let you return here. Your time here is finally at an end." Dispassionately, she wiped away crust until Emmeline could open her eyes.

She heard men at the door. John Neville came in first, followed by Peter and the day porter.

"Who?" Peter demanded, striding to the bed.

"A Russian," Olga said. She let the other two men enter but put her hand on Peter's chest and pushed him out of the room.

"What?" he demanded, his eyes hot and unfocused.

"Listen to me," Olga hissed, closing the door behind her.

"We can talk later. I need to see if she needs a doctor."

"Of course she needs a doctor. More than one kind."

"I'll call for one." He turned and started for the door.

"Peter Eyre Redcake, you listen to me," Olga said.

He stopped and turned, his expression harsh on his fine-featured face.

She poked a finger into his chest. "Emmeline tried to blame the attack on you."

Peter's hand went to his pocket, where he kept his cigarette case. His fingers made a clutching motion; then, his hand dropped to his side. "I need a drink," he muttered.

She wanted to scream. Why couldn't he protect himself from Emmeline? "No, you don't. You need to get this disturbed woman out of your life before she destroys you. I don't care about your past. We have a past as well, and I am not trying to kill you or ruin you."

Peter's chin set. "You weren't here during the war."

"No, I was in Russia, which was infinitely worse," she said. "You have no idea. Ask Lord Walling what the war was really like. Ask me how it felt to see Maxim shot. And now the war comes here, with the Hand of Death upstairs and your mistress entertaining Russians in her bed."

His eyes went blank. "You are certain a Russian did this?"

"Yes, but I don't know who. You sort it out." She walked to the door. "Never ask me to help with your mistress again."

Peter put his hand on her arm. She smelled clean, pressed wool and his sandalwood cologne, nothing like that Russian stench on the pillow. "I tried to get the Russians out of the hotel. Your bloody Lord Walling overruled me."

"He has to consider the greater good, Peter. There are larger priorities than yours." She pulled open the suite door and went out into the hallway. Suddenly, the wall had to prop her up. She put her hands to her face.

Should she contact Peter's sister, try to go back to Leeds? Find some other employment entirely? She couldn't stay at the Grand Russe any longer.

* * * *

"Where did Olga go after she left you?" Glass asked. He sat on the other side of the hotel manager's desk, opposite Eyre. Most of the congenial air of previous encounters was gone. The other man seemed to be reigning in his temper with a mere thread, and the air of dissolute glamor had vanished.

Eyre's gaze went to the drinks table in his office, but he didn't get up to pour anything. The cigarette smell was stale, as if he hadn't been smoking that day either.

"I can tell you she is on the sixth floor now," Eyre said after a pause.

Glass drummed his fingers on his knee. "Have you had anything from Miss Plash?"

Eyre's nostril's flared. "I know it was Ovolensky, same as you."

"It could have been him," Glass said, "but what about Lashevich? He might have the same tendencies."

"Does it matter?"

"I'd much rather deal with Ovolensky than Lashevich." Glass's tone was dry. "I'm more likely to survive the encounter."

"She wouldn't say. For all I know it was Judd Anderson, the piano player. But Olga swore it was a Russian. She smelled Russian hair oil."

"If we took Olga to the Russians' suite and took inventory of the bathrooms we could sort this," Glass said.

"She wouldn't go near that suite."

"It would have to be when the Russians were gone, but I've heard from the floor butler, and they have guards posted again. You won't be able to get into the suite. Should I call the police?"

"Won't do much good," Glass said. "No, I just have to pick one. Ovolensky it is."

"What are you going to do?"

"Have a word. What else?"

"Emmeline's been taken to hospital." Eyre's shoulders stiffened. "But I don't know for how long."

"Grand."

Eyre picked up his jade elephant. "I want the Russians gone. This is on your head. If they'd left when I wanted them to, Emmeline wouldn't have been hurt."

"No, she'd have started an affair with a musician instead, and you'd probably end up with syphilis. Peter, your mistress is going to wreck you."

One side of Eyre's mouth lifted. "Olga said much the same."

"Cut line," Glass said. "You have some sense of self-preservation, don't you?"

"Apparently not."

Glass thought about what motivated the hotel manager. "What's it going to do to the hotel's reputation when a chambermaid finds her dead body some morning? This experience won't stop her. She seemed to find it amusing."

"She likes a fuss," Eyre said.

Glass pushed back his chair. He knew the signs of a man too shocked to function. No point in belaboring the issue. "I'm going to confront Ovolensky. There will be marks on the man who did this. Can I make a call to Dent first?"

Eyre pushed his telephone across the desk.

* * * *

Ten minutes later, Glass stepped onto the lift. Detective Stone was being dispatched to the hotel. They had the issue of diplomatic immunity to wrestle with, but at least they could have Georgy Ovolensky expelled from Great Britain.

He considered exiting on the sixth floor to check on the princess but couldn't see the point. Peter had relayed her anger, and he was afraid their next conversation would be her telling him that she was terminating her employment and going elsewhere. He'd have to either propose and send her to his father's house or let her go completely. This wasn't the moment for that conversation.

The Russians had posted two guards in the hallway. He had no doubt one of the two top men had beaten Emmeline, for them to put this level of precaution in place. Oddly enough, though, the guards didn't engage him as he rapped on the suite door. A third Russian thug opened the door.

"Ovolensky," Glass demanded without any hint of courtesy.

The man shut the door, leaving Glass in the hall, but only a couple of minutes passed before he opened it again. "In meeting."

"I am next door," Glass said. "Tell him to come to me when his meeting ends."

He walked down the hall to order a tea service. When he returned to his room he found his telephone had been installed. He quickly checked the equipment to make sure it hadn't been tampered with. When he was satisfied, he placed a call to the front desk and asked Hugh Moth to send security upstairs to watch the Russians' suite. Such a relief to stop passing messages through the floor butler. This was the future, running operations from a convenient telephone.

Twenty minutes later, he heard a rap on his door. The tea had come ten minutes before and would be barely drinkable now.

He greeted the so-called Russian trade delegate. "Mr. Ovolensky."

"Lord Walling." The Russian rearranged one of his shirt cuffs. His knuckles were reddened. He'd been hitting something, or someone, and he also had a fat lip. That evidence was enough for Glass.

"Come in. Have tea with me." Glass didn't couch his words as a request.

Ovolensky stepped in and gestured his bodyguard to follow. Glass stepped neatly behind the door and closed it on the hulking figure's nose.

"We won't be needing him." He gestured toward the pair of armchairs in front of the fireplace, a tea table between them.

"Civilized conversation?" Ovolensky said with an oily smile. "Hoping to receive a report on the delights of Villiers Street? Too timid to visit yourself?"

"I don't think that is where you were last night, Georgy," Glass said, pouring dark tea into the teacups on the silver tray as the Russian sat. He liked rich teas but not overbrewed ones. "Milk, sugar, lemon?"

"Lemon."

He doctored the Russian's tea and added cream and sugar to his to cut down the tannin.

"What do you think you know about me?" the Russian asked as he peered into his tea.

Glass rolled his eyes and drank. He could have drugged the man but hadn't.

Ovolensky followed his lead, took a sip, and set down his cup. "Nasty stuff."

"I'm afraid so. You took too long to arrive."

"I am not a trained dog."

"No? I thought you were Stalin's."

When intense, it was easy to see the resemblance between this man and his cousin, Ivan Salter, head of the hotel's security. They both narrowed their eyes the same way and set their jaws.

"Are we going to discuss politics?"

"No, women." He tilted his head and flashed a cynical smile "As always, it seems."

"I can assure you, Lord Walling, that you have not heard any shrieking harpies in my suite recently."

"I'm more concerned with the condition of Emmeline Plash."

Ovolensky's thumb twitched where it rested on his leg. "She is not your property."

"She belongs to Peter Eyre."

Ovolensky tilted his head. "What does it matter to you?"

"The person who found her is of interest to me—as much as you are of interest to me."

Ovolensky sneered. "Not your whore, not your concern."

Glass pushed back his chair and was on his feet before he realized what he was doing. "Emmeline Plash is not a whore but a well-bred woman who isn't, frankly, very well. I don't think you understand the social order here. I am a viscount, the son of an earl. Peter Eyre is the son of a knight and the nephew of a marquess. Emmeline Plash is the daughter of a deceased, well-connected businessman. She is the sort of woman who will be protected by me and mine."

Ovolensky rose slowly, not losing his sneer. "And Olga Novikova, where does she fit into your social order? Because as best as I can tell, she is just a maid and a whore."

Glass saw red. He kicked the table out of the way, sending china and lukewarm tea flying. Shortbread squares ground under his feet as he rushed forward. He took a wild swing at Ovolensky. The Russian stumbled back, his head stretched back on the stem of his neck.

They moved into the center of the room as Glass slammed his foot against Ovolensky's, ready to grab his hand in a judo hold. Ovolensky attempted to reverse and clipped his foot on Glass's. He twisted, lost his balance, and went down.

Glass heard a terrible cracking sound. Ovolensky's head caught the coffee table in front of the sofa and slid limply. His head landed on the white carpet next to the table. The corner of it was dark with blood. The Russian's eyes were open.

Glass knelt beside him and checked his pulse. Still beating. He'd never even touched the man. Ovolensky had tripped. But thick blood spread on the carpet around the back of his head. Glass suspected he wouldn't last long.

Why couldn't killing Konstantin have been so easy? The brief fight, the one swing, swam through his mind, mixed with images of Bill Vall-Grandly's last moments. Fighting for calm control while his heart pounded in battle mode, he reached for the telephone.

"Operator?" he said. "Send a doctor to my suite immediately with the head of security. A man has been injured."

"My lord?" squeaked the switchboard operator.

"I've given my orders." He placed the earpiece back on the telephone.

On the floor, Ovolensky's lips moved. Glass knelt next to him, but the words were in Russian. He had no idea what the man was saying and doubted it would be of use, but he attempted to write the syllables down phonetically on a notepad.

It took twenty minutes for the doctor to come, accompanied by Peter Eyre, Olga, and one of the day security guards. When Ovolensky stopped speaking a couple of minutes into Glass's vigil, he called the hotel operator and had them connect him to Special Branch. After that, he put in a call to Quex.

Olga's mouth dropped open when she saw the corpse on the floor, but other than that, her expression remained serene. None of the three men reacted in any discernable fashion. The doctor shook his head, checked Ovolensky's pulse, and shook his head again.

"Do you need to be arrested?" Eyre asked with a dispassionate air.

"Never touched him," Glass said. "I expect those bruises on his knuckles are from the attack on Emmeline. He didn't explicitly confess, but he in no way denied it either."

Eyre's mouth thinned as he glanced at the dead Russian's swollen mouth. "Thank you."

"How did he die?" the doctor asked.

"He stumbled over my foot." Glass shrugged. "Hit his head on the table."

The doctor's eyebrows lifted.

"Bloody silly way to die," Glass said. "Couldn't have happened to a nicer fellow, though. Liked to hurt women."

The doctor knelt to take a closer look at Ovolensky's hands.

"He has diplomatic status," Eyre said. "We'll need to send word to the Soviet Union's embassy. Chesham Place, I think."

"No, we won't," Glass said as a knock came on the door. "That will be Special Branch. Let them deal with it."

"Olga?" Peter said behind him as Glass went to the door.

"I wish it were the other one, but Ivan Salter's sister has her revenge," Olga said.

Glass recalled that the plot to bomb the hotel had originally been a simple plan to murder Ovolensky for his crimes just after the revolution. The Salters finally had their parents and sister avenged.

By the time Glass returned with Detective Inspector Dent and two of his colleagues, Olga had a sheet and was about to drape it over the body.

"We'll need to take photographs," Dent said, holding her off. "Call for a gurney, Stone."

"Yes, sir." One of the men went to the telephone.

"First Emmeline and now this," Eyre said to Olga as she stood, motionless, the sheet in her hand. "I think you can do with a day off."

Her eyes were dark pools as she turned to the manager. "I like to keep busy, and I like to earn my wage."

"I'll keep you busy," Glass said. He didn't like the look in her eyes. "Where is Miss Plash?"

"Still at the hospital," Peter said. "We won't be seeing her here at the Grand Russe any time soon."

Olga caught Dent's attention. "This man assaulted a female hotel guest last night."

"So I heard." Dent stared at the body, as his colleague readied a camera. "A good death from everyone's perspective but the Russian government. We'll take a statement from Lord Walling and be done with it, ship the body back to Russia."

* * * *

Late that night, the new telephone rang. When Glass picked it up, he heard his princess on the telephone for the first time. "You have been gone all evening," she said. The line seemed to make her voice even huskier, her accent more pronounced.

He leaned against the wall in his suite, the telephone receiver against his ear. "I had to make a statement down at Scotland Yard. I also made plans for us for tomorrow."

"I see."

"Where are you?"

"Peter's office. We ate at the Restaurant together. He is starting to feel the loss of his Coffee Room compatriots, so I need to take down my art exhibit soon."

"I'm sorry. I know you like to visit it."

"I persuaded him to reinstall some of it in the conference rooms on the first floor."

He could hear the smile in her voice. "Clever girl. Where are you sleeping tonight?"

"I had thought with Alecia, but she is going to a musical comedy with some of the switchboard girls."

"I'll come and get you," Glass said.

"But you are on the seventh." Her voice caught.

"I don't think the Russians will be prowling tonight after what happened." He heard her sigh. "They might try to kill you."

"Dent let two of the thugs examine Ovolensky's body and the table. There are no marks on him other than where he fell. They showed enough rudimentary intelligence to understand."

"I don't know," she said slowly. "The Hand of Death is still there."

"Also, I have my own guard in the hallway. The Russians have pulled theirs back into the suite."

"I see."

"I will collect you in a few minutes," Glass said and hung up the receiver. He double-checked the recording to make sure he had plenty of time on the disk. The Russians had been silent after a flurry of activity. He thought they had drunk enough vodka while eulogizing Ovolensky to quiet even them.

When he reached Peter's office, he found Olga in her old Vionnet, sitting in one of the guest chairs. She needed something new to wear given how often she went out now.

"Is the hotel shop open at this time of night?" he asked.

"Peter would open it up for you." She stood and went to Peter's desk.

"No need to bother him."

"I have the keys in my handbag," she told him. "All I need is his permission." She quickly made the call to Maystone's, tracked him down, and secured his permission.

"Shall we go?"

* * * *

Olga had no idea what Douglas wanted to see at the shop. Douglas was a decisive man, to say the least, but shops didn't figure into her experience with him. Still, she followed him out in the Grand Hall and unlocked the iron gates and the glass doors of the shop.

Douglas closed them behind him as she turned on the lights. "What lines do they carry for women?"

"Lucien Lelong. Some Patou, Chanel. There isn't much, but what we do sell is exquisite, whether for evening or sportswear."

"What do you like best?"

She showed him a navy dress-and-coat combination with silvered designs that looked like keyholes along the hem. Sometimes the seventh-floor guests asked what was in stock, so she kept an eye on the shop's contents. "I think this is darling."

"It's a day look."

"For evening, I like this Lelong." She went to a mannequin and pointed at a delicate, embroidered sea-blue dress. It had a square neckline and thicker shoulder straps.

"It's boxy, but I like the scarf trailing down the back. And the color would be perfect on you."

His words sounded forced. She suspected he was trying very hard to forget the events of the day. "You've turned into a critic," she teased, tracing the embroidery on the bodice.

"I am a connoisseur of you."

His eyes had gone hot. She swallowed. "Do you want me to try it on? I can be careful."

"Is there a place?"

"Yes, a little dressing room."

He nodded. His voice came out hoarse when he said, "Yes. But try on the navy design first, the day look."

She took them both and went into the little dressing room. It only had a curtain for a door. She felt oddly exposed, though only her feet could be seen, and Douglas would have had to kneel on the floor to see them. She slid the brighter blue shift on first, then set the exquisite navy coat on her shoulders, and belted the look.

When she stared into the three-way mirror, she fell in love. This was how a modern princess should look. She tilted her head and pursed her lips, an impervious gaze even the dowager empress might have worn. She pulled the curtain away and walked toward Douglas.

He whistled low. "It might be a day look, but it is beautiful. You must wear it tomorrow."

She smiled. "Peter didn't mind us coming in here, but he probably thought you needed a new hat or something. I can't borrow Paris fashion."

"We'll put it on my account." He lifted his brows. "Now go try on the evening dress."

"You're going to buy this for me?"

"You need a treat." He lips curved boyishly. "And it is a treat for me, looking at you."

Her nipples hardened at his words. She was grateful for the coat, which hid the evidence of her body's reaction. His smile did things to her. She trotted behind the curtain, having quite lost her grace, though she was careful as she replaced one exquisite garment with another.

She stood on her toes as Douglas circled her in the sea-blue embroidered dress, his eyes heavily lidded and his gaze intent.

"Yes," he murmured finally. "You definitely need some new clothing."

"I can't believe these fit. I used to be quite plump. But today's fashions are forgiving."

"It's been many years since you were plump I'd guess, with the life you've led." He smoothed his hand down her bare arm. "I cannot express properly how beautiful you are."

"Douglas!" she protested.

"This is all I can do, frame your exquisite face and body with clothing."
She licked her bottom lip. Her insides had gone liquid. "You
needn't do anything."

"I want to. I want to see you properly, as you should be."

Heedless of the expensive dress, she crushed her torso against him
and sifted her fingers through his hair. She found his mouth and pressed
against him. His lips opened underneath, instantly taking control, though
his hands didn't touch her.

I have to take this dress off. He wasn't touching her because he worried
about the exquisite embroidery. The dress was loose. She removed her
fingers from his hair, tugged at the hem of her dress, and easily pulled
it up over her slip. When the fabric reached her breasts, he slipped his
hands along her torso, moving his thumbs up the sides of her breasts, and
pulled the dress over her head. She heard the soft rustle of fabric as it fell
to the side. Then his leg was behind her knee, bending her leg so that she
collapsed into the fainting couch behind them.

His body was hot over hers, overwhelming in its hardness, and his hands
moved everywhere. Had she given him an invitation? She wore nothing
under the slip but a thin-to-translucent pair of step-ins. He pulled off her
stockings first, his knife clattering to the ground as her garter slid down
her lower leg. The slip went next, over her head; then, he nudged off the
loose straps with his nose, holding her step-ins over her breasts. When the
fabric had bunched at her waist, his mouth closed over one nipple.

She gasped, moaned. The shifting of her torso pressed the intimate
crevice of her lower body against him, and instantly, that part of her that
he'd explored so thoroughly rubbed against him. Her hands went to his
bottom, pulling him against her so that she could rock, find that explosive
place he'd introduced.

Instead of letting her do what she would like, he lifted his body. Before
she could protest, he'd pulled the last of her clothing completely off, leaving
her in nothing but a cheap necklace.

With that realization, she lost all reason. She tore at his jacket, molding
her mouth to his again. He helped her with his clothing, whispering approval
as each piece fell to the carpet next to them. Each removed item gave her
more of his scent, more of his skin, more of him to learn and adore, taste
and lick. When he slid between her legs again it felt natural to wrap her
legs around his, slide the soles of her feet up the furry backs of his legs,
tilt her pelvis.

All of a sudden, he went rigid. She felt something hard nudge her intimate place and then press against her inner thigh.

"What?" she asked without completely removing her mouth from his.

"I thought you didn't want this."

"I need you." She kissed her way across his cheek and sucked his earlobe into her mouth.

His gasp sounded like surrender, and when she did it again, she felt the hard, smooth tip of him at her center again. It pushed into her, spreading her inner petals. He stilled when her body protested and moved deeper when her body dampened and relaxed for him. Her arms were locked around his waist, her mouth against his neck.

"I love you, Douglas," she said, as he seated himself fully in her virgin body. "No one could love you more."

His arms shook as he braced himself over her. He lifted his head, his eyes dark pools of lust. "I believe you." Then he reversed the movement of his hips, pulling out of her slowly, and dipped in again.

Her gasp stuttered as he repeated what he'd done. She lost track of her breaths then and just held on for dear life as the sensations concentrated in her lower body, her skin slick with their combined sweat.

When her body seized, he shuddered into her, finding his bliss at the same moment. A wedding of souls, it seemed to her, and she regretted nothing.

Chapter 15

"Has the carpet in the Artists Suite been sufficiently cleaned?" Peter Eyre asked his day manager late on Saturday afternoon. He sat in one of his own guest chairs, too weary to even walk behind his desk and take his usual command post. His clothing, still yesterday's, had lost its usual crispness, and he could feel sweat had hardened the fabric under his arms. He probably smelled like he'd done manual labor for his daily bread.

"It will need replacing when Lord Walling moves out," John Neville said, his face betraying nothing at the sight of his disheveled manager.

Peter rubbed his hands over his eyes, digging into the sandpaper-dry corners with his index fingers. "At least we know he can't request another suite from us. We've nothing free on the seventh presently."

"That is a good thing"—John paused—"although I'm eager to hear the status report on the eighth and ninth floors on Monday. I'm certain some of our suite guests will want to move into the new flats."

"They will. The pricing is a bit better than the seventh, but the rooms are similar, except for the lower ceilings."

"I haven't seen the interiors yet. Are they similar to the rest of the hotel?"

"Very luxurious. Lots of golds and reds and greens. No white carpet or upholstery as we won't have as much ability to clean long-term residences."

John pulled off his spectacles and wiped them on his handkerchief before replacing them. "I see. Speaking of rooms, what do you want me to do with Miss Plash's suite?"

Peter closed his eyes for a moment, but he couldn't give into sentimentality. He was worried about bloodstains there as well. Georgy Ovolensky had been a scourge on his hotel. "Have her belongings packed. Olga can do it. Then they'll need to be stored. After she was released from hospital this morning I had her packed off to a sanatorium for a long rest. She won't want to appear in public with her facial injuries."

John's eyes widened as if he desperately wanted to say something but couldn't get his mouth to obey. "So we can rent the suite again?"

"Yes, after an exquisitely thorough cleaning."

John cleared his throat. "You gave Olga the day off. She's not working until Monday."

Peter frowned. "Then have another chambermaid do the packing, under your personal supervision."

"Of course, sir. Anything else?"

Peter shook his head. He waved off the man and leaned back in his chair, weary to the bone. The two people he was closest to in the world still living, his brother and Emmeline, were both hospitalized. Would they ever be freed from their mental prisons?

Restless energy born of exhaustion made him want to move. He needed fresh air. For the first time, even his hotel didn't feel like a refuge. His own mind felt like a prison, too.

He caught a whiff of his day-old clothing and frowned. But no energy remained to change or bathe. No, he'd find a taxicab to somewhere with people who smelled no better, a suitably lowbrow public house where he could get drunk in peace.

Not that he went to places like that normally, but he'd heard enough about where Ivan Salter had lived before taking up residence on the tenth floor to know that Poplar was the neighborhood for him right now.

* * * *

"How does it feel to have two days off in a row?" Glass asked as the taxicab pulled up in front of his father's house on Hanover Square. Behind them, a taxicab expelled three fashionably dressed women eager to enter the French dressmaker's next door. More and more businesses involved in women's fashion were moving into the square. The house was not entailed, and Glass expected he'd be approached to sell it to some fancy milliner or furrier when his father died.

He might even sell and find a house less eighteenth century. Security was hard to manage when your front door immediately abutted the sidewalk with no filter and people could stare right into the windows on the ground level, even climb through them without lifting their legs very much. And with so many tradespeople on the square, strangers wandered about constantly. Not a home for a spymaster, even a retired one.

"I feel like the leisure class," Princess Olga said, "with a proper weekend."

"Err, yes," he said as the butler opened the door and inclined his head. "So sorry. I was woolgathering."

They walked through the decidedly old-fashioned foyer, with its Gothic wood-paneled walls. One of the earls had been a weapons collector and crossed battle-axes decorated the space.

When they reached the small drawing room on the next floor, he felt relief. He noted the instant the princess's attention was captured by the family portraits. "My mother is there, and my brothers, just there. All the rest are older, of course. We were an expansive lot in the early years of the last century, but the family has been on a sad decline since."

"My family has faced a similar fate," she said.

Glass heard a cough behind him and turned to see his father at the door. "My boy." He gestured Glass to him and handed him a worn velvet case. Glass opened the case and found the Crewe diamonds.

"I didn't remember those two," his father said, pointing at the rings tied to a dusty pillow with faded white ribbon. "But these brooches were my grandmother's favorite. And, of course, my mother wore the necklace."

"Yes, even in her portrait." Glass peered at the rings. "I think they must have been made from earrings. There is a Regency-era portrait of some long-ago countess with this necklace as well as earrings."

The earl tilted his head. "Let us take a look. We will be back in a moment, my dear."

Olga didn't respond, completely entranced by the portraits.

Glass followed him his father into the corridor. "I think I know the one you mean." They climbed the steps up to the next landing, halfway to the floor with family bedrooms, and stopped in front of a three-quarter-length portrait of a woman in flowing draperies.

"Yes, that's her."

"A second wife as I recall," his father said. "Not our direct line."

Glass took the velvet case and untied one of the rings. "Exactly the same number of diamonds as in the earrings."

"You are correct. I wonder what happened to the pearls?"

"Probably strung into necklaces."

"No," his father exclaimed. "I remember now. My great-grandfather had five daughters, and they were given two pearl rings, one for each hand. I'll bet that is where the pearls went."

Glass silently counted the countess's pearls. "Five pearls in each earring. How clever you are, Father."

The earl chuckled. "Those rings made from the countess's earrings are long gone from the direct line, but by Jove, we kept the diamonds. And now you have a ring selection for the princess."

"I do indeed."

"I must say she is looking particularly smart today."

"I treated her to some new clothing. Dreadful business with a man dying in my suite yesterday. She had to view his body and clean up the woman the deceased man had beaten the night before, a friend of hers, no less."

"Poor dear, but she'll have seen worse in Russia I expect. Will she have any family at the wedding?" The earl scratched his chin.

Glass inclined his head. "I haven't told her yet, but I tracked down her sister in Shanghai, and I'm bringing her here. Also, I'm sure any number of Russian royalties will come to the wedding. If there are free food and champagne, they will descend like pigeons to a child's bread crumbs."

His father patted his arm. "Jolly good business with the sister. Why haven't you told her?"

"I don't know what state's she's in. She's an elite taxi dancer."

His father sighed. "I see. I suggest finding her a good dresser and a companion. You can lodge her at the country house, make sure she's presentable."

"Thank you. I'll consider it."

"Will you wed soon or make it a society affair?"

"I don't know yet. I'd like it to be both, for her sake, but with her dangerous cousin on the loose we can't risk it."

His father had been staring at the portrait again, but his head snapped back to Glass. "What's that?"

Glass spoke more slowly. "Her cousin is a killer, and he's escaped the authorities up until now. Until we find him, it wouldn't be safe to have a large wedding."

The earl clucked his tongue. "Then he'd better be found."

"I quite agree. It's heating up. He's involved in the recent bombings."

"After your engagement is announced, I could take the princess out of London while the police sort out the situation," his father offered.

"I don't want Konstantin to target you, sir," Glass said. "He has a tendency to find the princess to get funds. Used her for years."

"We need to keep her safe. Be practical, Walling. As soon as she's known as yours, this man will know her pockets are full. He might even kidnap her for a large ransom."

"Then the safest thing to do is not announce the engagement."

His father took the velvet box from Glass's hand. "Or not propose yet."

"That would be unwise," Glass said, untying the second ring from the pillow and slipping both into his handkerchief pocket.

His father searched his face. "I see. Anticipated, have you?"

"Emotions ran high." He kept his gaze on the pillow.

"Then you had best marry quietly, and before May. We don't want tongues wagging if your heir comes too early."

"Yes, sir," Glass said. "With any luck, her cousin will be dead by then, and we can use mourning as the excuse for a quiet ceremony."

"I'll speak to the bishop of Waketree," his father said. He'd been at Eton with the future bishop, and they still stayed in touch. Glass had eaten dinner with the man at their family table many a time when he was visiting from West Yorkshire.

"We could marry out of the Redcake family hotel in Leeds," Glass said. "The princess worked there last year. It would be easy to explain here in London why we would choose to marry there."

"Excellent. It's practically sorted already."

Glass nodded. "You speak to the bishop, and I'll have something organized at the hotel. We'll plan on a month from now and hope I have the matter of her cousin sorted before that."

The earl clapped him on the shoulder. "I only have one of you left. Don't get yourself killed just when I finally have plans for another generation."

Glass grinned. "Are you taking all the responsibility for my marriage, sir?"

"Someone had to. A Russian princess, indeed." His father shook his head and stared up at the portrait of the long dead countess. "At least she's a looker. Almost up to your mother's standard."

Glass smiled at his father and went downstairs to the small drawing room. The princess stared intently at the 1913 brothers' portrait.

"You all look so similar," she murmured as he reached her.

"That may have been the artist's fault," he said, feeling his smile still dancing on his lips. Finally, his personal life would suit the position he'd never wanted. He would have a wife and the heirs his family needed from a suitable bride. "Come here, would you?"

She let him take her hand and escort her to a wingback chair with chintz upholstery. The reds and yellows clashed with her beautiful blue-and-silver coat, but he only noticed her face as he knelt on one knee before her and pulled out the set of rings.

Despite his pleasure, he had to focus to keep his arm steady as he held them out. "Your Serene Highness, I wanted to bring you here to propose marriage. A woman does not only marry me, but a long, respected family history, and an estate as well. You wouldn't just be taking a husband but a position in society and a great deal of work."

"Lord Walling," she whispered. Her cheeks had gone pink. She looked flustered, as if she truly hadn't anticipated his proposal.

Her obvious state of nerves made him a little less sure of himself. "I know you are equal to the tasks of Lady Walling," he said, stuttering slightly, "that of being my father's hostess in his declining years and estate management. You are more than equal to the title. What I am afraid of is that I am not equal to you."

"You know I love you," she said. Her lips parted; her chest rose.

"I know you've said such things in the heat of the moment, but it has been a very trying time for you." He took her hands. They were cool like his. "I promise you my protection and support in all things. I will do my best to keep you and our children safe."

"I knew you to be an honorable man. I expected your proposal after last night," she said, very low. "I am sorry you have been forced into this."

"You know I wasn't," he exclaimed. "I'm a cautious man. Here." He turned over her hand and dropped the rings into them. "My father had to get these out of a bank vault. There was forethought in this, even before last night."

Her lips curved slightly at his words. "He likes me, the earl."

He folded her fingers over the rings. "Yes. I'm stubborn enough to marry without his approval, but I'm glad I don't have to."

"Of course, you need to secure the succession."

He nodded. "As an aristocrat, you understand these things."

"Yes, although I am a Russian, we are at least of equal rank. I wish I brought more into the marriage. There was a time when I would have. We might be able to fight for property someday, but my sister is the elder." She opened her fingers when he took his hand away.

"Don't worry about it." He stared at the rings on her palm. "We're going to be very wealthy. You'll never want for anything."

"Unless the British government falls as well," she said. "We must fight, Douglas. You must continue your work."

"Will you be my helpmate?"

"Yes." Her gaze was fierce as she folded her fingers around the rings. "I will marry you."

He dropped his chin to his chest, unaware until that moment quite how nervous he had been. He'd finally made his choice of a bride at thirty-one. There had been times when he doubted this moment would ever come. "You do me a great honor."

He leaned forward to kiss her, but she didn't notice. Her gaze had gone back to the rings.

"They are about the same in terms of the stones," he said.

"One band is larger than the other." She tried the smaller one first. It didn't slide on easily. "I think my knuckles are larger than they once were."

"Try the other."

When the second one slid on smoothly, she smiled and held her hand up to the lamp on the table next to the chair. It sparkled. "It's perfect, Douglas."

He took the first ring from her and tucked it away. "You can decide what to do with this other ring later. I thought we could marry in Leeds. My father's dear friend is a bishop in West Yorkshire, and he can arrange a church there. We could stay at the hotel."

"Eloise's?" She rubbed her lower lip with her finger, unconsciously showing off her ring. "Yes, it has a lovely suite on the top floor overlooking Park Square. I wouldn't mind spending my wedding night there."

His lips curved as he thought of the delights he had to look forward to that night. "Very good. We'll speak to Peter about your final day, and when my father arranges a wedding date we'll book the hotel."

"When are you thinking?"

"Mid-April, if that suits you."

She folded her hands together, suddenly looking very narrow in the vibrant chair. "I suppose it is necessary."

He caught the hesitation in her voice. "Would you want to wait?"

"I'd prefer to wait until Konstantin is finally out of our hair."

"I hope that is my wedding gift to you. If I can manage it, we will be free of him by then."

She sighed. "Not a happy topic. But you will keep him safe, won't you? Just have him sent away somewhere so he can get the care he needs?"

"I'll do my best." He patted her knees, remembering how he'd caressed most every inch of her on the fainting couch the previous evening.

"It's hard to remember my cares when I'm with you." She put her hands over his. "Oh, Douglas. We're going to be wed, and soon."

As she leaned forward to kiss him, he wondered if he should excuse himself long enough to lock the door. But he didn't want her to think he was marrying her only for the sake of their sex life. Then again, Princess Olga Novikova knew her own worth, even if it had been shattered these past few years.

He pulled his hands from under hers and sat back on his heels. "I'll tell you what, darling. Let me check the corridor and make sure we have privacy in here. You relax for a minute, and I'll be right back."

She settled into the chair, losing a little of her well-trained perfect posture. "Very well. But I don't want an early baby if we can avoid it. Too much can go wrong."

He nodded and flashed her a grin. Smart princess to keep him on point. "We can be creative."

He went out into the corridor, shut the door behind him, and moved swiftly to the telephone room. His father had installed one on each floor of the house. He instructed the operator to connect him to the police and then had Dent tracked down in Special Branch.

"What's the word, Glass?" asked the detective inspector.

"I've just proposed marriage to Princess Olga," Glass said.

"You don't say. Congratulations."

"Thank you. Can you keep an eye on her for me? Konstantin is out there somewhere, and we're going to be married next month. She's going to be leaving the hotel more than usual, planning her trousseau and such. It will be hard for us to keep an eye on her as we have been."

"Of course. We've already put the uniforms on the main entrances, and we'll have them contact us when they see her leave. Or give us a heads-up if you know she's going."

"I will. Thank you." Glass hung up and rubbed his chin. The last thing he wanted was to lose his future bride just as he'd finally chosen her. Olga deserved his protection.

* * * *

Douglas had agreed to her plan to stay out of her bed with surprising alacrity. As Olga attempted to stretch upon waking on Sunday morning, she found her arms hampered by the back and arm of the Salters' sofa on the tenth floor, where she had spent an uncomfortable night. She couldn't wait to be married and live in Douglas's flat, which wasn't far from the hotel. It was on the wrong side of Marble Arch in terms of social superiority, but it was still close enough to be quite smart, and it would be her own home for the first time since she'd fled her family's mansion in the wake of Maxim's murder so many years before.

She rolled over, giving up on stretching, and lifted her new engagement ring from the table. Sitting up, she stared at the ring: quite a large, expensive stone, cornered by four smaller diamonds. If nothing else, this punctuated the fact that she would someday be a countess.

Kicking off the coverlet Alecia had leant her from her own marital bed, Olga stood and went into the bathroom. Ivan must have still been working, and Alecia had managed to leave the suite without waking her. She went into their bathroom and redressed in her smart blue dress and navy coat, then pulled her outer things off the peg, and took them with her.

Lazy butterflies drifted in her stomach, so she bypassed the shared kitchen and went straight to the lift, holding her breath until she reached the ground floor. *Freedom.*

She walked past the reception desk. Peter was standing there and caught her eye. He nodded animatedly at a young man with flattened dark hair and a wide part.

"Please take Mr. Haldane to his room, Jeremy," Peter said as Olga walked up to the desk.

The bellboy appeared from behind the potted fern where he waited unobtrusively for orders and reached for the man's case.

"Is that mine?" the man asked, smoothing his bushy mustache.

Jeremy frowned at Peter.

"Yes, yes," Peter said. "Honestly, Mr. Haldane, you'd lose your hat if it wasn't on your head."

The man lifted his eyebrows dolefully at Peter and followed the bellboy to the lift.

"Who was that?" Olga asked. "One of your mother's first husband's relatives?"

"Distinguished scientist. Haldane, not Haldene," Peter said. "Very absentminded."

"Ah, I see. That's a new class of guest for us."

"A bit worried about his politics to be honest," Peter said in a lowered voice. "Sympathizer with the Soviet Union."

Olga winced. "I'll stay clear of him."

Peter's eyes narrowed. "The scientist may miss what is right under his nose, but I do not. What is that on your finger?"

Olga grinned and showed him her ring. "Lord Walling proposed yesterday."

"So the princess is to become a countess? I say, old thing, congratulations!"

"Thank you." She flattened her fingers to admire the sparkling stone.

"When will the great day occur?"

"About a month from now. Lord Walling wants us to be married in West Yorkshire because his father is friendly with the bishop there."

"Will you stay on St. Martin's property?"

"We thought your sister's hotel, honestly. But he is making the arrangements."

"Very good. I am glad the British aristocracy is gaining such a perfect flower. It is a loss for the Grand Russe." He smiled.

"I'll be here for another month."

"No," Peter said. "You can't keep working here. Let's face it. You can't even stay in your room because of your cousin. Of course we'll keep protecting you, but your work has to end. Really, you should move into St. Martin's house immediately. I'll speak to your fiancé."

"But I need to work," Olga protested.

"No. It is our loss, but you need to stop." He picked up her hands, turned them over, and clucked his teeth. Reaching under the desk, he pulled out some coins. "Start hand treatments tomorrow."

"Hand treatments?"

"Yes. You don't have viscountess hands. Get a manicure and whatever treatments you can order to get them soft again. You don't want to be criticized."

"I'm not ashamed of hard work."

"No, but you don't want to be out of place, either. I won't even stop your salary, Olga, but you will cease employment immediately."

"But," she protested.

"But nothing. Go paint something. Better yet, get the art installation moved upstairs like we planned. We'll call it a promotion. You are now the Grand Russe's art consultant."

She narrowed her eyes but was too happy to be truly upset. "Fine. I'll consult with Mr. Neville about scheduling the men we'll need to move the paintings."

He nodded. "I'm proud of you, Olga. Well done."

She growled at him, then smiled, and put on her hat. "I'm proud myself. And the earl is as dear as his son. I love them both."

"Yes, he's a good old boy. You've landed a very elusive fish."

* * * *

A few hours later, Olga was taking an uncharacteristic afternoon nap. She woke sometime later when the Salter's sofa dipped. Head swimming, she sat up, almost murmured Douglas's name before she recognized her cousin in the afternoon light.

"Cousin," Konstantin said, turning his head to her.

She scrambled back. When she was off the sofa and pressed up against the wall, she fumbled under her skirt, opened the scrap of leather, and pulled out her knife. She held it his eye level and started to edge toward the front of the room.

"You aren't going to hurt me, Olga," Konstantin said, sounding far more calm than she felt.

"I might. You're a killer now." She adjusted her shoulders to remove the hunch. The blood of tsars ran through her veins, and she wouldn't be frightened of one man.

"I took precautions before I came. I have friends in Shanghai."

She stopped moving and faked a laugh. "Why should I care about that?"

"Fyodora is there, you know. She's a taxi dancer. Not a whore, not yet." His voice lowered. "Not dead, not yet."

Her brain could scarcely take in all his claims. She folded her arms around herself, her hands trembling. Could any of it be true? "Why would you threaten her?"

"Because I need your help. I shouldn't have killed the spy. I need a place to hide."

She latched on to his words of regret. Yes, he knew right from wrong, he knew he shouldn't have killed the spy. "You can't stay here. It's the Grand Russe!"

"I know that. You need to find me a telephone, or Fyodora is going to get a knife between the ribs during a tango. You want her to be buried in China? I understand that foreign paupers are buried to the west of Shanghai, at Zikawei. It has a lonely sound, don't you think?"

Tears pressed behind Olga's eyes. Surely Konstantin was bluffing, but she'd never known who his associates were. She had to ignore his games. "Why is Maxim's murderer here in the hotel?" she asked. "Is he your employer?"

Konstantin sat up, a bear on a child's sofa. "I never knew your precious Maxim. I have no idea who his killer was. Time is ticking away, Olga. You had better find me a safe telephone."

Olga stared at her knife, useless now. As saddened as Douglas had been by his operative's death, he would understand she couldn't risk her sister, no matter how slight the chances were that she was at risk.

But that was the point. Her sister must be dead by now to have been out of contact so long. And Konstantin couldn't possibly have contacts in China. How ridiculous.

She hefted her knife. Her cousin had killed Bill Vall-Grandly. She took a step away from the wall. Konstantin saw the movement and shifted to a standing position, pulling a gun from his pocket.

He grinned at her. "Gun beats knife, little cousin. If you don't value Fyodora's life, what about Lord St. Martin's?"

She stiffened, her fingers numbing. "What?"

"I saw your dinner with them. You seemed so fond of the old man."

Her heart began to pound. Her vision narrowed. "Don't you threaten Douglas's father. He is all that is left of Douglas's entire family."

Konstantin's smile went crocodile, showing all his teeth. "Just a little bomb in St. Martin's house. Not even inside. The garden wall would do. I'm very talented."

She took another step toward him. He pointed his gun at her heart.

"Don't be so evil." Olga said. "I believed in you, Konstantin. I believed you could change."

"You don't have a telephone, but there's one in the boardinghouse on Montagu Square. Take me there."

"Will you promise to leave the earl alone? I'll take you to a telephone box. I'll dial the numbers myself."

"I'm not going to make my calls in public so I can arrange to disappear. You want that, right? For me to leave London?"

"You just want a private place to make a call? Then you'll leave London?" *Bert Dadey. Please forgive me.*

He nodded.

"I'll take you to the boardinghouse," she said dully. "Mr. Dadey does have a telephone."

Konstantin tucked his gun away and held out his hand for her knife. She hesitated, but displaying a grace obscene in one his size, he had his hand closed over her upper arm in an instant.

She wrenched her arm away and found her coat and hat. He followed closely behind, standing just behind the door as she checked the corridor. "We'll go down the stairs."

"It's ten flights. No, we'll take the service lift."

She knew he was intimate with the hotel, so she didn't argue. About half an hour remained until shift's end, so if the service lift came up here, it would likely be empty.

When they were in the lift, she said, "Let me do the talking at the boardinghouse. I'll keep a taxicab waiting so you can leave after."

"As long as I have access to a telephone you have nothing to worry about."

She had a moment of fear, but if the cost of a telephone call was the earl's safety, she'd take the risk.

Chapter 16

The Russians had been curiously absent from their suite again on Tuesday morning. Glass had helped Olga measure walls all morning, to rehang her art exhibit in the hotel, and left her well attended by bellboys and off-duty waiters who had been brought in to pound nails and lift artwork.

He had to attend a private meeting chaired by Quex to discuss the Russian problem. His secretary, Miss Drover, had handed him three file folders just before he entered the meeting, but he hadn't had time to so much as open them before Quex launched into his interrogation.

The focus of the meeting had been him. Government ministers and other Secret Intelligence section heads sat nodding and smoking as Quex fired questions and secretarial pens scratched away at the seats along the wall.

"We need more agents focused on the Russians," Quex said. "Please review the current assignments of your section."

Glass went through what he had. "Not surprisingly, we continue to watch the trade union protests, as well as shipping in case there is more human cargo coming in."

"Any word on where this Lashevich appeared from?" asked the section head for German operations, cigar smoke wreathing his bald head.

Glass flipped open the folder containing notes from Les Drake, his man in the north. "His best guess is a ship that came in from Finland. It held timber by-products, and the captain is a known Soviet sympathizer."

He set the folder aside while the men around the table conferred, and opened the next folder. It wasn't from one of his own men, but a man from Special Branch. As he read, he couldn't help blinking. He glanced up at Miss Drover, feeling the dread freezing his upper chest.

"I'm sorry," she mouthed. She glanced down, clearly upset.

His leg jerked, but nothing could be seen above the table. He set the folder down, wishing he could shout at Miss Drover for not warning him, but it wasn't her fault. There hadn't been a private moment, and he hadn't expected a news ambush, so he hadn't planned to meet with his secretary or his section before now. There were so few of them. They needed to work, not speak.

Of course, as if some subterranean signal had been produced, Quex asked the important question. "What is the update on Konstantin Novikov?"

"He's been spotted outside the Grande Russe harassing his cousin." Glass cleared his throat. "I put surveillance on Princess Olga, his cousin, after I proposed marriage."

Quex's eyebrows lifted. "How did this meet occur?"

"She must have slipped her watchers at the Grand Russe hotel, though Special Branch kept an eye on her." Glass scanned the report. "Looks like they left the hotel in a taxicab."

"She didn't tell you?"

"No. I can't imagine why, except that she's terrified of him." He recalled her words. "I can see now that she warned me about this sort of thing."

"Ordering surveillance was the right thing to do," said the German-focused section head. "Women aren't as strong as we are, and family loyalties are keen in the royal ranks."

"Besides, she's Russian," said another man, in charge of Eastern Europe. "Are you really planning to marry her, Glass?"

"Yes," Glass said. "Other than her cousin, she has many fine qualities."

The man chuckled, but Glass bubbled with red-hot rage underneath his calm exterior. He'd get to the bottom of this betrayal. How could Olga not trust him? Lives were at stake.

* * * *

When the meeting ended, Glass left the room, followed by Miss Drover.

"I do apologize, sir," she said. "I was hoping you knew about the princess's contact with Konstantin. Special Branch only had one man on her and couldn't follow the bomber."

"How many people had to make mistakes for it to come to this?" he snarled. "This sighting of Konstantin was yesterday. Disregarding the personal betrayal this represents, this is an intelligence failure."

"I tried to reach you, but you were not at the hotel," Miss Drover said. "I am so sorry, sir."

His lips clenched. "We'll discuss it later. I have a princess to come to terms with."

Glass left the unobtrusive row house where the meeting had taken place and began to walk, ignoring his driver. The peeks of sunlight through the clouds did not improve his mood during his half-mile journey through teatime London.

When he reached the hotel, Johnnie Miles gave him the usual wide smile, but it faded quickly. Glass, realizing he did not wear his habitual impassive expression, forced a grimace and walked through the door the man held open for him.

When he was through he turned back. "Call a taxicab for me and hold it. I'll be down in ten minutes or so, and I need to leave immediately."

"Yes, sir," Johnnie responded.

Since Glass thought he knew the princess so well, he assumed she would have remained on the first floor, working on her reconstituted exhibit. The fact that he was right did not mollify him. She stood on a stepstool, her shapely ankles and calves on display as she righted a painting of Mary Magdalen weeping next to a large outcropping of rock.

"Do you identify with her?" he asked, gesturing to the Magdalen's face when he reached the princess.

"Douglas?" The princess stepped off her stool and turned, smiling. Her smile melted slowly as she looked at him, even though he thought his impassivity remained. Had he always looked at her with calf eyes before now?

"Do you? Mourn for your cousin every time we close in on him? Do you weep?"

Her eyes widened and she shook her head. Hands reached out to him. "No, of course not. He's a killer. He's mad."

He closed the distance between them and took her arm, ignoring the outstretched hands. "You need to come with me."

"Yes, of course, Douglas. I'm just finishing here."

Ignoring her glance back at the painting, he pulled her out of the room. "Where is he, in the hotel?"

"Who? No, what?" She glanced around.

"Your cousin. Is he here?"

"I don't think so. What is this about?" Her skin creased between her eyebrows.

He pulled her down the hall, into the service lift. As they descended, she asked, "Where are we going?"

"To Konstantin. Where is he?"

"I don't know, Douglas. What is happening?"

She pulled her arm, but he didn't release it. He shook her arm as the lift stopped on the ground floor. "You were seen with him outside this hotel.

Where is he, Olga?"

Her lips parted and her shoulders shook. When she said nothing, he dragged her out of the lift and past the Reading Room and the shop where he'd made love to her such a short time ago. He forced those thoughts to the back of his mind.

Pushing through the front door of the hotel, he saw that the clouds had moved again. Sharp slashes of rain descended, catching his cheeks with bursts of cold.

Johnnie dashed up to them, holding an umbrella. "I have your taxicab, sir."

Glass pulled Olga underneath the umbrella and marched her toward the cab. The driver had remained in his seat. Johnnie opened the door, and Glass pressed Olga's head down so that she'd enter.

"Excuse me sir, but the princess doesn't have her coat on."

"Unfortunate," Glass said, flipping the doorman a coin. "Thank you."

When Johnnie had shut the door, he leaned forward to speak to the driver, ignoring the princess's frightened eyes. "Holloway Prison, my good man."

As the taxicab pulled away from the curb, tears formed in the princess's eyes and dripped down her perfect cheeks. He ignored the subtle histrionics. If she wanted to wait until they reached the women's prison to tell him the truth, it didn't matter to him.

They would be going to the prison either way.

"Why?" she asked in a low voice.

"The prison is only about four miles from here," he said in a calm tone. "You have that long to tell me where he is."

"I don't know." Her voice shook a little. "He threatened your father when he found me.

"Where was he living when last you knew?"

Her head drooped on her elegant, regal neck. "I don't know."

"You saw him in the hotel. Where else?"

"I took him to the boardinghouse to make calls. I thought that was the last I'd see of him."

He leaned forward and tapped the driver's shoulder. "Change of plans. Montagu Square."

"Right you are, sir." The taxicab came to a stop at a street's end and turned.

Glass sat back and returned his attention to the princess. "What else?"

"Nothing else," she whispered. "After you gave me the knife. It didn't do any good. He was in the hotel again, in the Salter's room. I didn't know what to do."

"So you risked poor Bert Dadey's life to save your own skin? Why didn't you tell me?"

"I was frightened."

"You were covering for him."

"He threatened my sister. And your father. But I only saw him once. I have no idea where he is."

"Your sister?" Glass asked. "What does he know about your sister?"

"He said she's in Shanghai, and he knows people."

"You don't even know if your sister is alive, and you are risking half of London or worse, not to mention betraying me." Glass stared out the window at the rain. No wonder he hadn't married before now. He couldn't trust anyone, not even a woman he'd cherished, caressed, perhaps even impregnated.

They reached the boardinghouse. "It wasn't like that, Douglas," she protested, but he pulled her from the taxicab and told the driver to wait. He rapped sharply on the door when he arrived at the top of the steps, the shivering princess next to him.

Bert Dadey opened the door after his usual fumbling with the lock. His wrinkled face was wreathed in a smile when he saw the princess. "Another week, another visit! So happy to see you, Yer Highness."

She forced a smile. "Good afternoon, Mr. Dadey. I wondered if you had seen my cousin since I brought him here to use your phone?"

"Haven't seen him at all today," Dadey said. "Would you like a cuppa?"

"Today? You mean you saw him yesterday?"

"Why yes, miss. He took a room here."

"We'll need to see the room. We're in a rush," Glass said, securing Olga's arm with his hand.

"Must be. You need a coat, Princess," Dadey told her. "Did you leave one here?"

"In a rush," Glass repeated. "When did you see Mr. Novikov last?"

Bert's eyes lifted skyward. "Not since yesterday evening. But he's not my only tenant. Someone else might have let him in, and my sciatica was acting up this morning, so I didn't come down early."

"So you think he might have been and gone?"

"Really couldn't say, my lord."

Glass nodded briskly, reached into his coat, and pulled out a card. He handed it to the man. "Please contact Detective Inspector Dent at Special Branch immediately if you see Mr. Novikov again. It's a matter of national security. Don't let the man know you are making the call."

Dadey's eyes rounded. "Yes, my lord." His head swiveled on its thin, sagging neck. "Are you well, Yer Highness?"

She didn't even fake a smile this time. "No. We need my cousin."

"You can trust me," Dadey said, thumping his sunken chest. "I'll call this man as soon as I see your cousin."

"I'd like to check his room."

"Of course, my lord." He pointed up. "Yer princess knows where it is. Her old room."

Glass went up the steps, followed by Olga. Konstantin's door, when she indicated it, wasn't even locked. The room bore few signs of habitation. He quickly went through the small chest of drawers, lifted the mattress, poked here and there, but there were no signs of bomb-making equipment, no letters or telegrams.

Glass nodded his thanks when they returned to Dadey, pulled Olga back down the short flight of stairs to the pavement, and thrust her back into the taxicab. "Thank you for waiting. Holloway Prison again, please."

"Sir," the driver said, and pulled back into the center of the road on the quiet street.

"Why are we going to a prison?" Her lips tightened.

"To keep you safe, Princess."

* * * *

On Wednesday morning, the telephone in Glass's suite rang for him for the first time. He took off the headphones, set them on the ledge behind the *Firebird*, and picked up the receiver. "Yes?"

"Quex needs to see you immediately," Miss Drover said. "He is at the Piccadilly safe house."

"The Russians are having a meeting," Glass said. "I shouldn't leave. They are discussing brandy, which might mean another smuggling campaign is underway."

"You don't have a choice, sir," Miss Drover said crisply. "It's Quex."

Glass placed the receiver back on its hook. He'd just changed the disk. Hopefully the Russians' meeting wouldn't last longer than his recording. Pain speared his palms. He glanced down and saw he'd been digging his fingernails into them. Half moons marked his skin.

He'd felt less stress in the trenches. But he hadn't slept a wink with his princess locked away in the hospital wing at Holloway. What choice did he have? She was in danger and was dangerous. He had thought they were past all subterfuge. She was Russian. He'd forgotten that. No end to subterfuge. And yet, he'd offered her everything she might have wanted: a home, money, a British title, a husband, an escape. Why throw it away on a mad cousin?

He pushed the thought of the threat against her sister away, her mutterings about a threat to his father. Surely she'd given up her sister for dead years ago, like he'd mourned his lost brothers. She could not have kept the hope alive that she'd see her sister alive in this life. It was only through the efforts of someone like him, a spymaster, that a lost Russian princess could be found in the Orient and shipped to London. If indeed she ever arrived, much less arrived intact and sane, whoever Princess Fyodora Novikova had been, she was surely a different person now.

Half an hour later, he rapped on the rear door of a milliner. The man who opened it was not the type to be involved in the making of hats. He grunted when he recognized Glass and let him through. A door at the back of the storeroom led to a set of narrow stairs. On the second floor was Quex's favorite meeting room, a floor below what passed as the safe house.

Quex sat in shadow, his chair against a wall. But next to him stood a man Glass recognized, an equerry to the king.

"Lord Walling," the man said.

"Captain Drew." Glass stepped forward and shook his hand. "Are the Bolshies targeting royal property? I've heard nothing of the sort."

"What are you hearing?" Quex asked.

"I think another smuggling operation is underway. The last time we heard this kind of coded conversation, we found the Russian prostitutes coming in at the docks."

"Did you get a firm date and time?"

"No, I was called away to this meeting. But I'm recording. Hopefully I'll get the information we need."

"Good," Quex said acerbically. "Now listen to this."

"His Majesty is very fond of Grand Duchess Xenia," Captain Drew said. "And the grand duchess is very fond of Princess Olga Novikova."

Glass winced. He knew what was coming. "Yes."

"You are engaged?"

"Yes, not formally announced yet, not with this business going on, but my father knows."

"So do we," Captain Drew said. "You have no right to arrest Russian princesses, no right to put them into Holloway."

Glass clenched his jaw. "She's not in the main population but the hospital wing. It's been done before with high-born women."

"What possible justification can you have?"

"How can you ask me that? She's been aiding her cousin, who is a bomb expert and who killed my operative a few days ago."

"Aiding?" Quex asked.

"I'm not saying it isn't under duress. He's made threats that she seems to believe, however intelligent she usually appears to be, but aiding him she is. I had her take me to his last known location."

"Gone, I suppose."

"Of course. He moves around like a rat. You never find him in the same place twice."

"You will release her today," Captain Drew said. "And take her personally to the grand duchess. I would suggest a special license and a fast marriage to erase the stain of what you have done with her."

"She's making a bad situation worse," Glass said, pounding his fist against the wall. "He always finds her and takes her money, then uses it to keep out of our way."

"She is a princess," Captain Drew with an inexorable air. "I don't care about that quasi-Egyptian princess who was in Holloway a couple of years ago. She was essentially a whore. This Novikova woman is anything but, and she has protectors."

"Then why has she been working as a chambermaid the last year?" Glass demanded. "Where were her protectors then?"

Chapter 17

I am having a weekend. Olga told herself this as she sat in the straight-backed chair next to a woman in labor, despite the fact that she was very sure it was Wednesday, and this bland hospital wing, with its prison officer always on duty and six narrow beds in her dormitory, was anything but a country estate where one might have gone for the grouse shooting late in the summer months. No, it was March, and her fiancé didn't trust her, and her cousin had ruined her life.

She had never in her life expected to be forced to succumb to a mental and physical exam by a prison doctor. She had never expected to sleep in a prison ward with drunks, baby killers, and the deranged. She had never thought Douglas, once having proposed marriage, would betray her so completely.

She rested her hands across her aching stomach and tried to focus on the panting woman. The food she'd eaten these past few meals had been atrocious and what little she'd forced down had not settled well. Thinking about her own physical discomfort had no value. She had to help this woman through childbirth. Leaning over, she blotted the woman's damp forehead with a rag, smelling her sweat.

The wardesses were busy with a woman at the end of the row of beds who was having a fit and needed restraining to avoid eating her own tongue.

Hours passed. She helped the woman through her labor pains, though she could do little more than wipe her sweaty face, comb her tangled hair. Her prayers came out in Russian instead of English, but the prisoner didn't seem to mind. Today she was more locked inside her own body than in Holloway Prison.

"Who will take the baby?" Olga had whispered to a wardess.

"The baby will go to an orphanage, poor mite," the woman told her.

"There's no family."

"Why is she here?"

"Killed her husband, the great brute." The attendant rubbed her nose. "Poison."

Olga's eyes widened as they stared at the exhausted, emaciated figure on the bed. She was skin, bones and a huge lump of belly. The attendant shrugged. "No poison here, and from the scarring on her arms, cigarette burns, I'd say he deserved everything she gave him."

"I wish she could have pinned it on someone else. She must have hoped to give her child a better life."

"Considering the hell she went through, maybe the child will have one. More than one kind of prison."

Olga heard a commotion at the other end of the hallway as the woman moaned. The prison officer held her hand out in a stop gesture to the shadowed man in the doorway. *Douglas.* Had he come to remove her from this place? Had her cousin been found? They'd taken her ring away, along with her clothing. She felt set adrift from that young lady she'd been only yesterday.

The female official's shoes rat-a-tapped on the floor as she walked across the ward. "Novikova? You're wanted."

Olga took one last glance at the laboring woman as a wardess took her place in the chair. She walked slowly to the end of the ward.

At the end, Douglas waited for her. She felt hot and bedraggled in comparison to him, an immaculate nobleman dressed in the latest fashion. How quickly she'd been brought low, a princess in prison garb. What did he think of her now? Did he feel any guilt? Douglas stared at her, almost as if he didn't recognize her in the prison uniform.

"You can use my office, my lord," the official said, taking them down the hall and into a narrow room that smelled of cheese and cold coffee.

"Thank you," Douglas said.

After Olga had stepped in, he shut the door behind her. "I'm sure you've had time to think about your cousin's present whereabouts. What conclusion have you reached?"

She stared at him, this cold face of a stranger. He'd been inside her, loving her, and now this—completely shut down, in a way he hadn't been even when Konstantin had killed his friend. It was as if he saw her as the betrayer instead of the other way around. His marble face invoked pity, despite her circumstances. But she was also frightened and couldn't hide it.

"He threatened Fyodora and your father," she said, wringing her icy hands. "What else could I have done?"

"Konstantin is a national threat. What could he possibly have done to your sister in Shanghai? And I've put my father under guard. Meanwhile, people are dying here. Konstantin tried to destroy the Grand Russe two months ago. He's bombed an art gallery, a theater. How can you aid him? Your sister is merely an excuse."

"I think you decided you don't want to marry his cousin and therefore will destroy me instead," she told him, her hand against the wall holding her upright despite her trembling knees.

"Why? You could be carrying my child, my father's heir. Why would I want that?"

She shrugged. "Tainted blood? I'm Russian?"

"The royal family is angry at how you've been treated." His eyes burned into her. His face seemed to have lost weight overnight. The skin stretched tightly over strong bones. "I am in trouble for my treatment of you, but I tell you this: You are the key to finding Konstantin, and I will find him. I will get Konstantin out of this country."

"You'll have your revenge," she said dully, "on me, if not on my cousin."

"I don't want you here," Douglas said. "But I can't have you aiding and abetting your cousin."

"I was afraid!" she shouted. "It is a good thing you didn't marry me as clearly you are incapable of putting your wife first."

His jaw set. "The royal family may want you released, but I'm telling you that you can choose to either stay here or be deported. As long as Konstantin is loose, I want you locked up, for both of your sakes."

"You can't possibly see this as the right place for me. Don't you have safe houses? I'm not a criminal." She smelled something sour and fought not to gag. Her stomach was already in such an uproar.

"I can't risk him finding you. Tell the ward mistress if you have information for me. Otherwise, I will see you when your cousin has been captured."

"You are a hard man." Her voice sounded dull and defeated.

"These are hard times." His lips worked, as if he wanted to say more, and the skin around his eyes drooped. But he said nothing, merely opened the office door and slipped out, leaving her there.

She sat in the hard-backed visitor's chair, happy to be away from the cries of desperate inmates for a moment longer, but the silence only made her wonder what she would have done in Douglas's place. Could she really be trusted where Konstantin was concerned? She'd betrayed Peter and the hotel because of him. She'd lied so many times, trying to protect the only family she had left. No wonder she was in prison. She deserved it for her crimes.

* * * *

That evening, Glass paced through his suite and debated if he could return to Knightsbridge for a time and refresh his wardrobe since the Russians appeared to be out for the evening. However, he didn't want to go anywhere his father could find him since he had no idea what to say about his relationship with Olga. He'd announced their engagement, then this mess had happened. He'd been harsh, but with people's lives and national security at stake, what else could he do?

At least Olga was safe, whether she wanted to believe that or not. He hadn't stopped caring for her. He knew Konstantin would really hurt her. That didn't make her innocent, though.

The trouble was she'd been helping him for years. Where did her loyalties lie?

The telephone rang. He pushed his thoughts aside, went to the table where it rested, and picked it up. "Yes?"

"Peter Eyre," said the voice on the line. "Did you know your pet Russians are whooping it up at Maystone's this evening?"

"No. Is that out of the ordinary?"

"They have some ladies with them we do not recognize. Not our usual class, based on the accents. The clothing is deceptive."

"Maybe the Russians bought them clothing first."

"My thought exactly." Eyre's tone was wry. "Why don't you stop by?"

"I'll need to change, but I'll be there in twenty minutes or so." He hung up the receiver and went to put on evening dress, thinking of the irony that he would be dressing for a nightclub while his fiancée languished in the hospital ward of a prison.

Twenty minutes later as promised, he found Peter Eyre's table just beyond the dance floor, directly in front of the band. A waiter was replacing an empty bottle of champagne with a newly uncorked one. Eyre filled both of their glasses and saluted him with one of them.

Glass took the other, noting the high color in Eyre's cheeks and the sheen in his eyes. "Drink the first one yourself, did you?"

"No, the manager here had a glass," Eyre said.

"That makes all the difference," Glass said as Eyre drained his glass and poured another. "What makes you so eager to down the bubbly this evening?"

As Eyre lifted his glass to his lips, Glass surveyed the room. The man they suspected to be Lashevich was on the floor. Two women were laughing loudly, teaching the alleged assassin the Charleston. Two other Russians of the thuggish variety were also on the floor with girls. They didn't look too out of place. Both knew how to dance.

"I don't understand why Olga was helping the bomber," Eyre said, pouring the last of the bottle's contents into his glass.

Glass stared at the empty bottle in shock. When had the man emptied it? Had he stared at the Russians for more than a few minutes?

"How could she risk the Grand Russe?" Eyre asked, his hair flopping over his brow as he set his glass down. "It was a chance at a better life for herself. Not only that; she loves my family.

"In fact," he continued, "there was a time, as a boy, you understand, that I had quite the calf love for her. But my parents discouraged it. Too far above me, they said. But a valuable friend." He laughed drunkenly.

"She's not a valuable friend?"

"I've been a valu-valuable friend to her," Eyre said, starting to slur and stumble on his words. "Helped her. And she betrays me and the entire family. We've invested a great deal in the hotel, my entire family. And she'd let her bloody cousin destroy it."

"She's naïve despite everything," Glass said, pulling the glass away from the man when he reached for it. "I think she believed Konstantin when he promised he'd stop. She thought he was trying to earn a living and if she gave him money, he'd stop."

"That's foolish. To make bombs you have to be s-s-suicidally mad."

"That's where the naivety is evident," Glass pointed out. "She did wise up, but then he simply stole from her. Threatened her with bodily harm."

"And now she's with him," Eyre said glumly into his empty glass.

Glass didn't correct him. He drained his to keep it away from the inebriated hotel manager. "Excellent stuff," he had to admit.

"We should order another," Eyre mumbled.

"I suspect you started even before that first bottle. Come, let's get you back to the hotel before what you just drank hits you."

"Legless," Eyre said. "I never get legless."

"Not true," Glass said, with a last look at the Russians. He'd have to give their party a miss for tonight. At least it appeared they were merely having fun. Maybe the violent streak had died with Ovolensky. Pushing his chair back, he reached for Eyre's arm, just as a waiter rushed up with another bottle.

"So sorry, sir," the waiter apologized. "I didn't realize you'd emptied it."

"We're done," Glass said. "Help me get him to his feet, will you?"

"I'm fine," Eyre said precisely. "It wouldn't do, you know, to show weakness. Never does." He put his hands on the table and levered himself up. After a chuckle, he said, "The last funny drunk I saw was Sadie Loudon. She sat on the floor. Her husband hit me when I took her home."

Eyre laughed again. Glass moved behind him to persuade him to walk out of the nightclub. "I do miss that Sadie Loudon Rake, or whatever her name is these days. Loads more fun than you've been, in the Artists Suite. Lost my best friend, you know."

"Who, Sadie?" Glass knew Sadie well enough since she'd joined his payroll but had never heard she and Eyre were close.

"No, you fool. Olga. Princess Olga Novikova. You going to marry her after all this?" Eyre turned suddenly, swayed, then poked his finger into Glass's collar. "She still good enough for you?"

"Her virtues are so much greater than her faults," Glass said. "But I don't wish to discuss my fiancée with a man who is half cut."

"So you love her, do you?" Eyre asked. "Well, good for you. I'd have said she was worth it, if not for this bombing mess. She's Russian, you know. A v-v-very complicated people, those Russians."

Glass offered up a prayer when they reached the bar. He navigated Eyre through the back. "Let's have your keys, my good fellow."

Eyre fumbled into his pocket until he found them. Glass unlocked the rear door into the hotel. They walked down the surprisingly opulent rear corridor after he relocked the door.

He recognized Olga's signature style in one of the pastoral paintings on the walls. "Did she put any of her own art into that exhibit?"

"No," Eyre said, after slowly processing the question. "Very modest for a princess."

* * * *

Olga was awakened in the dark by the wardess. She pushed aside her thin prison blanket, in the bed next to where the woman who'd finally given birth in the wee hours was recovering, and sat up. "What is it?" she asked drowsily. When she focused on the watch pinned to the wardess's coat pocket, she discovered it was just after 6 a.m.

"Had a cable," the woman said. "You're free to go."

Olga wiped sleep from her eyes and blinked. "I am?"

"Yes. One of the king's equerries is here to escort you to a relative of yours."

For a moment, Olga panicked. Surely this wasn't some rouse of Konstantin's. He seemed to prefer brute force to anything so intelligent. "Which relative?"

"A Russian duchess?" the woman asked uncertainly.

"You mean the grand duchess Xenia?" Olga asked, anxiety spearing her empty stomach.

"Shhh," the wardess said. "I do not know."

"The equerry, did you get a look at his eyes? Are they amber and blue?" Olga asked, worried that it was Konstantin.

"Brown as mud," the woman said. "Never seen him before, but he gave his name as Captain something, and he had the proper credentials."

"I guess I had better go with him then," Olga said, her stomach calming.

The wardess snorted. "As if you have a choice, princess or not. Time to stop making enemies and get along, I say."

Olga stood and stared at the woman. "How dare you."

"Don't you take that tone in my prison," the woman warned.

"I've done nothing wrong," Olga said with dignity. "I was a political prisoner, nothing more."

"If you say so. I might even believe it, with all this royal business. But it don't take much to lay a woman low in this world, and you had better mind your p's and q's. I don't want to see you again."

"I feel quite the same way, madam," Olga said.

They stared each other down; then, the woman pointed, and Olga walked down the ward and out of the door, to the woman's office, where she was allowed to dress before leaving.

Half an hour later, as she was driven to Windsor in a square black car to be rejoined with the grand duchess's household, she realized that Douglas had been lying to her about how dire her circumstances were. The slow burn of anger overtook her senses. She fought to maintain an aloof, regal appearance.

It took immense effort to keep her feet from tapping against the floor of the car. Her expression was carefully neutral, ignoring her emotions, the way her hair itched, her empty stomach. Spymaster or not, how dare he? She wasn't the bomber. She was the bomber's victim. Oh, he'd have a taste of her sharp tongue when she saw him again.

She twisted at her engagement ring, which the wardess had retrieved for her from the safe, though only after she'd made a point of asking for it. How she'd like to throw it in Glass's face, though that was something a lady wouldn't do.

But why, why must she be a lady after her fiancé had clapped her in prison? She remembered her mother's softness. How ill equipped she would have been for the 1920s. How grateful Olga was that she and her sister had inherited their father's more sporting blood. Her mother would have spent the last seven years in the grand duchess's Russian Orthodox shrine praying instead of doing anything. She'd never have had an art career, though she was quite as good an artist as Olga. She'd never have been a chambermaid. And she certainly would never have attracted a man like Douglas.

Why had Douglas chosen her when he could have had any woman? Even this angry, she found the idea of him still intrigued her. She still wanted what he represented: that painting of parents and four boys, a family unit. The thing they had both lost, a family. She and Douglas could start over together. Anyone other than him was unimaginable. He understood her twisted, stunted life. The war had changed him too. She didn't need the money or even his title. She'd proved she could earn a living; she had a title of her own. But a family? That she'd long since lost. She'd been right to attempt to protect the earl.

By then, they had driven into Windsor Park and were arriving at the gleaming white Frogmore House. The long line of windows on the ground floor made the palatial house seemed curiously blank. Olga wondered if the grand duchess would find a measure of happiness here or if it would be just one more stop on this long journey of exile she had suffered since the Romanovs had lost power.

* * * *

Glass woke suddenly, uncertain of his whereabouts. Dimly, he remembered champagne with Peter Eyre, drunk in his suite in the hopes of lessening the hotel manager's consumption. He fumbled for a lamp and discovered he was stretched across his sofa in the suite, alone. Had Eyre drunk him under the proverbial table? He heard banging on the suite door and realized that was what had woken him. Standing, he rubbed his eyes, buttoned his coat, and reached for the knife he kept in the side table next to the door. He hid his knife hand behind the door as he opened it.

Princess Olga stood in the doorway, her expression quietly furious. She wore a fur jacket with matching cloche, and he could see a black wool dress underneath, nothing he'd seen her in before. Even the shoes were unfamiliar to him.

"Hello, Princess." His voice came out gravelly. Surely from sleepiness and not emotion. He'd treated her terribly yet she still came to him. "Here to slap me?"

"No," she said. "May I come in?"

He nodded and stood aside. She stopped still after he closed the door, and he realized he still held the knife. "My apologies," he muttered.

"Do you think my cousin is coming for you?"

"More like the neighbors," he said, "though I am certain to be on your cousin's list."

"I take it that imprisoning me did not help you find him." Her jaw worked.

"No, but you are still alive," he said.

"Do you think he will kill me?" she asked.

"I don't know. Not if he still hopes to take money from you, but he's carrying weapons, and he's unafraid to threaten you. I want you safe, but obviously your family intervened."

She shuddered slightly. "How could you leave me there?"

"I was angry, but I also wanted you safe," he repeated.

"Was that your way of canceling our engagement?"

He shook his head. "No, but I understand if you feel that way."

She slowly unbuttoned her coat. "How absurd that it took a trip to Holloway to put me in the latest Paris fashions? The grand duchess dipped into her latest acquisitions to dress me."

"I am sure they are very righteously angry on your behalf." He stepped behind her to receive the expensive coat and placed it on the bench in the entryway.

Underneath her dress was shapeless, but fashionable, sportswear in the color of mourning.

"I had a bath and washed my hair at Frogmore House," she said in an almost musing tone. "I even put on perfume, Chanel, I think."

"It smells wonderful."

"It keeps changing," she said. "Very complicated notes. Right now I'm smelling the floral notes, but I think it gets woody at the end before it wears away."

He appreciated her feminine dithering, but it wasn't like her. "Whatever it does, I like it now." He waited for her to take a shot at him.

"I should hate you, Douglas."

"I know." He shrugged because what else could he say?

"No argument?"

"I am suspicious and have too much power for my own good."

"Did you really send me there to keep me safe?"

"It was about half that and half anger."

"I see." She walked past him into the sitting room.

He changed his mind about the dress. It only seemed shapeless, but he could see her hips moving beneath it, her torso slim and straight above. He hardened instantly, his body notifying him of where it wanted to be led.

"Why didn't you stay at Frogmore for the night?"

"The grand duchess told me my place was here," she said, picking up the bottle of champagne. "Good year."

Amusing that the grand duchess had told Olga to return to her fiancé when the imperial been separated from her husband for many years. "It's probably gone flat."

She poured the last couple of ounces into his empty glass and drained it.

"I see." He crossed his arms over his chest, observing her. His princess was faking her bravado. He saw it in the faint trembling of her fingers on the glass. She held her head like a dancer would, well trained, a royal to the last.

What would she do if he responded to the woman beneath the exterior, the one who must be desperately in need of comfort after such an ordeal? "I am so sorry, my dear girl."

Her head tilted. "Are you?"

"Of course." He removed the empty glass from her fingers and set it down. "I wish we could just run up to my father's country seat and have a rest. But you know it isn't possible with your cousin on the loose and the Hand of Death sleeping comfortably next door."

"You cannot still want to marry me." She twisted her engagement ring but, tellingly, did not remove it.

"On the contrary. I know you are loyal. As my wife, you will be completely loyal. An excellent quality. Also, I know a little hardship will not break you."

"Do you expect your enemies to imprison me as well?" She sounded sarcastic.

"I hope not, but these are uncertain times."

She muttered something in Russian and sat gracefully on the sofa. He took the champagne glass to the bathroom, rinsed it out, filled it with water, and brought it back to her.

"Drink," he said. "Your skin looks tired."

"Really, Douglas. What a thing to say to a lady." But she set the cup to her lips and drank it down.

"You need fresh air, something to put the roses back in your cheeks. But it isn't safe for you right now."

"Am I safe anywhere?" She toyed with the glass stem.

"A valid question."

"I do not feel safe with you." She said it casually, as if toying with the notion.

"I am a dangerous man. I won't deny it." He sat next to her, pressing his advantage with his larger body. His thigh brushed her skirt. He could smell dust, as if her clothing had been stored some place unused, but underneath was still the faint citrus scent of her.

"It is ironic, is it not, that my biggest enemy is my closest relative."

"And your biggest tormentor is your future husband?"

"No, you aren't my greatest torment." Her lips curved. "A momentary aberration. I expect you do not think you have a temper, but you do."

"I'm very clearheaded," he protested. "You should have seen the risks I took in the war, delivering messages behind enemy lines to saboteurs. A temper will get you nowhere but dead."

"Douglas," she whispered, "allow your fiancée to know you a little better than you know yourself. A calm man would have kept his fiancée safe by hiding her away on royal property or such, not clapping her in prison." She moved her hand to his thigh. "You are a man of passion."

Chapter 18

"Passion." Glass chuckled, brushing her leg with his thigh. He could hardly believe she was back in his suite, on his sofa again, after everything that had transpired, and looking so lovely. "There is more than one kind of passion."

"I disagree," Princess Olga said. "Passion is a man's fighting spirit in any endeavor."

"Well, if that is true, you bring out the fighting spirit in me."

"I know," she said, and her smile looked like the *Mona Lisa*'s as she turned her body toward him. "Show me that you love me, Douglas. I need to feel like this is real."

He cupped the back of her head with his palm. He could feel the pins tight against the base of her skull, her unfashionably long hair coiled as if to hide it from prison's dirt. This woman belonged in a palace, not a prison. For the first time, he felt shame for what he had done. "I'm sorry."

She tilted her neck so that her breath brushed his lips. "I know, Douglas."

"How? Do you know me better than I know myself?"

"You didn't take the ring back." She turned her hand so that the diamond was toward his cheek and brushed the cold stone down his stubble. "Feel that? It's still mine."

His erection swelled painfully. Focus narrowed to her puffy lips, her pale skin. Oh, he'd make those cheeks bloom again. He captured her mouth, roughly, inelegantly. Her hands tunneled into his hair, tugging, the sensation almost painful.

He welcomed the burn and pulled her into his lap. He heard a seam pop. Tugging at her dress, he managed to get it up to her waist and slid one hand through a leg of her knickers while he opened his trousers.

Oh, God. She was wet, moaning when he touched her. Her hips shifted, pressing the apex of her sex against her fingers. In such a short time, he taught her well.

"My darling." He reached for one slim leg and pulled it over his lap, exposing her completely to him; then, he tore the center seam of her knickers, baring her sex.

She was so wet that he slid right into her.

"Douglas," she said, then whispered his name again, clutching his hair even tighter, her mouth still against his.

He reached for her bottom, not giving her any quarter as he thrust into her with the hard, desperate strokes from a man who could give her nothing but his all.

They panted together, their lips fused open. His fingers moistened as sweat rose on her back and dripped. But it didn't matter; he couldn't hold back. He spent himself utterly, dropping his head to her shoulder, but thank God, he felt her body pulse. He'd taken her with him into the madness.

When she stopped vibrating against him, her breathing slowed. He felt his legs could carry them, so he spread his feet on the thick carpet and rose to a standing position, her legs wrapped around his waist, her sex still stretched around his.

He took her into the bathroom, reluctantly disengaged her, and turned on the taps to fill the bathtub.

"Now what do we do?"

He quickly stripped off his clothes and wrapped a towel around his waist before turning back to her. "You can't stay at the hotel."

"I know that," she retorted with alarming venom.

Why was he surprised? She'd met his desire with the craving of an attacking jungle cat, and her orgasm hadn't softened her spirit any.

"After we bathe, could we please gather the rest of my things from my room? I was never able to pack," she said.

"Yes, of course. I just need a minute to think. I'd take you to my flat in Marylebone, but I've always been troubled by how close the art gallery bombing was to it."

"If Konstantin knew the British Secret Intelligence Service had a flat in a specific location, I'm sure he'd have sold the information to one of his paymasters," she said, her ire still obvious from her tone. "It was pure luck."

"Still. I'll take you to my home in Knightsbridge."

After they bathed, Olga dressed as best she could. Glass felt guilty about putting on clean clothes himself. "You can change upstairs before we leave."

She nodded as they went to the lift. The tenth floor was silent, more so than the lower levels of the hotel since everyone who lived here worked hard for their living, but Olga let out a wordless growl when she unlocked her room and entered.

Glass surveyed the clothing scattered across the room. "What happened?"

"He's been here." She pointed at her dressing gown, on the floor just opposite the door. "That's where my money was, what the Plash boy paid me for the painting. How long did it take him to find it in such an obscure place?"

"Konstantin," Glass said in an answering growl. "He knows this hotel far too well. This floor has been empty for hours."

She gathered a handful of clothing from the floor, went to the trunk at the foot of her bed, and dumped it in. He watched her change out of her ruined knickers, enjoying the brief flashes of her body revealed. Then, she went through the room, dropping everything into the trunk. A smaller trunk was against the wall, and all of her art supplies went into that.

Glass had already called downstairs from his suite's new telephone for a bellboy to bring a cart. He didn't like to risk tipping off Konstantin if he returned, but they needed a cart for the trunks. When a knock came at the door, he was surprised to see Peter Eyre, rather than a bellboy.

"Removing her things?" Eyre demanded. "Where is she going to go?"

"It's no business of yours. She is my fiancée now."

"She is still my art consultant," the hotel manager retorted, "if not my friend."

Glass gestured him in and closed the door as Olga exclaimed, "Peter!"

"How could you have helped him after what he did?" Eyre glanced around the room.

"I was trying to make him stop," she protested. "I thought if I supported him he would stop making bombs, but it didn't work. He's greedy. He's been in here again, stolen my money again."

Eyre's mouth tightened. "How did you have any left?"

"From Harold Plash. He paid me for a painting."

"The money isn't important," Glass broke in. "It's the fact that Konstantin still has full access to the Grand Russe. How is he getting in? He must have keys."

"Did you give him keys?" Eyre demanded of Olga.

"No." She sounded uncertain.

"What?" Glass asked.

"I would assume he has Russian spies among his contacts. They would know how to make copies of my keys without me even noticing, don't you think?"

"Wax impressions and that sort of thing," Glass said.

"That's probably it then." Olga's tone was glum. "It's me again."

"I'll have the locks changed tomorrow," Eyre said, in a slightly calmer tone. "But you need to give me your keys, Olga. I can't trust you while your cousin is on the loose."

She went to her handbag, pulled out the ring, and slapped them into his palm. A moment later, she apologized. Tears came to her eyes. "I'm so sorry."

Eyre shook his head. "So am I. You have been my friend for twenty years and, as such, so familiar to me that I forget you are Russian."

"Not for much longer," Glass said. "Soon, she'll be an English viscountess."

Olga's lips were pressed thin, but at least the corners turned up.

Eyre pulled out his wallet, ripped out a sheath of bank notes, and shoved them at her. "Why don't you check into the Savoy? Konstantin won't look for you there because he knows you don't have the money. I'll pay your fare until your wedding."

"You don't need to do that," Olga said, lacing her fingers together.

Glass shook his head. "I'm going to put her in a flat. Better security than a hotel, even a good one. Almost no one will see her, and if she stays away from the Grand Russe, he won't be able to put a tail on her."

"I want to know how to reach her," Eyre said.

"Very well." Glass gave him the telephone number for his flat, and the two of them loaded Olga's trunks onto a cart.

"I have a car waiting off the service entrance," Eyre said. "I assume you will be able to lose any tails if you are spotted?"

"Of course," Glass said.

Eyre stared hard at Olga for a moment and shook his head. "First Emmeline and now you. I don't appear to be able to keep any women in my life."

"You should look for less dramatic companionship," Olga said softly. "But I'll be back when this is all over. I'm not about to say good-bye to all your beautiful art."

Eyre nodded and put his hands on the handle of the cart. Glass pushed open the door as Olga took one last look around.

"You didn't stay here very long," he said.

She pulled on her hat and wrapped a muffler around her throat. "No. I thought I might be here the rest of my life. But life has a way of surprising one."

"Indeed," he said. "At least you'll be comfortable in the flat."

She nodded, though he could see she was too drained to pull out any real enthusiasm. He had a moment's worry that she'd find it unsuitable. While he thought of her as the chambermaid from the boardinghouse at times, this was a woman who'd lived in palaces for much of her life. At least his flat was full of modern comfort.

* * * *

As much as Glass wanted to spend the night with Olga at his flat, duty called. He needed to return to his surveillance at the hotel. After he showed Olga the locations of such food as he had, made sure the sheets and towels were fresh, and settled her in, he kissed her cheek and departed. She hadn't complained or said anything much. He knew he was on unsteady ground with her after everything that had happened. While she undeniably had a strong pull toward him, his behavior had done a great deal of damage to their relationship.

So, the next evening, he retrieved her from her exile in Knightsbridge and brought her back to the Grand Russe. He'd missed her all day, and she'd be safe enough in his suite. After ordering food to his rooms, they passed a quiet evening, not talking much but starting to relax around another again.

Just after nine, a bellboy knocked on his door to tell him he was wanted in the Coffee Room.

"Thank you." Glass shut the door and went back into the sitting room, where Olga stood in the center attempting to dance the Charleston to a record Glass had on a portable gramophone.

She stopped, breathless. "Who was that?"

He drank in the sight of her. "Eyre wants me downstairs."

"The Russians aren't in their suite."

"Never are at the dinner hour. Sometimes they reappear about now."

"I'm glad I'm here," Olga said. "I like feeling like a regular girl sometimes."

"I have to change my shirt, but keep talking," Glass called, as he went into the bedroom to put on evening dress.

"I painted all day," she called. "I think Harold's painting is done. I have to wait for it to dry. Do you think he'll be in the Coffee Room?"

"Probably. I'll have to bring it to him. Where does he live?"

"I have no idea. He's mentioned his father, so he must still be alive. Must have been quite a bit younger than Emmeline's father."

"I'll make arrangements tonight if I see him. But I should probably put you in a car before I go into the Coffee Room. You won't want to be there if Lashevich is lurking about."

"No." The music abruptly turned off. "Peter wouldn't call you downstairs for anything else?"

"No. I shouldn't think so."

"Then I can go down with you and go straight to the front door. The

Russians won't see me."

He came back into the room, adjusting his bow tie, and picked up the telephone. He told the operator to find Ivan Salter and send him to the Coffee Room so he could escort Olga into Knightsbridge. She would enter through an attached row house, unlock the door between the buildings, and go upstairs to his flat. A nice extra bit of security. He had never forgotten that Ivan Salter's sister had been an associate of Konstantin's, though she had fled the country and had been seen in Paris. They had the police there keeping an eye on her.

When Glass and Olga reached the Grand Hall, Olga in her fur coat and Glass dressed for the Coffee Room, Salter hadn't arrived yet. Glass peered between the doors and saw that the Russians were in the Coffee Room, though people were starting to depart the dance floor, ready to head to Maystone's for the remainder of the evening. They stayed in the corridor.

A minute later, Salter appeared.

"Can you escort the princess to my flat?" Glass asked.

"You want me to leave the hotel?" Salter's *w*'s still sounded like *v*'s, despite more than three years in London and his much-prided Britishness.

"She can't go out alone with mischief on the loose. Would you rather I call Special Branch?"

"It's not far," the princess said. "You'll return in well under half an hour."

Salter inclined his head. "Very well."

The two went toward the main entrance, and Glass stepped into the Coffee Room just as Teddy Fortress and his wife, Honor Page, were stepping out. Fortress was whistling jauntily, not a care in the world, but his wife's lips were moving. Glass read them quickly. For some reason the famed film star Miss Page was mouthing "I hate you" over and over again.

"There you are," Eyre said as Glass sat down at the small table where the hotel manager held court. As usual lately, an empty champagne bottle was in the bucket in a silver stand next to the table, and he was alone. "Any contact with our p-princess today?"

"We had dinner here," Glass admitted. "But I've just sent her away."

"I've thought about it, and I agree she should have been arrested," Peter said, overpronouncing his *s*'s. "Untrustworthy women might as well be locked up. For their own good you know. Look at Emmeline. Got a man killed and herself beaten. Deserved it of course, both of them."

Glass patted his shoulder. "I don't know about that, but I'm in charity with you. Emmeline has put you through more than most men would take. You're a loyal soul."

"Wish my brother was here," Eyre said, staring at the table. "Oh well.

She damned us both."

Glass ignored the melancholy statement. "The Russians are leaving."

"We'd better follow them," Eyre said with a long sigh. "Off to Maystone's."

"Why don't you stick to water," Glass suggested as Eyre moved to stand, then swayed, and sat again before successfully rising, "for the rest of tonight?"

"Whatever for?"

"To help me observe. You're no good to me half cut."

"Ah, I see. Going to make a spy of me yet." Eyre grasped the edge of the table.

Glass kept his expression neutral, though he was quietly furious. Just what he needed. A drunk outing him. "On second thought, why don't you stay here in case the Russians double back?"

"Don't be ridiculous." Eyre straightened fully and looked him in the eye. "We'll go through the back so we don't appear to be following them."

Glass inclined his head and held out his hand, following behind as Eyre swept from the room, his head held high. He walked well for someone feeling the effects of his champagne. Perhaps he wasn't as drunk as he had seemed.

They went through the service corridor. When Eyre paused at the rear door into the club, Glass asked, "Were you able to change the locks?"

"The service doors, yes, like the basement entrance and this door. Getting to every hotel room door will be a different issue, and to be realistic, if we change the doors on the seventh floor, the Russians may just give Konstantin a new key."

"A fair point. But the Russians have no special access, correct?"

"Correct. They never asked to search the hotel." Eyre pulled out his ring of keys. Glass saw some of them looked shiny and fresh compared to the dull, well-used ones. "They've never tried to get master keys to the hotel to the best of my knowledge."

"We have never really been sure if the trade delegation was connected to Konstantin." He followed Eyre through the door into the nightclub's storeroom. Boxes of liquor, glasses, and cutlery were stacked on shelves. Silver trays were piled neck-high in one corner.

"No?"

"We believe one of the delegates attempted to make contact, but he was expelled from the country some time ago."

"Are there other Russian bomb masters about?"

"A couple of Irish ones," Glass admitted. "No Russians that we know of. But won't it be exciting to tell your grandchildren that a famous Russian assassin once stayed at the hotel?"

"Let us hope I have the sort of grandchildren more interested in tales of film stars than assassins. I did hope we'd have some old-fashioned royal assignations here, but so far the Prince of Wales and his brothers haven't shown an interest."

"Unfortunate," Glass said.

"We did have the Duke of York's mistress in for dinner one night, but she came with friends."

Glass patted Eyre's shoulder. "You'll get there. This generation should start having children soon enough. In twenty years there will be a new bunch to be scandalous here."

"It might be at the hotel or in Maystone's," Eyre said, his gaze taking in the storeroom. "It's sexy enough, for all that some of the most favored clubs are little more than basements. But I can't stand some of these dances that are popular. The Twinkle? The Shimmy?"

"Effeminate," Glass said. He followed the man through a service area where the last touches were put on the food they were forced to serve at the club to keep the liquor flowing, and then behind the bar.

"Russians, Friend?" Eyre asked.

The club manager turned. His shadowed eyes looked tired, but he was nonetheless a handsome man, the kind any girl would be thrilled to dance some twinkly song with. He had the upright carriage and lean, broad body of a military lineage. Glass wondered what his service record was. He looked just old enough to have been in at the end. Maybe never made it out of training.

The man held out his hand, and Eyre shook it. Eyre nodded at Glass. "This is Lord Walling, Cuddy. Walling, Cuddy Friend. He's keeping a close eye on the Bolshies when I'm not around."

"They just came in. Their women were waiting outside, and we've just let them into the nightclub. Already on the dance floor." Friend shrugged. "Can't see the harm."

"Not if they are paying," Eyre said. "This way, we know where they are."

"Fair enough. Same group of women exactly as before?"

Friend nodded. "Yes. My doorman has a photographic memory."

"Good. This lot aren't being beaten then—or at least not badly."

"So what do you want to do then?" Eyre's words had begun to slur again.

"A quick look," Glass said. "Then a night off for both of us."

Eyre attempted to clap him on the shoulder, missed, and stepped around the bar, grabbing a glass of champagne off the edge as he did. Glass followed but was distracted by the sight of his princess coming into the club. He went toward her, taking her elbow. "I thought you went home?"

"I don't have keys to your flat," she said. "I know how to get as far as the door, but—"

Glass frowned. "How stupid of me." He reached into his pocket but was distracted by the sight of Eyre turning around, an expression of stupefaction on his face.

"What?" Glass mouthed.

He watched Eyre's half-full glass tip. Following the tilt of Eyre's hand, he saw who had shocked the hotel manager. He'd recognize that face anywhere. *Konstantin.*

Chapter 19

Glass shoved his keys at Olga as the Maystone's band moved into position on their small stage. "Go."

"What?" she asked. A couple brushed past her, intent on the dance floor. "What's wrong?"

"Just go," he said in a low voice, hoping his lowered brows and stern expression would make her obey.

But she wasn't that sort of woman. She followed the line of Eyre's lifted chin and stiffened when she saw her cousin. "What on earth is he doing here?"

They all watched as Konstantin weaved his way through the room from the bar, heading toward the dance floor.

"Maybe the Hand of Death bought your cousin a woman for the night," Eyre said with drunken ire.

Glass attempted to turn Olga around. "You need to leave."

Eyre spoke. "You need to arrest him."

"Exactly." He gritted his teeth in Olga's direction. Why wasn't she moving? "I don't want you here. A man died the last time I tried to capture him."

She clutched his arm. Her brow furrowed. "It isn't safe here. I can lure him outside, Douglas."

"I want you to leave."

She shook her head and darted forward. He grabbed for her, missed, just as the cornet blared out the opening passage to "Blue Paradise," a one-step from a decade ago.

With that unfashionable choice by the band, the dancers, who had been shimmying to a gramophone recording, left the floor en masse to seek refills on their drinks and chat. Konstantin paused, suddenly unsure of his destination, it seemed. Was he heading for Mikhail Lashevich or someone else? The crowd surged around him. Glass grabbed for Olga's hand, trying to keep her close.

As he pulled his princess out of view, he saw Konstantin's eyes narrow as he caught sight of them.

"Sodding bloody hell," Eyre muttered. "I really need to start carrying a gun."

Glass shoved Olga at Eyre and pushed between two flappers in beaded black-and-white gowns, their hems rippling around his trousers as he moved. He smelled the heavy rose perfume on one of them, the sweat under the arms of the man in front of the women.

Konstantin, light on his feet despite his height, drifted to the wall and moved speedily in the opposite direction, toward the bar. Glass turned but was trapped by the women again.

The rose-scented one fingered his dinner jacket. "Buy me a drink, Valentino?"

Glass ignored her and tugged his sleeve away. Konstantin had gained several feet. As Glass followed, he crouched, slipped under the hinged bar counter, and headed into the shadowy recesses behind, ignoring his cousin.

Glass swore. Had Konstantin been getting into the Grand Russe through the nightclub service door this entire time? He lifted the bar counter and went through, followed by Olga and Eyre. He reached under his jacket to unsnap his holster and pull out his pistol.

In the dim light, confused by dots of light shining off silver trays, he saw Konstantin try the door. The knob rattled but didn't turn. He pulled out a key and shoved it in the lock. It didn't go all the way in. Must have been an old key. With a growl, the man reached into his own dinner jacket.

"Stop right there," Glass said, wishing he had Special Branch as backup. "Hands over your head."

Konstantin didn't turn, didn't lift his hands. Glass took a step, raising his weapon.

"Go ahead, don't lift them," he taunted. "I want you dead. I'm no bobby. I'll drill your heart so full of bullets that no one will ever know it was missing in the first place."

One of Konstantin's hands lifted. Glass moved in closer. He heard footsteps coming close to him from the nightclub. Glass stayed focused on his target. He couldn't make the same mistake twice.

Olga screamed. Glass glanced over his shoulder despite his better judgment. What was going on? Then he heard the sound of wood splintering. He glanced in the opposite direction to see Konstantin punch through the door above the handle.

Glass sighted down his pistol. Konstantin shoved his hand through the broken part of the door and pushed it open, separated from the locking mechanism. He broke into a run just as Glass fired his first shot, missed.

Konstantin picked up speed as he ran down the service corridor. Glass heard screaming, realized it was just to his right, a reaction to the gun in his hand not a bullet hitting the wrong target. He took aim and fired again, missing because the Russian was already too far ahead of him.

He made it to the end of the corridor and turned right.

"The lifts!" Eyre called.

Glass picked up speed. He didn't want a race through the guest floors. But Konstantin didn't head for the lifts. He went past the back of them and turned left into the Grand Hall.

Glass could still hear the band playing in the Coffee Room. Inside the Reading Room he saw men in evening dress pouring over the day's papers. Couples sat on the banquettes in the center of the hall. Konstantin ran full tilt into the marble table in the center. The enormous glass vase, full of hothouse blooms in riotous red and yellows, tipped and fell, crashing loudly on the floor. The flowers spread across several feet.

Konstantin turned toward the Coffee Room.

"Is there an exit in there?" Glass called, knowing Eyre was behind him.

"Yes, to the service corridor."

"He's doubling back," Glass growled, checked his gun, and ran in.

Konstantin passed between the tables. Glass followed, gaining speed. He tripped over an outstretched foot and moved into a run to keep from falling.

Then, he saw it. His shot. Konstantin, no one in front of him, in relief against the silver-and-blue far wall. He couldn't let the man move between the dancers still on the floor, get behind the band through the door into the corridor.

He stopped, spread his stance, and lifted his gun.

As his fiancée screamed behind him, he fired.

At first, nothing. Then, Konstantin's head turned. Glass pressed his lips between his teeth and fired again. Blood spattered against the silver and blue. Konstantin sank to his knees, his head sliding down the wall.

People screamed and scattered. Glass pushed past the last two tables, ignored the waiter, who stood open-mouthed, still holding a tray just feet from the dead Russian.

"Dead?" Eyre asked, much too close behind him.   –

Glass reached the body and kicked the gun away from his hand. He stared at the hole in the Russian's head. "Yes."

"I'll call DI Dent," Eyre said.

Next to Glass, his princess crouched, keening next to her cousin. Poor thing, having to see yet another death at close hand.

Glass waited for the footsteps to tell him Eyre was moving away, but instead, the hotel manager stepped alongside him.

"How dare you," Eyre said in a strangled voice.

Glass stared at him. What was he blathering about? "What?"

Eyre's voice rose. "Olga!"

She didn't turn away. Glass shoved his pistol back into its holster and tried to take Eyre's arm, but he wrenched it away.

"How can you mourn him?" Eyre yelled, spittle appearing in the corners of his lips. "You brought this into my hotel. You tried to ruin us. After everything we've done for you."

She didn't even look up, just reached a trembling hand out and held her fingers over Konstantin's back.

"We're done," Eyre said, staring down at her. "I never want to see you again. Any association with my family, with this hotel, is over."

Slowly, Glass turned his head to look at the man. Their eyes met. Eyre's eyes were glassy, fixed. He shook his head, shoved his hands into his pockets, and turned around. "Call Dent," Glass said, more harshly than intended.

At some point, the room had emptied. That door into the service corridor was open. The musicians had fled, followed by the dancers.

But he heard heavy footsteps. Ivan Salter entered the room. Wordless, he reached Glass and surveyed the scene. "What do you want me to do?"

"What I asked you to do before. Take the princess to Knightsbridge."

Salter said something in Russian, then reached forward, and wrapped his arm around her waist. He pulled her up, still speaking softly in Russian, and turned her around. She put her head against his shoulder and didn't look at Glass as they left the room.

Glass sighed and pushed Eyre out in front of him, then closed the doors. At least the princess's precious artwork had been removed before he'd ruined one of the Coffee Room's fabled walls with bullets and blood.

* * * *

Olga had scarcely noticed the Edwardian cast-offs that littered Douglas's sitting room, the wicker tables and Sheraton side chairs. The matched love seats were a riot of chintz. She doubted Douglas would be able to bring himself to sit on such feminine things. No, she suspected he holed up in his flat's office, which was a darkly paneled masculine preserve, on those rare occasions he could be home.

This would be her life, pacing the floors until the babies came, unless he let her have an artist's studio, some light-filled attic in Chelsea. She'd need such a place to be able to breathe.

While she forced herself to have all these commonplace thoughts, she didn't believe any of them. Behind every moment where she identified a piece of furniture or a *tchotchke*, had a thought about their married life, she heard Peter's cold words.

Had she ruined the Grand Russe with yet another murder? It had survived Richard Marvin's attempt to rape Alecia Loudon Salter earlier in the year. No one had even known about it. The bomb attempt had changed nothing; government officials were having meetings in the hotel.

Perhaps it had been a mere drunken outburst, but Peter Eyre wasn't a dramatic person, and his words had seemed final.

She found herself on her knees without knowing how she had fallen to them.

No Peter. No Eloise. No Grand Russe. The art she'd created, the art she'd curated, lost to her. Her friends, the Salters, new still but precious nonetheless. Her position. All gone, because of her cousin.

Her fiancé had shot him in Peter's hotel. After Douglas had promised to keep Konstantin safe.

"Olga."

She shook her head. Why hadn't Douglas told her to call the police? Anyone could have done it. He could have cornered Konstantin, overpowered him somehow.

Revenge, she supposed. Such a masculine province. He was repaying Konstantin for killing Bill Vall-Grandly—and betraying her trust.

"Olga."

She rubbed her temples and glanced up at the huge cottage roses on the sofa to her left. Why not sit there instead of on the floor? She didn't know.

Feeling a hand under her elbow, she rose unsteadily to her feet but sat gracefully enough, her ankles and knees together.

"Olga."

Someone was being terribly forward. She glanced up and saw a tall man, with lips that quirked up slightly even though his thick, dark eyebrows were drawn together. Douglas.

Douglas? She stiffened.

"You have been up all night," he said, "judging from those dark circles."

"Did you sleep?"

His eyebrows lifted. "No. Too much explaining to do. Difficult to keep a story like that out of the papers. Quex was able to bury it a bit. Page three."

She forced herself to sound reasonable. "I'd hate to see Peter's hotel go under over this."

"It won't. It seems to stimulate the film people, being involved in such drama. Might see a few less titles around, but then, Peter's bread and butter seems to be film people and commercial travelers."

"Just marrieds," she said.

"Yes, I imagine so." He cleared his throat. "Difficult to repair the Coffee Room. I understand the wallpaper is one-of-a-kind, hand-drawn, and the artist killed himself shortly after the installation. The understructure can be repaired easily enough, though. It will all be sorted in time."

She stared at the floor.

"I'm not sorry for any of it, though," Glass said quickly, "for killing him. I had a clear shot, no one behind him. And I'm a good shot. Did my bit as a sniper when I first joined up. Had an eye injury that put me on courier duty for a while, and I was good enough at that not to go back to the other."

She didn't look up. "You shot him in the back."

He tipped up her chin with a gentle finger. "He was running away from me with a gun out. You think he wouldn't have killed me? Or innocent bystanders? He made bombs, Olga. He killed Bill and another man in the tube station."

"He was my family." Her voice sounded distant. "You promised me."

His rose. "Bloody hell, Olga. He was a killer. Don't canonize him now that he's dead. He was a sodding Rasputin for heaven's sake. Besides, I promised you nothing."

"How dare you," she said coldly.

"Rasputin did his bit to destroy Russia, just like Konstantin was doing his bit to destroy England. So there you go."

"I hate you," she said. "You know he considered himself an artist. He was misguided and ill."

"He terrorized you, Olga." He tried to take her hand. "Please, I know you're hysterical. You need sleep. I can get a doctor in here to give you something. You can sleep all day."

She pulled her hand away. "I am not weak."

"No, of course not. But I don't really understand why you would mourn him. He wasn't a part of your childhood."

"You also cost me Peter and the Grand Russe."

He winced. "I admit that's a situation worthy of an apology. But he was drunk, you know. One says things. I'm sure he'll see reason when he's slept, sobered up."

"You think so?" She kept the hauteur in her voice, but a prick of hope darted up her spine.

"I do." One of his cheeks lifted, a half smile.

He was so terribly handsome. Even now, she felt the tug of his personality, of his masculinity, but he knew how to use it, too, and that made her angry. She reached for one of the hideous pillows resting against the sofa's arm and pulled it against her chest.

"You need a bath," he said. "You have soot on your cheek." He lifted a finger.

She batted it away. "Don't touch me."

He stilled. His gaze searched her face. Then he nodded, some decision being made. "I have some wonderful news to balance the hard night."

She said nothing as she seated herself gracefully on the ugly chintz. He put his hand on her shoulder, ignoring her tense muscles. "It's about Fyodora."

She had been staring straight ahead, but the name made her jump. Her head turned. "What about her?"

"She'll be in London in about ten days."

"What?" The word came out of her throat in a croak.

"A British warship has her, like how you came here all those years ago. Princess Fyodora Novikova has been found in Shanghai and is on her way to you."

Olga's brain went blank, but then, out of the gray haze, a question came. "How could you have known?"

"I had a search ordered for her."

"When?" She kept her voice even with difficulty.

He shrugged, his hand dropping from her shoulder. "A little while ago. I wanted her to be a wedding present for you."

Oh, did he? "She's a human being."

"I wanted to know if she was well," he said with no uncertainty in his voice.

She'd been an utter fool to trust anything about him. Why had she given him another chance after the prison? Because the grand duchess had all but forced her, that was why. And she couldn't stop loving him, even now. "You've played with our lives, hers and mine."

"Darling, I wanted to help. She might be ill, in body or spirit. I wanted to know it would be a good reunion."

"Do you think I have no unfamiliarity with illness of body or spirit?" she demanded. "Do you think I would care? I did what I could for my cousin, and the same will apply to Fyodora for all that you've cost me my position yet again."

"We're to be married next month. If your sister is well enough, you can spend the time shopping for your trousseau, doing what you want to the flat. Or we can rent a house, or move in with my father. So much to do."

She stood, shaky on her legs. "Oh, Douglas, you do wonderful things— and horrible ones."

"I am sorry for what I have put you through." He lifted his hands and dropped them again, an uncertain gesture for such a self-assured man.

She faced him squarely. "I would prefer to spend my time with my sister. I do not want to marry you. We will return to the grand duchess's care. I have lost the protection of the Redcakes. So be it. We will begin again. I will sell more paintings."

"Konstantin still had your money on him," Douglas said. He put his hand into his coat and pulled out an envelope.

She didn't recognize it. Was it really her money, or had he just pulled the funds from somewhere? Either way, she couldn't afford to be choosy.

"I understand you are highly emotional right now." He held out the envelope and sat.

She wanted to scream, to strike him. But she swallowed the bile in her throat. She had Fyodora to think of. She needed that money. Her hand went to the envelope, and he released it. "I appreciate that. Ten days, you say?"

"Yes."

"I shall see if Bert Dadey will take me back at the boardinghouse. Konstantin didn't do any damage there, thankfully. And I'll find another chambermaid job. I'll try at the Savoy."

He stared at her, all that scarcely contained masculine energy seated on that appalling sofa. "Stay here, Olga. You'll feel differently with some rest."

She glanced down at her ring. The diamond seemed to wink at her, as if trying to share a joke, but she could see no humor. She pulled off the ring and set it on a little candy dish, empty, on one of the wicker tables. "No. With my cousin's death, I have no more ties to the world of espionage, no more ties to my childhood visits to England. I do not want this life of lies and danger."

"Very well." His mouth had lost all its usual mobility. "Send a note to the hotel if Bert Dadey takes you back, and I will have your trunks delivered. They are still in my suite."

"Good." She shoved the envelope in her pocket and went to find her coat. In the front hallway, she was able to get her arms into her sleeves, but she couldn't seem to sort out the buttons.

Hands came out of nowhere, helping her button it up and then helping her with her gloves. She felt a small, cold circle thrust between the leather and her skin. Her engagement ring.

"I don't accept that this is over, Olga. You are grieving, and I'm trying to accept responsibility for that. There is no logic to pain. But you are still my fiancée, still under my protection."

She lifted her chin, scarcely able to see him through tears she didn't remember shedding. "When will you finally let me go?"

"Strawberry season. If that comes and you still hate me, well, you can return the ring then."

She wondered why he had made a face, as if something in his mouth tasted foul. "That's months from now. I've only known you a month."

"You knew your cousin all your life," he said. "It's only right to give you time to process his death."

She folded her fingers over her palm. "Why aren't you angry with me? I'm being very hateful."

"I'm sad and sorry," he said, "not angry, at least not with you."

"Then who?"

"Konstantin. Peter Eyre. Your ties to them were stronger than your ties to me."

His eyelids lowered, and she had a vision of him older, the skin around his eyes loosened, still handsome, still distinguished, but burdened by ever-increasing cares. Someone had to support him.

But it couldn't be her.

She slipped her hand through the straps of her handbag and opened the front door. When she had it open, she put the key to the building next door and the door between on the small table. The ring as well.

"Funny, isn't it? You gave me two of the three keys I needed to get in. I wonder what kind of metaphor that might be for our relationship."

He shoved his hands into his trouser pockets. "Not a good one."

She left then, somewhat blindly, but was careful to go out the way she'd been shown so that she wouldn't be seen leaving his actual building. When could she let caution go and finally be like any other woman?

* * * *

Glass went through the motions the next couple of days. He listened to the Russians, wrote his reports. When Redvers Peel came to spell him at his listening post on Monday so that he could attend a meeting at Special Branch, he found himself in front of the Imperial Art Gallery instead of at the meeting place.

He went inside and headed for where Olga's paintings had been located the last time he was there. He found the section of the wall had been rehung with some rather muddy religious paintings, definitely not hers.

"Lord Walling!"

He turned around and found Margery coming toward him. She wore a loosely draped day dress with wide pockets at the waist. He could tell the crisp fabric was brand new. She reached her hands out to him and clasped them.

"What brings you in?"

He tilted his head toward the wall. "No paintings from the princess?"

"No, we sold what we had, and she hasn't brought anything else. Too busy?"

"Her cousin died," he said, leaving out all of the pertinent details.

"Oh, I see."

"Have you heard from her at all?"

Margery straightened one of the new paintings. "No. Why?"

"She's having a difficult time of it. Not employed at the Grand Russe any longer. Back at the boardinghouse."

"I'd rather she focused on painting," Margery said frankly. "She's too talented to waste time with other things."

He suspected she wouldn't be pleased to know Olga had wasted time considering marriage. "Is there anything you could hire her to do for now? So she can spend her days around art while she's regrouping? She did that lovely installation at the Grand Russe with the hotel art."

"I saw the exhibit," Margery said. "I'd be happy to hire her to supervise rehanging our walls. Where the eye falls is very important, the lighting, all of that matters."

"That would be good. I don't want her to sink into depression, and I know too much has changed in her life in a short time."

Margery's eyes went shrewd. "You can't help her?"

He lifted his shoulders. "She doesn't want my help. Her sister is coming from Shanghai finally. I don't know what effect that will have. She'll need her friends around her."

"I never really thought of her as having friends. She's so quiet and self-assured."

"I can see why you would think that. She's so competent, but she's a social being like the rest of us."

"I'll write her a note and ask her to come and see me," Margery promised. "What about you?"

"Busy," he said. "Need to get to a meeting."

"Don't want to answer questions?"

He shook his head.

"Some days, I miss your brother so terribly." Margery sighed. "Now that we're in touch again, let's stay in contact, shall we?"

He smiled. "I'd like that. Remember the good times."

She nodded. "Something's terribly wrong with you, Douglas. I knew your family well enough to read your emotions."

"It will be sorted or not." He shrugged again, realized there was nothing more to say. Turning on his heels, he lifted his hat to her and went to his meeting.

* * * *

On his way back to the hotel more than an hour later, he found himself wishing he dare stop at Montagu Square and speak to the princess about the disturbing news. Full translations of his surveillance caught news from Moscow read aloud. Mikhail Lashevich had been officially made head of the trade delegation. Mail intercepted at the hotel indicated a new romance as well. He was exchanging letters with Queen Mary's dresser.

That intel gave him a sick feeling in the pit of his stomach. The princess would have the best insight since Grand Duchess Xenia was friendly with her cousins, the king and queen. But he knew he couldn't approach Olga, even though he'd refused to accept her termination of their engagement.

He touched the pocket over his heart, where her ring rested. It wouldn't leave him until she accepted it back.

* * * *

Olga stepped into the Imperial Art Gallery on Tuesday as per the owner's note that had requested a meeting, eager to put her hands on her money. For the first time, she'd opened a bank account the day before, sure with Konstantin's death that there was no one to borrow, steal, or be gifted her meager savings. She'd also given Harold Plash his painting, and he'd seemed delighted. In her sketchbook, she had ideas to show Mrs. Davcheva. If the gallery owner approved of any of them she planned to start painting immediately.

Instead of Russian memories, she'd thought to do some London paintings. She had three nice sketches of Hyde Park scenes, all of them with children. If she painted them, she knew she'd do it with tears running down her face, sadness over the children she would never have with Douglas.

"Why so mournful, Your Serene Highness?" Mrs. Davcheva asked, coming up to her in the small gallery entryway. The space wasn't decorated. The walls were stark white, all the better to soothe the senses before the riotous colors in the rooms beyond. Olga sat on the bench next to the door and placed her sketchbook in her lap.

She avoided the question. "I have some ideas for new work. I wanted to see if you were interested or if I should continue as before."

"I'm sure I'll be interested in anything you try," the woman said, dropping her formal address as Olga had previously requested for their business dealings. She took a seat.

Olga stared at the reds and golds in the panel of patchwork sewn into the woman's dress. They reminded her of the Grand Russe uniforms. She blinked and clutched at her notebook. "Well, then. Did you just want to pay me for the work you sold?"

"Not just that. Come into my office." She rose and gestured for Olga to join her. When they reached the office behind the gallery, she unlocked one of her desk drawers and pulled out an envelope. "Here you go. That's everything, so we do need more work from you."

"Yes, I intend to paint a great deal," Olga said, taking her money. "My life will be quieter now, and my sister is coming soon. I want to be able to see her."

"Were you planning to change your style?"

"No, just the subject matter. A bit of London for a change."

"Very good, as long as it isn't dreary. We do have a steady tourist trade, and they will snap up a good London painting. The Russians, though, they want Russia."

"Maybe half and half then," Olga said. "I want to be sensible."

"Yes. Keep one clientele happy while building another," Mrs. Davcheva said. "I had another idea for you as well. Actually, Lord Walling's idea, though I quite agree with him."

"What is that?"

"I understand about your sister coming, and of course I want you to paint as much as possible, but you did such a lovely job with your exhibit at the Grand Russe. I did wonder if you would help me rework the exhibit space here to make it more inviting. I believe you have a gift for drawing the eye."

Olga nodded. "Interior design was very important to my mother. We learned to create an inviting home. Of course, I've learned color theory as well."

"Artists do, but you have an extra talent, I believe."

"What did Lord Walling have to do with the suggestion?"

"He feels that you need work. I don't think he understands how talented you are as an artist."

"He's used to thinking of me as a chambermaid with a hobby," she sighed.

"Oh, I don't think so."

Olga glanced away. "He feels guilty, even though I broke off our engagement."

Mrs. Davcheva's eyebrows rose. "You were engaged?"

"Yes, I had his father's approval, a family ring." Olga shook her head.

"Love?" Mrs. Davcheva suggested.

"I loved him," Olga said. "I don't know how he feels. But I broke it off, not him; he's steadier than that."

"Of course." Mrs. Davcheva sat in her desk chair and Olga followed suit. "I've known Walling since we were quite young. It's my belief that he loves you. I hope you didn't break it off because of that."

"He didn't propose because of love."

"That doesn't mean it isn't there. The Walling I know is very detached, but he didn't act in that manner at all when I saw him. Genuinely concerned for your well-being. Looked ill, really." She trailed off suggestively.

Olga wanted to believe Mrs. Davcheva's words, even as she protested. "He seems foolhardy. He takes risks."

"Really?" She smiled. "Some ex-soldiers do, you know. Makes them feel alive. They need the juices in their blood rising."

"Is that what it is? I don't want that at all. I want peace."

"You're an artist. He's a soldier. With marriage, you have to accept some fundamental differences. Men will do silly things, dangerous even. Driving in races, for instance. I don't understand it, but my husband finds the sport fascinating."

"Lord Walling likes action," Olga agreed. She wanted to put her head in her hands, but, even though this woman was kind, she was still the closest thing Olga had to an employer right now. "Thank you for your counsel."

"Will you take him back? I wish you would. He needs a strong wife. He and his father are so alone, just rattling along. Plus, all that money needs a good chatelaine." Mrs. Davcheva grinned with vulgar cheer.

"Do you miss his brother, the one you loved?"

"So terribly. But you have to cultivate amnesia about certain things. And so many of us lost our boys in the war. We didn't marry our first loves, those of us who have husbands. I know your first fiancé died."

Olga was struck by that, by the realization that Maxim's killer was in London now, and that people like Douglas were all that were standing between the Hand of Death and another girl bereft of her loved one. "Yes, he did. I lost him to murder and now Douglas to foolishness."

Mrs. Davcheva leaned forward. "Don't let foolishness keep you from happiness. You deserve it, my dear. We all do."

Chapter 20

It had been nearly two weeks since Glass had seen Olga. His pulse raced as he ushered Princess Fyodora Novikova into a government-chauffeured car to deliver her into her sister's care. How would she respond to seeing him again?

Olga had sent him a polite note a few days after he'd last seen her, thanking him for his intervention at the Imperial Art Gallery. He'd seen the Davchevas socially, at a benefit dance that he'd attended at his father's bequest, and Margery had insisted that Olga would return to him in time. She had counseled him to let Olga be.

Olga had done no such thing. While it made sense for her to stay out of the Grand Russe, since Eyre had banished her, she could have asked to meet him somewhere else. But, nothing, just the note, as formal as any communication between two strangers.

Even now, she could be growing his child in her belly. But it had only been three weeks since they'd made love for the first time. Plenty of time to mend things and marry if she'd only forgive him.

"Who does my sister reside with?" Princess Fyodora asked, in a much thicker accent than her sister's. She didn't have her sister's curves either. Glass knew they were Irish twins, just under a year apart, and this was the elder. Fyodora's hair was darker, and she had a couple more inches of height, with a pronounced elegant angularity. He wondered if it was by design or lack of money for food.

Her clothing, like much of Olga's, looked like it had been purchased the previous decade and had been carefully preserved since. Fine quality, but faded and threadbare, the hems too long for current fashion.

"Her Serene Highness is residing in a boardinghouse. My secretary spoke to Mr. Dadey, the owner, a couple of days ago, and we understand she has taken the parlor suite now, which has a sitting room and two bedrooms."

"Who pays for this?" the princess asked.

"She does. Her finances have been difficult due to your late cousin's perfidies, but she is selling her paintings as well as consulting at a gallery."

"Good. This work is suitable. She can take care of me?"

Glass, watching closely, saw the tremble in her gloved fingers. "I believe so."

"I had understood she worked in a hotel, for our old friends the Redcakes," she said. "This is what I was told when I was contacted by the British consulate."

"She, err, had a breakdown in that relationship."

"My sister was burdened as a child with a sharp tongue," she said. "This is still the case?"

"It was my fault, ma'am," Glass said. "Your sister did nothing wrong, and I am terribly sorry I caused the breach."

"The Redcakes are a tolerant lot, as I recall. Quite Bohemian. You must have done something terrible."

He regaled her for the rest of the drive with the story of her cousin's death and the attendant strain on Peter Eyre and Princess Olga.

"Has she called off the engagement?" the princess asked as he finished.

"She returned the ring." He touched his pocket.

Her shrewd eyes followed the path of his fingers. "I see." She patted his arm. "We shall soon set her to rights. My sister is headstrong but not a fool."

"I love her," he said softly. "I dream about her at night, but then I wake, and she is not with me."

She nodded but stared straight ahead.

He rubbed his eyes. His sleep had been interrupted nightly with these dreams. He was not himself.

At Montagu Square, the princess asked about the faded girls' school sign still etched into the bricks and slowly walked up the front steps, leaving Glass and the driver to wrestle with her two worn suitcases.

Bert Dadey appeared after she'd allowed Glass to ring the bell, dressed better than usual in a suit, his tie crooked. "Your Serene Highness, such a pleasure," he exclaimed and hobbled backward so they could enter.

He led them toward the parlor. Princess Olga was seated there, and Glass drank in the sight of her, hands folded as she sat next to the silent gramophone. When she caught sight of her sister, she gave a wordless cry and stood. He recognized the blue day jacket he'd bought for her as the women flew into each other's arms, simultaneously bursting into tears.

Several minutes went by as they said a few words in Russian, then cried, and repeated the exchange. Mr. Dadey excused himself bashfully after a couple of minutes to make tea. Glass remained, holding up the wall next to the gramophone until he could see some sense returning to the princesses

He'd been learning more Russian, thanks to his immersion in it, and made out a few words here and there, but he was used to men's voices, and the women's higher pitch threw him. A little while longer, the house owner returned, his arms shaking slightly from the effort of holding a tray piled high with seedcake and tea things. He set it down with a rattle, and the women sat.

"Will you pour, Miss Olga?" he asked politely.

Her sister's eyebrows went up at the familiarity, but Olga gave her sister a defiant look. "My sister may have the honor, sir. I will say good-bye to Lord Walling."

He took that as his sign to depart the room. She followed him into the hallway. "Not fit for tea, me?" he asked.

She took his hands in hers, squeezing them slightly. "Thank you for returning my sister to me."

He inclined his head. "You are very welcome, Princess, but what I wish most is that you return to me. You don't have to live like this. Every property my father or I possess is open to you."

"Meaning you consider our engagement still on, despite everything?"

He nodded. "I can't let you go. Perhaps these are not the words of a gentleman, but, Olga, darling, I can't help thinking of you. I dream of you. I want to marry you."

"Oh?"

His voice dropped into a harsh whisper. "Did I ever tell you I loved you? I do, so much. It's broken me to lose you. Almost two weeks of exile. You know how that feels, exile."

"I feel it most keenly, and not just from you," she said in a tone rather more dispassionate than his.

He cleared his throat. "You need more time. I understand that. But anything you need, ring the hotel and ask for me. I'm still there."

She seemed to stare through him. While her gaze met his, he had the sense it was a trick of the light, that she really was fixated on his nose or forehead. Had she never loved him?

"Your sister comes first right now. I understand that." He reached into his pocket and pulled out an envelope with banknotes, and came up with a convenient lie. "This money came from Buckingham Palace, to refurbish Princess Fyodora's wardrobe."

Olga took the envelope, the smallest hint of a smile curving her lips.

"How kind of them. I will have to write Queen Mary a note."

"You do that," he said. "I hope to see you very soon."

She didn't say anything. The faraway look had returned to her eyes. He took his hat from the entryway table, clapped it back on his head, and returned to the street and the rainy March day.

* * * *

"You felt you had to write Peter a note to be allowed into the Grand Russe?" Fyodora asked in Russian on Sunday evening as they returned from Windsor after spending the day with Grand Duchess Xenia.

Olga held tightly to the bouquet of blue delphinium and white lilies on her lap as the taxicab turned onto Park Lane. She'd had them placed in a cheap glass vase and didn't want it to break. "He did forbid me to enter, but he was drunk at the time."

"I've never thought of the Redcakes as over-imbibers," Fyodora said.

"The war was so difficult on his generation. Eloise's fiancé died, and Noel is too damaged to live outside of a hospital. Peter, the youngest, seemed to have escaped their curse, but he's had his own issues of late."

"It was a war to end all wars," Fyodora said in a faraway voice and stared out the window as the taxicab pulled up under the awning.

"Are you going to come in with me?"

"No." Her sister forced a smile. "I am not ready for society. A cup of tea and my bed are all I require after this long day."

Olga kissed her cheek as the door was opened for her. She hadn't seen her sister since she was nineteen years old. In some ways the years had been kind; Fyodora was undeniably a beauty, but to Olga's eyes, she looked older than twenty-six. In her eyes at least. She'd seen too much. At the grand duchess's urging, Fyodora had shared the bare bones of her story, but Olga knew she'd left a great deal out.

"I'll bring us something nice to eat," Olga promised as Johnnie Miles helped her from the taxicab.

He grinned at her as it drove away. "Those for me, Princess?"

"No, for one of the guests. A thank-you."

"Well, they are beautiful, Princess."

She smiled at the doorman, instinctively plucked off the smallest delphinium bloom, and tucked it into his buttonhole. "There you are, Mr. Miles."

His white teeth showed as he grinned. "Most kind, ma'am."

Feeling lifted, Olga winked at him as she went inside. But once in the

Grand Hall, her floral offering seemed tiny as she saw the beautiful blooms in the enormous bouquet in the center of the room. She remembered how they had been toppled during Konstantin's run through the area weeks ago, minutes before he'd died.

Taking a deep breath, she reminded herself of everything that had come to mind these past few days and walked to the lift. Her feet seemed extraordinarily heavy as they crossed the tricolor marble, but they moved.

A few minutes later, she'd plucked another bloom for Rohan, the lift operator. She fluffed one side of the bouquet as she left the lift, hiding the damage. Hesitating, she checked the corridor for Russians, but they didn't have a guard posted. She knew they were usually all out at this time of evening.

In front of Douglas's door, she stood for a moment and polished the tips of her shoes on the backs of her stockings. *Silly*. She knew her shoes were just fine. Feeling light-headed, she took a deep breath, filling her lungs, and rapped on the door.

When Douglas opened it, she took full measure of him and found nothing wanting. The time away had refreshed his power of personality. So tall, so dark and handsome. He seemed to have lost confidence, though. His expression was uncertain, instead of the usual mocking grin around the corners of his mouth or the sternness.

"Princess?"

She thrust out her blooms. "Thank you."

He tilted his head and stepped to the side. She debated for a moment but walked in. Her head drooped as the door closed behind him. It seemed to intensify his masculine scent, reminding her of those few times she'd been with him, naked in his arms, surrounded by and accepting his masculine power over her body.

"What brings you by?" he asked.

She turned back to him. He stood strong, his feet firmly planted, his arms crossed. She offered him the bouquet again.

Slowly, he unfolded one arm and took the flowers.

"I needed to thank you again for rescuing Fyodora."

"You risked coming here?"

"I wrote Peter. He sent me a curt note back allowing me to visit you."

"He needs a wife," Douglas muttered. He went into the sitting room and placed the vase on the table between the seating.

"He seems desperately unsettled."

"Why don't you set your cap for him?"

"First of all, he never wanted me. Second, I haven't forgiven him yet, not for sacking me and banning me from the hotel."

Douglas's lips curled into the familiar yet faintly feral grin she remembered. "Maybe he'll take your sister on. Will I ever be forgiven?"

She unbuttoned her coat but left it on, pulled off her gloves, and sat on the edge of a chair. "I've thought about it. A life for a life, that's what you've done. Having my sister back is payment for Konstantin's death."

"Very Old Testament of you."

"I realize Konstantin had chosen his evil side, if he'd ever had a good one. He was always wrong, somehow. I don't know how else to think of the situation."

He sat across from her on the white sofa. "I might have used Fyodora in an operation in the future. I can't claim my intentions were good."

"You didn't love me then. But you claim to love me now."

Her breath caught in her throat as he rose from the sofa and went to his knees in front of her. With a swiftness that belied his large body, he wrapped his arms around her waist and buried his face in her lap.

She stroked the back of his head as tears pricked under her eyelids. "You never let me call off our engagement."

His words came out muffled. "No, I didn't."

"I've missed you terribly, Douglas," she whispered.

He nodded against her thigh. "I'm usually sure of myself, but you've had me at a loss."

She sniffed. "How can I love someone when they are likely to drive me mad?"

He chuckled, the sound reverberating up her legs until her body all but melted with longing.

"So you do love me, Princess?"

"Yes, but I want to only love my Douglas. No more secrets."

He let out a breath. "It's time for me to leave the service. I need to help my father, and dangerous work might leave my own children without a parent. I can't abide that."

"The times are so very complicated," she said. "But I couldn't bear the thought of losing you to the man who killed Maxim."

"Other men can fight that battle." He looked up. "We'll retire to the country estate for a time. Your sister can regain her strength there, and we can make the St. Martin's title an heir."

"Promise?"

He nodded. "We'll marry in Yorkshire by the end of the month."

"Just as we'd planned?"

"Exactly."

She stroked her fingers through his hair, then inclined her head, meeting his lips with hers. There had been moments where she thought they'd never kiss again, but now, he was hers forever. Her heartbeat quickened as he accepted her kiss, her love.

* * * *

Two days later, Glass, the two princesses, and Peter Eyre stood on the pavement in front of Kings Cross Station. Eyre took one last drag of his cigarette, dropped it in front of his left foot, and ground it out.

"Must I?" he said, with just the taste of a whine in his cultured voice.

"John Neville can keep the hotel running for a few days," Olga said. "You need a vacation. I did not like the look of you when I called on you Sunday night."

"I'm a disgrace," he said easily.

"Take a few days," Fyodora said. "Embrace your cousins; appreciate your family."

"Why don't you come with me, Fee?" Eyre asked. "I'm sure you could do with some bracing country air."

The princess shook her head. "Too much to do for the wedding. Yorkshire," she sighed. "We have much shopping to do."

"You have to think of yourself, too," Eyre suggested. He pulled out his wallet and thrust a handful of bills at her.

Fyodora shook her head quickly and patted his cheek. "No more cigarettes. They make you pale. You were a red-cheeked boy."

"I grew up."

Her eyes narrowed. She poked him in the chest. "Fresh air and exercise."

His nostrils flared. "I remember you as plump and sweet, not a termagant."

Fyodora threw her head back. "I am professional dancer for years now. No place for fat."

Eyre winced and moved his gaze to Olga. "Will you come back to the hotel? Help Neville for a few days?"

"No."

Olga's one syllable answer made Glass smile. He wrapped his arm around her and pulled her to the side of the door to allow others to enter. "You need to get to your train, Peter. Must we walk you to the platform?"

"I can manage."

"And no flask, correct?" Olga asked.

"No." Peter's lips thinned. "I shall leave you three before I become extremely cross with you."

"You'll be at our wedding?" she asked.

He nodded. "Probably."

Fyodora's eyes narrowed. "You will be, Peter Eyre, or I will find you and drag you there by the ear."

Eyre smiled, the first time Glass had seen anything resembling pleasure in his face for quite some time. Could there be romance in the air? After all, springtime was for lovers.

Glass squeezed Olga's shoulders and held out his other arm to Fyodora, his soon-to-be sister-in-law. They watched Peter Eyre doff his hat to an elderly matron and follow behind, a single suitcase in his hand.

Glass was very happy to know that the next time he'd be boarding a train, it would be with his Olga by his side. He no longer liked the look of a single man about to travel. It smacked of desolation, a feeling he was most happy to leave behind.

"Better days ahead," Olga said and smiled up at him.

"Better days ahead," Glass said. "Time to leave the past behind and shout, 'Tallyho,' to a new tomorrow."

Keep reading for a special excerpt of the first book in The Grand Russe Hotel series.

IF I HAD YOU

The Grand Russe Hotel by Heather Hiestand

Inside the glittering walls of a famous hotel, an ingénue experiences first passion . . .

As she stands before the gilded doors of The Grand Russe Hotel, Alecia Loudon is poised on the threshold of a profound awakening. It is the Roaring Twenties, and London is buzzing with opportunities for adventure . . . and indiscretion. The young personal secretary knows nothing of the ways of men, but a chance meeting with the hotel's handsome night watchman sets her imagination afire.

Ivan Salter has noticed the quiet Englishwoman and wonders what delicate beauty might be lurking behind Alecia's plain clothes. As the handsome Russian draws Alecia further into the hotel's luxurious world, he introduces her to fine food, cool jazz, and forbidden assignations. Their dalliance is tested, however, by a surprising link between Ivan's family history and Alecia's bosses. Tangled up in international intrigue, the lovers must decide if their sparkling new romance is worth the cost . . .

Praise for Heather Hiestand's novels

"*One Taste of Scandal* is a delicious, multi-layered Victorian treat."
—Gina Robinson, author of *The Last Honest Seamstress* and the Agent Ex series

"A fast read with a different view point than many novels in the genre."
—*Library Journal* on *His Wicked Smile*

"This is definitely one for the keeper shelf."
—Historical Romance Lover on *His Wicked Smile*

"A delightful, sexy glimpse into Victorian life and loving with two wonderfully nontraditional lovers."
—Jessa Slade, author of *Dark Prince's Desire*, on *His Wicked Smile*
Available now!

Chapter 1

Jazz.

The saxophone wailed and screeched over the piano. A trombone blared in, deepening the rollicking sound. Alecia Loudon's foot tapped as a female singer sang the words to the newest tune from America. Underneath the music beat the sounds of the nightclub: cups rattling on plates, champagne glasses clinking, and matches being struck for innumerable cigarettes.

Alecia longed to see the action, but it was hidden from her on the other side of the nightclub's rear door. Cocooned in the luxury hotel that shared the club's wall, she couldn't see the dancing. Styles changed so fast, and she wished she knew the current fads. Of course, the song had about as much relevance to her sex-free life as the dancing. "'My baby don't love nobody but me . . .'"

No, the life behind that door bore no resemblance to hers. She was a questionably modern secretary of twenty-two who'd never been kissed. Oh, but she'd thought about kissing, fantasized about kissing, daydreamed about kissing one certain handsome man here at the Grand Russe Hotel . . .

She pushed the thought away and tried the handle of the door. One inch to the right, two inches . . . it caught. Frustrated, she turned the knob again but it only rattled, metal against metal. Securely locked. She considered leaving the safety of the hotel, darting onto busy Park Lane at Hyde Park Corner, going into the alley where the main nightclub door was. But she wasn't dressed for the nightclub.

Giggles emanating from a dark corner on the far side of the door stole her away from her thoughts. She peeled away from the wall where she'd been leaning, in what was little more than a service corridor between the nightclub and the newly reopened hotel. Even back here, the opulence of the Grand Russe Hotel continued undiminished. The tops of the walls were stenciled in a forest green and red-brown geometric pattern that reminded her of teeth. Colorful paintings of ballet scenes done by itinerant Russian artists dotted the walls every six feet, uniform in size and frame.

The hotel's decorations had been inspired by *The Sleeping Princess* ballet performed at the Alhambra in Leicester Square a few years ago, but for sure, the couple on the dark velvet sofa in the corner were no Sleeping Beauty and her Prince Charming. The man in the clinch did not meet any masculine ideal. She'd seen a man who did, though, late at night here at the hotel. Alecia ghosted her way through the somnolent hotel in the wee hours, escaping her ever-present nightmares, while he protected it. A night watchman. She'd never spoken to him.

Dark waves of hair gave him a rakish edge. He possessed eyes of a brown that were closer to amber. Thick chocolate brows overshadowed his eye sockets, making for a fiercely probing gaze. Sculpted, full lips, the rosy bottom just slightly larger than the top. A nose almost too expansive for the face, but imposingly masculine. Angular cheekbones and triangular jaw with a mildly cleft chin. Golden sand-colored skin. A real sheik, though she was no sheba to find herself bent back over his arm and ravished. How she wished.

Oh God. The mere thought of that man, those broad shoulders and trim hips, six feet of masculine perfection, made her weak in the knees and damp in places her late grandmother had told her never to think about. She ought to set her sights on the kind of man who could take her to the nightclub, but her imagination hadn't released the night watchman yet.

The man on the sofa though, leaning over the woman in the revealing champagne-colored French dancing frock, was the type to be able to afford London nightlife. Unfortunately, he was young, balding, stoop-shouldered, and tending to embonpoint around his midsection. The expensive clothes did not make up for this. The gleaming gold bands on the couples' ring fingers told the tale. A Christmas season wedding, followed by a honeymoon in the most scandalous hotel in London.

The hotel owners no doubt hoped the complete refurbishment of the place, and the name change, would rescue their investment from the ignominy it suffered as the location of the infamous Starlet Murders of 1922, but even she, living then with her vicar grandfather and younger sister in Bagshot, Surrey, had heard the stories. With all the inns nearby, the London news could not help filtering in. Rumors of gin and cocaine and sex and sex and sex and, well, death.

Nothing like the quiet life her employers, Richard and Sybil Marvin, had introduced her to when they took up residence here at the hotel, though they, like the rouged and lipstick-wearing murder victims, were actors.

The bride giggled again as her new husband kissed her décolletage. The man ran his tongue along his wife's collarbone. Alecia's eyes widened as his hand went up her knee-length skirt. Were they actually going to have sex, right there on the sofa?

She cleared her throat loudly, but they didn't hear her, or didn't care. The silver tray holding two empty champagne bottles and two overturned glasses explained why these two were in their own world. Drunk as lords. What should she do now?

When she glanced away, she saw *him*. The handsome night watchman wore his uniform of gold coat and deep ruby trousers. Black chevrons were appliquéd on his sleeves. All the buttons were gold, matching the trim on his ruby cap. Underneath the bill, his eyes narrowed as he saw her. He heard the moan behind her at the same time she did. They both turned to see the couple on the sofa. The woman's marcel-waved hair was crushed against the armrest as her husband knelt between her splayed legs and fumbled with his trousers.

"*Hvatit*," the night watchman ordered.

Alecia didn't know what the word meant exactly, but knew his intent. *Stop that, you sex-starved just-marrieds.*

Her dream lover moved past her. She smelled birch oil. This was the closest she'd ever been to him. Though his coat went almost to his knees, she could see the contours of his well-muscled backside underneath the fine wool.

"You must return to your room," he said in a Russian accent. His Rs rolled in a way that set Alecia's heart to fluttering.

The woman screamed when she opened her eyes and saw the watchman standing not three feet away from her. Her husband scrambled to his feet, still fumbling under his jacket. Alecia could see the tops of the woman's stockings, the lace edging on her camiknickers. She was too drunk to close her legs properly. Her husband finished fumbling and hauled her to her feet. Without speaking, the duo stumbled down the hall, past the night watchman, their gazes downcast.

Alecia still didn't know if they'd ever noticed she was there. When she lifted her gaze, the night watchman was regarding her steadily.

"Voyeurism is not polite, even at the Grand Russe." He said "is" like "ees," so sexy. The word "polite" rolled off his tongue in a drawl. *Heaven.* Oh, he was the cat's meow to be sure.

"I didn't know they were there at first. I've been listening to the music."

She nodded at the nightclub door and tried to channel her flirtatious sister. "What is your name?"

"Ivan." He paused. "Salter."

"I'm Miss Loudon," she said. "I work for the Marvins on the fifth floor."

"I know who you are," he said, each word clipped and disapproving. "If you want to hear the music, you can go into the nightclub."

"I don't have the right clothing," she said, pointing to the long, shapeless gray frock she'd sewn herself.

"Mrs. Marvin must have trunks full of suitable garments."

"Not for me. I'm just the secretary."

"*Myshka*," he said, his eyebrows coming together. "That is what you are."

"I don't know any Russian," she said. "What does that mean? Are you really from Russia, or are you playing a role?"

He narrowed his eyes. "Do I seem false to you?"

"No, of course not, but you know how it is. Ladies' maids and cooks and shopgirls pretending to be French, actresses pretending to be Russian. It's all the rage."

"The rage," he growled. "Such a funny expression. When you've seen true rage, it does not seem so fashionable." His gaze wandered to a painting of peasants in a yellow field, before returning to her.

She wondered if he'd been in the Russian army. "At any rate, Salter doesn't sound very Russian."

"It wasn't always my name," he said evenly.

"Ah." She cast about for something to say, but words failed her. How could she stay with him, keep him talking, so she could watch the way his sensual mouth formed each word? "I fancied that staff was given a handbook of Russian phrases and an accent coach, that you're really from Islington or someplace."

He shook his head. His shoulders relaxed. "I was born in Moscow. But I am English for three years now."

"There must be quite a story there," she ventured.

A whistle blew in the distance. A summons? His gaze shifted back to the corridor. "I must go. Return to your room, please. It is late for a young lady to be wandering alone."

She knew she wandered too much, late at night, but she had to wear herself out completely or she saw the submarine approach in her dreams, the *Lusitania* sinking, her parents' drowned faces. He stood, unmoving, until she began to walk again, quick, nervous little steps. He escorted her as far as the bank of lifts, then continued his path toward the Grand Hall at the front of the hotel.

The lift operator let her out on the fifth floor. She could never remember which direction to turn. The pattern on the wall here, a thick red-brown line underscored by a sharply jagged stripe of forest green, had dots around it, like tiny green berries. A distracting pattern. Staring at it, she nearly stumbled into a fern. She blew a frond out of her face, then noticed the elderly woman standing behind it.

"What are you doing?" Alecia asked.

"Good afternoon," the woman said. She wore a frightfully Edwardian costume, much too rich and decorated for 1924. And a straw boater. And galoshes.

"It is the middle of the night," Alecia said carefully, not wanting to frighten the woman.

"Is it? I seem to have lost my way. On a garden path, are we?" She touched a frond.

"No, at a hotel. Is there someone I can fetch for you?"

The elder's heavily-lidded eyes drooped even further. "Oh dear. A hotel?"

"The Grand Russe."

She made a congested noise in the back of her throat. "Never heard of it."

"It used to be the Grand Haldene."

"Very dreadful place. One hears things." She sniffed.

"Yes, well, it's been rather quiet lately."

"My daughter is a bit of an adventuress," the woman said. "Too old for it, though."

Alecia's interest pricked. "Is she staying here?"

"With me. Daft girl. The younger set, all frivolity."

"Can I see you to your room?" Alecia asked, since the woman seemed to be making more sense now.

"It's just down the hall, ducks. Not to worry. Room 502." The elder's gaze lost focus. "Don't know why I was standing outside. Probably didn't want to listen to all that tee-heeing. And the cigarette smoke. So vulgar."

Her daughter must be having a party. "Yes, ma'am."

"Well"—she nodded—"good morning to you."

Alecia didn't correct the woman. At least she had her key out now. Alecia waited until she shut the door, then went down the hall to her own room. She had been housed in the valet's chamber attached to Mr. Marvin's room, since he didn't have a man with him. Mrs. Marvin, however, had a maid, a grumbling, poorly-used person named Ethel.

Her room held none of the decorations of the public spaces. Only three pieces of furniture were present: a bed, a dressing table, and a chest of drawers. The chair at the dressing table had splinters in the seat, and a door connected her room with Mr. Marvin's, which was not proper. She kept her side bolted at night and hoped never to hear him knock in the wee hours. Aside from marital fidelity, something she was not sure applied to actors, he was fifty-one, almost thirty years older than her, and had a luxuriant mustache that all too frequently had food in it.

Nothing like Ivan Salter. She sat down on her bed and removed her shoes, replaying their conversation in her head, reveling in his voice, just as sexy as she'd imagined.

* * * *

Greetings from Peter Eyre.

The next evening, Ivan stood in front of a notice pinned to the employee board in the hotel's basement. The place was a dank, groaning hive of activity. He suspected the scarred furnishings of the employee dining hall had been in place since the hotel was first opened in the 1890s, but the daily notices from the fastidious general manager were always crisp and clean.

29 December! The increase in petty theft is alarming. Watch for pilferers of ashtrays, glasses, furniture cushions. If you see any Gypsies entering the premises, please escort them out right away. We don't want them stealing our rugs and chairs. Please report any concerns, or concerning persons, in full detail to your supervisor. Your servant, Peter Eyre.

"Now we are to man all the doors and still make our rounds to the second?" complained Ivan's fellow night watchman, Norman Johnson, tucking his pocket watch away.

"Not you," Ivan said, pointing to the day's roster. "You've been assigned the top floors. Extra security."

Norman squinted at the roster. The habitual expression had left premature lines around his eyes. "Who is in residence?"

"Some American businessman. A film actress. Lady Cubult," Ivan recalled.

"Who is the actress?"

"I don't remember. I don't go to the movies."

"You should. What else is there to do?"

Ivan shrugged. "Family, friends."

"You have some? I thought you were from Russia." Norman straightened his cap and licked his teeth.

"I came here with my sister."

"The rest of your family still there, then?"

"Dead," Ivan said through clenched teeth. He didn't like speaking of them.

"Awful thing, the wars. My little brother died in the trenches, you know.

Don't know why I survived." Norman sniffed.

"I should not have survived either. But we go on. We remember our dead." *Catherine. My parents.*

Norman nodded. "I'm off to prowl the halls. Maybe I'll be invited in for a drink. Someone must know who that actress is." Whistling jauntily, he strode off.

Ivan went to start his rounds on the main floor. It was still terribly busy at ten P.M. because Peter Eyre was holding court in the glittering, silver-and-blue Coffee Room. The real draw, despite the gorgeous geometric wallpaper and stunning parquet floor, could be said to be the glamorous Eyre himself, wandering through most evenings, greeting the anointed, glaring at the out of favor. His eyes would narrow at times as he decided who would be paying the champagne bill for everyone that night, as if mentally calculating the worth of each visitor.

Eyre was an obscure fellow, about the same age as Ivan, and much whispered about in the dens where the maids and valets waited for summonses. He might be an offshoot of some German royal family. Or the son of an Irish peasant. No one knew. He hadn't been to Eton or Harrow, but that crowd adored him as much as they were adored by gossip columnists. He'd sprung whole from the hotel the day it had been reopened. Who knew? He might even be the owner.

But Eyre wasn't the ever-present figure that most intrigued Ivan as he left the Coffee Room and made his way through the web of corridors on the main floor. Miss Loudon, the little mouse who had not run away when that dreadful twosome were coupling on the sofa behind the nightclub. A woman who would not avert her eyes from sex and insisted on listening to jazz.

It would not take much to turn her from a mouse to a cat. She had the very English peaches-and-cream skin, large bright-blue eyes, and yellow hair. Classic beauty, hiding in a dress that was too large. A boyish figure that was all the rage. She could be in style if she wore red lipstick and cut her hair. A little paint, some money for better clothes, and she might be on the arm of some man, entering the club instead of skulking behind it.

He made his way past the Salon, the Reception Room, the Ballroom, the Restaurant, the Reading Room. The only trouble he found was a damp wad of chewing gum decorating the armrest of a chair, and two occasional tables that were missing their ashtrays. He made a note in his book and moved on.

By eleven P.M.., he had done a full round of the two main floors of the hotel and had circled the outside of the building. Part of the duties of the night watchman downstairs was to keep an eye on the nightclub. Drunken dramatics tended to spill into the hotel.

After the previous night, he decided he'd better check the service corridor where the honeymooners had been canoodling the night before. He also felt duty-bound to make sure the carpet had been cleaned where champagne had been spilled.

"Excuse me," said a man Ivan recognized as being in sales, stopping him by the lifts. The man had taken one of the rooms with a parlor set up with a display area for his wares. Garden products. "Can you recommend a place where I can get a plate of kippers this time of night?"

"The Restaurant is closed, sir, but if you go into the alley around the block, Maystone's, our nightclub, is still serving."

"But will it be edible? I know these places have to serve food to keep the champagne flowing, but I want a meal."

"You can ask the hall porter to have sandwiches delivered to your room," Ivan suggested.

"No. I don't like to eat alone."

"Flash your money around inside Maystone's and you'll have companionship soon enough," Ivan said.

The man winked and moved off. Ivan wove deeper into the maze of service corridors. Rarely did he find guests, but when he did, they were usually up to no good.

And there she was, the *myshka*. Leaning up against the back door of the nightclub again, still in that same foul dress. Did she not know the Grand Russe Hotel was an elegant place?

* * * *

"It isn't midnight yet," Alecia said when she spotted Ivan Salter coming toward her. She told her traitorous heart rate to slow. While he might be handsome, he wasn't kind. She'd asked the Russian chambermaid who cleaned her room what *myshka* meant. Little mouse, indeed. An insult. She had thought him a creature out of a fairy tale.

As he approached, not speaking, she lifted herself from her slouched pose along the wall and straightened her shoulders. Pins holding her too heavy hair in its prim bun dug into her scalp. She needed to take it down and go to bed, but the music had drawn her. Better than a lumpy mattress, the *Lusitania* sinking.

When he was two feet from her, he stopped. His gaze wandered the space, taking in the empty sofa, and, oddly enough, the carpet.

"What?" she demanded, very un-mouselike. She had resolved to be as belligerent as a maiden aunt. "There isn't a sign saying hotel guests are not allowed back here."

He cocked his head. She wilted when he sucked in his cheeks, highlighting the magnificent structure of his cheekbones. No. He may have every blessing God might offer a man, but he was only a night watchman. She was just a secretary. Unless she was breaking a rule, he had no right to intimidate her. She would not be cowed.

"Say something," she said very crisply, as if she was dressing down a young nephew.

His lips curved. She felt a sinking sensation in her midsection. How dare he look so knowing?

"Young ladies wandering about unchaperoned are looking to be kissed."

"By you?" How stupid she was, to say this.

His teeth were exposed by his widening smile. The top row was perfect, but his two lower front teeth were just a little crooked. She fell in love even more. In lust?

"You knew you would see me tonight. I am the watchman."

"Very well then." She lifted her chin. "It is unlikely that I am looking to be kissed. I like to wander and have never been kissed."

"Never, *myshka*? Such a pity. You are somewhat pretty."

"How dare you!" Outrage bubbled in her lungs. She could not find any other words.

But the truth was, she could find another thought, even if she couldn't say it aloud. She wanted to be kissed. By him.

And don't miss Sadie and Les's story . . .

I WANNA BE LOVED BY YOU

The Grand Russe Hotel by Heather Hiestand

For a young woman swept into international adventure, romance can't be far behind . . .

The 1920s are in full swing when Sadie Loudon leaves her grandfather's stodgy vicarage, and she dreams of the glamour and excitement she's seen on the silver screen. But before she even begins work at the storied Grand Russe Hotel, she is ushered into London's glittering nightlife by a handsome young businessman intent on introducing her to the pleasures available to a Bright Young Thing. Is it a fleeting romance...or something even more intriguing?

Les Drake is on the lookout for Bolsheviks when he encounters sweet, sexy Sadie. A British Secret Intelligence agent, Les has more experience with the seedy underside of the city than with innocent chambermaids, but he can't deny that Sadie tempts him. Using her as part of his cover seems like a brilliant plan until the danger of his assignment threatens what has suddenly become a love he can't bear to lose . . .

Praise for Heather Hiestand's novels

"You've got to admire Hiestand's moxie for setting her latest romance in an era rarely portrayed in today's historical romances."
–RT Book Reviews

"*One Taste of Scandal* is a delicious, multi-layered Victorian treat."
—Gina Robinson, author of *The Last Honest Seamstress* and the Agent Ex series

"A fast read with a different view point than many novels in the genre."
—*Library Journal* on *His Wicked Smile*

"This is definitely one for the keeper shelf."
—Historical Romance Lover on *His Wicked Smile*

"A delightful, sexy glimpse into Victorian life and loving with two wonderfully nontraditional lovers."
—Jessa Slade, author of *Dark Prince's Desire*, on *His Wicked Smile*

Meet the Author

Heather Hiestand was born in Illinois, but her family migrated west before she started school. Since then she has claimed Washington State as home, except for a few years in California. She wrote her first story at age seven and went on to major in creative writing at the University of Washington. Her first published fiction was a mystery short story, but since then her primary focus has been romance. Heather's first published romance short story was set in the Victorian period, and she continues to return to historical fiction as well as other subgenres. The author of many novels, novellas, and short stories, she has achieved best-seller status at Amazon and Barnes and Noble. With her husband and son, she makes her home in a small town and supposedly works out of her tiny office, though she mostly writes in her easy chair in the living room.

For more information, visit Heather's website at
www.heatherhiestand.com.

Want to stay in touch with Heather and receive exclusive information about her new releases? Sign up for her newsletter at heatherhiestand.com/newsletter/.

CPSIA information can be obtained
at www.ICGtesting.com
Printed in the USA
LVOW07s1612131017
552340LV00001B/150/P